The Seas Come Still

J.P. Jamin

ISBN-13: 978-0-9966996-8-6
ISBN-10: 09966996-8-6

2015 Edition
Akelarre Press

CONTENTS

Prologue v

1 Tears of Heaven 1

2 Roots of Exile 21

3 Figures in the Dust 33

4 Lady of Spain 49

5 Spinning Island 65

6 Duty Bound 79

7 Crystallizing 95

8 Paying Out 111

9 Initiation 129

10 Safe Space 145

11 Lotus Blossoms 161

12 Heresy and Blessing 173

13 Inner Treasures 191

14 Pivot Point 205

15 Life Devotions 223

16 Pulse of the Heart 235

17 Spring of God 251

18 A Singular Debutante 263

19 Swords and Cedars 281

20 A Cry from the Gap 297

21 Serpents of Fire 315

22 Bread and Blood 333

23 Ladder of the Rock 353

24 An Imperfect Divinity 369

Epilogue 391

J.P. Jamin

Prologue

October 2015
Kuzaki, Japan

Doctor Yumi Daikokuya kneels in the tidal shallows, in the shelter of the *shima*—the coastal rocks of the Kuzaki peninsula where she was born.

Her head lies half in the water, as though straining for a whisper. As her tears dissolve in the sea, it occurs to her that the sea, in its turn, dissolves in them, each drop absorbing all the majestic sadness of the Pacific.

"Umi wa gyōsan no Ama no namida ga fukuma rete oru." The last words she heard her mother say, so long ago.

"The sea holds a multitude of Amas' tears."

That rustic Mie-ken dialect she struggled to shed like a snake skin after her departure. Suffering its itch all through university, then Osaka Medical College. So awkward she thought she sounded to her professors, the big city students. The handsome residents who invited her for coffee and ice cream. So much the daughter of a sea woman.

She lets the salt water fill her nose.

So much an Ama.

As hard as she once pushed her mother from her mind, she labors now to remember her. Dirty complexion, lined by the sun and salt. Hands mottled with the scars of sea rocks and shellfish spines. Graceful as a minnow in the freezing water. But stooped and waddling as she shouldered her catch up the beach each morning to warm her sinuses by the fire before starting back down. Already old, more than twenty years ago.

The eldest dive longest, and deepest, Yumi remembers.

The few Ama that remain in Kuzaki are all old now. Hundreds once dove the coast, its treasures buying them a freedom enjoyed by no other women of Asia. Independence from convention, government, husbands. In prolonged cold water immersion, a woman's body is her advantage, a physical inheritance that can be passed from mother to daughter. If the daughter wishes to follow in that life.

But that was before. Before the time of expansion and depletion. Before post-war populations whose appetites grew with their means, consuming more shellfish than Japanese waters could produce, no matter how carefully the Ama conserved their harvests. Before corporations cultured the pearls and turned the Ama-san into tourist exhibits. Before the tsunami and the great poisonous wound it opened. It bleeds still, the people as afraid to eat from their coastal waters as they are to speak of it.

Her mother looked strangely younger in her frail coffin the night before. Death smoothed the deepest lines from her face. Her kimono inverted, wrapped right over left, white kerchief marked with the multi-pointed *seiman*. A symbol of witchcraft in many cultures. But for the Ama, spiritual balance, protection from malignant fortune.

Yumi had arrived late from Osaka. Barely time enough to moisten her mother's lips and light incense to the tiny household shrine, shielded with rice paper from the corrupting presence of the body. She accepted the stone from her aunt, nailed the coffin shut, and prepared it for the fire.

Could there be a more suffocating regret, she wonders, than to be ashamed of one's own shame?

Misunderstood words, so unimportant now. During her second year at university, she brought a friend home to Kuzaki to visit. Her only close friend, a *nisei*—a Japanese born abroad. Chika's Australian accent and manner, her status, made Yumi feel less an outsider. In Japan, all *nisei* are treated as foreigners.

But not by the Ama. Her mother and the others were accepting of her friend. And Chika was fascinated by them. She shared their cloudy homemade rice wine, relished the spiny lobster grilled on their open fire, laughed at their bawdy jokes. She sampled the dried abalone—the *awabi nori*.

The ancient, sacred harvest. Fabled food of princesses offered at the temples of Ise, and in thanks to Amaterasu, the sea goddess. It is said the Ama brought the technique of salting and drying it when they arrived long ago from foreign shores. Japanese as they look, the belief that they are from elsewhere persists. Older than the Ainu, more closely related to the Haenyo—their counterparts from coastal Korea. Some legends say they came three thousand years ago from China. Perhaps from much farther.

Certainly, they came by sea. As certainly as an Ama's educated, vegan daughter despises *awabi*. The old sense of alienation came washing back over Yumi as she stared in silence. Watched as her friend was enchanted by the their easy smiles, their Bohemian candor.

"Tastes how it looks," Chika said. "But it's delicious." The abalone's elliptical folds are the figure of womanhood. The Ama howled in approval.

"You see, Yumi?" Her mother's top-heavy seaside laugh, embracing Chika in those thick arms. "You cannot run so far you will not find another Ama! Like knows like!"

The mounting chagrin burst forth then. Hand over face, Yumi tripped from the hut to find what privacy she could behind the laundry lines. Chika did not understand that true Japanese women need be alone to weep. She followed and knelt to comfort her, perfecting her indignity.

"All right, love?" Australian English. Intrusive and infantilizing. Foreign.

"Ignorant *gaijin!*" Yumi whispered fiercely, shrugging off the arm.

It was then her mother's loud words reached them through the thin walls and hanging linen: *"Umi wa gyōsan no ama no namida*

ga fukuma rete oru"
   "The sea holds a multitude of Amas' tears."

1 Tears of Heaven

Where the wave of moonlight glosses
The dim grey sands with light,
Far off by furthest Rosses
We foot it all the night,
Weaving olden dances,
Mingling hands, and mingling glances,
Till the moon has taken flight;

Come away! O, human child!
To the woods and waters wild.
With a fairy hand in hand,
For the world's more full of weeping than you can understand.

—From "The Stolen Child" by W.B. Yeats

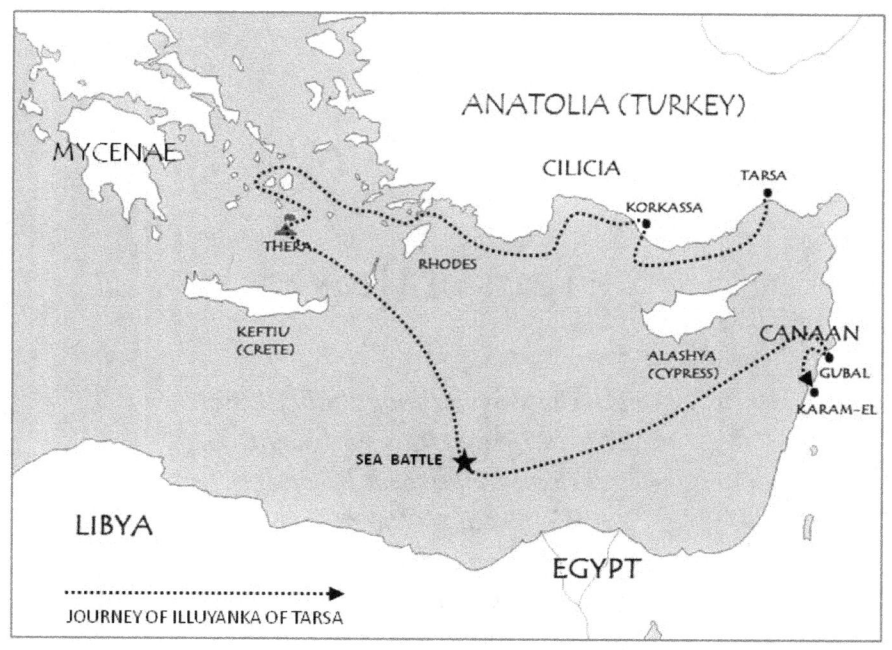

ANATOLIA (TURKEY)

MYCENAE

CILICIA

TARSA

KORKASSA

THERA

RHODES

KEFTIU (CRETE)

CANAAN

ALASHYA (CYPRESS)

GUBAL

KARAM-EL

SEA BATTLE

LIBYA

EGYPT

JOURNEY OF ILLUYANKA OF TARSA

1602 B.C.E.

Eastern Mediterranean

The Middle Bronze Age

"UPON YOU I BEND MY HORN. THAT WHICH LIFTS AND TOSSES MOUNTAINS, I BEND IT. AS I LAY YOU LOW, SO SHALL I RAISE YOU UP. AND TOGETHER WE SHALL CONQUER THE SEA."

In his dreams, it impaled him, the masthead. Its splintery groan became an incantation. The unrelenting rhythm of a lover-god he dared not name.

He awoke with a start and buckled his tender legs once more against the galley's lurch.

Bare reflex for the young lookout. He was long numb to any conscious fear of falling to the deck, twenty meters below. The Akkadian words faded as his mind cleared. He rubbed his salt-matted auburn hair from one eye and raised a thin rectangle of wood. Minutely angling the device sharpened the pinhole image.

A square sail, backlit by the golden dawn, cut the far eastern horizon.

He considered the possibilities. Merchants were rare in those waters, well off the coastal trade routes. But so were Keftiun warships. The late spring Mediterranean skies were routinely clear; no storm could have diverted the distant vessel. If the wind didn't veer more than a point, and the oarsmen kept up a steady pace, it might be identified before raising suspicion.

He spat to wet the skin of his left inner thigh. It was more inflamed than the right. The Cilician raiding galley had been pitching through a sharp starboard heel on its easterly heading. Long weeks he had straddled the rough mast, scanning the blinding sea, braced only by the bronze rings that led the brailing and bunting lines from the cross spar.

Yet the endless watches were ease compared to the life of the rowers. That he did fear—more than pain or blindness or backbreaking plummet. He thought of their battered, twisted shoulders, constant confinement below decks, baking in the reek of the galley. The salt water immersion which kept the whole of each palm a never-healing blister. The fate of one hated by the gods. There was little he would not do to escape it. Little he had not done.

His seamanship had been honed by that fear. He knew the horizon's exact distance as viewed from the mast-top. He looked down for the commander. The Hittite appeared small and bored, seated in his padded sling on the stern quarterdeck below. He was picking lazily from a platter of grilled sardines and preserved black olives, dipping at a delicate lentil stew with motes of dried flatbread.

The lookout fought back the urge to spit again. He cupped his hands and gathered breath.

"One *iter* ahead, Master! A sail!"

He hailed in Akkadian, the universal second language of the

eastern Mediterranean. But *iter* was an Egyptian-borrow-word: six and a half miles by other measure.

The commander stood up, licked his fingers, and took a swig from his wineskin before ordering the ship to fall off one point from the wind—a course calculated to gradually close the gap without raising alarm. The burly coxswains each took a tighter grip on one of two massive steering paddles suspended against the outer hull. As they leaned to their task, the commander stomped his foot three times in steady succession. The rowers below would match the rhythm.

Errant quarry, if quarry it was. But neither had the raiders expected to find themselves so far south in those open waters. They were seven weeks out of Tarsa, their home port. After rowing westward along the Anatolian coast, they had lain over in Korkassa to reprovision and fill out the crew.

All the ship's company identified as Cilicians, but profound social distinctions divided them. The leaders and most of the ninety warriors were members of the Hittite master class. The deckhands and rowers, like the lookout, were slaves: Luwians and other upland natives.

They had entered the Aegean north of Rhodes, hugging the land as long as possible before losing sight of the familiar contours of the channel islands and making a difficult crossing to the Cyclades. The vessel's single square sail made her fast before the breeze but inefficient when bearing up into it. The northwest Etesian winds had remained stiff and steady on their starboard bow, forcing them to tack often to northward to regain leeway and avoid being blown too close to Crete.

The Cilicians maintained a habitual distance from that greatest and southernmost of the Aegean islands they knew as Keftius, whose northern harbors held the bulk of the Keftiun war fleet. The island gave its name to all the Keftiun peoples, whether living on Crete itself, Thera, Delos, or any of their many other settlements. Powerful warships patrolled the Sea of Crete as far as thirty miles offshore, protecting the island's trade, guarding its rich cities and villages. The northern Cyclades, less defended, were the preferred hunting ground of Cilician pirates.

There was discontent on this voyage, however, and the commander sensed it. The raiders were frustrated by the almost total absence of vessels and land stores and no opportunity to carry off slaves. After vainly scouring the shores of Delos and its neighboring islands, sparsely populated at the best of times, they threaded south toward the outer coastal villages of Thera. These too they had found empty, save for a few clay amphorae storing what little dried fish, fruits, and olives were left behind in the inhabitants' hurried departure.

Thera was a ring-shaped island with an interior lagoon four miles wide, broken only by narrow straits at its southern quarter, and dotted by a separate island of volcanic rock, like the pupil of a vast eye. To enter the inner harbor under sail alone was impossible. The channel was situated to require rowing almost directly against the prevailing wind, funneled in powerful gusts by the northern peaks. Any exhausted interlopers who succeeded would be met by a fresh force of a dozen or more Keftiun warships, attacking with the breeze behind them and their driving hail of arrows, maneuvering to board or burn them into the water before they reached the lee of the caldera.

None, to the commander's knowledge, had ever made it back out.

Protected by their war fleet, the inhabitants of the villas and palaces lining the inner shores of Thera needed no walled fortifications to safeguard their peaceful prosperity. Keftiun seamanship held a mythical status among contemporary nautical peoples. Their trade empire extended throughout the known world. And, if the fables were to be believed, well beyond.

But this voyage was different. His empty holds and glowering crew, the desolation of the villages on the seaward coasts, even the acrid air, had emboldened the commander to venture into Thera's interior. After a backbreaking pull through the narrow channel, with apprehensive amazement, the Cilicians had entered the internal caldera unopposed.

None had dared break the dank silence in the lee of the cliffs. A sporadic shivering had rippled the surface of the lagoon—a sprawling, steaming soup of hundreds of species of fish floating belly up, smelling of rotten eggs and death.

Cautiously skirting the interior shore, alive with activity just months before, they'd found the pillared temples and mansions stripped and empty. Even the gold plating on the roofs and columns had been pried off. Had the Keftiu fled to the shelter of the island's towering ring of mountains? Gathered their treasure and set to sea?

Not so much as a mermaid, live or fanciful, could be spied off the coastal rocks or among the handful of worthless fishing boats remaining in the bays.

Disappointment had given way to superstitious dread. Without touching upon the inner shore, the raiders had hurriedly made sail, put the wind at their backs, and shot southeast out of the channel with all possible speed.

More than an hour later, watching Thera sink below the horizon off the stern, a burst of crimson, like a false sunset, had jolted the lookout, quickly obscured by a gray column filling the distant sky. Thirty heartbeats, then a shattering rumble, too deep for thunder.

After another hour passed, a ghostly white dust had begun to drift down with the Etesians. The crew's terror so mounting that he feared a mutiny, the commander had ordered the ship kept full before the wind. They threaded Karpathos and gained the open Mediterranean, but did not stop. Only when the Keftiun gods' anger was altogether behind them had they felt safe hauling up northeast for home.

Their flight had left them in their present position, more than twelve *iters* south of Rhodes, closing steadily upon the unknown vessel.

The lookout squinted again through the viewer, slung on a

leather cord around his neck with a skin of water and a slab of reeking salt mullet. A slim, sweeping prow became visible as the distant ship pitched. He waited, following the image for another five minutes, before he was certain.

"Keftiun, Master! Perhaps forty oars, and a passenger deck!"

The commander ordered the crew to alter course due east and spread full sail.

The lookout needed no reminder to stay aloft and alert. He smiled down at the figures of his father and cousins, watched them loose the hemp brailing lines with sharp, efficient motions. Their limbs appeared comically long as they strode the deck—an optical artifact of his bird's-eye perspective. The sail, made of greased wool and linked along its upper edge to the pivoting cross spar, shook out to its full surface area, and the ship gained speed. His father glanced up and winked as he hauled its leeward corner hard and low and clamped the clew sheet with a practiced knot.

The family group kept their relationship a secret. Raiding ships were prone enough to mutiny by Hittite freemen; the commander would never have knowingly risked alliances among slaves as well. Taking advantage of the crew's distraction, the youth relieved himself into his loincloth, gritting his teeth to the shame and sting as the warm urine burned the stripped skin of his groin. He would be flogged if he left the mast-top for even a moment. Or accidentally fouled the commander's banquet.

This last image made him smile again through the pain as he shifted once more on his perch. He gnawed at his dried fish, took a swig of water, and reflected.

The commander's fears of mutiny were well founded The warriors were still choking up Thera's dust and making little effort to hide their dissatisfaction with the cursed expedition. The lookout felt opportunity in the air.

He and his cousins had long spoken of the day they would cut out a vessel and set themselves up in their own coastal raiding enterprise. Among them, they already had knowledge sufficient to pilot and navigate. If the commander and the senior Hittites were dead, even the warriors would have no choice but to defer to them. An audacious fantasy, but not an impossible one.

And not entirely without precedent. Piracy presented a rare means of escape for the slave class. The Hittites deemed themselves a sacred race, sealed to their potent father god, and those they subjugated, mere chattel. But all of Anatolia had been ravaged by war for generations, and the culture, language, and values of its peoples were becoming blurred with those of their conquerors. Attaining power was increasingly a simple matter of acquiring wealth.

The lookout had been too young to fight in the last great uprising. His mother had died in childbirth, his father and uncles taken captive in battle in the rough western highlands. Unaware of their fate, for years his cousins and aunts tended the modest family olive groves in the foothills of the Pyramus River valley. When not keeping watch in the fields, he'd studied history, poetry, and mathematics until the day their land was overrun by the Hittite overlords, the family dispersed into bondage.

He'd been carted off to Tarsa, two years' service as a bath attendant the price of his youth and beauty. Not long after his twelfth birthday, a devoted client had purchased and taken him to sea. Several voyages, several masters, and the gods at length reunited the family—a grateful consolation.

There were many roles within the Cilician slave class, some more bearable than others. He was determined to better his position and took every opportunity to improve his seamanship. Unlike his father—graying and fatigued by battle and long servitude—the youth dreamt one day of escaping the hierarchy altogether.

The day passed, and the chase ship was visible from the Cilician deck. The lookout knew his value depended much upon his eyesight. While light remained, he strained to provide more details of their quarry.

"Master! Forty-two oars and at least twenty passengers! I count no more than twelve hands on the upper deck!" He paused. "Some passengers, I think, are ladies . . . females!"

The commander was puzzled. Keftiu rigged a canopied passenger platform only when carrying nobility, typically on short coastal cruises for diplomatic or ceremonial purposes. On merchant voyages, they crammed the upper deck with stores, placing heavier goods below to stabilize the ship: amphorae of oil and gold ingots. Or the far more valuable copper.

Why transport a bunch of lords and priestesses so far out to sea? What did her holds contain? He scratched at his braided beard. Unless they were packed with hidden swordsmen, she could be no warship.

"Has she altered course at all?"

The lookout grimaced and peered through the viewer. Yes, an almost imperceptible widening and squaring of her visible sail area betrayed a small increase in her starboard tack.

"*Annu*, Master! She has fallen off one point, heading now south by southeast!"

A frown creased the commander's brow. Surely, this deep in the Mediterranean, the Keftiu could not be worried about straying close to unfriendly shores. Keftiun vessels had the advantage sailing to windward. If they wished to outrun their pursuers, why were they veering farther south with the Etesians behind them?

Perhaps they meant to turn and fight, he thought. But he shook his head. If so, they would still have first beaten northward to gain the weather gage. With the the wind at their back when the Cilician's intercepted, the Keftiu would have had the edge in mobility and archery.

He kept the weary lookout aloft all night, scanning for the shadow of an escort in the reflected moonlight. None appeared, and by morning, both reason and greed had convinced the commander that the vessel was easy prey. Even with all her oarsmen taking arms—Keftiun rowers were volunteer freemen, never slaves—her visible force was little more than half the number of his trained fighters. The Cilicians could board and take her with minimal losses.

He hooked a thumb into the wide woolen sash girding his prosperous midriff and smiled. The hostages would bring a bonus, and if the ship held even a small portion of the riches hauled away from Thera, after sharing out and paying tribute, he could still look forward to a winter of ease and excess. He thought of his wives. A creamy Keftiun noblewoman would be a diverting addition. In Tarsa, a man's status was measured by his household.

Hour after hour, the Keftiun ship continued to edge southward. At their relative pace, they would not long delay their fate. The Cilician navigator, who had been marking the height of the sun since late morning, nodded to indicate high noon. The commander arched an eyebrow at the man's nervous demeanor and walked his own fingers at arm's length from the horizon up to the edge of the sun's disk. He moved his lips in a short mental calculation, then blinked several times.

At this latitude, they would pass well clear of the southern coast of Alashya. Neither he, nor any coastal raider he knew, had ever been south of Alashya. He chewed his beard.

No matter, he decided. He had come this far, and his holds were still empty. He would pursue the Keftiu on their present course, matching their southerly adjustments point for point, and attack from the north when he overtook. He, not his prey, would have the weather gage.

By late afternoon, the Keftiun ship lay at less than a quarter mile, its deck clearly visible. While nearly within downwind speaking distance, there was no point in either vessel hailing the other. Cilician raiders never attacked without advantage and had no reputation for mercy. Close sea action resulted only in the taking of the quarry and all its stores and the brutal death of anyone without worth as slaves or hostages. This far south, facing a long upwind beat back home against the Etesians, the Cilicians could afford to carry none but the most valuable. However dearly they sell their lives, the Keftius' end loomed certain. The commander feared only they might first tip their valuables over the side.

He stomped the deck again in faster tempo.

Reluctant to arm the disgruntled warriors earlier, he now ordered weapons distributed: short swords with leaf-shaped bronze blades, equally effective when employed in a slashing or stabbing motion. Molded, not forged, they were strong and heavy along their center but narrowed to thin outer edges, both durable and razor sharp.

The powerful, well-fed Cilician fighters were among the most capable killers of their time. They wielded the swords like an extension of themselves, swinging them in double arcs around the smooth olive wood handles, their eyes keen for the coming slaughter. Pumice sharpening stones began to circulate, along with skins of flat beer and a slab of honeyed seed cake.

At just a few hundred paces, the commander took measure of his prize. It was longer and narrower than his thirty-five-meter vessel, and fronted by a curling, tapered prow. The mast was of similar height, but its sail was substantially broader. His eyes fell upon the external gallery, which flanked its outer hull. Unlike the Cilician rowing galley, a suffocating hold pierced only by small oarlops, the open Keftiun gallery provided their oarsmen fresh air and the ability to swim free should the ship founder. It also allowed water to drain off when heeling in heavy seas. The Keftiun rowers could pull from a seated position or back their oars by standing and pushing them on their rotating bronze oarlocks.

While the finer points of Keftiun seamanship were poorly understood by other cultures, the mystique of the prize would enhance its value. The ship had traditional double steering paddles but also bore the broad, curved Keftiun stern fin. Controlled by a hardwood lever from the quarterdeck, the fin could be raised or lowered in the water and fixed in various positions. In its vertical shark-fin configuration, it stiffened the ship and reduced leeway. When deployed parallel to the surface like a whale's fluke, its curve could be rotated to raise or lower the bow, lengthening or shortening the hull's waterline and angle of attack. Skillfully handled, the feature maximized a Keftiun galley's efficiency under almost all conditions. It was the fastest and most weatherly seagoing vessel of its age.

The Cilician commander's nautical knowledge, considerable as it was, did not extend to such subtleties. He would order the external rowing galleries sawn off and the hull drilled with standard oarlops before placing the vessel for auction in Tarsa. The bronze locks and stern fin hardware were more valuable to him for their material than their cunningly molded shapes. They would be melted down to make weapons.

The faces of the Keftiu were distinct now. Their deck crew had not armed themselves: not a bow, sword, or spear appeared. Seated on hanging benches under the mid-deck canopy, he counted eighteen passengers, twelve of whom were women. Like the crew, the passengers, both male and female, were bare to the waist with the exception of one older woman, likely a priestess, who wore a fitted bodice of blue cotton. The females braided their dark black hair and tied it in a bun at the top of the head, shorter ringlets hanging in front, secured by gold bands. They wore layered leggings of belled contour, wider toward the ankles, easily mistaken for a skirt when seated. The men were dressed only in loincloths, their hair bound in clubbed tails.

Unlike the commander's shapeless flaxen tunic, even the rough seagoing Keftiun wardrobe was woven to fit its wearer and tinted with the rarest of dyes—a testament to the Keftiuns' wealth and far-ranging resources.

Their demeanor was oddly placid. The passengers murmured together, glancing back from time to time at their pursuers, as their crew continued to steer the ship farther off the wind. For most of the day, the course of the chase had been due south—far deeper into the eastern Mediterranean than any Cilician coastal raider had been before. The northwest wind was gradually diminishing, backing and clocking in a lazy, random manner, rendering the sails all but useless. The sea roiled in an irregular chop.

The commander was becoming impatient. He did not stop to

order the sails lowered, but pounded the deck faster and directed his coxswains to run the ship shoulder to shoulder with the Keftiun vessel a hundred paces off its port beam. In his long experience cruising the Aegean and the coast of Anatolia, the clear, cooling Etesians had blown from the northwest all summer, reliable as an old friend. He was certain they would pick back up. When they did, he would abruptly cross the bow of the Keftiun ship, stopping her dead, and board her. It was a tactic he often used when he did not wish to damage a prize by ramming it.

As the Cilician vessel began to overtake, the Keftiun rowers slowed their pace. The commander eased his exhausted oarsmen in turn. He was bemused to see the Keftiun priestess mount the prow of her ship.

Lips moving rapidly, she plunged her hand into a leather purse and faced the Cilicians. She drew a handful of bright silver ingots and hurled them in a backhanded arc. The precious pieces dotted the sea as they fell. The commander's eyes followed the flight and fall of the wasted wealth, as did those of all his crew.

They failed to remark the Keftiu reversing their sail and sheeting it slack to port.

A desperate offering fallen short? "Surely, the gentle fools can't think we'll be satisfied with tribute," the commander chuckled to himself.

Still at the masthead, the lookout, too, was distracted by the priestess's strange ritual. He did not notice a score of bronze, naked bodies spring over the rails of the starboard rowing gallery on the far side of the Keftiun ship and dive silently into the water. When he did raise his head, he was fixed by the sight of a line of strong wind rippling the sea beyond.

A wind he had never known before. A wind approaching rapidly from the *south*.

"*Shla yima! Ariyako!*" The cry of the Keftiun priestess ripped him from his stupor.

At her command, the Keftiun oarsmen on the near port gallery stood up as a group and pushed their oars to back them while the starboard rowers pulled powerfully in the opposite direction. The coordinated maneuver spun their ship ninety degrees and pointed its high prow directly at the starboard flank of the Cilician galley. The Keftiun sail cracked like a wet whip as it filled with the warm southern gale.

The dry cumin scent of the Khamsin—the Egyptian sirocco— was wholly foreign to the lookout's nose. Already sheeted for a broad port reach, the Keftiun ship leapt forward under combined wind and oar power and bore down upon the Cilicians' exposed flank with startling speed, her foamy bow wake cleaving the sea.

To the Cilicians, who had never experienced the Khamsin, the phenomenon was indistinguishable from sorcery. Panic gripped them, and they began to shrink back from the rails.

Despite his own confusion, the Cilician commander knew the delicate prow of the Keftiun ship was unsuitable for ramming. A suicidal tactic in any case, this far out in open water.

"Hold fast, there!" he shouted.

A bare quarter turn to starboard, he thought, and the Keftiun vessel would glance off his stern and settle gunwale to gunwale, undamaged and in an ideal boarding position.

He barked at the coxswains. "Hard to starboard! Now!" They leaned all their weight into the steering paddles.

The lookout scanned between his father, trying desperately to loose the sheets of the tightly backed sail before the unexpected blow capsized them, and the crew of the Keftiun ship, who were pushing on the lever of the strange tail fin. They plunged the device vertically into the foamy wake behind their stern. The drag immediately yanked their bow to starboard, pointed again at the side of the Cilician vessel.

The waves were mounting. The Keftiun crew set the fin's axle in its toothed slot and reached up to grip the long bars that radiated from the end of its handle like the spokes of a wheel. They watched the priestess on the prow. She raised her arm as it topped the pitch, and they pushed and pulled with their combined weight, rotating the fin to its horizontal, curve-up position.

The sudden downward force of flow at the stern caused the front of the Keftiun ship to vault upward like a crocodile's jaw, seawater streaming from its canvas-reinforced bottom.

The commander's gaze followed, his face slack. He saw the Keftiun priestess high astride the raised prow. It crossed his vessel amidships just as his starboard gunwale was rolling low. The Keftiun crew released the stern fin lever. Their forepeak plummeted and settled full over the Cilician galley, splintering its rail, pressing its deck below the surface, crushing or mangling a half dozen warriors, and flooding its lower compartments.

The priestess began spinning a bright object on a line.

Swimming ability was rare among Cilician mariners. With the abandoned terror of drowning cats, some tried to mount the mast, others hacked futilely with their swords at the timbers of the Keftiun ship. Those with the presence of mind to attempt to climb aboard her were dispatched by the scything of the priestess's weapon. The commander saw it clearly now. A double-bladed bronze axehead affixed by a swivel to a long leather cord.

She swung it with otherworldly skill, controlling its arc by paying out or coiling the line around her shoulder and arm. Those she missed were impaled by the Keftiun rowers, who had drawn short bronze-tipped javelins from concealed beckets and were hurling them with power and accuracy.

The commander's voice cracked. "We founder, dogs! Hold the rail and take their ship! Hold for your lives! We *must* take their ship!"

The admonition had some effect, and the Cilician swordsmen forced a desperate rally. Crouching in the rising seawater behind the stern bulwarks to avoid the flying javelins, they uncoiled grappling lines, tossed them over the Keftiun gunwales, and prepared to climb.

Pacing behind the line of boarders, the commander ducked to evade the priestess's ax. As he straightened, a shocking weakness overwhelmed him. He crumpled to the deck, as if his body had turned suddenly into a mass of wet seaweed.

He felt no pain. But through his narrowing field of vision, he remained conscious just long enough to witness a whirling flock of the bronze double axes, flung from behind him, bury into and sever the spines of five of his men at the base of their necks.

All along the starboard rail, Cilician warriors and crew were dropping, few having the bare time to turn and face the assailants at their backs. Each double-headed ax was retracted on its cord after it did its work. The lookout twisted in his perch and saw who wielded the vicious weapons. Still streaming with seawater, twenty or more female swimmers crouched along the port deck, hair twisted in tight clubs, naked but for gleaming golden cinctures and scabbards at their waists.

They had boarded over the undefended port rail. But how had they swum so far without him spotting them? He could only surmise that they'd crossed completely submerged below the keels of both ships, fully exploiting the element of surprise. No war cry or other sound escaped them.

He had failed as a lookout. He compelled himself to watch as one of the women recovered her weapon, reeling its cord about her arm, and flung it again with a sidearm wrist motion. The double axehead spun horizontally, almost floating on the air as she arched the coil high and clear of its flight. He gasped when it found its target, cleanly severing the upraised sword arm of a Cilician warrior.

The Cilicians offered no further hostility. All their swordsmen and leaders were dead or dying, the few remaining crew, the lookout's father among them, squatting mutely on the quarterdeck to avoid the rising, blood-tinged water. The lower galley was flooded, the rowers no doubt already drowned in their chains.

The old man motioned his son to stay aloft. There was still a chance the Keftiu might find some of the slaves worth saving. His gray head cleared the stern rail as he pulled himself up, and he waived his arms for the attention of the Keftiun priestess.

He pointed at the mast-top, then folded his hands in a pleading gesture. *"Remu!"* he cried. "Mercy!"

The priestess glanced briefly upward. *"Shlak'usura eya!"* she said. "They are done!"

With long, nimble steps, the warrior women reboarded their ship over extended oars, and the Keftiun rowers began their standing reverse paddle to back it off and away from the sinking Cilician vessel.

The priestess gazed up again at the lookout. She studied him, then beckoned.

"Pekdol tzetaru, kitmayo!"

He could not understand Keftiun. Her eyes darted with a strange intensity—fierce, ancient, yet somehow childlike. He did not move.

From the quarterdeck of the Keftiun ship, one of the male pilots repeated more loudly in brusque Akkadian: *"Uwid katta!* Come down!"

The priestess extended a finger to silence the man and beckoned again.

One of the youngest of the female warriors, ax now sheathed at her waist, climbed past and balanced upon the highest point of the prow. She began spinning the opposite end of her leather cord, weighted by heavy, polished wooden balls. Peering up intently, she slowly let it play out through her fist, lengthening the radius of its circular motion.

He would not wait to die by her weapon. He felt the descent of a silent clarity. The sea itself seemed to tarry and anneal. He scanned once more the bodies of his kinsmen wafting in the bloody wash. With a last look at his father, he loosed his grip and dropped, slack and soundless, toward the deck below, offering an inward prayer to Ishtar that the fall might end his life quickly.

Before he dropped five meters, the bolo end of the young woman's cord whipped out and upward, wrapping his leg. She leaned back, jerked him clear, and deposited him with a booming splash, uninjured, in the water between the two ships. She unbound her belt and dove, emerging beside him, supporting his unresisting head until the Keftiu fished him out by the arms, limp and naked onto their deck. He had lost his sodden loincloth.

Coughing, he wriggled for the gunwale, stretched his arm over the water toward his father. A futile, hopeless gesture. Their eyes remained locked as the raiding ship disappeared beneath the swell, dousing the screams of its wounded.

"Abu?" his rescuer asked, still holding his other elbow.

She pointed toward the foamy eddy and tried again in her limited Akkadian. *"Abu-kku-nu?"*

Still he did not answer.

"Qibid!" the Keftiun pilot barked. "Speak!"

"Annu!" he wailed and turned to the warrior. *"Anna, eesta abitusmaas!* Yes! Yes, he was my father!"

Fear wholly broken by grief, his words began to flow with his tears. *"Ata? Eesta muzzaz biti—edanis muzzaz biti!* Why? He was a servant—a mere servant!"

The young woman could no longer follow the rapid, wracked Akkadian. She sat against the bulkhead and lowered him gently between her long, muscled legs, the wet skin of his trembling back against her bosom. She surveyed the rawness of his thighs, livid from the salt water, as his head lolled back upon her shoulder. She met the priestess's eyes.

Receiving a nod, the warrior set into a gentle whisper-song, breathed it in the young man's ear, tracing deft spirals in his wet hair with her fingertips.

The Keftiun crew retracted the stern fin and put the ship on a more easterly tack, the warm, steadying breeze just forward of her beam.

The Cilician winced, then relaxed as another woman washed his groin with fresh water, then applied a liniment of sweet terebinth resin, mint, and dead nettle. She offered an alabaster chalice, containing an amber tincture of wine and lotus blossom. Despite his thirst, he averted his head.

"Di, pasahid libbu. Here, calm your heart," the healer said in Akkadian and held the cup to his lips with an encouraging smile. A cool, piney bite of cedar resin met his tongue, softened by the kiss

of juniper.

"*Assus.*" She nodded, and his gulps came faster.

When he finished, his rescuer wrapped her arms about him. His pain and fear abating, his eyes rolled up to meet hers.

"*Edanis muzzaz abiti.* Just a servant." He held his wrists together to illustrate.

"*Duritzi kashyaru tzeroru-min kai yibasa yatzu eya,*" she whispered back. He did not understand the Keftiun words, but they danced off her tongue like a well-tempered proverb, and he was comforted by them.

"The most unbreakable binding is the illusion of liberty" was their meaning.

His heaving slowed. The tender grate of her fingernails against his scalp helped still his trembling core. Her black forelocks swayed and dried in the Khamsin as her amber eyes panned the twilight sky. A thin drift of Thera's ash, stirred for days by the four winds of the high heavens, finally reached them and began to fall like silent sorrow upon the deck.

"*Kai'yak tzo Yanu pakyo, kahu'tzin. Kai'yak tzo Yanu pakyo,*" she repeated in airy rhythm, so close to his ear that her velvet voice seemed born within his head.

"Weep with us and God, little brother. Weep with us and God."

Some corner of the bewildered labyrinth of his heart understood. The salt of her tears mingled in his mouth with his own and that of the sea. His chest drew calmer, deeper, a powerful, purging discharge with each breath.

2 Roots of Exile

Hark back within, embrace that wond'ring child
  Whose native bud blooms in your bosom yet,
  Your years a composition in its debt;
Sober poise is but its caprice, a mild
Divertissement satirically styled
  By younger humors innocent of fret;
  Still unsnared, then, in worldly sorrow's net.
Remember when we wafted rivers wild,
Sprites unabashed by rain or vernal wet,
  Nursing love like orchids; how thus became
  That ravaged heart? I would that love still grew
  Behind fogged windows, lucent eyes I knew
Before this time of mists. And when they clear
  I'll flay your weary petals each by name—
Anon, in downy dishabille appear.

3 March 1769 AD
Lt. S. Singer, HMRN
At Sea

Darling Girl,
     As I run, I salute you. Not the babe I left you in your mama's arms scarce a week ago, for though the crisis of my recent injuries is passed, I know not if, or when, I may ever look again upon your sweet face.

An exile, sure, but I do not feel a fugitive. A fugitive runs to evade punishment, some loose bight of line left unknotted. He flees to preserve himself from justice, whereas I run because I have presumed to be its measure. I run in hope of the welcome of unacquainted family, toward warmth and sunlight, deep mountains and whispering streams, which I wish their draught may restore me.

A curious thing, to write these words without a figure in my mind of who you shall be when you read them. Are you an older child? A young woman? A mother?

You may not have heard much of me, and what little, of littler truth. Yet be assured that once we did—we *did*—share the most precious congress, for an interval that fled so to break my heart, and that happy memory the lingering reason for me to write these letters. Be they correspondence or journal, it makes no odds; as I live, I will write and preserve all, that I might one day commit them to your eyes.

I chill to think I may never learn your name.

I pray you better know your mama, that she has you now and always near. Howbeit, it is well I acquaint you of her. This against fate, or that crueler power as would fain separate you, which the same it has done us.

The mama whom I hope you know is Eleanor Blunt, née Singer. She is my aunt, although sufficient close in age that she has always called me cousin, and the bond we share is that and more. Whatsoever her disposition as you read this, be assured that before she knew your father, she knew happiness.

In her youth, Eleanor had prodigious gifts for music, arts, and letters; her esthetic sensibility so compelling that she needed no self-discipline to master them. She adored the eccentric pearls of the Baroque as much as the modern perfection of the younger Bach, Sappho as much as Shakespeare. She was petite and pale, speckled blond, a gray-eyed, unselfconscious beauty—yea, her own millpond aspect the sole *magnum opus* which failed ever to move her.

She doted upon me, her little Sebastian, and I upon her. She was used to put herself to sleep with candle and book; and so I gifted her one Christmas with a sturdy crystal lamp, its bright flame protected by a glass chimney, that her mother Nessie might cease her voluble speculation upon which night the house should burn.

Eleanor was oft so affected by the sublime that she would bite her lip and dig her fingernails into her palms at exhibitions and recitals, or if she fell upon beauty in obscurity or by happenstance, as when a magpie pecked at the window, or a visitor turned an apt phrase at table.

Nessie found her daughter's peculiarities rather more amusing than worrying.

"Look! There she's struck dumb again!" she would exclaim in her scant brogue, eyes steely blue with mirth.

My mother, Arima, however, would gently grasp Eleanor's little fists and whisper in her ear until she came back to herself.

There were other predilections as well: a misdirection of gaze, a hesitancy of speech, myriad inexplicable habitudes and anxieties. I make no doubt that some great continental men of physic have a term for the condition, as if classification were cure. After

Eleanor's marriage to your father, it matured into a frank malady of spirit, which grieved me as deeply as once the little tendencies had enchanted.

But I overtake myself.

The casual sonnet with which I prefaced this letter was inspired by a journey through the French countryside your mother and I made together when I was twelve and she sixteen—a few months before her marriage. Nessie was to host a gathering of her Irish relations at the Portsmouth house, which she did infrequently, and only in summer when her late husband's family were mostly abroad.

Nessie was born a Laughlin, a papist Ulster clan of which she remained the reluctant matriarch despite her conversion from the old faith and marriage to an Anglican parson. In her view, the Laughlin women were as unpredictable as they were undomesticated, and she no more liked to expose them to her offspring than to her in-laws.

And so she dispatched our little band to Burgandy for a month's party tour by barge of the Loire River and the Canal de Briare. We learned with satisfaction that we were to travel not only with my mother, but also with our adored pair of bachelor "uncles"—in fact, her particular friends and business agents.

Arima, then just thirty, was rather more friend and confidant than chaperone. Eleanor being betrothed, and I to enter the Royal Naval Academy upon our return to Portsmouth, the adventure was to prove the final frolic of our childhood, and we reveled in the carelessness from which we were neither of us long for a disagreeable weaning.

A number of my Singer uncles were in active naval command and had already enlisted my name on the muster roll of various vessels, as who should say *in absentia*, to gain me nominal sea time. This little legal fiction aside, my actual experience had been very scant indeed, and I longed to know blue water, if only as a passenger. I pled that we should sail out the Channel, round Brest, and take the ocean route, putting in to the Loire riverhead at St.

Nazaire on the Atlantic coast.

Yet alas, Arima's bittersweet memory of her migration from Spain via the Bay of Biscay put her off, and a direct line across the Channel from Portsmouth to St. Malo on the northern shore of Brittany won the decision. This route offered the dual charms of brevity and the opportunity to discover the monastic city of Mont St. Michel, which rises like a desert mirage from the tidal flats. Thence, a long day's overland journey to board a waiting *futreau* on the Mayenne River, which flows into the Loire south of Angers.

As we approached the Channel Islands, the ferry was compelled to stand off northwest of Guernsey before putting into St. Malo with the high tide. The swell lessened a bit, and Arima desired me to tarry with her on deck. Looking down over the rail, her habitual placid smile grew thin, and her eyes took on the gray of the sea as she mouthed a silent prayer. She opened an oiled paper bundle and offered me one of two large flowers of delicate purple, pink, and white. She called them *orkidea gizon biluzik* in her Basque language, which is, I blush to say, the "naked man orchid," and each of their numerous petals did indeed bear that resemblance, down to the tiny smiling face and unmistakable *membrum virile*.

She led me in one of the many little mystery rituals which had become the custom of my childhood. We held our orchids out over the rail; squeezing them until our fists ached, she recited in her piercing whisper, *"loreak beti dute arantza,"* which is to say, "every flower bears a thorn," then we cast them into the sea.

I knew better than to pose importunate questions when my mother was in that state of quiet reflection, and I wrapped my arm around her waist as we watched the flowers toss gently upon the swell for a time before repairing below to rejoin the rest of our party.

Arima evinced no desire to nurse her melancholy—indeed, she seemed relieved to have surrendered it—and cast herself fully into the spirit of our adventure. Our exploration of the towering monastery island and the passage through the mountains by open carriage flew by in a breathless buzz; only once aboard our canal barge did our pace of experience slow and our excitement give way to lingering rapture.

Can anything in youth be more romantic? Long, languid days passed in contemplation of the lilac that swept broad the river's margent, and the gentle dragonflies, whose name I asked Arima, as I was wont to do, to give me in Basque.

"*Sorginorratz,*" she replied.

I searched my mind for its etymology. "Needle . . . witch's needle?" I giggled.

Arima frowned. "Do not say 'witch' for *sorgin.*"

I spoke Basque with no one but Arima in my infancy, but I knew I must have derived the connection from some source, perhaps the proverbs of Oihenart, or the stories of Axular, which she had given me to read.

"Why do others call it so, Ama?" I asked her.

Her face clouded slightly. "Because to them, a woman who is free must be wild, and if wild must be destitute. A woman without the support of a man, in their thinking, must necessarily live under bridges, use thornwood to comb her hair and dragonflies to mend her tattered garments. It is a word used at once to wish ruin upon a woman and to mock her poverty."

After a moment, her smile brightened. "But it is just a word, in the end. And an amusing one for so beautiful a creature," she said, carefully cupping a dragonfly in her hands and releasing it with a puff of breath.

Every day of our little journey offered new glamours. My uncles and I helped the bargeman step the slender masts of our *futreau,* which held its odd, square topsails high enough to catch the wind above the canal's banks. We tasted the splendor of the rustic delicacies, each meal a *pique-nique* of samplings urged upon us by proud villagers: *rillettes* of pheasant and venison spread like butter upon crusty baguettes with preserved black cherries, trout caught and pan fried before our eyes by the bargeman's wife, eaten fresh and fresh in their own unctuous essence, deglazed with just a splash of the local white table wine.

Ah, and the freshwater *langoustines* we caught below the rocks along the banks of the canal! All that was needed to tease the shy crayfish from their hiding places was a bit of shiny metal on a string and patience. Once having seized the dangling lure, they would not leave off and could be pulled straight out the water, victims of their own stubbornness. I laugh to remember how Eleanor winced the first time Arima pulled the head off one, hot from its brief boiling in the stockpot, and sucked with her native Basque relish. Their tails were shelled, coated in a *velouté* of their own *court bouillon* thickened with cream, seasoned with nothing more than white pepper, salt, and a suspicion of nutmeg, and baked *en croute*—in a flaky pie. Each bite, followed by a sip of the cool Anjou wine, elicited a silent prayer of gratitude for the joy of life; as did for me, each glance at the contented, sun drenched face of my beloved Eleanor.

I learned much on that short holiday. I learned to tell good wine from great, the essence of sublime food, which abides in its source, not its preparation. Neither more did I overlook the delicacy of color nor the subtlety of scent. Simply, I learned to love. More than the needful love of a child, but the discriminating *amour* of a balanced being: the wisdom of rejecting what did not appeal, and choosing that which spoke to my heart.

And like the antique troubadour, I learned that our passions neither obey nor direct our destiny. Our beloved belongs to us only inasmuch as we make love itself our own; to be *fedeli d'amore* is no less than to be a confidant of Venus through all her chaotic mischiefs, and to surrender ourselves not to the beloved, but to providence.

And yet, for all that, the pang of loss nags as I pen these happy remembrances and again puts me in mind of how little you may know of your family; and so permit me for the instant to put that journey aside and revert to antecedents.

Of your Singer great ancestors, I have already written: Nessie, whose maiden name in its Irish form was Neassa Laughlin. The history which follows must stand on your appreciation of Nessie's ambitions in marrying David Singer. The Laughlins are a fish-and-pearl merchant family of some local renown in *Gaoth Dobhair* (or Gweedore, as we say in English) in Ulster's county Donegal. You may know that the body of Ulster escheated to the crown, and most of its prime tracts were deeded over to Scottish and English immigrants during the great plantation of the last century.

Nessie is one of two surviving daughters of Seamus Laughlin, the other being her younger sister, Roinseach, whom she calls Rhona. I have learned much from my great aunt Rhona; and because Nessie spoke precious little of her life in Ireland, most of what I write now is as Rhona related it to me.

Donegal is the westernmost and least arable part of Ulster, with its rocky, windswept Atlantic coast, boggy rosses, and lofty mountains, and lies farthest from the prominent eastern seats of provincial power. Some might say that the new landowners usurped little, therefore, when the region was apportioned into British baronetcies, but in any case are scarce loved by their native Irish tenants. While Romanism is suppressed under the Penal Laws, Anglican congregations coexist with the Protestant Church of Ireland, the only remarkable distinction being the language in which services are conducted.

Despite all, many Roman Catholics continue to practice their faith and educate their children in the remoter parts of Donegal, though some papist landholders have professed the Communion of the Church of Ireland to protect their interests. Nessie's father, Seamus, the eldest of his brothers, made such a nominal Protestant conversion to gain the right to keep all the extended family's lands, fishing fleet, and other properties in his name, as who should say a trustee, leaving the rest of the Laughlins at liberty to continue in the Roman rite if they chose.

The Laughlin women, whose commercial contribution to the family derives principally from the article of pearls, have for generations drawn the disapprobation of the local clergy; this for their deemed independence and atavistic way of life amidst the coastal sea caves and grottoes. Which particular style of Christian might claim their allegiance makes little odds to most of them.

Nessie's own conversion was widely seen as a matter of ambition conquering conscience, as the Penal Laws prohibit papists from wedding Anglicans, and she was determined to marry into property if she could. Her deeper reasons had much to do with Seamus, with whom she had always shared a particular bond. Her father's apostasy had left him nigh friendless in the county, shunned by papists, neither well accepted nor trusted by lifelong Anglicans. Many believed his isolation contributed to his early death by drink.

As for your Singers, they are a prominent Scot family with close ties to England established over several generations. Having earned preferences from the crown more than a century ago as military servitors during the Nine Years' War, several large and valuable tracts of land in East Ulster remain with them to this day.

The lesson of ascension through martial service was well taken, and several generations of Singer men obtained naval commissions which they contrived to work to their considerable wealth and interest, those few not attaining post rank profiting the family's mercantile endeavors as captains of private vessels. By David Singer's generation, the family well afforded him the means to read his divinity at Oxford, which he did, and afterward determined to return to Ulster to support the expansion and Anglicization of the Church of Ireland. He accepted a shabby benefice as parson of the small congregation at Donegal Village.

Having passed some years of his youth in the province, David's accent of speech was not strange to the local ear, and he had a good deal of the Irish tongue as well, which served him in what he called his "missionary situation."

I learned that it was Rhona, and not Nessie, who first caught young David Singer's eye one winter Friday morning at the market in the Donegal Diamond, as the village square is known. Talk of the new parson's arrival had spread quickly. Rhona admired his tall stature, fine but rumpled waistcoat and cloak, and properly affable manner as he tarried by her stall. There on offer was the daily haul of herring and mackerel from the Laughlin fishing fleet at nearby Killybegs, together with live shellfish from the islands of Gweedore Bay. Alongside was a simmering cauldron of stew made from the otherwise wasted meat and liquor of the many oysters shucked in suspicion of pearls. At a halfpenny a bowl, its price barely covered its cost, but it served to feed the poor of the town, and the fragrance and warmth were a clever draw to trade.

Rhona smiled mischievously as David asked in his stilted Irish, *"Cé mhéad é cochall?"* He supposed this to mean, "How much for cockles?"

Now all the Laughlin children of both sexes were educated at home—many by their uncles, who had studied at the Irish Colleges abroad—and Rhona spoke tolerable English, French, and Latin. She well knew the source of David's confusion but played along to prolong the dialogue. Spilling her long copper tresses, she unbuttoned the red felt hood from her woolen cloak and offered it to him for four shillings.

David flushed. He removed a glove, picked up a cold handful of the little bivalves, and said, "Forgive me, miss, but cockle . . . *cochall*, no?"

"Forgive *me*, kind reverend sir," Rhona replied in English with her most engaging smile, "but, if it pleases you, *this* is a *cochall*," again exhibiting the hood. She extended her arm and folded her fingers over his raised hand. "*These* we call *ruacan*, the creatures, and barely boiled in fresh cream and butter, they make the most delicate of potages."

"But I was certain . . ." He frowned, unable to disengage from her cobalt-blue eyes.

Rhona took pity. "Perhaps the reverend has been misled by our expression *'cochall mo chroí*?" she volunteered, still grasping his hand.

His face brightened. "Just so! As one should say, 'the cockles of my heart'!"

She tilted her head. His honest delight in her language was rare among the Planters, as the English and Scottish interlopers were known; his looks a cozy, virile balance of gentility and birr.

"Yes, Reverend, a common mistranslation. The warmth we describe from strong sentiment is within the *cochall*—the hood, or covering, encompassing our heart," she said, wrapping her palm firmly round his chill fist to illustrate. After a pause and a smile of bolder directness, she began filling a damp sack with the cockles, adding in a goodly portion of live oysters.

"A parish offering," she said, refusing his payment.

After thanking her and learning her name, he made a leg and said, "Surely, you have warmed the *cochall MO chroi,* Roinseach Laughlin."

Rhona curtsied, and as David turned his back, leant athwart the counter of her stall to watch him leave.

I grow prolix, my dear, and I pray this history not fatigue you so in the reading as does it me, in the instant, to write it; but my wounds, though healing, still bite, and my blood has not yet recovered its vigor. I shall rest awhile and continue when refreshed.

Your affectionate,
S. Singer

3 Figures in the Dust

But when you have bad governance, of course, these resources are destroyed: the forests are deforested, there is illegal logging, there is soil erosion. I got pulled deeper and deeper and saw how these issues become linked to governance, to corruption, to dictatorship

—Wangari Maathai

1602 BCE
Eastern Mediterranean

The lookout's next memory was nine hours later, drawn up from a sleep that was dark and bodiless. A niggling rasp. Sunlight edging through an open scupper. Behind his eyelids, the burnish blinked like a channel beacon as the ship rocked the low hammock in which he lay. He groped for his viewing tool, his mind not yet alive to what had passed since last he scanned the eastern morning skies.

"Yibri Sephuru." Friendly, unfamiliar words. He opened one eye. Seated by his side was his rescuer, her legs crossed, circling an arm within a large blackened pot.

She was scrubbing its interior with salt, watching over him as he slept. They were on the Keftiun ship's lower deck, alone in a tiny but airy compartment cordoned by translucent tapestries.

"Shulmu," he replied in Akkadian.

She shook her head, folded her rag, and knelt beside him. Parting his legs to inspect his lesions, she repeated with emphasis, *"Yibri SEPHuru!"*

He rubbed his eyes and tried the Keftiun greeting. *"Yee-bree SEF-oo."*

She smiled at his effort and turned to face the morning sun. Its rays framed her aquiline profile, gilding her amber eyes and bronzed skin. When she looked back, the meaning struck him.

He pointed toward the dawn. *"Sephuru?* Morning?"

She nodded.

"Yibri Sephuru!" he said. *"Good* morning!" She squeezed his foot.

Folding his hands beneath his chin, he addressed her in rudimentary Akkadian.

"Nabu-ka?"

She playfully mimicked his gesture and translated into similarly simple Keftiun. *"Yam namu?* My name?" She took his right hand, placed it atop her bowed head, and said, "Hibya."

"Hibya," he repeated. He reeled at its beauty, wondered if she knew how it resonated in Akkadian. *Hibti*—my beloved.

And from one of the oldest prayers, *Hibti Hebat.* Beloved mother of the gods.

For a long moment, her chin remained lowered as he mused, fingers still entwined in her hair. Coming to himself, he blushed and jerked away. She looked up with an arched brow.

He strained to say something in her words. *"Yi—yibri namu.* G—good name."

She sprang to her feet, spun, and clapped in approval of his simple but clever construction. Her laugh was like a sudden rainfall. Natural and tenderly penetrating.

The tapestries parted, and an older woman entered, silent and fluid. The healer who had treated him the day before. She set her tray and frowned at his still brightly inflamed skin. She scooped a reduction of wood ash and sheep's fat from a wooden bowl and smeared his inner thighs and genitals. It stung and foamed like the mouth of a rabid dog when she cupped fresh water and rubbed. He glanced at Hibya, then turned away, picked a tapestry, and fixed upon it.

A woman's face in bold black lines, framed by a woven border of gold and violet, eyes rimmed in dark kohl. It stared back at him with the same self-possessed intensity he had seen in the Keftiun priestess. The image seemed to come alive as the diaphanous material played on the breeze from the scupper. The healer rinsed his body with more fresh water. He contemplated this generosity, so far from land, as she spread clean linen and applied more soothing balm.

The pain eased, and he looked around the chamber. The

hangings shared a similar design, but each portrayed a different female face. Icons of the warriors' ancestors, perhaps. The reflection brought a throb for his father. He wondered why he—he alone—had been left alive.

Before exiting, the healer addressed him in simple but clear Akkadian.

"Diqqum dakkukutu takalas? Shatas mu?"

He hesitated to accept more freemen's drinking water after so much had already been used to bathe him. But his stomach groaned at the wafting scents of cooking.

"Anna, diqqum akalas, hod."

She returned to leave two long-handled earthenware bowls. A steaming saffron-scented chowder of freshly caught skate thickened with olive oil, bulrush root, and dried nettle. They sipped it down in companionable silence.

In his life, he had never tasted anything so delicious.

Hibya rose and stood over him, extending her wrist. His eyes flickered up over her lithe body and met hers. The current he'd felt on the deck, in her arms, revisited, stoking the warmth in his belly. She took his fingers, wrapped them around her wrist, and nodded.

He understood. He guided her hand to his own head and said his name.

"Illuyanka."

"Yi-loo-LYAN-ka?" she ventured. A fair attempt, but he offered the simpler form. The name his masters called him.

"Luyan," he said.

She shook her head. *"Li. Itzmo. Vam namu kebi.* No. Once more. Your true name," she demanded in Keftiun.

He uttered it slowly and distinctly. "Il-lu-YAN-ka."

"Iy-loo-YAN-ka."

"Yibri." he nodded.

Still stroking his hair, she repeated the foreign syllables several times. She paused, circled a finger toward the deck above, and said, "Luyan." Then touching her forehead to his, whispered, "Illuyanka."

Luyan for the rest of the world. But his sacred name was hers alone.

Still ignorant of the Keftiu's motives for saving him, Luyan was anxious to work, show his value, distinguish himself from a menial, unskilled slave. Two days passed, however, before Hibya permitted him to leave the curtained compartment other than to ease his needs off the leeward rowing gallery. She made him understand he was to speak only to the *serkarui*—the female warriors.

The days that followed seemed to rush past, lost in the buzz of learning. Hibya was not only eager to teach him, but to know his capacities, his habits of mind. She instructed him in their counting words, using the opportunity to discover his age.

"*Itz, vi, shlan, arsh, ko, zai, zhi, hyu, kya, yam, yamitz, yamvi, yashlan, yamarsh, yamko, yamzai . . .*" She stopped and pointed to her chest. She was sixteen years old.

She turned her finger to him.

"*Yamarsh.*" Fourteen. "*Kedosh itzmo tsukaru, yamko.* But one more moon, fifteen," he quickly qualified, tracing an arc in the sky with his finger.

"*Itzmo-TI tsukAIru YA EYAKAYA yamko.* IN one more moNTH, I WILL BE fifteen," she corrected.

Her brow creased. Malnutrition had given him a deceptively lank, boyish frame. But most Keftiun men were several years married by his age. Luyan was very much an adult.

He took her expression as impatience and began counting again with his fingers, repeating the series perfectly on his second attempt. He pushed to go higher, correctly constructing some multi-digit numbers from their root components. "*Yamvi*"— twelve. "*Viyam*"—twenty.

It became clear to Hibya that Luyan's capacity surpassed her own as they covered addition and subtraction, multiplication and division. She did not know the meanings or words for negative numbers, fractions, the many symbols he traced on the deck. To these, she merely shook her head and said, "Kozhiniru."

An uncertain look. She made a backhanded casting gesture, the motion with which the Keftiun priestess had started the sea battle. The conflict that had destroyed his ship and killed his father.

He winced and lowered his eyes.

She took his wrist and spoke slowly. "You will speak to the Kozhiniru. She knows much of sacred numbers and symbols. She is the teacher of all our *serkarui*."

He ate the same food as she did, shared the same simple chores, and, at her firm insistence, spoke only her language. He was not invited to participate in religious exercises, but she performed them freely in his presence. They cleansed themselves together each morning off the leeward rowing gallery, a ritual which she always preceded with a swim. When the ship was hove to or making slow headway, she beckoned him to join her and worked to improve his ability.

They sat together, whispering long into the night, facing one another, he in his best approximation of her erect posture, feet crossed over thighs. He attended closely to her Keftiun phrases, her gestures and pantomime. He soon began to associate the words with ideas, within a few days hearing her soft tones in his sleep.

Luyan's ability to acquire language was exceptional, even for one born in a multilingual society. All the same, Hibya pressed him hard and denied any attempt he made to communicate in Akkadian. He would rarely defy her, but he often burned to phrase a question, to understand an important nuance.

He picked up the word *zhyuzhurai* from context. Hibya uttered it in a low hiss, finger to her lips. "Whisper." Extending her arms about their shared compartment, *"Zhyuzhurai hitzwatu."*

"Whisper place," he guessed, but her reverent tone carried more. In a moment alone with the healer, he asked her to translate the phrase into Akkadian. She considered and said, "Whisper cave."

While most of the *serkarui* slept on piled skins around the foot of the mast, the sides and corners of the lower deck were separated into a number of "whisper caves." Each contained two women who shared their lives and hammocks. The scant tapestries doing nothing to muffle sound, it was apparent these couplings were more than friendship. The Keftiu, both male and female, were to Luyan's eye a generally quite beautiful people, and his culture was all but indifferent to alternative forms of sensual expression. Still, he found it odd so many women had no male counterpart or even interest in occasional pairing with the crewmen and rowers.

His reflections, despite himself, turned to Hibya.

Grief gradually ebbed as he eased into the familiar rhythm of life at sea, his mind alert to the novel complexities of the vessel and its people. He had some knowledge of the Keftiu, of course, as did all nautical Mediterraneans, but this ship's company—and its mission—was decidedly unique. The crew treated the passengers with the deference due nobility, and the *serkarui* a distinct class of no lesser rank. All demonstrated deep reverence for the Kozhiniru. And a general, but palpable anxiety.

Luyan's own foreboding remained, questions which he lacked the words to pose. The purpose of the Keftiu in preserving him. The urgency he sensed in Hibya's teaching. How eager he was to please her, he thought, biting his lip. In Cilicia, there was no lower status for a male than that of a woman's concubine. If his usefulness remained uncertain, so must his fate.

But the gods could not have brought him so far to die a failed bed slave. He would do all to prove his worth as a mariner.

As the days passed, he kept careful mental reckoning of the ship's heading and speed, watched the crewmen throw the cork line, noted the curve of the wake, learning as much as he could about the unfamiliar waters. The ship was creeping northeast by day, only a few starboard oars working to counteract leeway, heaving to at night for safety, and keeping a good offing from shore, presumably to avoid being sighted by coastal vessels. He knew that at their current rate and heading they would soon be approaching the eastern limit of the known sea—the Levantine coast.

He shot the height of the noonday sun with his fingers as he had learned by watching the Cilician navigators, making a deliberate show of skill in hope his seamanship might attract favorable notice. He estimated the ship's position to lie along a line a day's journey due south of Alashya, a latitude to which he had never before traveled and knew only by its designation.

"*Gubel,*" he muttered absently.

Hibya turned sharply. "*Doshyi va yaposai kozhmai yakom kageru?* How could you possibly know our destination?"

He did not follow.

"*Gubel . . . doshyi va kozhmai Gubel-min?* How do you know about Gubel?"

He gestured at the sun with a proud grin. She sighed, grabbed his palm, and traced a rough rectangle, pressed her finger at the right edge, and repeated, "Gubel."

Only when she pointed east did he understand. Gubel, like Alashya, was not just a latitude. It was a specific place.

"*Va yaka Gubel?* You go Gubel?"

"*Ayi!* Yes! We are all going to Gubel!" she said, her exasperation showing.

The ship's sail plan did in fact take them to that most ancient port city of the Levant. Although she pressed in simplest words, how Luyan had apparently guessed remained a mystery to Hibya. She vowed to redouble his language lessons.

He followed her to the foredeck. The *serkarui* were at exercise, a raucus athletic game. Facing the forepeak, each woman spun and cast the ball-weighted end of her ax cord toward the prow. As the line wrapped itself, the thrower took a turn around her arm, sprinted, and dove over the side. Swinging through the air in a wide arc around the front of the ship, abdomen rippling as she folded at the waist to propel herself though the upward leg, she cleared the starboard rail and alighted at the starting point. The others celebrated with a keening wail.

How praiseworthy, their grace and prowess, he thought. Their energy so wholly foreign. The *serkarui* were loudly and openly reveling in their physical power, something Luyan had never before witnessed outside a company of men.

Panting and flushed, Hibya smiled. "We find the ship so confining, so small." She gestured to make it clear. "We have to improvise in our exercises." Luyan nodded mutely.

"Would you like to try?" she asked, holding the line out to him and motioning. She tugged hard to show him the bolo end was still wrapped tightly around the prow.

He hesitated but felt the eyes of the other *serkarui,* as well as several crewmen, upon him. She gave the cord a double turn around his shoulders and upper arm. He made to mount the rail in preparation for a halfhearted jump, but she shook her head and led him back to the center of the deck.

"You must run and leap hard. Cast yourself out against the line as strongly as you can." She pantomimed the movements.

"Start head first, finish feet first!" another shouted. "No fear!' They all echoed these last words.

Amid the current of encouragement, Luyan leaned back until the cord was semi-taut, ran hard toward the port rail, leapt, and dove over. He suppressed a shout as the cord snapped tight and sharply redirected his momentum out and forward.

He visualized the necessary physics, pressed his legs together, extending first straight out behind, then tucking under and swinging them to waist level as he rounded the bow.

But his upward momentum began to flag as he neared the starboard rail. He reacted with a panicky pedaling, managed only to hook one heel over before Hibya and two others pulled him aboard. Their congratulations tasted of charity.

He declined a second try. He was tired of being fished helpless into boats by these women. Fascinating as their abilities were, they seemed far beyond him.

But as his father had often said, Luyan's curiosity burned brighter than his fear. After their sunrise ablutions the next day, he and Hibya shared an idle moment, standing at the rail while the crew scoured the deck. He touched her elbow and pointed at the ax at her waist. No reaction.

He made an open-palmed chopping gesture. *"Khasinu?"*

She shrugged. He turned to a nearby *serkaru* named Raya, who he knew had better Akkadian. Little older than Hibya, Raya was shorter and sturdier, her square jaw softened by a mouth and eyes suited to mirth. She was using a heavy broom strawed with dried sage to sweep the remnants of salt and sand from the quarterdeck.

Without stopping, she shot a sly glance at Hibya. *"Shla vam yalanu mera-hyo.* He wants to see your ax."

Luyan colored at the women's laughter. His question must have carried some comic undertone. Hibya asked Raya to explain in Akkadian.

Her culture's humor always posed a challenge to translation, and she spoke hesitatingly. *"Yalanu* is the word for ax, but also power. Woman's power, yes?" Her grin widened. "Already, Hibya shows you her power."

Finished sweeping, Raya set the sage alight in the swinging firepot and circled the purifying smoke in the direction of the four winds. The end of her staff was not scorched, but rather tempered from the long repeated custom. She leaned upon it, and turning back to Luyan, tapped her hand on the ax scabbard hanging from her cincture.

"This, we call *labrysu.*"

"Vami kudaro-y. Lumo Aggaderi," Hibya said to him. "Ask me yourself. No more Akkadian."

He struggled to form his request in Keftiun. *"Vam . . . labrysu ya mera eya yibri?"*

She nodded, unsheathed her own *labrysu*, and held it out.

He found it lighter than he had expected. Its braided leather cord was whipped in several layers and lashed tight about the handle, providing a comfortable and sure grip. The remaining line and wooden balls hung in a neat coil. He fingered the edges with respect. They swept back to sharply bearded points. A deadly instrument from any angle, even stabbed directly forward. The bronze handle was hollow, accounting for its light weight.

Hibya asked Raya for her broomstick and showed Luyan how the *labrysu* could be threaded over its length and secured at the end to create a sort of poleax. With a nod, she placed it in his hands. He lifted it by the end and grunted with the added weight of the thick oak staff. Checking his clearance, he raised and swung.

He lacked the strength to stop its fall, and it sank into the deck with an awkward ring, sending up splinters. He had cut many cords of firewood with axes, but fixed on its long handle, the *labrysu* was distinctly more weapon than tool. Its heft seemed suited only to the most powerful of warriors, and he marveled that the *serkarui* had the strength to wield it.

Hibya levered the ax head from the planking and directed his grasp to the center of the staff. Supported at its balance point, he barely felt its weight. She guided him, hand over fist, the skin of her wrists like spring olives, palms nearly as calloused as his own, revolving the *labrysu* between them. Sweat studded his chest by the time she stepped back, released him to windmill alone, the deadly blade flashing in the sun.

She led him through basic defensive exercises: cross-guard, high, low, and side strikes. He warmed to the lesson, prayed it go on, if only that he might know more of her, like this.

With an impish glint, Hibya seized the poleax and leapt up on the rail. She swept it in wide, flowing arcs, pivoting on one foot, spinning it behind her back and over her head as she dipped in a catlike crouch, flowing into a blinding double-winged flourish. Here she stabbed it into the deck and vaulted into a perfectly balanced handstand off the shaft. For a moment, she came still—a lissome figure framed against the dawn—then an arched somersault, planting her feet before Luyan and an affectionate bite upon his nose.

She giggled at his recoil, turned to share her exuberance. But Raya was looking past her, eyes wide with alarm.

"Kozhiniru!"

They wheeled about and saw the priestess watching them.

Luyan bowed and lowered his eyes. Hibya tempered her grin

but met the stern, wrinkled face directly.

"Do you teach the *vitz-yturi* your own errors, Ser-Hibya? Pride before devotion?"

Hibya blinked. "The 'twice-born' is inquisitive, Kozhiniru, as we had hoped. Am I not to satisfy his curiosity?"

Luyan did not fully follow the exchange, but his face reddened. His desire to learn had cost Hibya a reprimand from the leader of the *serkarui*. She who had ordered the death of his father and cousins. Who had rescued him, yes, but still held his life in her hands.

The Kozhiniru regarded him and touched his chin to raise it. He searched his mind, but there was no specific way to beg forgiveness in Keftiun. Debt and retribution were not notions the *serkarui* readily embraced. She angled her head as he struggled for words.

"*Ya . . . kudara'sh mera, Kozhiniru. Labrysu-min . . . kozhma.* I . . . asked to see, Kozhiniru. To know . . . about *labrysu.*"

As though borne upon her wan smile, insight pierced his fear, and his mind registered the root relationship between the priestess's title and the Keftiun word for knowledge. She beckoned him to follow her, down the quarterdeck steps to the foremast area, still unswept. There she unsheathed and handed him her own highly ornamented *labrysu*.

He held it carefully, afraid to drop it or smudge its brilliance. Bending at the waist, the Kozhiniru fingered several images into the salty dust. A neat circle; beside it, the flanking figure of a bull, head turned to display its curved horns. An image sacred also to Luyan's own people. He whispered a short prayer. The last was an eccentric oblong, which held no meaning for him at all.

Without a word, she guided his wrist to place the *labrysu* within the ring. It fit precisely, the curved double blades a symmetrical remove from a perfect circle. She tapped the weapon's center of balance, where the swivel attached to the cord, and spun it like a top. She shifted it to the second figure, showing him how the blades' insets followed the outline of the bull's horns.

Pointing to the third image, she said "Keftius." He understood the name of the island of Crete, but could not associate it with the strange shape. To depict Keftius, he would have sketched its mountain ranges as viewed from an eastern seaward approach. The vertical profiles of most Aegean islands were familiar to him. Line-of-sight memory was a coastal raider's primary navigation tool.

His brow remained furrowed. Next to the island, the priestess traced the hull of a ship, in bird's-eye view.

This shape he recognized. As a masthead lookout, he had seen his ship from a top-down perspective thousands of times. She erased and redrew it, made it progress around the island. He audibly drew breath as the idea began to take hold.

The figure was Keftius as seen from the *sky*—a true geographical map. She made a circle around the horned bull's head, then another around the island's double-pointed northwest headland. Next, the phallus of the bull, followed by the island's similarly shaped southern cape.

Luyan's mind raced, but his jaw remained slack. The Kozhiniru reached up and strongly gripped his genitals through his loincloth. He cried out in pain and astonishment but also understanding. Her point was made.

All his life he had pondered the sacred figures of the gods in the stars but had never considered what they saw when they looked back down. Keftius *was* a bull.

The Kozhiniru locked him with her golden eyes, and he was penetrated by the significance. Its symbolic relationship to the *labrysu*, its empty spaces as important as its points, and usefulness derived from the balance of both. Form drawn in substance, but function arising from the void.

Her words, his voice, but the thought pealed clear within him: our essential nature lies not in the shape we take, but in that eternal circle from which we have been removed.

The priestess smiled again and broke her gaze, releasing him to his own awareness. "The twice-born is a fast learner," she said to Hibya and the other *serkarui* gathered to watch the lesson.

It was not finished. She traced a number of pinnate figures on

45

the island. Bending on one knee, she drove the *labrysu* into the deck, the center of her map, and immediately erased the trees with her hand.

Luyan understood. The island had once been heavily forested but had been denuded by lumbering.

She stretched a finger to encompass the island in a broad, irregular rectangle. The whole of the Mediterranean, from the narrow western straits to the sprawling Levantine coastline in the east. She figured Rhodes, Alashya, and other islands. The coasts of Italia, southern Iberia. Then a fleet of ships off each landmass, progressing farther and farther west.

The pattern repeated wherever her ships went: once limitless woodlands, depleted, eradicated.

She raised her head to gauge his comprehension.

He nodded. Even in his own lifetime, the worth of bronze, the cedar needed to fire and smelt it, the prices of copper and tin, had climbed. And the value of the blood spilt to get them spiraled downward every day.

He hesitated. *"Kedosh domin mayagru yaka . . .* But then why does the ship go . . ." Not knowing the Keftiun for "east," he pointed in the direction of the bow.

The Kozhiniru grew stony. She outlined a circular island north of Keftius and formed a high pile of debris at its center. She pinched off the top of the little mountain, raised her arm, and splayed her fingers, raising a miniature dust cloud.

Luyan shrouded his recognition in silence. He feared revealing his personal witness of the event, feared reminding the Keftiu of his former ship's purpose in those waters. The meaning, however, was evident.

She was depicting the eruption of Thera.

Even had he the courage to tell them his ship had survived the disaster from no great distance, that it posed no further danger, he lacked enough Keftiun. Instead, he bent and marked their current position, nearly two hundred miles southeast of the volcano, well clear of the debris.

The Kozhiniru's face darkened. She remained on one knee as she surveyed her creation. A simple map of the known world. Glancing up at Luyan, she reached out with both hands and scooped up little Thera—its dust in both figure and fact. She stood, raised her arms, and smashed the pile back down upon the deck, obliterating the island, clouding the air about them.

Luyan coughed and rubbed his eyes. As they cleared, he saw the Kozhiniru press the flat of her forearm to the deck. She pushed along a mounting wave, sweeping away his mark, blurring the coasts of Alashya, Egypt, and the Levant.

He met the eyes of Hibya and the other *serkarui* each in turn. All nodded somberly.

Thera was going to erupt again. And this time, there would be no running away.

4 Lady of Spain

Combien de choses nous servoyent hier d'articles de foy,
qui nous sont fables aujourd'huy?

"How many things served us yesterday for articles of faith,
which today are fables for us?"

—Michel de Montaigne, *The Complete Essays*

4 March 1769
Lt. S. Singer, HMRN
At Sea

D arling Girl,
The ship pitches this gray morning, and I beg you forgive my uneven hand. Despite the stiff breeze, we are scarce making three knots; I stood at the rail and watched two packets pass us within an hour.

How I come to be lodged in so sad a state upon this sluggish merchant vessel you have a right to know, and I shall discover it to you in due course, but permit me first to place a finishing point upon your family roots.

The next Sunday found Rhona at David's church, seated on a forward pew between her father and Nessie, the latter dressed in her finest blue taffeta and matching bonnet, which admirably complimented her carefully pinned golden hair. In his cassock and surplice, David seemed more dignified than he had shivering in the cold by Rhona's market stall, the Anglican vestments being not so very different from the papist ones to which she was accustomed. She was fascinated to hear what amounted to a Mass spoken in Irish instead of Latin, and the masterful ecclesiastical timbre in which David recited the liturgy moved her much; but it was for Nessie's benefit that she was in attendance, not her own.

Despite the evident mutual *interesse* between David and Rhona, it would have been unlawful for them to wed unless she converted, which, less from papist loyalty than general disdain for dogma, she would never do. Nessie, on the other hand, was already confessed of the Anglican creed and hence a member of the communion of the Churches of England and Ireland. While Rhona shared neither Nessie's ambition nor values, they were, as I will explain to you, joints of a sisterly race that demanded selflessness, and learning that Nessie was willing, she turned all efforts toward linking her with David.

Now I'm given to understand that Nessie had no pretensions to exceptional beauty as a maid, but I know her to be a women of substantial parts, if little kindness. A certain grace of bearing survived into her later years, as well as a precious, engaging keenness of eye. Though not possessed of Rhona's glamours, I make no doubt she cut a handsome figure and was without question a more suitable bride, Penal Laws or no. Rhona's liberty of manner, alluring by a market stall, might have proved wearing in a marriage; and she anywise had little inclination toward the estate.

At all events, whether through the power of Nessie's own blessings, or some indirect emanation of her sister's charms, the spell was cast, and David proposed. Seamus readily consented, and the couple were wed by the Archbishop of Armagh in June of 1725. A year later, David inherited and had his choice of several livings. Nessie longing heartily to live in England, and having just given birth to my father, Hagen, David chose to accept an Anglican benefice at Portsmouth. A congeries of David's cousins resided in or near that crowded port city, where was soon to be established the Royal Naval Academy, and it was thought the boy might follow his Singer relations into the service.

While not, as who should say an absentee pastor, David began spending a good deal of time away at London soon after taking up the situation, leaving liturgical duties to his deacon of many a Sunday. Nessie, you see, betimes grew bored of the establishment at Portsmouth and devoted increasing attention to the much grander house David had inherited in May Fair, where she launched an unpromising campaign to insinuate herself into the good graces of her metropolitan in-laws.

Rhona tells me that Nessie's delivery of baby Hagen was uncommon difficult; but it being a son, upon which she pinned all her hopes, and not the least of these the safeguarding of the Singer estates to her control should David predecease her, she cherished the child. She did not carry another for many years, whether due to a cooling of passions between the couple or Nessie's subtle artifices, I cannot tell. I learned of how elementary such workings were to her sisterhood.

Nessie had many ambitious hopes for her son, of which some likely stood upon his effecting an upward-reaching marriage, like her own. She encouraged Hagen toward a naval career rather than a clerical vocation despite the example of his father. England was at war with Spain during Hagen's childhood, and I daresay Nessie dreamt of him one day winning a title through wartime naval service.

To hear Nessie tell it, Hagen was a willful boy, but by no means a spoiled one, despite her lavish attentions. He exhibited a generosity of spirit and a sensibility for the transcendent, and David oft made poorly received remarks upon how suited he might be for the ministry. Possessed of the Laughlin curly red locks and green eyes, he had also inherited a moral courage which indeed would have served him well in either an ecclesiastical or a military career.

Nessie once described to me how Hagen, at the age of seven, had been lost for the better part of an anxious day, separated from his father in the jostling port district. They found the boy, not as young Jesus teaching the lawyers, but squatting on his haunches before a dockyard public house, engaged in conversation with several bereft sailors. Spellbound by stories of adventures far foreign, he'd emptied his little purse to stand them treat in the article of rum. Hurried off and roundly scolded, he was not too shy of his father's anger to besiege him with questions of how heroic men could sink to low estates and God suffer undeserts to brave mariners who had faithfully served their king.

Naval commissions were becoming scarcer and more difficult to acquire. The old scheme of appointment by king's letter was being done away in favor of commissions earned by sea service; young gentlemen took in what seamanship they could along of acting as shipboard servants to senior officers. Mark you, this new system was no more appealing to the Singer mind than the old, their interest having never attained to the level of royal notice; and possessed of prodigious *restants* of Scottish pride, they were blood disdainful of personal servitude. They therefore welcomed the opening of the Royal Naval Academy at Portsmouth, which, upon any student who completed his three years of study, conferred an ordinary midshipman's rank as well as a reckoning of two years' nominal sea time.

Nessie's persistence prevailed, and Hagen was there enrolled in 1739. Having already done some service as a reefer, upon graduating at the age of sixteen, he was more than well qualified for his first midshipman appointment aboard a royal frigate. He had attentively learned his navigation, mathematics, geography, French, and naval history from the academy's illustrated primers, and his exemplary Singer figure—he was already nearly six feet in height and seemed to carry the bulk of his thirteen stones in his broad shoulders—was an added benefit. His dunnage for the academy comprised a brace of dragoon pistols given him for his twelfth birthday by his father's brother.

While the continental war with Spain had been over for several years, Nessie's importunate letters to the Admiralty office and other exertions permitted Hagen to see service off the Continent as well as the Americas and Africa. He passed for lieutenant after returning from his first cruise but continued to accept commissions as second aboard sundry men-of-war, as few commands were available in that relatively peaceful period.

Indeed, as the years went by, disposed by love of the world's beauty and its peoples—and disdain for Nessie's social machinations—he pursued nearly any commission to remain away from England, the farther foreign the better, and most of little benefit to his advancement. Like David in Gweedore, Hagen would fain have read divinity and voyaged as a missionary rather than a warrior, serving God before king. His natural inclination to reject the responsibilities of marriage and higher command drove an inexorable distance between mother and son. Nessie exercised effective control over the Singer estate while Hagen remained at sea; but because he was her only son, and defiantly unbetrothed, that control was also dependant upon his remaining alive.

I daresay it was for this reason she permitted herself to conceive again at the age of thirty-nine, which to her disappointment yielded not a second son, but little Eleanor. David's death by apoplexy settled the matter of further attempts, and Nessie thence grew increasingly isolated and embittered.

I come now, darling girl, to tell of how my parents met, and I make no doubt you will have discerned from the piecemeal nature of my history thus far that I never knew my father, Hagen Singer. Discounting Nessie's rare and self-serving disclosures, all I know of him, and this history as I recount it in its particulars, I learned from Arima and my uncles.

Arima Zarazua, that is my mother's maiden name. She was born in a mountain village outside the port city of Donostia, in the coastal province of Gipuzkoa. France closely borders that region of Spain, but its people are of neither race—they are Basque and have features, customs, cuisine, and language which share no conspicuous similarities with any others of Europe.

In the late autumn of 1751, Hagen was second in command of the king's frigate *Merrow*, which had made a difficult return from southern Brazil, becalmed for several weeks in the doldrums off West Africa. Short of water, the ship gained the estuary of the River Gambia and laid up to reprovision near Fort James. The Gambia is navigable far inland and of great interest to naturalists; I make no doubt it was amongst its lush flora and warm tidal pools that Hagen, as well as the ship's captain and many of its company, contracted that pernicious variety of ague to which they succumbed less than three days back out to sea.

When they did get wind, it came on to blow something fearful and ran them hard into the Bay of Biscay, whence they could not in any event have proceeded farther without they made repair to their standing rigging, spars, and sails. Thus they put into the port of Pasaia in Gipuzkoa again lain idle a few weeks for a refit.

Recent to that time, the long dispute between England and Spain over colonial trading rights had been put to rest by the Treaty of Madrid, and our ambassador, Benjamin Keene, contrived to improve relations. At the price of much blood, the Basque provinces had won home rule and trade exemptions from the Spanish Crown, profiting principally from the exporting of iron to America. This traffic is now diminishing, however, as the region's mountain forests have been cut clean, and wood to fuel the forges has risen so to make Basque iron too dear.

The diplomacy of Britain and Spain being neither here nor there to the Basques, I make no doubt the *Merrow* received fair treatment at the shipyards of Pasaia—which offer capital materials and fine, if unhurried, workmanship—and its people a warm welcome, for so long as the drink-loving foremast jacks behaved civil.

Hagen's fever had been somewhat relieved by frequent and liberal dosing of Jesuit's bark—a supply obtained in South America, alas, since exhausted. He explored Pasaia's protected bay, its steep hills lined on all sides with antiquated churches and houses of red tile and whitewashed plaster; then he took the ship's little cutter and a small crew round the cape to the harbor city of Donostia, or as some say, Saint Sebastian.

Neither did he long tarry there. He chose to journey thence upland along the River Oria to the village of Lasarte, where he had been informed the local winter festival would provide an agreeable spectacle. Some may call this a frivolous stretching of liberty under the circumstances, but as I have written, it was not in Hagen's frame to over-confine himself to duty when the chance offered to discover unvisited regions and peoples.

Now I have never been to the Basque country. It is my present destination, God willing—a point which I hesitated to write when I began this letter in my precipitous flight.

Never been, though half of Basque blood, and understanding of the Gipuzkoan dialect I learned from my mother, along of so many dear particulars that I oft fancy it home. During the winter, its coastal regions are subject to a nearly constant fine rain—more than a mist, but never as who should say a deluge, which the locals call it the *txirimin*. As Hagen and his shipmates made their way up the valley on hired asses along the rushing Oria River, these cold, falling damps cannot have failed to rekindle his fever, and indeed, Arima's first notice of him was his deep cough, resounding above the music.

My mother, then nineteen years of age, was taking part in a ceremony called *sorgin dantza*, or "witches' dance" as it would grieve her to hear it translated. At all events, it is a celebration in remembrance of the time before the witch burnings and an homage to the *sorginak*, the term by which that group of women call themselves who live apart from the congress of farmers and villagers, holding title to no land and shifting by their own means, trading in their healing arts, their service as midwives, and divers other skills and goods. Some take the word's meaning from the Basque *sortze*, for birth, or creation, but Arima gave me to believe it was derived from the Latin *soror*, or sister, and that surely is the significance it carries to those women themselves.

I say women; some are men, though precious few, and often when the sisters go abroad in settled parts by day, they do so in men's array, and in more than this they have from antiquity provided a span of union between male and female, as between old and new, mountain and sea—indeed, the world and the wilderness, howsoever understood. In times before, each community would leave their upland and coastal haunts once each year at winter solstice and visit the nearest village *en masse*. This to give occasion for the *sorginak* to express their appreciation for the villagers, and the villagers for them; to share music, food, and gifts. The *sorgin dantza* is a species of lively *rigaudon* in which the couples exchange roles, the women dressed in men's breeches and tall red pointed caps, and the men in frocks, aprons, and bonnets, as a sort of tribute to the sisterhood.

It was as she danced thus, in manly attire, that Hagen first looked upon Arima. Girl or boy, her enigmatic beauty would have drawn his regard: her balletic grace, the clear gray eyes, the alabaster cheeks tinged by the chill mountain air to match the scarlet hat, from under which her inky black tresses fell despite her tucking.

She recalled to me how, when his cough turned her glance, Hagen smiled at her through his remounting fever, for which several dishes of warm spiced Basque wine had done little. She held his gaze, first out of curiosity of a foreigner and then frank admiration of his uncommon figure; finally, in concern of his wan and sickly complexion—his brow shining with sweat despite the cold.

After the traditional conclusion, other music continued and the company and spectators joined in a general revel, from which Hagen abstained. Arima approached him as he sat trembling upon a low log bench near one of the smudge pots which provided some warmth to the outdoor festivities, his damp surtout drawn tightly about him. Without leave, she pressed her hand to his forehead and frowned at its animal heat.

He tried to rise, but she pressed him back down by the shoulder.

Making a seated bow, through chattering teeth he said, *"Tengo mucho gusto en conocerla señorita."* I daresay he may have felt some relief to confirm, upon closer inspection, that he had not indeed been so charmed by a *señor.*

"Enchantée, monsieur," she replied in French, an understanding of the Spanish being widespread but rarely acknowledged in rural Basque country. *"Vous savez bien que vous avez de la fièvre. C'est dangereux rester en plein air comme ça."*

He did by all means know, but had not wished to admit to his companions how dangerously his fever had risen in the damp open air. Arima supported him toward a nearby stone building, the home of her aunt, his shipmates making vague obeisance and remarking of his worsened condition as they passed, though it would seem not sufficient troubled to cut short their debauch.

Scarcely had Arima and her aunt removed Hagen's boots when he collapsed insensible upon the little bed, and they had no small difficulty to remove his sodden clothes. They sponged him with spirits to reduce the fever, which was rising by the minute, and then wrapped him in fresh sheets and every blanket the little house possessed. Arima banked the fire and sat by him through the night, but he was not much improved by morning, the fever sweating out only to return with renewed malice, as is typical of the ague. During his periods of mindfulness, she asked him of the history of his sickness and treatment; she lamented that his best chance would have been to continue his course of the Peruvian bark, a physic all but unobtainable in Gipuzkoa at the time.

Hagen's company appeared at the house near midday, in a precious crapulous state, to inquire after him. She having no English, and they neither Basque nor adequate French among them, Arima grudgingly switched to Spanish to explain to the master's mate that his lieutenant's life was in the balance, and he could by no means pass back down to Donostia in his condition. They appeared not at first to credit this, but she recounted the lack of Jesuit's bark, which she had sent word of its need already to her sisters on the coast with little hope, and that her upland relations had been set to searching for an alternative. These remarks sufficed to establish her authority, especially in the minds of the foremast crew. They were several of them of rustic origin and not without confidence in women of herbs and roots, and at all events the *Merrow*'s surgeon knew little better how to cure the marsh fever.

Hagen's companions remained in the village for three days, waiting often upon him to know when he might be well enough to travel. Arima contrived to find a small patch of sweet wormwood, a *sorgin* remedy for ague that many others apply ineffectively by brewing a hot tea from the dried leaves—an all but worthless method. She knew better and gently ground generous quantities of the live herb in her stone mortar with cold rainwater, making Hagen to drink the strong infusion down while still bright green. He began to improve, but Arima also well knew that the fever would return if he were not dosed with the fresh article three times daily for a full fortnight.

Howsoever, that long his men would never tarry, as they were anxious both for the *Merrow*'s cutter docked at Donostia and of the risk the frigate might depart Pasaia without them, at once stranding them and risking a mark against their names as deserters. With a final call upon the lieutenant to urge him to join in their departure—he could not have bodily complied even had Arima permitted it—the crew left Hagen, with their pledge to explain matters to the ship's captain and return for him in time if ever it proved feasible.

Neither were Arima's relations entirely comfortable of Hagen's continued presence. Hospitality, especially to sick travelers, was *de rigeur* in rural Basque culture, but Arima had been meant for greater responsibilities. Since childhood, she had been a prodigy of doctrine and devotion, this demonstrated no better than in the healing arts, every broke wing baby starling her charge and patient. Yet after her mother died, many remarked in the girl a burgeoning restlessness and thought it far too much time she passed gazing at the sea, making charcoal drawings of the port traffic and perfecting foreign tongues—more indeed than was fit for a dedicated initiate of the upland communities of *sorginak*.

Arima was born of a line of spiritual leaders and rebels, notable women necessary to the defense and continuation of a doctrine and people that had scarce survived the burning times. Whether Arima would assume such a weighty mantle time would tell; but the picture would be painted, her aunt was certain, in the colors of her passions, and it was those passions she most feared now as Arima poured out her care upon the beautiful and helpless foreign sea officer.

By the morrow Hagen was somewhat improved, the fever having broken during the night with a fearful profusion of sweat and quaking chills, which so fretted Arima that she'd wrapped him in her close embrace to still them. As the dawn came, it was an astonished and grateful Hagen who roused her; he able to converse at length, and that with his full presence of mind, though the crisis had left him weak as a lamb. He posed many questions on her subject: her family, her history, and from whence came her knowledge of healing. Before engaging, however, she counseled him in the strongest terms upon his condition.

The ague, she warned, must be driven out completely or not at all. Taking a partial or abortive course of physic would cause the fever, sooner or later, to return all the stronger and more resistant on the subsequent attempt to the same cure. Sweet wormwood was not as powerful a remedy as the Peruvian bark, and therefore nothing less than the full fortnight's dosage would do. He was too feeble to demur and merely thanked her for treating him of a sickness which he made no doubt could be mortal, having seen a number of his shipmates die of it on the voyage.

At length assured that he credited her advice, she put aside her stern manner and accepted his thanks with her placid smile. Arima's face was as fluidly mutable as the heavens, now tempestuous, now clearing of a sudden into a tranquil, prepossessing contentment, a beam which lit both eye and mouth. It was this quality of her countenance, as much as its uncommon beauty, that held the regard even of strangers and made one so desire to please her.

In the days that followed, the couple—for love made short work of them—spoke for hours unceasing, not only beguiled by one another's evident charms, but each fascinated by the other's parts and acquirements, family history and formation. Arima always wondered how two creatures of such disparate cultivation found themselves so sure and precipitous bound; but bound they were, fast as long-parted siblings.

Nay, not veritable siblings, for she spoke also of a passion distilled into those short days like fine brandy from a lifetime of sweetening fruit, and which it burned agreeable in the draught.

For all his many prior fond fancies of jumping ship in exotic ports of call, Hagen now found himself wholly laid by the lee: an irresistible squall of happiness, a force to overcome any sensibility of duty to comrade, kin, and king. The still small prayer that had been echoing in the deep holds of his mind became a conscious wish that the ship might depart without him.

Besides the remedy, she lavished him with the fruits of her country: first simple consommés of fowl with lashings of *ezpeletako biperra,* the smoky local red pepper, to steam the cavities of his head and reduce its ache; later, as his stomach could bear it, she fed him playfully out of hand thin shavings of ham of the local wild black boar—creatures which grow richly fat on chestnuts as they roam the mountain woods.

The good food helped his fragile stomach suffer the taste of his physic, and in the dark of the night, as my story demands I tell, in their tender ardor, Arima gave to him of more sublime dosings.

Accordingly, and as soon as Hagen could manage the walk, on a rare sunny morning the couple stood before the priest under the antique arches of the little church of Saint Paul the Apostle in the village center. The die being cast, her aunt proffered naught but her blessings, though her heart was torn.

"Beldurra dut hau agurtuko da, nire iloba," she whispered in her niece's ear as they embraced after the ceremony.

Arima took her face. "No, do not fear this is good-bye, Aunt. Love is always a beginning, yes? And true love casts out fear." She kissed both of her cheeks several times and smiled. "Besides, it is not for us to doubt. Providence may work to keep us both in Gipuzkoa."

Revived by his joy of the short ceremony, Hagen sat in the sunshine taking small sips of sparkling deep yellow *txakoli*—his first wine in nearly nine days, chosen for its kindness to the digestion—and greeted many members of Arima's family, these being principally women, as most of her male cousins had gone off to the colonies for emigrants or iron traders. The couple patiently embraced each relation, not neglecting to share a few cordial words with any, and then repaired as soon as was proper to an empty room prepared for them, in as close an approximation of nuptial custom as time and circumstance afforded.

Neither could contain their rapture on that rare night, nor Hagen the increasing strength of his resolution to remain. His happy but palpable exhaustion—and slight fever—as the morning dawned gray and rainy, drove Arima hurriedly out to harvest more of the remaining wormwood. As she ran back to him after diverting to her aunt for the forgotten mortar and pestle, her heart skipped a beat to see a cordon of uniformed English sailors and stiff red-coated soldiers riding in loose formation up the trail from Donastia. She drew her hood and made her way past, praying none might recognize her, as some were of Hagen's original band.

They were bound for her aunt's house, where they assumed Hagen still to be. When they were out of sight, Arima rushed open the door of their little haven, bolted it behind her, and roused her new husband with a an urgent brush of his warm cheek.

"Mon amour, ils arrivent te chercher!" she said in a stricken whisper.

"Who? Who has come for me?" he asked, still half-asleep.

"Vite!" she said. "Hurry, I must give you your medicine." She began tearing the fresh wormwood into the mortar.

He brought himself fully to his senses. *"Calme toi,"* he said. "It is my shipmates returned, surely."

"You did not see—there are pistols and red soldiers," she said, breathlessly pounding at the plants and adding water from a bucket. "You cannot—must not—be taken from here yet. The treatment is not finished!"

A tear sprang heavily from her eye, the first he had seen of her to weep, and it was a torment to him.

"Redcoats?" he asked with lowered brow. "Why would the captain send a file of marines for me? I have taken sick, not deserted."

Arima gasped as a heavy knock shook the little room. Unable to deny the plea in her eyes, he swallowed the green draught in several gulps directly from the heavy stone mortar before pulling on his shirt and breeches and striding to the door. Arima stepped around in front of him as it opened on a dark-eyed marine officer, standing stiff and tall.

"Lieutenant Singer, sir, forgive the intrusion." The man lowered a quick but discernibly critical glance at Arima before bringing his eyes firmly forward and continuing. "With the captain's compliments, you are required back at the ship. We are under orders to escort you without the loss of a moment, if you please, sir."

Hagen replied in a reedy but authoritative tone. "Surely my coxswain reported my situation. I have been laid up here with the marsh fever for more than a week. If the ship is ready to sail, that's all well, but a couple of foremast jacks could have been sent to report of it."

Lieutenant Matthew Porter was one of Hagen's dearest friends with whom he had served on a number of cruises. Nonetheless, the marine remained rigid and silent.

Hagen assumed a more intimate tone. "Come, what's all this row, then, Matthew?"

Porter still hesitating, the gunner's mate touched a crooked finger to his brow and broke in. "It's the captain, sir. He's as sick as ever you were, and worse, and the surgeon says he may not live. The fever's taken five of our men as they lay in town hospital. The gov'ners at Pasaia has ordered we clear port directly, as the ignorant scrubs is dreadful of plague. If I may so express myself, sir."

Hagen found the sailor's casual air disagreeable, and he scowled as he summarized in French for Arima. If indeed the captain were disabled or dying, then the frigate would be sorely endangered were Hagen left behind. The wardroom had been much reduced on the return leg from Africa, and their few remaining midshipmen lacked the experience to properly navigate. The order to depart left no time to fill out the crew; far less to dispatch requests for new officers.

Hagen's clear duty was to return at once, for what might well prove to be his first command. The reason for Porter's deference became clear: in his mind, Hagen was already ship's captain.

Arima grew stolid as he related the circumstances; she knew it futile to attempt convincing the Basque port officials that this calenture was not of a species to be catching in the manner of a pox or plague; and she discerned from Hagen's tone that there was no use in protesting his decision.

She quickly bundled the few belongings she had to hand, and while Hagen was drawing on his boots and the seamen loading his dunnage upon the hired donkeys, burst out through the mist and ran toward the opposite end of the village.

One foot still bare, Hagen called after her until his voice broke, then resigned himself with a sigh. Porter, now aware the attachment was far more than sensual, made an amiable but awkward attempt at sympathy as he held the reins of Hagen's donkey.

"Well, farewell and adieu to your fine Spanish ladies, eh, sir? I do hope you shall have the happiness of seeing her again ..." He trailed off with a blush.

Hagen shot him a cold stare and mounted, folding up the collar of his uniform jacket against the fine rain.

I fade again, my dear, and must change the dressings of my wounds before succumbing to sleep. Forgive me. I shall write you more tomorrow.

Your affectionate,
S. Singer

5 Spinning Island

"Superstition would seem to be simply cowardice
in regard to the supernatural."

— Theophrastus

1602 BCE
Eastern Mediterranean

L uyan had derived more understanding from his wordless encounter with the Kozhiniru than all the stumbling conversations which came before. But he remained uncertain of how much time remained and thirsted more urgently than ever for answers: how to escape, how to reach the safety of his Anatolian highlands.

Knowledge of the coming cataclysm did not, however, fully stifle his instinct for opportunity. Although he continued to be closeted with Hibya during the night watch, his acknowledgment by the priestess gave him greater freedom of access during the day. Luyan took every chance to scan the holds of the opulent ship in hope of identifying its more valuable cargo.

He began the next day working alongside the *serkarui*. Hibya showed him simple chores such as fire tending and cooking. He longed to assist the crew and learn more of Keftiun seamanship, but it seemed the *serkarui* had other purposes in mind.

The *serkarui* attached a ritual significance to many routine tasks. Certain ingredients were not to be used when cooking for them, nor would they eat food prepared in the same ovens and vessels in general use for the crew. While the Keftiu made cultivated grains such as wheat and barley into familiar flat breads and porridges, the *serkarui* would not touch them. They called these staples *taibu yibetzi*, or "slave food."

Luyan found this curious. There were, as far as he could tell, no slaves on the ship. Even the rowers were a free and socially powerful fraternity who enjoyed priority in food, water, and beer.

Any one of them, if he became ill or fatigued, could demand as of right that another member of the crew take his shift at the oars.

Maybe the Keftiu defined slavery differently than did the Cilicians, he considered. Or perhaps he was the only *yibetzu* on board.

The *serkarui* baked their own *banu,* or bread, a formulaic recipe which seemed to comprise specific wild grains and seeds. The heavy cooking vessels of the *serkarui* were unique, and each woman possessed at least one, along with her *labrysu* and staff.

Hibya told Luyan that the pots were to be cleansed only by salt and fire. He watched her scrub its interior and reheat it to burn off impurities. She whispered a short prayer as the smoke rose. He was reminded of the ceremonial altar where the pilots offered incense to the sea gods.

Luyan was uncertain how to feel when Hibya made him a gift of one of her own cauldrons. In the two-story earth hovels of Tarsa, food preparation was exclusively women's work, several wives sharing a central oven for baking bread and parching grains for brewing. The large fire-blackened pot had a round belly and a broad, flat bottom. Its weight felt more like stone than clay when he lifted it.

He wondered if he was to be a kitchen slave.

Other possessions were universal among the *serkarui.* Each owned a set of tightly fitting leather leggings, cut in lapped layers. The monk seal hide extended in wide cuffs below the feet, worn rolled up to the calf when walking. Every *serkaru* also had a long hooded cloak and a pair of thick webbed gloves made from the same soft skins, scraped thin and supple, tanned in acacia bark and waterproofed with the seal's own train oil.

Luyan noticed a pile of them in the cargo hold. It contained stores of other textiles, including raw and dyed linen and golden sea silk—a material of which he had only heard stories—woven from the ultra fine beards of giant sea mussels. The floating banners that framed the whisper caves were made of the rare and precious fabric, so delicate that a bolt one meter in length could be crumpled and hidden in the palm of the hand, as Hibya demonstrated. When she opened her fingers, the banner sprang back to its full size, smooth and unwrinkled.

Luyan watched the *serkarui* weaving large, elongated reed baskets. When completed, they were filled with seawater to prove them watertight, then coated with a thick mixture of resin and mutton fat. A sturdy rim of boiled and bent willow was fastened around and several curved ribs hammered in to brace the bottom. Luyan's nautical mind perceived the function: the baskets were coracles—stubby kayaks designed to carry a single passenger with a paddle. The owner's wooden staff was snugly wedged along the bottom as an internal keel, stretching the little craft lengthwise, reducing its instability and sluggishness

Before launching the coracle, the *serkaru* lashed her sealskin cloak tightly around the outer hull, folded the hood and loose edges in the bottom, and jammed her inverted cauldron tightly between two of the wooden ribs. She half knelt and half sat as she paddled, her legs pressed against each side of the pot, the folded leather cushioning her knees.

The *serkaru* was the best long-distance swimmer Luyan had ever seen, but the coracle extended the range and conditions of her mobility. In heavier seas, she could stretch the hood of the cloak around her waist and tuck it into her cincture, or fully over her body, hood upon head, to create a watertight skirt. The boat could be laden and pushed ahead while swimming or ridden through rough surf by mounting with the upper body and kicking, protecting both the rider and her cargo.

It occurred to Luyan that he could travel a considerable distance in one of the little coracles. For the first time, he envisioned a possible means of escape. And not necessarily empty-handed.

Late one afternoon, as he stoked the swinging foredeck brazier, his empty cooking vessel by his side, Luyan was beckoned by one of the passengers. She was near Hibya's age, seated beside an older couple engrossed in a board game played with small bronze pegs.

Her dark black hair was strikingly offset by her ivory skin the result of a Keftiun noblewoman's obsessive avoidance of direct sunlight. Delicate of frame, her myriad little graces at first struck Luyan as superficial, self-indulgent in comparison to the *serkarui*. She wore sumptuously tailored garments: belled, layered leggings and a fitted bodice that framed her breasts, patterned in bright dyes of pomegranate and saffron.

She carried a subtle scent of lilac and myrrh, her smile a languid invitation to his gaze. She was skillfully expressive. Luyan followed her conversation with little trouble. And she understood his broken words without once making him repeat himself. She launched a breezy history of her father's merchant travels in Cilicia, during the time before "the pirate troubles." She spoke of the mythic ancient relationship between the great houses of Keftius and the ancestors of the Hittite kings. Luyan wondered if she thought this flattered him.

He could contribute little. As the conversation wound down, she removed a brightly polished copper pin fastener from her bodice and held it out. It was worked in an elaborate spiral design. He had never owned anything made of copper.

"M'hara," he said. An expression of acceptance.

She returned another charming smile, laid his hand upon her head in the Keftiun naming gesture, and said, "Talyera."

He heard Hibya utter a distinct "baaah!" from the foredeck. Stifled giggles from the younger *serkarui*. Luyan quickly reciprocated Talyera's introduction and stepped out from the cool shade of the passenger canopy into the midday sun.

He frowned as he rejoined the group. Raya explained that *talyera* meant "lamb" in Keftiun. All the same, it seemed dangerous for him to be the cause of a noblewoman's humiliation. Hibya refused to meet his eye as she snatched the copper pin and fastened it to his lanyard, patting his chest facetiously. He had never encountered jealousy before. Her feelings eluded him.

"Nadoru eya. It's copper," he said.

She reached down for the handle of the cooking pot she had

given him and held it out, her other arm crossed around her chest in a ridged self-embrace—a posture he had never before seen her assume. His own anger dissolved as he realized he had somehow wounded her. She scooped a handful of rock salt and sand from a nearby basket and rubbed the outside of the sooty vessel vigorously. The spot revealed an underlying bright burnish. Luyan's mouth fell open.

The cauldron was made of pure copper—almost five kilograms of it. He skipped back to save his toes as Hibya dropped it at his feet. She spun on her heel and strode toward the companionway.

He pulled his eyes from the upended vessel and started to follow her, but Raya gently gripped his arm.

"Not now," she said. "You will see her later. You have power for Hibya as well. She too is *vitz-yturi*."

Luyan made a mental note to learn more of this expression— twice-born—which he had several times heard himself called.

He took Raya's broom and finished her sweeping. He needed time to think. His mind turned with calculations of what the sale of the copper vessel might bring if he could get safely away with it.

But if the Keftiu were so wealthy they made cookware from copper, what other portable fortunes might the ship contain?

Just after sunset, the Keftiun navigator stepped off the quarterdeck and approached the rail. He wore a while linen robe and purple-striped turban. From a goatskin pouch, he removed a thin, rectangular copper plate sttached to two flexible willow handles. A flaxen cord, knotted at regular intervals, was affixed to the plate's center. He placed its free end between his teeth. A young nobleman joined him to assist and mounted a frame on the deck, supporting a free-swinging leather foot cradle. The navigator stepped in. Flexing his legs to compensate for the ship's motion, he lifted the plate to the sky. Toward the constellation of the Great Bear.

Long accustomed to learning by stealthy observation, Luyan swept more slowly and worked his way closer. The navigator's posture reminded him of a praying mantis. Swinging in smaller and smaller arcs in the foot cradle, he used the bend of his thighs and the spring of the willow handles to float the plate motionless against the pitch and roll of the galley. The assistant noticed Luyan's interest. A finger to his lips, he beckoned him closer.

The navigator gradually drew the cord through his teeth, one knot at a time, keeping the lower edge of the plate level with the horizon as it neared his face. The assistant pointed out Kochab— the shoulder of the Great Bear, and the brightest star of the northern sky. Near it was the fainter Thuban, the tip of the dragon's tail. Luyan knew that the midpoint about which the two stars slowly rotated was due north. He traced a circle with his fingers, and the young man smiled and nodded.

The stars that never set. The spinning island.

With the minutest of compensatory motions, the navigator inched the plate nearer his face until, with the string fully taut, Kochab peeked through its tiny upper notch, its lower edge perfectly aligned with the horizon. He clamped off the string with his teeth and counted the knots in the cord. The assistant took his place on the sling and repeated the measurement, followed again by the navigator. They compared their results and calculated the average by the flickering firelight.

They unrolled a long parchment and weighted it flat. Luyan peered over their shoulders. A top-down view of the sea and land, like the priestess had drawn on the deck, but much more detailed. The whole of the Mediterranean was lain out, from the Levantine coast on the right to the Pillars of the Gods on the far left—the western limit of the world he knew. He recognized the bull shape of Keftius and what must have been the great island of Alashya. The navigator used the plate's straight edge to trace a horizontal line with a sharp stylus. Luyan guessed it represented their latitude.

The assistant next removed a set of nested copper circles from the pouch. The upper was sprinkled with silver dots and rotated upon its base, rimmed with tiny pegs. Luyan noticed a silver crescent.

"Eya tsukaru?" he whispered.

The assistant nodded. The crescent represented the moon. After affixing the disk to the rail, he unspooled two smaller copper plates and hooked the line that joined them into one of the wheel's pegs.

The navigator took them, stepped back into the sling, and began the same skilled, subtle dance. He aligned one plate with the star Kochab and waited. As the first glimmer of the gibbous moon peeked above the horizon, he set the other plate against its silver edge. The assistant turned the circular device until the left leg of the bent cord lay directly over the tiny moon image. He then dialed the upper disk until the silver stud representing Kochab sat below the right leg of the cord and carefully counted the notches that now separated them.

They alternated, made the angular measurement several times, and again averaged their results, this time consulting figures on a thick scroll. While the men were lost in their calculations, Luyan leaned in for a closer look at the chart.

The first line the navigator had drawn lay between two of many horizontal bands that covered the map. Luyan had been right. It clearly represented their latitude—the ship's position along the world's north-south axis. It crossed the Levantine coast slightly north of Gubel. Not far off Luyan's own crude solar estimate of the prior day.

But the map also featured a series of fixed *vertical* bands. And the navigator now drew another vertical line at a measured distance between two of them. He then made a small circle around the point where his lines intersected.

Luyan was thunderstruck. Could such a close estimate of their position on the vast open sea be possible? He could not control himself.

"What are these lines? How are they known?" He pointed to the vertical lines.

The navigator frowned. But the assistant rolled the chart out farther and beckoned Luyan closer. He showed him that each of the bands extended through one of many landmarks. Their last line of longitude passed just east of a ring-shaped point in upper Egypt, which he named Nabtu. This evening's lay between the eastern tip of Alashya and the band intersecting another of the strange circles, this one on the coast of lower Canaan. The assistant called it Kyartu.

The navigator interrupted impatiently, and the assistant handed him a polished olivewood box. It contained one of the most remarkable objects Luyan had ever seen. A shallow chalice of translucent emerald, mounted on a copper stem. Like the astrolabe, its base was notched at regular intervals, its bowl etched all around with linear Keftiun characters. The assistant filled the cup with clear olive oil and delicately floated a long shard of dark stone on its surface.

He held the cup to the light of the brazier. The needle trembled, then slowly rotated until its tip pointed north, in the direction of the polar stars. Luyan failed to grasp its significance at first. The assistant placed the object in his hands and pressed his shoulders to turn his body.

A superstitious awe mounted within him. Whichever direction he faced, the floating needle settled back to point north.

He trembled as he returned the device. The assistant set its base upon the map and rotated the entire table until the chart's vertical bands aligned with the the compass needle. He whistled for the attention of the coxswains and stretched his arm to indicate their new heading. Keeping the ship in the same relative alignment with the pole stars would ensure it stayed on course throughout the night.

Luyan's mind reeled. Cilicians could calculate their position north or south relative to the latitude of known major port cities. But the Keftiu had knowledge of lines of intersection on the east-west axis as well. The resulting grid covered the entirety of their world map. Luyan grasped the reading of latitude by the ascension of the pole stars above the horizon. But how did the navigator, by measuring the angles between the moon and stars, calculate the ship's *longitude?* And what magic kept the needle in the emerald chalice pointing always north?

Cilician ships were compelled to sail north or south until they reached the known latitude of their destination. They then turned due east or west, tracking the line as closely as possible, hoping their lookout spotted the intended landfall. If not, they might be lost wandering on the open sea or wrecked upon an unknown lee shore. Mariners who could calculate both their latitude *and* longitude, even at night, and know their heading in the heaviest cloud cover, could undertake long-distance deepwater journeys with a reliable chance of reaching their destination safely.

He burned with frustration. He did not have the ideas, let alone the words, to frame his many questions. The navigator carefully re-bundled his instruments and, with a disdainful glance at Luyan, left the foredeck.

Well into the night, Luyan made his way down the companionway, guided by the braziers and oil lamps of the lower deck. He parted the tapestries and sidestepped lightly so as not to disturb Hibya's meditation.

"Did the pilots press you to take the evening deck watch?" She spoke without looking up.

He dropped in front of her and set the cauldron between them. After his navigation lesson, he had spent an hour at the sand basket. The scoured copper gleamed in the lamplight.

Hibya smiled and took his hands. They were chapped and red. She reached for the healer's jar.

"I want . . . wanted to honor so great a treasure," he said.

She worked the terebinth balm between his fingers. "This ship bears a treasure far more precious than a few copper pots."

His breath caught. In any port city, he could sell the cauldron for more than he could spend in a year. What the ship might carry that was "far more precious," he could not guess.

He missed some of her words in his distraction.

". . . look like you have been playing in the snow." She scooped another gobbet. "One of my earliest memories was of my father's hands, cold and red, after we made snow sculptures on Mount Ida."

"Hibya's father . . . he lives?"

"I had reached my sixth year, the time of my dedication. We burned herbs in the great cave, then mounted the winding trail to the western summit. He carried me on his shoulders when I grew tired. I remember the laurels that lined the path, more dwarfish as we neared the top. He broke a leaf and held it to my nose. Their scent is more powerful the higher they grow. My first glimpse of snow was on those shiny green leaves . . ." She trailed off.

Luyan struggled to commit to memory some of the unfamiliar phrases. He sensed she needed to speak, uninterrupted by his questions.

"He held me out over the valley. I felt no fear looking down. My father's hands were powerful. Like yours. I trusted with all my being he would never let me fall."

Luyan squeezed her fingers.

"I can't remember his prayer," she continued. "All I have left of him is the name with which he consecrated me. I learned later that the ceremony was a remnant of a much older ritual, a practice long abandoned."

"*Yibri*. He did not cast me in." She raised her eyes and smiled. "So, Talyera is beautiful, isn't she?"

He could detect no lingering anger. She had never explicitly claimed to own him, but her behavior on deck had been unmistakably possessive. He chose carefully from his limited vocabulary.

"Illuyanka . . . is for Hibya."

Her eyes darted, then softened. She sighed, pressed her forehead to his, and began spreading the sweet balm over his inner thighs.

There was more in her touch than healing, and he felt it. She splayed her fingers as she glided over his tender parts. His body reacted, and he flushed, began to pull away. She wrapped him tighter and gently bit his lower lip.

He wished he knew more of Keftiun custom. But his

inexperience only seemed to ignite her. She offered the front of her long throat to his kisses, each less timid than the last.

"My Illuyanka . . . my dragonfly." She found his mouth again.

He bit back this time. The pain unfolded into pleasure as their lips took on a mutual tumescence.

"How is . . . Keftiun way?"

"What is the Keftiun way?" She shrugged. "*Serkaru* love begins with *zhinkatu*."

He tried to interpret. Spirit . . . sharing?

She sipped at the chalice, then held it to him as she unfastened her cincture. The lotus wine partially numbed his lips. He touched her skin where the sun had not, traced the white outlines to their juncture, stopping at a curious marking just above the fringe of her down.

A tattoo like a star. An internal spiral and nine points.

Her golden eyes searched his face. Then she took his ankles and crossed them behind her, reached up his back, and gripped his hair. She sealed her mouth to his and slowly exhaled. He was unsure of what she wanted. To show him, she reversed the ritual, drawing the breath from his lungs.

He hesitated for a moment, then inhaled. She released her breath in synchrony, depleted and warmed by her body. This deprivation, combined with the wine and lotus tincture, induced a sharp, deliciouis delirium. Still, she did not break the *zhinkatu*, and he slowly exhaled his even warmer and more divested air back into her. She reclined, as if retaining hemp smoke for more potent effect. He took a few gulps of the pristine night breeze from the scupper as he studied her. Head hung back, lips clenched and curled, hair teasing his toes.

With a blissful smile, she finally expelled, leaned in again, and kissed him the way he had kissed her. Then down his chest and ribs, pressing him back to the deck, savoring his scent, already familiar in the tiny space they shared. The bite of him, mingled with terebinth balm. She mopped with her hair as she cupped, his desire heavy and urgent in her hand, ran the other up his torso, admired how quickly the ship's food and varied work had filled him out. He could no longer be mistaken for a mere youth, as other *serkarui* remarked with irritating frequency.

She suckled and pressed closer, her bosom itching for contact. Feeling a tremulous flutter, she caught a fold of skin in her teeth, just hard enough to delay him. He gripped himself—an immature instinct for self-relief. But she took his wrist, turned his back against her, as when the gods first joined them, and trapped his hand beneath her. His fingertips began to explore, their rugged callous piercing the slurry of balm and the flow of her body. She sighed and reciprocated the rhythm.

Sooner, more powerfully than she could have expected, they reached a mutual point of no return. She turned his jaw, sealed him once more, drawing hard as he exhaled. Savoring but a moment on the ship's rise, the top of its pitch matching theirs, she gave all back, as they swallowed one another's tearing cries.

An hour later, they lay across the hammock, blanketed only by the warm Khamsin flowing through the scuttle. Luyan's musings turned once more to Hibya's words.

"What is *vitz-ituri*?" Second generation, perhaps, he'd been thinking.

She mumbled her answer, eyes still shut, hand upon his chest. "I am twice-born, and you are twice-born. One is born to the world, or to the *serkarui*. Some to both. We are twice-born, so that we may beget the once-born."

He was more puzzled than before. "How can twice-born beget once-born?"

She scratched lazily at her throat. "You were born once to your mother, yes? And again . . ." She hesitated. "Again when you abandoned your life and were reborn from the sea. Reborn to me. Twice-born, you see?"

The notion seemed to menace her with sadness. But he sensed its importance to himself as well. His value to the Keftiu. Perhaps his fate.

"So you are my mother?"

A creeping, ironic smile. "I am your mother like you are my sister."

His brow furrowed as her palm strayed lower.

She cleared the husk from her throat. "Illuyanka, the *serkarui* are a sisterhood apart from the world. When a child is born to one of us, is it said to be 'once-born' to the sisterhood. But many are given to the *serkarui* by worldly parents. As when a mother dies in childbirth, and the baby has no one to care for it. Or when a blessing comes unlooked for, and a woman would let her infant die. When *serkarui* midwives save and protect such children, these are twice-born."

"But not only daughters?"

"A boy may be accepted, but fewer are unwanted by the world. Already the priests call us baby thieves, but they do not grieve the loss of girls. When the *serkarui* beget once-born sons, they are easily placed with worldly families to raise them. Few boys, few . . . men," she glanced at him, "are suited to our mysteries. To life in the *yridinu tzerori.*"

Her gaze grew distant and her voice thick. "Also, there are those who prove that they do not wish to live longer in the world. When they are saved from death by the *serkarui,* then they too are *vitz-ituri.*"

Luyan had heard the crewmen say the word *yridinu* for "current." Her language was going beyond the pedantic simplicity she used for his benefit, taking a more complex and personal form.

He softened his voice. "And you. You are twice-born of this kind."

Her eyelids remained half-lowered as she nodded. *"Etz eya va.* As are you. We swim together now, Illuyanka." Her breathing became more even as her words trailed off. "But the current is swift. And so little sea room remains . . ."

He held her and let the ship rock them to sleep.

6 Duty Bound

Since man cannot live without miracles, he will provide himself with miracles of his own making. He will believe in witchcraft and sorcery, even though he may otherwise be a heretic, an atheist, and a rebel.

—Fyodor Dostoyevsky, *The Brothers Karamazov*

5 March 1769
Lt. S. Singer, HMRN
At Sea

My Dear Girl,
We are near to passing Brest, and the sun shines fine this morning. I breakfasted alone in my little cabin, feeling as well as I have since the ordeal of my departure. And so to continue.

Hagen gave a final long look in the direction Arima had run as the cordon of donkeys began picking their way down the misty river valley. Turning forward, he made an effort to restore his composure by asking the boson's mate for an account of the ship, its stores, water, and provisions. Major repairs to the rigging were complete, he was informed, though leaving the ship lacking in spare spars and cordage. It would have by then fully watered, a point upon which the ailing captain had pressed the port admiral on humanitarian grounds, and to gain time sufficient to the retrieval of Hagen.

The gunner's mate, who had been acting as master gunner since his chief had been sick listed, and was likely to receive his warrant when they reached England, interrupted without leave to speak. Pulling closer to Hagen, he offered to acquaint him that the ship contained a full complement of powder and shot and then stated in a more conspiratorial tone that the fever was not the whole story. Certain insolences had been offered to some ladies of Pasaia; he was not in the way of naming the crewmen implicated, but knowing them not to pique themselves on politeness, nonetheless doubted the merits of the fuller accusations, if the lieutenant smoked his meaning.

This discourse, accompanied by a suggestive arch of the brow and a finger aside the nose, put Hagen so thoroughly out of countenance that he pulled the column up short to rate the gunner for his impertinence. This he did so roundly and imperiously that the little company continued on in stunned silence for the next several wet, slogging miles.

Hagen's assertion of officer-like authority, which both the substance and manner of the gunner's observations evinced had been sorely lacking among the ship's company for several weeks, exhausted him. He was still in the grip of sad and fevered reflections when startled by the beat of cantering hooves on the winding trail behind. To the astonishment of all, Arima overtook them, wrapped in a thick red felt cloak and riding a stately chestnut mare with a tooled, silver-studded saddle.

"Donnez le moi! Je connais un raccourti a Pasaia par voie de terre," she exclaimed breathlessly, standing in her stirrups to make room for Hagen in the saddle behind her.

Porter replied in his officer's French. *"Impossible, mademoiselle.* We can neither render Lieutenant Singer to you nor follow your overland shortcut. We go to Donostia to retrieve our cutter—our small sailing boat—and return to Pasaia by sea to rejoin our ship."

The smolder in my mother's eyes flared as though sloshed with pitch. *"Non!"* she cried. *"Il est malade! Il peut mourir!* He must get warm in his cabin and take his medicine *tout de suite,* do you understand?" This last she shouted standing in her saddle, glaring down at the marine officer's face at a remove of inches as the powerful mare jostled his donkey.

Hagen intervened after a coughing fit and said, "Porter, my dear fellow, I beg you will address my wife in proper fashion. Mrs. Singer has all our welfare at heart, I do assure you."

The marine's jaw fell slack for a moment. Gripping the mane of his rearing donkey with one hand, he removed his hat. "Your humble servant, *Madame* Singer."

Turning to Hagen, he said, "I give you joy of your marriage, sir." Still endeavoring to calm his beast, and with a final glance at the glowering young woman, he added in muttered English, "And wish you the best of luck."

Beaming with happiness despite his condition, Hagen held Arima's bridle and said, *"Mon amour*, these good men in red are royal marines of the first colonial regiment. They are under orders to return me bodily to the ship and would hang for dereliction of that duty. They cannot let me out of their sight until I am delivered to the captain, do you understand?"

She merely touched his cheek in reply, brushing back his sweaty red locks with a concerned tilt of her head.

He kissed her hand. "Porter, may we not send the seamen on down to Donostia to retrieve the cutter, and you and your marine cohort run with us overland to Pasaia? The captain wanted me back without the loss of a moment, did he not?"

Porter guarded a skeptical expression. With her fast horse and knowledge of the mountains, Arima could easily outrun them.

Hagen sensed his reticence. "Surely, you would not object to my good lady wife's kindness in guiding us?" he asked.

"No . . . oh no, sir!" Porter replied. He reflected for a moment. "One of my men would take the lead, if that's all the same to you, sir, and if you do choose to ride with Madame, you would oblige me exceedingly if you handled the reins yourself."

Arima consented, and after a seaman helped Hagen into the saddle behind her, she flipped her heavy red cloak back to encompass them both. Hagen placed his arms around her and took the reins in hand. The great mare evinced no difficulty in bearing the weight of two riders. Indeed, the slow trotting pace of the donkeys vexed her, and she more than once nipped at the tail of the lead animal, ridden by a ruddy-cheeked marine sergeant named Turnbull whose direction, when the trail became faint, Arima was frequently compelled to correct.

Several times Arima called a halt, once to grind Hagen's

medicine, she having pulled all the remaining wormwood plants she could find and wrapping their root-balls in wet burlap. It did not seem to have answered, as the plants had already wilted and were turning dark and slippery. She doubted their curative essence would much longer survive.

As the trail emerged from a forest of beech trees and opened to a high mountain meadow, Arima spied a stand of blackthorn, its rich blue fruits, which in Basque she called *aranza*, ripe and sweetened by the winter frost. These she gathered, carefully avoiding the tree's wicked spikes, and fed some to the mare. She popped one into Hagen's mouth and filled his hands with more; he chewed and swallowed with some difficulty but gave her a feeble smile and shared them out to the marines.

Sergeant Turnbull, though no lackwit, was of a marvelous and superstitious frame and had watched Arima at the grinding of her herbs with extreme interest; he now reverently studied his portion of the fruit at arm's length with an imbecile grin.

Porter upbraided him through his own mouthful. "Its refreshment, booby, not magic." Turning to Arima, he commented cordially, "They eat rather like little plums but with a hint of sloe gin. *Merci, madame.*"

She flickered a smile in acknowledgment as she remounted.

By noon the path was descending steeply. Hagen had been dozing for an hour and more with his head upon Arima's shoulder; their hands invisible to Porter under the great cloak, she had taken the reins. The trail joined a forest road lined by old oaks and a sprinkling of pines and eventually cut a number of fallow fields, disclosing the pass ahead through the steep hills which ring the port of Pasaia.

"We are nearly there, my love," she said to Hagen, whose fever she could feel in his trembling hands as they sleepily cupped her bosom through her blouse. "One more climb and we shall see your ship in the harbor below."

The mare broke finally into a light sweat as they ascended the pass. Porter and several of his men turned in their saddles to take in the fine vista of valley behind them, colorful in its quilted loveliness even in winter, before gaining the top of the hill where the whole of the calm, blue, protected harbor opened before them. The sergeant and Arima stopped briefly to permit the others to catch up and to profit from the spectacle. Hagen pointed to the tall masts of the *Merrow*, no longer in the shipyard's dry dock where he had left it, but now at single anchor at a moderate remove from the shore due to the fear of contagion. Several crewmen could be seen in the upper rigging hurriedly knotting and splicing, others rowing the ship's launches to and from the ship, transporting fresh water in barrels.

The portside road was steeper and wound into several switchbacks; they worked down past churches, houses, and inns before the animals' hooves began to clop along the boards of the docks. Hagen dismounted with difficulty as Turnbull signaled for one of the ship's launches to pick them up. Arima made arrangements in rapid Basque with some local youths to return the line of hired donkeys to Donostia and her horse to her uncle's *baserri* near Lasarte. Hagen took out his coin purse, but Arima shook her head; a foreigner's gold was always too free—her uncle would give what was due when the boys appeared with the mare.

The launch drifted in alongside the dock, and the six crewmen backed their oars, the empty water barrels having been cleared to make room for the passengers. Hagen stepped into the boat first, extending his hand for Arima, and the marines followed. The rowers pulled them quickly to the frigate, stretching out in long powerful strokes.

The Basque are a nautical people, and as the launch drew near, Hagen lamented the pride he should have felt in showing Arima his ship. The stains of reeking runoff from the quarter galleries, the lines left hanging helter-skelter about the unvarnished rails, and the lack of a lookout confirmed his guilty suspicion that discipline had gone by the boards, the captain likely being too low from fever to enforce it.

They boarded the frigate over the untended port side netting.

Hagen's concern for Arima proved unfounded when she leapt for her grip and climbed with able grace. The launch tied along to wait for the last of the empty barrels to be lowered over. Hagen settled his tricornered hat upon his sweaty head, tossed off the red cloak, and smoothed his uniform before ascending, wishing to present as robust a figure as possible to the anxious ship's company.

Though received without boatswain's pipe, Hagen gave the traditional salute to the foremast, where in olden times a crucifix hung, and then lifted his hat to return the salutes of the small assembly of seamen and warrant officers who had been milling about amidships.

"Turnbull, show Mrs. Singer to my cabin, if you please. I shall report immediately to Captain Norton." The marine sergeant bowed solicitously to Arima and began to back down the companionway. With a skeptical look at Hagen, she followed.

The ruddy ship's surgeon, Dr. Grimmer, was just exiting the door of the captain's stateroom, followed by an attendant bearing an unemptied chamberpot and a basin of thick blood.

"I hope I see you well, Lieutenant Singer," the surgeon said with indifferent sincerity, his breath rummy in the tight passageway. "Don't trouble yourself to knock, I pray you."

Hagen composed his already unsteady stomach with an effort, gave his sticky forehead a final wipe with his sleeve, and entered the cabin.

The captain did not rise from his bed as Hagen removed his hat, shocked by the man's condition. The formerly powerful officer greeted him through a fit of weak coughing, adding to the speckling of blood, old and new, upon his beard. His eyes were sunken and sallow, his skin jaundiced; his bulging abdomen an absurd contrast to the emaciated legs which protruded like matchsticks from beneath the naked shirt in which he lay.

"I regret being unable to report sooner, sir," Hagen said, 'but I was myself beset with a fever fit of this damned ague while taking my little liberty."

The captain gave a feeble waive of his hand. "Yes, yes, Singer, it don't signify. The lobsters was but a preventative. I'd not have sent them out after you without I thought you might need some help getting back, and the situation here in such a delicate low state." He pointed toward the flagon of rum and water the surgeon had left beside him, and Hagen held it to his lips.

"The fact is, I've not got long, Singer, and we've already lost most of the wardroom and half the experienced warrant officers. The port admiral, as it were, compelled us to cancel all liberty and shift our bob from dock a week ago when it became evident how much sickness there was among the crew. To make matters worse, a couple of tavern wenches made accusations of ravishment against three of the foremast hands. I take responsibility for all of it, Singer—it's all in the log, shaky as my hand may be. This ague has long since passed to my brain, I'm afraid, and it's run discipline all to hell. I order a man placed on the defaulter's list Thursday, and by Sunday I've forgotten, and he avoids his flogging." He tried to clear his lungs with the help of the grog. "I'm not crying mutiny, mark you, but the crew knows I'm adrift, and with no senior officers to superintend, it's in the nature of tars to kick up after such a hard service as they've seen on this cruise." He broke off into more coughing and lay back, silent for several moments.

Hagen blotted the captain's brow with his neckerchief and gave him another drink. "Most kind of you Singer," he said, making an effort to sit up. "Now if you'll pass me that folio on the locker there . . ." Hagen complied.

"These are the ship's papers, as well as your acting command. Don't stand on loyalty, man. Read yourself in as soon as ever it suits. The doctor will certify that I've been unfit for duty these three days and more, and there's no use waiting until I'm dead." He waived off Hagen's protests and continued. "The shipyard bill is all settled, and we are under orders to sail with the tide, now we are well-nigh fully watered. You would oblige me extremely if you will deliver these upon reaching England—one is my report to the Admiralty. The other is a letter to my wife."

Hagen swallowed. "I pray it does not come to that, sir," he said.

"I shall put things right on deck and wait upon you again in the next watch, if I may."

The captain's voice grew thinner. "Yes, all a-tanto on deck. Make it so, Singer. And for God's sake, search the holds and put off any females those hang-arse whoremongers may have cached aboard."

"Aye, sir," Hagen replied, closing the door quietly as Norton lay back in evident relief, wrist to forehead.

Hagen called for the bosun and ordered preparations for weighing anchor at the next morning's high tide. The presence of a commissioned naval officer back on deck had a powerful and immediate effect: rope ends were flemished, reefers run aloft, parties organized to holystone and swab the decks and to pump the noisome bilges. A brace of Porter's marines "discovered" three women who had been living in the forehold, their presence verily known to the entire crew. They were put off in the launch, to the consternation of many a foremast hand and at least one young midshipman, who wept hearty.

Hagen knew the cutter would not enter the harbor after dark on the incoming tide unless it came on to blow, but rather stand off and on and await the frigate to be hauled up in the bay on the morrow. Having occupied himself with the immediacies, he again attended the captain.

Norton could not be roused. The surgeon had let more of the poor man's blood before retiring to his own cabin much in rum, as he frequent was by the end of the afternoon watch. The captain's breathing was assuming a stertorous quality that concerned Hagen and put him once again in mind of his own condition, from which his duties had until then distracted him.

He left his senior midshipman—a youth of fourteen—on deck at the turn of the middle watch and went below, where Arima was waiting. He found the cabin sweeter not only for the thorough paced scrubbing she had bestowed, but for her very presence. She straightaway gave him to drink of the last dose of sweet wormwood, this having a dank and slimy quality, and the rest of the herb barely worth the grinding. She was discontented with the state of his fever, and after a hasty washing, bundled him into bed.

He was roused at the beginning of the morning watch, a mere four hours later, by a cook's mate carrying a tray of tea. Arima, used to coffee, wrinkled her nose at the brew and made Hagen to drink both cups before hurriedly buttoning his coat. She stopped him to feel his brow before he took to the quarterdeck, and to ask if she, too, should be put off the ship like the other women.

Hagen smiled. "*Non, mon amour.* You are a naval officer's wife being carried home, all proper to custom. The crew will extend the fullest courtesy. Porter will station one or two marines by your cabin for peace of mind, and I shall present you to the captain. It would please me if you were to examine him, in any case."

He pricked the chart by lantern light and marked the course out the bay and into the Channel, desiring the two remaining midshipmen and the master's mate to observe him, to whet as fine an edge as possible upon their navigation skills. He could not discount the possibility that he himself might be laid low before reaching home port.

Once done, he brought Arima to the stateroom. They entered without knocking to avoid deranging the captain should he be sleeping, as he indeed was; but his eyes fluttered open to the touch of Arima's hand upon his clammy forehead.

"A most agreeable *levee.* Your servant, *senõrita*," he said in a thin but clear voice.

"Captain Norton, sir, may I present my wife, Arima Singer?"

She curtsied quickly and began palpating the captain's abdomen.

"Well, Singer, I see you have made quite a profitable liberty here in sunny Spain," he groaned as Arima pressed his spleen, caked as stone.

She sponged the man and attended efficiently to the relief and tidying of his simpler needs, which had been neglected by the surgeon and his mate. She neither scrupled nor blushed to shift him into a clean shirt. Hagen was astonished at the condition of his wasted limbs and grossly swollen belly. When he reached at his flagon of rum, Arima offered fresh water instead.

Hagen might have found some sign of improvement in the captain's condition, he no longer coughing and in a weak but wholly sensible state. Arima shook her head slightly when their eyes met, however. As is so often the case, an ailing subject seems to quicken as the body prepares to give up the ghost.

"Sir, is there anything we can do to make you more comfortable?" Hagen asked.

"No, my boy. I am quite settled, thank ye, and more than content, Mrs. Singer being the first and loveliest of the angels I can hope to meet this day. I give you joy of your marriage. In a Spanish church, I daresay?"

"Yes, sir. The charming little Roman chapel in Pasaia."

"Just so. Well then, we best tuck a reef in it. No need for ceremony. Just avow the union before me, and I'll list it solemnized."

Hagen took Arima's hand uncertainly, never having witnessed a shipboard wedding.

Captain Norton prompted him. "Lieutenant Hagen Singer, before God and king, is this woman your wife?"

"She is, sir," Hagen replied.

The captain turned to Arima with a saintly smile. *"Y usted, hermosa Señora, este hombre es su marido?"*

A bit muddled but pleased by the question, she nodded and looked up at Hagen. *"Seguro que sí, Capitano."*

"Bueno," he said. "Singer, pass me the log, will you?"

With difficulty, the captain scratched out and signed his entry in his stricken hand as Hagen supported the heavy book for him.

All hands were called at four bells—break of day and an hour before high tide. Deck hands busied themselves at the winch to weigh anchor, and reefers ran aloft to prepare to let fall the topsails. Hagen was pleased by their alacrity and the return of the joy which is right and proper to sailors in the final leg of a long journey homeward. They recovered the cutter with some little difficulty in the bounding chop outside the mouth of the harbor, and set west-northwest under all plain sail to stand well off the coast of Brest and seek the westerlies, which would complete their wide loop back toward England.

The next day they buried the captain over the side with full ceremony, and Hagen read out his formal order of appointment as commander before the assembled company.

The ship heaved mightily; its early course flung them against the Portugal current, the wind stiff on their forward beam, and the Bay of Biscay notoriously rough at the best of times. Hagen was pleased to see that Arima suffered no seasickness during the first few days, when even some seasoned hands were not unaffected.

It came, therefore, as a surprise when she lost her coffee into a washbasin on a relatively calm morning six days out.

Brushing her hair back, Hagen assured her in a gentle tone. *"Ce n'est qu'un peu de mal de mer. Ça passera."*

She laughed. "Basques do not suffer *mal de mer*, my love. And have you ever known *mal de mer* to first set in this long into a Bay voyage?"

Her gist he did not at once divine, but as the nausea visited each morning for the next week, disappearing each afternoon, the happy truth soon appeared. He urged her to see the surgeon to confirm her condition, but she refused to submit to the examination of whom she called, "that tippling horse leech," whose bloodletting, she was certain, had hastened the already anemic captain's demise.

The westerlies set uncommon north that year, and the ship's course required a long northwest arc into the southern Celtic Sea before it could turn east toward the Channel. The lack of experienced officers compelled Hagen to take more than his share of deck watches, and the constant driving rain took its toll on his already delicate constitution.

The marines being of little use on passage, Lieutenant Porter and Sergeant Turnbull, both among the few French speakers aboard, were welcome companions to Arima, frequently waiting upon her in her cabin or taking a turn with her upon deck when the weather allowed. She noted the longstanding camaraderie between her husband and Porter; the latter, though no seaman, being the only commissioned officer left aboard under Hagen himself, and the only member of the ship's company qualified to approach him on the quarterdeck and address him on a personal footing. Hagen had long admired Porter for his judgment and discipline and readily trusted him as chaperone to his new wife; she in turn shared an increasing confidence with the marine officer.

And she did not fail to discern the more than brotherly tenderness between Porter and Sergeant Turnbull. The pair palavered intimately with her for hours over endless cups of coffee in her little cabin, the men gradually revealing their privy habit of addressing one another by their Christian names—Matthew and Christopher—despite the disparity of rank. Just as their frequent visits gave Arima to feel secure, the cabin became a cloister for the men's own conversation of heart, her presence checking the rumors that might otherwise arise were the two to closet themselves alone, expression of such passions being subject to the harshest of penalties under the Articles of War. The trio, when communing together in whispers, took to calling their circle "safe space," and this was among the first English phrases Arima acquired.

The ship was a day south of the latitude of Ushant, which marks the southern limit of the Channel, when Hagen surrendered to his mounting fever, he having by bare force of will and duty kept it at bay until then. While charting for the midshipmen the landmarks and waypoints, the knowledge necessary to safe winter passage through the Channel, he collapsed insensible. His foul weather kit having obscured the wasting of his body, Porter remarked his lightness as he lifted him upon his shoulder.

He laid Hagen down in his cabin and not the sick berth, in

accordance with Arima's strict instruction. Her eyes shone with tears as she stripped his outer garments and wrapped him in a blanket. He was burning again with the fever, the skin of his face yellow with jaundice, and his distended belly tight as a drum.

There are few secrets aboard a vessel of that size, and Doctor Grimmer soon appeared at the cabin door. His burley loblolly boy carried a rusty thumb lancet, an encrusted fleam which might have seen prior service on farm animals, and a bleeding bowl. The surgeon bore a bottle of brandy.

Arima blocked their path to Hagen and appealed to Porter to prevent them from touching him. When Grimmer persisted, she thrust out her jaw.

"Il est deja anemique bricon! Vous voulez le tuer avec vos conneries de put aire?"

As the surgeon composed his startled countenance, Porter merely shrugged. He had seen Arima's protective wrath before then, and in truth credited her diagnosis above Grimmer's. The jaundiced color was not the result of imbalanced humors, as the surgeon would maintain, his medical training consisting of the award of a book on nautical disease and a certificate from the Sick and Hurt Board. Hagen was in point of fact anemic, his spleen swollen to bursting and his liver failing—as well as his lungs, to judge by the pink tinge of his spittle. Bleeding and a draught of spirits were a prescription for murder, not cure.

"L'ecorce de saule! Y'en a-t-il au moins, l'incompetant d'un fils de bas?" Arima addressed this to Porter.

The marine turned to Grimmer, whose lack of French further evinced his meager education, and translated Arima's comments in their less provocative aspects.

"Doctor, Mrs. Singer begs you will reconsider phlebotomy, as her husband is already quite anemic from the ague. She further is concerned to say that his liver may be compromised, and, under correction, of course, asks if spirits may be best omitted? Finally, she begs to know if the, er"—"useless bastard" had been her actual words—"good doctor . . . may not have some willow bark is his dispensary?"

"Rubbish!" Grimmer replied. "I adjure you respectfully not to presume to supersede a ship's surgeon in medical matters, Lieutenant Porter, sir, or my report to the admiralty will bear notice." He turned to his assistant. "Restrain this woman, Ben, if she makes the most trifling attempt to interfere, and gag her if she emits that harpy shriek into my good ear but once more again!"

After rolling his sleeves, Grimmer pulled the cork with his teeth and took a swig of the brandy, then placed Hagen's trembling arm over the iron bleeding bowl. Arima grasped at his elbow with a cry, and the assistant held her back from behind, a grimy hand across her mouth. When the surgeon unfolded the corroded lancet with his thumb in a practiced motion and held it to the crook of Hagen's arm, Porter saw Arima's eyes go dark. In one stroke, she reached up to her mouth and broke the little finger of Ben's hand as if snapping off the wing of a roast chicken, folding it with a wet crack all the way back to his wrist, and wormed herself free of his grasp. He wailed as loud and shrill as ever Arima had done. She snatched the fleam from the bowl and whipped its bayonet-like point to the side of the surgeon's neck, her other hand on her hip in a fencer's pose.

"Lachez le, putain!" she said in a compelling whisper.

Ben's mewling was the only sound in the cabin for several long moments before Porter spoke.

"Madame Singer regrets she must importune your kindness in standing down from the procedure and dropping your lancet, if you please, Doctor," he said.

My dear, I have again taken the greatest solace in passing all this day in writing. I remark that I am nearly out of paper and ink and will beg some from the purser tomorrow.

Adieu!
S. Singer

7 Crystallizing

"The people never give up their liberties,
but under some delusion."

—Edmund Burke

1602 BCE
Eastern Mediterranean

Luyan awoke alone in the hammock to a stiff morning breeze through the scuttle, scented with cedar resin. He was disoriented by the rearrangement of the tapestries bounding the sleeping space. They had been moved, along with a number of others, to form a single circular area at the center of the lower deck. He took a drink from his waterskin, wrapped his loincloth and padded softly over to the new enclosure. Through a small gap, he saw the entire group of twenty or more *serkarui*, Hibya included, seated in meditation, their eyes fixed upon the floor in front of them. The Kozhiniru was in the middle, her back straight against the mast.

He quietly mounted the companionway ladder, noting by the height of the midmorning sun that he had slept later than usual. He found most of the crew and passengers lining the forward rail, peering into the distance off the bow. He scrambled up the mast, grabbed a bronze ring bolt with one hand, and shielded his eyes. A thin line of greenish gray, capped by a broken range of clouds, was visible in the east.

Clapping on to a back stay, he slid easily down, dropping near the passenger deck. The mood of the company seemed muted, and Luyan thought it odd that after a long open-water journey, they were not more jubilant at the sight of land.

He crossed the deck, took a grip on a becket, and flipped himself over the gunwale, his feet landing on the port side rowing gallery. He wound his way aft past the broad-backed rowers, one of whom clasped his shoulder in a strong grip and offered him a draught from his skin of beer.

Luyan replied, *"M'hara,"* and raised it to his lips. But the crew leader grabbed his wrist, shook his head with a smile, and said, *"Li! Harol, Ser-Luyan. Eyal vamtami!"*

Luyan realized that the man was addressing him as he would one of the *serkarui*. He wondered if he was mocking him. Beer was evidently another of his tastes that was *eyal vamtami*, or "not for you." The rower took the beer, lifted his head above the rail, and called out, *"Phinyu!"*

Rapid footsteps, and an earthenware decanter was handed down. The rowers grinned amiably as he savored the amber wine in slow gulps. They wasted none of what remained when he passed it back.

He stepped to the stern end of the gallery and relieved himself. In what was now, thanks to Hibya's lessons, a natural and confident habit, he mounted and dove off the rail and into the cool sea. With long strokes, staying below the water to challenge his breath as well as his muscles, it was not too difficult to keep up with the ship, and after several cable lengths, he scaled the port steering paddle and remounted the gallery's stern quarter. He took a rough rag from the bucket of warm soapy water kept there for washing. When done scrubbing, he poured some over his head and tried in vain to work out his matted locks. Finally giving up, he shook himself off, rinsed, and wrung out his loincloth.

Conscious of the eyes of the rowers upon him, instead of crawling easily through the scuttle, he leaped to grab the rail of the upper deck, and with a slight grunt, pulled himself waist level and swung a leg over. He remained straddled there for a few moments, enjoying the effects of the wine, thoughts of Hibya, and the warm sun on his wet skin and hair. He could not put a name to what he was feeling. He wondered if it was related, or even connected, to what the *serkarui* were experiencing in their silent meditation below. If it was freedom, he thought, it might be foolish to get too used to it.

And just as foolish, while the ship's company were all on the upper deck straining to see the landfall, not to take advantage of their distraction. He made certain no eyes were upon him, and crept down the companionway. On the lower deck, he lit an oil lamp and descended a ladder to the holds.

He made his way in a crouch past the dense corral of pigs, grateful for their seasick silence, along dozens of clay amphorae and bound stacks of skins and textiles, to the far aft section, where a number of chests were stowed. He looked behind to be sure he had not been followed, quietly unlatched one, and opened it— silver ingots, more than could be carried in a single coracle. He suspected he could do better. He tried another, larger chest. It contained a number of ornate boxes, perhaps intended as diplomatic gifts. Sampling a few, he found jewelry of dazzling design, all wrought of precious materials: amber, gold, and pearls. Tempting and portable, but difficult to sell. It was copper he was after. If he could half fill a coracle with ingots, he could buy his own ship and crew at any major port.

He listened carefully but heard no footsteps above. He wrestled part of the stack aside, trying to make mental note of the containers' original positions, and crawled between, pushing his candle on the planks and knocking gently to guess their contents.

As he spread two containers apart, he was startled to see a burley foot in a laced sandal, inches in front of his face. He struck his head as he recoiled. A strong hand gripped his hair, yanked him up, and flung him on his back.

The navigator stood over him with the scowl of a man who'd found a maggot on his spoon.

Luyan was dragged to the upper deck by two crewmen and thrown again to his knees. Durzhyar, the navigator's assistant, tried to intervene, but the older man silenced him with a loud command.

The Kozhiniru was called from the forepeak. The navigator recounted the situation in irate, rapid Keftiun. Luyan could not fully follow, but the accusatory tone was unmistakable. He was certain his life hung in the balance.

Hibya came running and dropped to her knees beside him.

"What has happened?" she asked.

"Do not speak for me," Luyan said in a miserable whisper. "I am unworthy of your protection."

"Curiosity again, Hibya?" the Kozhiniru asked.

The navigator interjected. "He is a pirate, infected with the morals of a nation of thieves! On such you hang our hopes?"

"You are wrong!" shouted Hibya. "I have tasted his goodness, his strength. He discerns much and intuits more. I need only a little time!"

"We have fewer days left than Alashya has cedars," the Kozhiniru said, regarding Luyan with stern sadness. "The navigator's concerns are well founded, Ser-Hibya."

Luyan felt a cold hopelessness. A tear sprang from Hibya's eye.

The Kozhiniru reflected, then turned to the navigator. "On the other hand, my lord, what else but time is left to us worth stealing?"

He glowered, unmoved. He glanced toward a crewman, who began to untie a javelin from its becket.

"*Eyshto'y!*" Hibya cried. "Hear me! *Shla tami kebulu-na zhyira . . . l'usuro'sh, Kozhiniru . . . turo'sh!*"

Her words carried uniquely *serkarun* implications, and even the navigator did not appreciate their deeper meaning. Luyan roughly understood, "He still lives in delusion . . . don't abandon him, Kozhiniru . . . beget him!"

The priestess met her eye. "You judge him ready?"

"He is *ituru ashyukyari*. I know you see it," Hibya replied.

Her eyes seemed to wrestle with the Kozhiniru's, now pleading, now determined. Finally, the priestess raised her hand.

She faced the navigator but addressed Hibya. "*Va ryasa shlan hyim, Ser-Hibya.*"

Her mouth fell open. "Three days?"

"No more," said the Kozhiniru. "And he must be a willing aspirant. You know what that requires."

The group slowly cleared, leaving Hibya and Luyan alone.

What was required was that he asked, of his own accord and with pure motives, to be initiated into the *serkarui* order. Hibya kept Luyan close during the remainder of that day and the next, a spectator to their devotions, in forlorn hope that something might inspire him.

The ship kept several miles offshore until the pilots could be certain of their landing and of avoiding detection by warships or more coastal raiders. The *serkarui* were preoccupied during this time with preparations. Communal exercises took place each morning and evening, and the Kozhiniru was holding frequent audiences.

The ship was hove to shortly before sunset, and the pilots and crew went below to dine as one shift, leaving only the *serkarui* and a coxswain upon the upper deck. Hibya instructed Luyan to sit quietly near the forepeak.

The devotions began with thirty minutes of still meditation. Luyan attempted to emulate the cross-legged, straight-backed posture, eyes half-closed, peering at a fixed point on the deck. Despite his long experience remaining unmoving in uncomfortable positions, he was quickly frustrated. A minor itch on his nose turned into a torment. His legs tingled painfully and then went numb. At first, he tried praying to Ishtar. Then he let his thoughts drift as they did before sleep. Finally, he tried deliberately not to think at all.

Nothing worked. Nothing staid off intrusive images, musings, and fears. He wondered again why the Keftiu had spared him. Why he might not be bound up and executed at any moment.

Just as he was sure he could take no more, the Kozhiniru got to her feet. The *serkarui* stood with her, remained in a quiet circle for several moments, eyes closed, before she said simply, "Begin."

They eased into motion in no particular pattern. Some hummed or sang softly. Others danced in slow circles, prostrated themselves, or simply walked. Luyan felt a guilty curiosity watching the exercise, as if he were spying on the women as they bathed.

Each gave the appearance of obeying her own inner voice or movements, but the result was far from chaotic. Luyan experienced a surging, numinous awe. It was as though the gods themselves were present, manipulating, harmonizing, speaking through the sisterhood. As the tempo increased, his body was seized with a deep, vibratory force. He had to resist to keep his limbs from rising and moving of their own accord. He stole a glance at Hibya as she passed him, eyes closed, humming to the skies with arms stretched wide. She had spoken to him of "practices of ecstatic motion." He knew he must be witnessing one.

After a little less than an hour, the cadence began to diminish. Some of the women were sprawled on the deck, some still traveling in slow circles at the periphery or merely standing with hands folded. They observed a few more minutes of silence, then began to wander off to other tasks.

Luyan and Hibya spent the night making subdued love, whispering in turn until sleep overtook them. They rose early nonetheless, Hibya not wishing to waste a moment of the time that remained. By the ribboned light of the Levantine dawn, Luyan saw small groups of *serkarui* on the upper deck, performing graceful postures and breathing exercises.

Barely two miles from shore, the ship had stood off during the night to avoid the possibility of grounding on the coastal rocks. Now the lightly manned galleries were rowing at an easy pace to edge slowly nearer to port. The morning land breeze carried the scent of warm bread baking in a thousand ovens, fired since well before sunrise to feed the great city of Gubel and the many towns and settlements of its northern environs.

Hibya left Luyan with a cluster of *serkarui*, who gladly tutored him in the rudiments of their practice, and went forward for her whisper council with the Kozhiniru, an audience held every few days in the ship's triangular forepeak cabin.

They showed him how to inhale deeply through his nose and into his diaphragm. They called the open-throated sinus flow *oramayari zhiniru*, or "ocean-like breath." He was discouraged from trying to imitate the advanced postures. They demonstrated more primary forms. It was the process, not the result, that mattered. The gradual expansion of physical awareness, mindful control of responses that were normally involuntary. As unsuccessful as he felt, after an hour he was left with a pleasant muscular exhaustion. His mind light and vital.

He thanked them and, stretching his hands above his head, looked toward the bow, where Hibya was still closeted with the Kozhiniru. He noticed a small group of *serkarui* perched upon the prow, performing single-footed balance exercises. Durzhyar was tenuously making his way up the rail toward one of them. Luyan had seen him pay special attention to the young woman before.

Still a few paces behind her, Durzhyar began quavering, shooting out his arms to balance himself. Luyan sprinted forward but was still out of reach when the ship gave an eccentric lurch, and Durzhyar fell. The strangled cry and splash as he hit the water were masked by the rush of the hull's wash.

The *serkarui* were facing in the opposite direction. Only Luyan knew his friend had gone overboard.

With the full force of the vessel's momentum, Durzhyar was struck in the head by an oar as he came up and buried back beneath the wake. Luyan jumped onto the rail and, pushing off as hard as he could to clear the port gallery, dove headfirst into the sea just inches beyond the wooden blades. Flipping and turning beneath the surface, he searched desperately. He finally spotted the unconscious young man, a cloud of blood orbiting his head, sinking slowly in the clear water several meters below and behind him.

Luyan reached him just as he saw the swift jets of three *serkarui* diving in from off the prow, now well ahead. He was unwilling to make the easy grab for Durzhyar's hair, as his scalp was already very damaged. Ignoring the burning in his lungs, he pedaled, pushed deeper, and managed to wrap an arm around his friend's limp body. He kicked back toward the surface, fighting not to black out as spots began to obscure his vision.

He emerged, gasping. The rowers had backed their oars and taken headway off the ship, but he was already almost a cable length off the stern in the choppy sea, and he struggled to hold Durzhyar's head above water until the *serkarui* swimmers could reach them. One approached from beneath, supporting the lolling head, and kicked backward, while the others each hooked an arm and set back for the ship with powerful sidestrokes.

"Yibri' eya!" Luyan shouted when they glanced at him, to assure them he was in no need of help himself. He was lagging only a few yards behind as the rowers reached out, raised Durzhyar aboard the gallery, and eased him through the scuttle to the lower deck.

When Luyan made it back aboard, Durzhyar was still unconscious, seated on the lower deck, his legs straight out before him. The healer was pumping him from behind, doubling and releasing, water pouring from his mouth.

She opened the deck hatch to admit more light and inspected the wrinkled flap of scalp that hung over Durzhyar's right eye. Luyan nearly sickened at the sight of the naked expanse of skull glistening above it. An assistant placed a cauldron of soapy water and linen bandages on the brazier and floated a smaller dish within it. It held a block of what appeared to be cloudy amber flecked with tiny metallic flakes. Luyan stoked the coals and noticed a sweet scent as the crystalized honey melted.

The healer submerged a handful of instruments into a bowl of strong wine, checked Durzhyar's breathing, and felt his neck for his pulse. She uncorked a bulbous jar and tasted the poppy resin to gauge its potency before giving a careful measure to her assistant to mix with wine. They held up Durzhyar's head and placed the cup to his lips. The healer could not give him much—with such a head injury, he could not be allowed to fall fully asleep—and there would still be some pain. She placed a thick leather bit in his mouth and enlisted a strong *serkaru* to brace his head firmly.

Luyan grimaced as the healer washed her hands in the near-scalding water, scrubbing until her fingers were bright red. She took a bone forceps from the bowl of wine and lifted the flap of scalp. After picking out several splinters of wood embedded by the oar, she ladled the steaming water, holding the flap up to ensure the exposed area was well cleansed. Despite the poppy, the sting of heat and caustic saponin shocked Durzhyar into full consciousness, and a mutter escaped his lips.

"We must work quickly," whispered the healer. She rinsed the wound with wine and kept the flap retracted. Her assistant raised the bowl of shimmering molten honey to permit it to cool as she poured and covered the exposed skull in a slow, thin stream. Durzhyar began to squirm.

"Be still! It is almost done!" The healer beckoned Durzhyar's love interest and directed the young woman to sit where he could see her, to make him more stoic in the face of his pain.

She pressed the scalp back in place, ensuring a good seal with the recrystallizing honey, and swabbed the beads of blood with the clean linen. She took several stitches with wine-soaked thread on a copper hook, tying each off with the forceps.

She held a silver hand mirror under the open hatch, directing a beam of sunlight to judge the response of Durzhyar's pupils, sprinkled more wine over the seam of the closure, and dressed his head in a fresh bandage. Luyan helped carry the unhappy patient to a hammock, where the healer would keep vigil through the night.

"Will he live and be whole?" Luyan asked Hibya.

She nodded. "I think so. His skull was not badly damaged, but there is danger that his brain may swell. The healer will give him willow bark, but if by tomorrow he does not speak normally, or if the responses of his eyes do not improve, she may need to pierce his skull to relieve the pressure. This is why she took so few stitches."

The healer's skills were beyond anything he had witnessed in Cilicia. He was even more astonished that Hibya seemed to match her understanding.

"Do all *serkaru* have the healing knowledge?" he asked.

"All pursue the devotions of community, service to the sisterhood and the world. All study the skills needed to care for others. The healer has pursued this particular devotion with more discipline because it was the spirit in which her heart was most lacking."

"Lacking? She seems specially *gifted* in it."

Hibya smiled. "We never fight our gifts. That would be . . .' She tried to think of words he would recognize. "Paddling upstream against the current. But there is no fruit to devotion without discipline. The path to which we are dedicated requires a balance, a fullness of being. So where the current is weakest, we swim hardest."

His mind felt exhausted as they mounted the companionway. He posed a more straightforward question. "What makes the honey sparkle so?"

She flashed a wan smile. "Your favorite metal. The copper filings are mixed in before it crystallizes to ward off the spirit of corruption."

Luyan passed the day in torn reflection. Having witnessed the healer save his friend, the practices of the *serkarui* took on a more personal relevance.

They referred to them as *bakzhinui*, or "devotions." Their exercises had an evident spiritual basis but were unlike any prayer or worship he had known before. Neither had they anything in common with the dream journeys of the Anatolian shamans, fueled by datura, hemp, or stronger substances. Hibya remained fully conscious, even hyperaware, while she meditated. If he disturbed her, she would sometimes give a slight start but was never annoyed or offended. She simply started over.

Having grown up in a religiously diverse region, Luyan had a natural reticence to question the pious practices of others. Hibya could barely mask her joy and renewed hope when he finally expressed curiosity.

"To which god do you pray when you sit?" he asked her the

next morning as she finished her meditation.

She stretched and rose to her feet. "It is *like* prayer, isn't it?" She performed a long straight-legged forward bend. "Why do you pray, Illuyanka?"

He hesitated. He'd noticed before that the Keftiu often answered a question with another question, especially when discussing abstract notions. Light banter on the subject of the gods could bring misfortune, especially in a language he did not fully understand. Only the ancient words, the ritual prayers and formal cycles, were wholly safe.

"I offer prayers to know the will of the gods or to place my needs before them," he said carefully.

"Like sacrifice?" She straightened back up and twisted at the waist.

"Yes, like sacrifice. We make . . . fire gifts."

"Burnt offerings," she corrected. "Why do you burn what you offer the gods?"

He considered. "To make clean . . . purify. And to raise the scent to the heavens. Like when you purify your cauldron with fire and smoke."

She smiled. "Yes, our cauldron contains the remnants of countless sacred meals, past generations of the Goddess's gifts. We cleanse it with salt and fire to raise our needs before her and make our vessel worthy to again receive her blessings."

He looked about before continuing in a hushed voice. "So it is the Mother—Ishtar—to whom you pray, like I do?"

"That is one of her names. Her myths," Hibya replied.

Her words alarmed his superstitious instincts. The "god-fear" which ruled his life. The sacred names were a dangerous topic.

"What, then, do you sacrifice when you sit?"

Hibya arched her long back until her hands and elbows rested on the deck behind her. She raised first one leg and then the other and inverted in a headstand. She considered Luyan's question through three long breaths, then vaulted back to a seated position in front of him.

"As in prayer," she said, "by sitting, we purify our will in the fire of silence and raise it to the heavens. It is an exercise of willful stillness. Just as this . . ." She kept her legs crossed as she tilted forward on her forearms and lifted them behind her. "This is an exercise of willful motion."

Luyan was piqued by her words, their conviction framing the flush and sheen of her skin. Cilician culture placed no enmity between sensuality and faith, yet never before had he experienced such a guileless desire, a yearning both physical and spiritual.

"And this practice?" He kissed her hovering thigh.

She yelped at the unexpected stimulation and plopped back down in front of him.

"That," she laughed, "is an exercise of ecstatic motion, if you are really interested."

Luyan smiled. Her classic Keftiun words sounded so formal a description of their physical pleasure.

"Will you teach me the sitting exercise?" he asked after a pause.

Hibya's face froze. "This is truly your wish?"

"*Ayi.*"

She searched his eyes to gauge his sincerity. Her response was her first formal words to him as a *serkaru*.

"*Kudaru Illuyanka'm yam kyikoru yibasai.* May Illuyanka's request bind my heart." She tapped her fingers between her breasts. "Follow with me in the rest of our devotions this morning. We will practice what you must say when you are initiated, and I will give the Kozhiniru the good news."

"Good news?" The Keftiun word *kirykmu* was unfamiliar to him.

Hibya gripped his fingers and sprang to her feet.

"*Ayi! Kirykmu!* It is *kirykmu* that you have asked—you have asked, Illuyanka—to be initiated into the mysteries of the *serkaru*. To life in the *yridinu tzerori*."

His smile became fixed. He had not known his simple request would carry such weighty implications. Was he in fact to *become* a *serkaru*?

"The Kozhiniru will make everything clear," she said, "but first I must prepare you."

The next morning, after a long night of instruction, rehearsal of the ritual responses for *serkaru* initiation, and little sleep, Luyan visited Durzhyar in his quarterdeck berth. He found the healer there, knotting a fresh linen dressing. She smiled at him and left Durzhyar a cup of pine-scented tea.

"Va eya yibri, Durzhyar?" Luyan asked. His friend nodded weakly.

"I had no memory of what happened until the healer told me," Durzhyar said. "You were a gift of the gods, Luyan—the other *serkarui* did not even notice I had gone over."

"My swimming lessons have been good for something," Luyan said, returning his smile.

Durzhyar's faded, and he turned his head toward the bulkhead. "Luyan . . . I helped the crewmen to turn the bars of the stern fin during the battle. My actions contributed to your father's death. Of this, especially now, I am very ashamed."

Luyan squeezed his shoulder. "Do not think of that."

"Your father was a mariner," Durzhyar said. "What you know of seamanship, he taught you?"

"Yes, much of it. The rest I learned like he did, from observation. My family were olive growers from the highlands. The sea was new to us."

"I, too, learned from my father. He is the man I assist. The navigator," said Durzhyar.

This surprised Luyan. "I have seen no one who knows the motions of the sun and stars like your father."

"Ayi," said Durzhyar. "It was men of his line who in antiquity invented some of the instruments you have seen. He is our court astronomer, one of the most learned men in the Aegean, and the second-ranking member of our royal academy," he said. His faced betrayed a mixure of pride and guilt.

"Who is the first?" Luyan asked.

"Your Kozhiniru. She is very dear to our nation, a leader of both our academic and spiritual communities, as well as the greatest of the living *serkarui*. She is a rare, true crossover. She seeks to reunite and preserve all our traditions."

"She told me the ship carries great treasure. Was she referring to herself and your father?"

Durzhyar met his eye again. "Perhaps in part. There are greater stakes in which we all share, but to which I am not fully privy. I am not of your order, Luyan."

"*My* order?" Luyan smirked. "Do you mock me like the rowers, Durzhyar? I am a seaman. Perhaps now a seaman reduced to a woman's servant. But I am not a woman."

Durzhyar looked confused. "Luyan, no one is mocking you. It is a rare and sacred privilege when we are given to know a male *serkaru*. You, too, are a crossover. You mediate between the sisterhood of the caves and the greater world."

"So far I have mediated only between the broom and the cook pot," Luyan replied.

Durzhyar studied him. "Don't mistake their intention, Brother. They are preparing you for momentous things in the little time they have. You would not be here if the Kozhiniru didn't see in you a unique and needed potential. My father will not harm you now, after what you have done for me. But whether you rise to the challenge of providence is up to you."

Luyan reflected. "What can a sisterhood of cave-diving warriors need from me?"

"Not all are warriors, but they are far more than cave divers. This I think you already know. In ancient times, the *serkarui* were the keepers of the deep sanctum of the Goddess—the very soul of the Keftiu—and their high priestess ruled us all. The group that has adopted you is the remnant of their most elite circle, that closest to the Kozhiniru. All *serkarui* develop their physical being along with their spirit, but this community served in former times as a sort of . . ." He searched his mind for a term Luyan would understand. "Palace guard?"

Luyan nodded. "But now they are separate. You also have a noble class."

"Yes," Durzhyar said. "The materials needed to make bronze were depleted in the Aegean more than a thousand years ago, and the skills of our seamen improved as we sought them out in more distant lands. We created mining colonies in Africa, Anatolia, and the Levant, all of which became wealthy centers in their own right. But now the cedar and copper are dwindling there as well, and the Egyptian appetite is as great as ever. We were the first to journey west to find new resources, and the wealth of our merchant class, those men who build and sail our ships, has become incalculable."

"With wealth comes power," Luyan said.

"And conflict. The nobility and the *serkarui* are hand in glove, wherever we journey. They keep us in balance with the gods. Remind us that our heart, our home, lies always deep in the sacred mountains of the Cyclades."

The bruises on Durzhyar's forehead were darkening. Luyan could see he was growing tired. After helping him sip his tea, he exited onto the main deck. Hibya approached him.

She beamed. "The Kozhiniru is waiting for you. She is ready for your first whisper council."

The time had come for him to be initiated into the *serkaru* order.

8 Paying Out

Power always thinks it has a great soul and vast views beyond the comprehension of the weak; and that it is doing God's service when it is violating all his laws.

—John Adams

7 March 1769
Lt. S. Singer, HMRN
At Sea

D arling Girl,
How much more lively is my narrative vision as I
pass through the same waters upon which I left Arima
and Hagen in my last letter. Of course, the condition of the Celtic
Sea in spring is very different from that which my parents faced in
winter, and you are to consider that they were traveling homeward
with the westerlies, and I south for the Spanish coast.

That wet season had left Hagen low with the revisitation of his
calenture, his new wife having menaced the life of the ship's
surgeon—a warrant officer of peevish and vindictive frame—to
protect him from his bloodletting.

Arima was of that sisterhood—the *sorginak*, as I earlier named
it in Basque—who recognize a shaman when they see one and
have long struggled to protect the people of that region from their
depredations.

It was not fear of magic, but the magician himself who burned
the Basque "witches." The priest, the pseudo-thaumaturge, with his
myriad screeds of dreadful belief, who painted them a species of
demonic pestilence, and his particular style of enchantment—
whether cast in grove or church—its only remedy.

But, my darling girl, I do not mean to say that the *sorginak* lack
belief, only that they nurture and practice the mysteries that abide
in all women. I speak of the universal sacraments rooted in the
tides of a woman's body, the phases of her life, the humors and

passions of her heart. Consider any woman—think of yourself. Survey your memories, your dreamings, your connection to earth and water, sun and moon, life and time.

Do you know a woman whose home, if but unwittingly, does not contain an altar to these? Look—and you will find a table on which are displayed relics of people of her lineage, a source of light, whether window or candle, to illuminate them. There will be something containing seed—flowers, dried gourds, or beans. You will find earth, stones, or a vessel of clay; and if not water itself, then something silvery and reflective.

But in the event, shaman or base buffoon, the surgeon did stand down, though not without muttered threats of official redress, and withdrew to his cabin to drink his bile. Porter ordered Arima access to the ship's dispensary, from which she profited in the first instance to splint and plaster poor Ben's dangling little finger and to dose him with a comfortable draught of laudanum for his pain.

That done in tender haste, she found the willow which would temporarily reduce Hagen's fever, though unlike the sorely missed Jesuit's bark, could have nothing to say to its cause; and she begged a jug of barley water from the steward, to which she added sugar and lime juice. In the passageway, she met Sergeant Turnbull, still grinning from Porter's recounting of her bedside swordplay, and asked him to fetch her a live chicken and some dried raisins.

"A chicken and *sultanas* it is, madame," Turnbull repeated with a touch of his forelock, hoping he got the French right, and anticipating with pleasure some "spanking mumbo," as he would phrase it. He trotted forward toward the galley.

On reaching Hagen's cabin, Arima cut open three boluses of the grated willow bark—a heroic dose by ordinary standards—and ground it into a fine powder in her mortar. She added several ounces of the barley water, then asked Porter to prop Hagen upright while she held the heavy stone vessel to his lips.

Turnbull entered the cabin bearing a fat hen under his arm, prised over no minor objection from the ship's poulterer, and a sack of dried raisins. Arima relieved him of the latter, put some the mortar, and began to bash away with her pestle. Stroking the chicken, Turnbull sat beside Porter on a locker at the head of the bed and shrugged in response to his quizzical regard.

The senior marine closed his eyes for a moment, weary from his long vigil, and was roused by the slower, louder character of Arima's pounding. She was glaring past him, and he turned to find Turnbull making circular passes with the chicken over Hagen's head while whispering the Pater Noster. Porter snatched the flapping bird, and placed it in Arima's extended hand, who, with a final glance of remonstrance, quite handsomely broke its neck.

Holding the hen over the surgeon's abandoned basin, she plucked a handful of its breast feathers and, with a single cut, removed the liver and tossed it into her mortar with the raisin pulp. Turnbull and Porter struggled to hold their gorge as she ground the bloody mash with more sweet barley water and made Hagen to drink the mixture down, which he did without objection, not being fully in his senses. Arima assigned the wide-eyed Turnbull to bring the bird's carcass to the cook for soup.

The bark succeeded in bringing Hagen's fever down for several hours, the sweet barley water and lime, drunk in quantity, cleansed his beleaguered organs and relieved a bit his jaundice, and the fresh liver and mashed raisins commenced to restore his blood. By morning, his vitality was discernibly improved.

Over the next five days, Arima repeated this regimen. Having at length picked up reliable westerlies—although farther north than calculated, the constant thick cloud making it difficult to shoot the noonday sun—the frigate was making steady progress in open water, permitting Hagen to leave navigation and piloting to the midshipmen while he laid up below. The regular dosings of the willow bark, while hard on his digestion, kept his fever down, and coupled with occasional use of laudanum, the aches in his head and joints manageable. His color continued to improve, as well as the vigor of his blood, and he spent most of the day conscious, enjoying the congress of his new wife and playing hands of piquet and games of chess with Porter. By the fifth day, he was taking a turn on deck once each watch unsupported, which was as capital a boost to the crew's morale as it was to his own.

Arima, for her part, remained gripped by quiet concern. The still turgid and swollen spleen, the wasting of the once well-muscled frame, and the periodic rigor and paroxysms evinced to her that the ague still lingered in Hagen's blood. She knew that none of her palliative measures would cure him of it for good and all or even continue long to relieve his symptoms. She cherished and cosseted him night and day, guarding him from the sensibility of her least solicitude; but her dread smoldered within her, and her silent tears often bathed his sleeping face.

At length, the all too brief reprieve expired. An uncommon dirty late November storm blew up, and they already slightly north of the Scilly Islands, threatened to drive them onto the rocky lee shore of Cornwall. Arima's tearful objections notwithstanding, there was nothing else for it but that Hagen go on deck to stand the middle watch himself. Drenched by the driving sleet and the chill waves which swept the deck, he remained at the wheel as the ship fought for sea room under double-reefed topsails all that night.

The task demanded every whit of his skill to keep the frigate on the needed tack to gain southing while preventing her from broaching to and capsizing in the chaotic gale. It also required of him all his dwindling bodily resources, and a prodigious force of will, to fight the pull of the double wheel and to project his cracking voice into the tops as the ship was brought about several times each watch.

He remained there as the storm continued unabated all the next day and throughout the night after. Each hour, Turnbull brought him up a flask of strong hot tea, and Arima's forlorn remedies, which the latter did little execution but in the beloved presence they kept before his fevered mind.

By the second morning, the frigate was safely mid-Channel, well east of Brest, and the worst of the gale had eased; but the deluge of cold rain and sleet continued until even the Thames over swelled its banks, it proving one of the most devastating storms in the near memory of southern England.

All that signified to Hagen was that the ship was out of danger. When he finally relinquished the wheel to his midshipman, he did so with a singular glisten in his eyes, an ethereal smile, and a reassuring clasp of the young man's neck, the skin of his wrist hot as a pudding fresh from the kettle.

"Pardon me, sir," the midshipman said, "but do you choose to see the doctor?"

Hagen was leaning upon the binnacle, looking off at the gray swells, his countenance steady, his hair streaming like the spindrift; and he made no reply.

The youth tried again. "If you please, sir, shall I call for a man to help you below?"

Hagen's eyes refocused as if returning from an inward distance, his smile still fixed. "No, no. Carry on, son," he said and picked his way down the companionway with the weary care of an old man crossing a winter stream, his head at length vanishing below the hatch.

"Bear a hand for the captain, one of you, do you mark me there?" the midshipman shouted to whichever crewman might first hear him, he daring not let go the wheel.

But Hagen was already leaning against the door frame of his cabin, gazing at Arima, his damp skin shimmering in the lantern light, his eyes with an inner radiance of their own. She had not slept all night and would fain have stood on deck with him had not Porter checked her. Her tears fell in their heavy, soundless fashion as she studied his face, where that most liberal spirit, having cast off at last the hopeless burden of moribund flesh, appeared in all its rarefied beauty. He held up a hand as she started to rise.

"No, just let me see you," he whispered. "Let us remember. Remember this always. How the seas come still . . . and wait."

Arima recalled Hagen's words vividly to me, years later, and how after speaking them, a tiny crimson drop seeped from the corner of his mouth, his eyelids fluttered, and he fell limp and light into her arms.

The frigate was close enough to port that it was offered to carry his body home for interment, but Arima chose to honor the nautical custom, much to the somber approval of the more superstitious seamen. And so they buried him, Captain Hagen Singer, in ninety fathoms as they passed northwest of Guernsey, the Channel's deepest point, and from there laid direct for Portsmouth with the welcome aid of an experienced pilot they pressed from a passing fishing vessel.

Arima spoke little of what remained of her voyage but to say that Porter and Turnbull were an ever-present comfort and pledged their unfailing service and friendship. Indeed, Porter's intimate knowledge of Hagen and his family background was all but indispensable and enabled him to acquaint Arima with many necessary particulars before she landed at Portsmouth, not the least of which being the difficulty she was to expect from Nessie.

Hagen, as a precaution guarded from Arima's knowledge, had written letters of introduction for her to his solicitor, the principal staff at the Portsmouth house, and to Nessie herself, who, since little Eleanor's birth and David's passing soon thereafter, had spent nigh all her time in London. These Porter had kept, and not wanting to compound Arima's grief, waited until shortly before they docked to confirm she possessed her marriage certificate.

His heart chilled when she told him what a close-run thing it had been—she having thought only at the last moment to retrieve it when she returned for her uncle's mare—and she shewed it up to him, unscrolling it from its leather-bound pewter tube. Porter was concerned to see that the document was written in Basque and Latin, plainly of papist consecration. There existing no separate will, he hoped fervently—for Arima's sake and that of the child— that it might stand up to the opposition Nessie was sure to lodge, it certifying a union she would have no means blessed even had Hagen been alive to avow it.

Porter's heart was penetrated by her sisterly trust when she asked him to keepsafe the certificate and furthermore placed three identical tubes in his hands, these filled to bursting with hundreds of the most exquisite pearls he had ever seen, many of exotic and precious color, they to have been an earnest on her dowry.

Porter and Turnbull placed their dunnage on a hack shay together with Arima's—comprising little more than what poor Hagen had shipped—then reported, as was their duty, to the regimental office. The remainder of the ship's marine detachment would make their way in time, Porter having presumed to give them a day's liberty, which he believed well within their deserts.

Turner was astonished to see how sparsely manned the barracks were, most of the guards being invalided, with patched eyes or uniforms neatly folded and pinned around the stumps of divers honorable wounds. One of these men they asked to watch over Arima and the shay until their return.

They were received in a tiny office by a double-chinned regimental clark whose air of complacence Porter found not quite the thing. He acquainted them with the news that their regiment, along with the entirety of the royal marine service as theretofore constituted, had been ordered disbanded by the new Lord of the Admiralty, the Earl of Sandwich, with the full support of the Duke of Cumberland. Indeed, he informed them, they were among the last marine units to return from foreign sea duty.

Porter, being an officer, was to be placed on half pay at an army lieutenant's rate. To his disappointment, he did not first receive his long hoped for promotion, despite having served as acting captain of marines during the last legs of the cruise and possessing more than adequate seniority. Turnbull, as a mere sergeant, received nothing more than the best wishes of the service. They had, simply put, been sacked while at sea, and that unbeknownst to them at the time.

The clark then assumed a conspiratorial tone and disclosed that he had "succeeded" in getting them paid through their debarkation despite the disbandment having an effective date more than a year prior. Porter and Turnbull looked at one another, and Porter saw to his alarm that Turnbull's face was assuming a hue not far different from his uniform tunic.

Porter asked if it would be possible to defer the discharge for three days, which would give him time to install Arima and then post up to London to deliver the late Captain Norton's official report and letters, a responsibility with which Hagen had charged him before his death.

The officious little man hesitated, raising an eyebrow in the most disagreeable manner. "You are to appreciate, sir, that I have already stretched a point to extend your pay through until today. My authority is more limited than you might credit."

Turnbull broke his stance to rest his fists upon the desk, which groaned under his hard weight. The clark opened his mouth to object but snapped it shut when he remarked Turnbull's ruddy glower.

"Let's be fair, cully," Turnbull said. "The Admiralty office already keeps us marines waiting like cadgers in the corridor in favor of any raggedy-arsed tar what staggers in for an audience. It's only civilians they abuse worse. You don't want to compel the lieutenant here to report without his nice uniform, do you?"

The man appeared flustered. "B-But the discharge is already dated. And three days' more pay . . ."

Porter winced and braced himself. Turnbull erupted in an earsplitting parade-ground din.

"Look here, you bacon-faced little whoreson, Lieutenant Porter doesn't give a rat's quim for your three-days' pay! He's the ranking officer on that king's frigate docked there within sight of your dreary little window and under duty to present the ship's log and the departed captain's final report at the Admiralty!" He leaned menacingly close. "Now make your change on that paper, or see if you can call enough invalids in here to keep me from ramming it down your fucking throat!"

The clark's chair was tilted fully back against the wall. "Lieutenant Porter, I appeal to you, sir," he gasped.

Porter sighed. "I'm afraid I have no further military authority over Mister Turnbull."

Ten minutes later, the pair emerged to remount the shay, amended discharge in hand and both still in uniform. Arima regarded with fascination the rout and spectacle of the teeming city as they rode north through the Commons.

Now, regardless of how Nessie might attempt to color it, Porter would in no event have believed his friend Hagen vulnerable to the bite of an opportunistic female, and he and Turnbull were already well acquainted with the nature of Arima's noble character and exceptional, if unconventional, breeding. That being said, the discovery that Arima was also not without means, while unaffecting of Porter's complete devotion to her, raised new occasions which he felt it his duty to address.

He proposed, if it be Arima's wish, to arrange passage back to Spain on the next merchant vessel and even to accompany her if she chose—which offer Christopher Turnbull heartily seconded. Porter came from a respected merchant family for whom his military career had represented, due to the rumors of his unorthodox *gouts,* a kind of not unwelcome exile; and Turnbull was an orphan. Indeed, nothing now bound the two men to the service, nor much to England—by no means to the degree they were linked to one another; and, they both avowed, they could conceive no greater happiness than to forge a life together on the Continent, in the friendship and service of their dear Arima and the fruit of her marriage to their fallen comrade. In such event, she could avoid Nessie's machinations altogether while lying-in and being delivered of her baby in the bosom of her own family.

She contemplated their kind words for several silent minutes and was much moved by them. When she spoke, however, she spoke decisively: she had shipped with her new husband as was her desire and duty; though she lost him on the voyage, she now found herself where he had wanted her to be, and this to say nothing of the patrimony and culture which would be his child's heritage. She would stay in England, and if Matthew Porter and Christopher Turnbull would consent, nothing could please her more than to convert their circle of mutual constancy and affection into a domestic establishment: they the guardians of her person and issue, and she of their privy felicity and public appearance.

"Safe space," she said in her charming accent.

They repeated the incantation, and both embraced her. The conveyance was already entering the *recherche* Kingston North End, and a short ride through its wide and tidy streets brought them to the corner lot dominated by the stately three-story Singer house.

Only the house steward, Mr. Bridger, and a single housemaid were on the premises when they arrived, Nessie having reduced the staff with she and Eleanor in London and Hagen at sea. Bridger took the news of the death quite hard, having known Hagen boy and man, but the letter of introduction and presentment of Arima brightened him considerably.

A messenger was sent for Hagen's solicitor, Porter wishing to make certain all was in order, and Arima securely installed at the house before he posted up to London. The elderly lawyer Mr. Shelby, sat with Bridger and Porter at the grand dining room table and examined with care all the documents in question, including the marriage license and letter of introduction.

The solicitor, having acted for Hagen and his father, now placed himself, with unfeigned sincerity, at Arima's service. He informed her, in excellent French, that all appeared to him in order. The letter of introduction, which expressed Hagen's desire that Arima should take immediate title and possession of the Portsmouth house should he not survive the voyage, did not, unfortunately, carry the full force of a last will and testament, it not having been fitly formulated and witnessed; but as Hagen's legal wife, she could not be turned out without process of law.

"Have no worry, madame, this is your proper home," Shelby assured her.

As for title to the remainder of the assets Hagen had inherited upon David's death, these would ordinarily pass to the control of Hagen's male issue, absent which they would revert to his nearest male relative, being the eldest of his Singer uncles.

Arima's first act as proprietress of the house was to confirm Bridger's permanent position under her direct employ, at a rise of three pounds over his current salary, and to hire Matthew Porter as her personal secretary and Christopher Turnbull as his assistant. These appointments, while extraordinary for the size of the establishment, were designed to allow them to travel and reside with Arima without social comment; her need for English translation and men of affairs being natural to her circumstances. She listed Turnbull at eighteen pounds—equivalent to Porter, and two pounds more than Bridger. This sum was uncommon liberal for such a situation, as the solicitor discreetly advised, but she meant it to compensate him at once for his service to her and his lack of a military pension.

The solicitor offered to consult at greater length, when the time convened, on the "opposition of the elder Madame Singer in the event of Arima bearing a child of the female sex." Bridger failed to suppress a slight grin when he heard this: Nessie's obdurate and illiberal frame had nurtured little love among the staff since David's death.

Before saying "Madame Singer" Shelby had stumbled over the word *veuve*. It was evident to Porter that Arima, whose countenance concealed little, had not before named herself the "Widow Singer" in her own mind, and the appellation stung her.

Thus installed in dome, if not yet fully settled in all her affairs, Porter left Arima at the house in the care of Turnbull and Bridger and made for the Blue Anchor Inn, where he caught a stagecoach to London to deliver Captain Norton's letters and the ship's report. This he accomplished without incident.

Exiting the Admiralty office, Porter directed himself toward Hatton Garden. Before he'd left Portsmouth, the solicitor had told and digested Arima's pearls upon the great table. The preponderance were white, of perfect or near perfect roundness, and of a size somewhat larger than a pea; of these there numbered about two hundred and fifty. The next most common were of similar dimension but variant colors, and others of divers shape, size, and hue. There were also eleven teardrop pearls of prodigious size, nine white and two of a charming light pink. Porter had lodged the collection with a reputable bank in Portsmouth but carried a sample of each category to London have them appraised.

He shewed them one at a time to the pearl merchant, a mellow Jew with a sincere and amiable mien, who studied each carefully. He pronouned the round white pearl of capital quality, such worth nigh five pounds apiece if sold individually. However, if a set of more than thirty could be assembled of equivalent size, their value would be much greater to a craftsman of fine necklaces. Those of variant color were worth quite a bit more, and given a surfeit of white pearls that had reached the London market from the colonies several years prior, he counseled selling the more exotic articles now and conserving the others for a time. Porter's mind reeled: the ordinary white pearls alone would bring Arima between one and two thousand pounds, if prudently marketed.

When he presented the large white tear-shaped pearl, the situation was altered. The honest merchant wiped his brow and looked up and down the alley, inquiring if Porter had traveled alone from Portsmouth with so valuable a stone. He beckoned him behind his counter to the back of the stall, bolting the gates behind them. He weighed it out at an hundred and ten grains. As he looked up, his jaw slack, he commented that such a stone was in the "five-pound range."

Porter frowned, asking why the merchant would offer no more for such a big pearl, despite its tear shape, than for one of the littler round ones of the same color.

"Oh no, no, my dear sir, I have expressed myself badly. I meant to say that such a pearl would be worth five pounds *per grain,* especially to a crafting house of fine pendant necklaces. And you may rely on me, sir, as this is far beyond my humble traffic to offer," the merchant exclaimed.

Porter mumbled aloud his mental calculation. "So each of the big white teardrops would bring five hundred pounds or more."

"Pardon me, sir, but did you say *each?*"

"Yes," replied Porter. "Are they more valuable in sets as well, like the round ones?"

The merchant drew air through his clenched teeth and stammered a bit. "S-Sir, a matched set of these . . ." He examined the large pearl again closely. "Of *these*, would bring more—oh, considerably more—than the rate I just mentioned, upon my word, yes."

"Ah, worth more as a pair are they? Earrings, I suppose?" asked Porter.

The man nodded as he mopped his brow again.

Porter pulled the final large pink teardrop from his inner tunic pocket. "I ask, you see, because there are two of these."

The poor fellow gasped, narrowly avoiding apoplexy, and begged Porter to at once put it carefully back in his pocket. Owning his insufficiency in dealing in stones of such quality, he told nonetheless a staggering sum upon which Arima could rely: all her pearls together would bring in excess—and perhaps well in excess—of fifteen thousand pounds sterling, if brought timely and selectively to market.

Porter paid the merchant a handsome *douceur* for his unbiased advice, and as he ambled absently through Covent Garden in the late afternoon sun, revisiting their discourse in his mind, realized the man's figures were based on his knowledge of only two of the great white teardrops, and not the full nine which Arima in fact possessed.

The last of his duties was to call upon Nessie Singer. This he was in no haste to perform, but remarking the worth of what he carried on his person, he hailed a hackney instead of risking the walk past St. James and through Piccadilly.

The grand Singer residence commanded a broad view of Hyde Park in the affluent St. George parish, the heart of old May Fair. Porter adjusted his hat and gave his gaiters and sleeves a brush before knocking at the great door. He had no calling card; he asked the butler whether Mrs. Singer was at home to Lieutenant Matthew Porter of His Majesty's Royal Marines. He stood at attention by the portico as he waited, his being a solemn and official errand.

He was announced into a rich parlor and presented himself before Nessie Singer, who sat straight and stiff in a high-backed Chippendale chair beside a small table, her yellow hair in a tightly curled *tete de mouton*, her clear, penetrating blue eyes intent upon his own. Nessie's bearing conveyed a matronly substance, and what appeared an extravagant *toilette* offered to conceal her forty-four years. Finding himself at length in her presence, having long known much of her nature through Hagen, strangely robbed him of his bowels. He braced to deliver his news.

"Dead or wounded?" Nessie asked before he could speak.

Porter was momentarily embarrassed by her question. He bowed and began his prevented words. "Your humble servant, madame. Your gallant son, Captain Hagen Singer, was—"

"Dead, then," she interrupted flatly. "In my fondness, I denied it to myself, but I knew. God preserve us, I knew. Buried at sea?"

"Yes, madame. It grieves me to say it, but with all possible honors and the love of his many comrades, myself chief amongst them." He continued to meet her eye as she studied him.

"Just so," she sighed after several moments. "And what have you for me, young man, besides your practiced words?"

He pulled Hagen's letter from his tunic. "Shall I withdraw, madame, and do myself the honor of waiting upon you tomorrow after you have . . . ?" But she had already unsealed it and begun reading.

As he had not been offered a seat, he stood cradling his hat, and regarded Nessie as she read. Her face betrayed little; she seemed every bit the self-possessed enigma that Hagen had described. He attempted to imagine what she must have been like as a mother, and it came more clearly to him why his friend had been so drawn to females of mysterious parts, learned women of will and wit—what Turnbull called "bluestockings."

Nessie slowly folded the letter and at length muttered, "Love, forsooth." She touched the bell. "Do be seated, Mister Porter. Will you take tea?"

"Very happy, thank you, madame."

A housemaid served. Nessie had the unsettling wont of holding one's eye when lost in her personal reflections.

"I entreated him, you know, for years. Made arrangements. Girls of family interest, of wealth. He would have none of it. One would almost say he had a wish to perish at sea without an heir, just to spite me. After his father died, we barely corresponded." She eyed Porter keenly over the rim of her cup.

"I will own he was a creature of ideas, ma'am. It made him a natural leader—his men had uncommon respect for him. And he had a great love of the naval service and the places it took him, which I hope it is some comfort."

She pursed her lips. "And what did it leave him, all his peacetime yachting? Advancement? A title? No—a hat to bury and an alien whore pleading her belly." She sipped daintily.

Porter was dreadfully astonished by her words, so cold in both substance and manner.

He placed his cup and stood. "I will not presume to defend your son to you, madame. Not in your grief, if it were ever so. I am sorry, however, to hear such words spoken of his widow and must persuade myself you will think better of them when you know her," he said. "I shall leave you with my condolences."

"Is she under your protection, Mister Porter? Do you speak for her?" she asked with narrowed eyes.

"I do not, ma'am. Your daughter-in-law has engaged me and my comrade, Sergeant Turnbull, as her men of business. We leave the king's service and are most grateful to be in her employ," he said.

"I see," she said. "And am I meant to support this queer establishment of wench's footmen?"

His face clouded. "No, ma'am. Mrs. Arima Singer is not without independent means—to so much I can attest with no indiscretion. Her other qualities you may judge when you make her acquaintance. I believe you will find she desires nothing of you and offers you a daughter's love."

He made to bow but paused. "And I will indulge myself to say, madame, that what I find most queer, for my part, is your having not so much as inquired of the circumstances of your son's death. There were an hundred and fifteen souls preserved from perishing on the rocks off Cornwall by Hagen's sacrifice, myself amongst them."

"And what did his sacrifice preserve to me? A widow's pension, gone snacks with his pretty Spanish relish and her whelp?" Her scant brogue was the only evidence of her anger. She squinted. "And a half-pay soldier to share in bed and bargain."

Porter reddened, and though he struggled to keep control, his voice rose in pitch and volume, and he touched the hilt of his sword by impulse.

"By God, woman, be grateful your sex shields you from the consequences of such a base utterance! My honor, you may be sure, would check such an inclination, even were it to exist!"

Nessie smiled for the first time, in satisfaction of finally having discountenanced him. With a tilt of her head, she seemed to regard him anew.

"Such an inclination . . . hmm . . . no, I imagine it would not exist. Not in *you*, eh, Mister?"

Porter only glowered in reply.

"*Eh bien, chacun a son gout,*" she chuckled dryly.

He matched her French. "*Sans doute.* 'Each to one's own taste,' surely. The last time I heard that little banality, it was uttered by another friendless old widow—as she was kissing her dog. Good day to you, Mrs. Singer."

She was without words until he was nearly at the door. "You are no longer welcome in this house, Mr. Porter!" she shouted, breaking at length into frank rage.

"You excoriate me, madame," he replied, turning to effect an antic bow, and strode out the door.

I leave you here for tonight, dear. Sleep knocks, and I dare not refuse her when she visits. I will write more tomorrow.

Affectionately,
S. Singer

9 Initiation

The man who believes that the secrets of the world are forever hidden lives in mystery and fear. Superstition will drag him down. The rain will erode the deeds of his life. But that man who sets himself the task of singling out the thread of order from the tapestry will by the decision alone have taken charge of the world, and it is only by such taking charge that he will effect a way to dictate the terms of his own fate.

—Cormac McCarthy, *Blood Meridian or the Evening Redness in the West*

1602 BCE
Eastern Mediterranean

Hibya led Luyan to the *zhyuzhurai hitzwatu* in the forepeak of the upper deck. Before parting the long banners, she whispered nervously in his ear.

"Clear your mind, keep your eyes confidently upon her. Above all, be true!"

In the back corner of the triangular space, the Kozhiniru was sitting in meditation, covered in a shimmering cloak of sea silk. A polished silver water bowl lay at her knees, a sprig of dried hawthorn and a small silver knife by its side. Laurel and sage had recently been burnt in the space, and its heady, cleansing smoke lingered. She said nothing for several minutes. Luyan kept his gaze steady, tried not to fidget. He fought to still the vibration in his stomach.

The priestess opened her eyes fully. "Luyan. How are you progressing with your Keftiun?"

"*Yibri, Kozhiniru.* But sometimes it seems the more I learn, the more it is difficult."

She nodded. "Hibya has had little time to prepare you. First I will give you the challenges. Then I will ask you the formal questions."

He readied himself. After a moment's gaze, she began with the simplest and most ancient of the *serkaru* greetings.

"*Kyom yaru etz maiteru.*"

"As above, so below" was the meaning Hibya had taught him. The words with which countless generations of *serkarui* had proven their kinship.

He took a slow breath and gave the response. *"Myeni yatzmi etz zhikai shl'myeni.* Like therefore knows like."

The priestess nodded. *"Yitz-min kumai kolyeru."*

Luyan knew the meaning. "All things arise from one." But her whisper seemed to directly engage his understanding, piercing his mind with alternative translations, deeper meanings. Among them, "from unity derives fullness." Luyan prayed these insights might not fly off as quickly as they came.

"Ya itzteru tzo cheru. I am the first and the last," he said in his turn.

"Ya zhyami tzo tahari," she replied. The significance drenched him like spring rain. "I am the filthy and the pure" and "I am begotten of earth and of nothingness" or "I am the whore and the holy one."

But also, "I arise at once in form and in the void."

Luyan swallowed. It was as though he were wading in a deep undertow. An undeniable current of shared understanding. She began the next sequence of challenges.

"Itzmi pekeru heshyo. First cast off fear," she said.

"Ayi, y'zhyaru-min tzo mayaru-min pekeru ya heshya," he responded. "Yes, all fear upon the land and sea, I cast away."

So doing, he deliberately plunged his mind, deeper this time, into the flow. The connections arose before him. The word *zhyami:* filthy, earth covered, of the world. Its relationship to *zhyaru:* dust, debased matter, chaos. He was taking a sacred vow to cleanse himself of fear, of man and of the gods. Of the void and the fullness, chaos and order. Life in this world and the great crossing to come.

They recited the culminating response in unison. *"M'aishya lu zharikai pekda.* With care, there is no need to be afraid."

But even more, "love casts out fear."

Luyan sighed. He had made it through the challenges. The priestess now began the formal questions, and for these he did not feel as well prepared. Hibya had tutored him in general principals of doctrine, but for what came next, there were no formulaic answers.

"*Doeya vam yichu duritzi?*"

He translated each of the archaic words in his mind. "What is your most determined will?"

"*Kirykmu-min yturai. Tzerori yridinu kai turai tzo kebulu usurai. Yami bakzhinai yibasalu doheru-ti.*" He spoke each word with increasing confidence. "That I may be born into the flow of the eternal doctrine. That I may beget the deep current and abandon delusion. That I may devote myself to the liberation of the world."

But as he spoke, the Kozhineru seemed again to silently unfold his understanding to added layers. The words carried related but deeper meanings. "To awaken to the good news. To express the unconquerable truth that is the path to freedom. To unbind myself from chaos through self-discipline." His mind wheeled with more.

"*Doeya zhiniru bakzhinui'ch-min?* What is the spirit of these devotions?" she asked.

"*Zhiniru yalanu-min, zhiniru aiyshyu-min, tzo zhiniru kozhmeru-min,*" he replied. "The spirit of power, the spirit of love, and the spirit of wisdom."

"*Tzo doshyi shiyaya bakzhinui'ch?* And how will you practice these devotions?"

"Through willful action, willful stillness, and ecstatic motion," he said.

"*Tzo leya mahusuri layseru-min shiyu?* And is there no practice of ecstatic stillness?"

Luyan's breath caught. He was completely unprepared for this question. The Kozhiniru ordinarily asked it only of the most advanced *serkarui.* She watched him closely as he grasped for the answer.

"*Li—*" he started to respond in the negative but stopped himself. He pushed aside his trepidation, opened again to that current in which they both now partook.

"*Ayi. Kedosh yako yaposayal kozhmai,*" he finally replied. "Yes.

But we can never know it."

The Kozhiniru released her breath. She marveled inwardly, realized the import of the presence in which she found herself. It settled full now, like the weight of providence. Her responsibility as a teacher in these, perhaps her final days. If time were not so short, she would not have pushed him so.

Especially to answer a question to which she herself did not know the answer.

She leaned forward. *"Domin, Luyan? Domin yako yaposal kozhmai?* Why, Luyan? Why can we not know?"

"Min yatzu . . . yatzmi . . . yatzumi shyameru eya." Although he stumbled for the words, they were as clear as thunder.

"Because this one . . . itself . . . the thing itself is death."

The Kozhiniru pulled her cloak fully around her to hide her trembling body. She would meditate upon his answer long into the night.

Only one thing remained now in the initiation sequence. She calmed herself and marshaled *orshiya,* the power of edification. It was her duty to offer the first of many spiritual gifts a *serkaru* would receive as he advanced in the mysteries.

"Doeya vam kyikoru-min orabitzi aishyeru?" she asked. "What is the greatest desire of your heart?"

Luyan didn't hesitate this time. "To know the heart of Hibya."

She smiled despite herself. Of all the requests he could have made, it was the most perfect. The Goddess herself was born of such passion. Divine power could not be importuned, much less commanded. Only with passion could it be seduced. She reached out and gripped one of Luyan's ears in each of her hands.

"Eyshto!" she commanded. "Hear!"

The Kozhiniru hugged a knee and leaned back against the bulkhead. The sequence of questions was complete.

Luyan felt different. Some great chorus, ever within him, never perceived by his conscious mind, was revealed by its sudden silence. What sounds, what thoughts remained were pure and more distinct. As if woken to whalesong on a ship hove to in the night, distant melodies framed by the hushing of its wash.

"Let us converse freely."

He touched his ear in disbelief. The priestess seemed to be speaking Luwian. His native tounge.

"Your second birth made you a part of our community, Luyan. But the loss of your ship, your family, must have left you with great sorrow and confusion. You cannot wait long to seek answers. Our voyage, like many things in the world you know, is nearing its end."

The priestess's touch had awakened more than words. For the first time since the death of his father, he felt gratitude to be alive. It poured out, now that he could express it in the language of his birth.

"I thank the Kozhiniru and the Keftiu for returning my life to me. I mourn for my father and cousins, but I know that had my Cilician masters taken this ship, all of my new friends would now be dead. And Hibya and others . . . ."

Her childlike laugh interrupted. "Answer in Keftiun, Luyan! I have never been to your Anatolian highlands."

He was perplexed. "But aren't you speaking Luwian?"

Even as he asked, he realized she was not. Her words were Keftiun, nuanced and complex. And he understood them perfectly.

"How . . . ?"

"The Goddess has honored your desire. You have been opened to the language of Hibya's heart. Your speaking it is another matter. To that, you must continue to apply yourself. You will have many important questions to pose in the coming days."

The god-fear began to creep back. He rubbed his neck and swallowed and continued in his best Keftiun.

"I was saying . . . words of gratitude. Despite the death of my father, I am grateful to be alive. I regret my faithless actions."

"There is no time for regret or to multiply one another's sorrows," she replied. "Death, at this very moment, heel-bites all of us like a wild dog. We are the believing remnant. Those who have remained to warn the nations of the sea."

He listened, understanding her words without difficulty.

"We might have evaded your raiding ship, but we could not suffer our presence in those waters to be known or even rumored. We carry an irreplaceable treasure. It needs to be lodged far upriver here in Canaan, our oldest colony. But we are uncertain of our welcome. Our ancient cousins have lost connection to their former Aegean culture and beliefs. They have abandoned the watercourse life."

Luyan finally received understanding of the Keftiun term *yridinu tzerori.* The watercourse, the bourn. His mind turned with a hundred questions, whose answers he could now comprehend.

"You call yourselves the 'believing remnant.' Are you all that is left after the destruction of Thera?"

The Kozhineru shook her head with a wan smile. "Oh my, no. Many other ships sailed, months and even years ago. Some bound for the Aegean mainlands and farther north. Others went to Libya, many to the west. The generations of the Keftiu are past our measuring. We have scores of cousin colonies far beyond the Pillars of the Gods."

Luyan suppressed a shudder. "Does the world not end at the Pillars of the Gods?"

"No," she said. "No, our Illuyanka, it does not. It only begins there."

He had never spoken his full name to anyone on the ship but Hibya.

"I could not have imagined, when you taught in signs and figures upon the deck, that we would be speaking like this. Kozhiniru. That such magic even existed."

"Magic is a delusion, used by shamans to control others with fear. Human languages are like the petals of a flower, layered over eons. The common bud lives yet within us all. No magic but love is needed to open it."

She served wine from a decanter. "And in any case, some thoughts are best expressed in symbols."

She rolled her cup in her fingers and savored a sip before continuing. "Durzhyar tells me you are especially gifted in abstract and numerical thinking. It was your hope, was it not, to become a master mariner among the Cilicians?"

Luyan nodded.

"To enter a life of piracy, like your former masters?"

He hesitated. "My cousins and I spoke of the day we would cut out a vessel and flee the port of Tarsa." His vow to be a follower of the truth was fresh before him. "Kozhiniru, I saw Thera's first eruption. Our ship entered the island days before we sighted you. All the people along the interior shore were gone, their valuables removed. The water and air were warm and full of death, so we fled before the wind as fast as we could. Fled for safety."

"We had many months of warning. Felt the tremors. Some *serkarui* took shelter in the caves of Thera and may have survived the rain of ash you witnessed. I have shown you that Thera's great destruction yet awaits us all. When it comes, there will be no safety along the coasts of this sea."

"Why did they not all leave with you?" he asked.

"In times of tribulation, the *serkarui* have always taken to their havens in the coastal caverns, where none but the monk seals can reach them. Some refused to leave because they did not believe the end was coming. Others did believe but had no hope that refuge could be reached."

"So Thera's next bellow will be its last and greatest."

"The island may speak again in warning. But the great calamity, when it comes, will send Thera's mountains crashing into the sea and the earth's black vomit high into the heavens. It will wound the land and sky, stop the progress of the seasons. There will be famine and pestilence throughout the world you know. On the seacoasts, it will be worse. Like a millstone flung into a pond, Thera's fury will push the waters outward, far into the inland valleys."

"But, if I understand, the *serkarui* live on the waterways and worship in the deep places of the earth," Luyan said.

The Kozhiniru held his gaze as he put the thoughts together. "Of all the *serkarui* on our ship, you and Hibya are the only twice-born. Like all twice-born, you stand in the gap for others. You bridge the separation between the bourn and the world. The sacred space where earth and heaven meet."

Luyan took a moment to frame the questions he most needed to ask. "In what manner was Hibya twice-born?"

"You sense the sadness she guards."

He nodded.

The Kozhiniru sipped at her wine. "Hibya was born on Delos, to a noble family. Her father, a younger son, looked after their merchant interests. One of our passengers, Talyera, is her relative—her cousin."

Luyan had not known. The two were so unlike in personality. But reflecting on their features, accounting for the difference in skin tone, he realized the similarity.

"When Hibya was nine years old, the family journied to visit relatives in Thera. As they passed through the Cyclades, their ship was surprised by pirates. Her father was killed. Hibya and her mother were carried into captivity in Rhodes."

Luyan squeezed his eyes shut and said nothing.

"Hibya's mother offered herself willingly to protect her as long as she could. Finally, believing it the only way to preserve her from a life of abject slavery, she promised the girl in marriage to one of their captors. The Cilician took his nuptial right immediately after the betrothal ceremony, an act unthinkable among our people. It left little Hibya broken in body and spirit. The next morning, she flung herself from a cliff on the western seacoast. Pearl divers pulled her from the water before she drowned."

Luyan sat in silence. Like himself, Hibya had known captivity. Horrors inflicted by the very peoples with whom he had shipped and served. Despite it all, she had rescued him. Cared for him.

"Kozhiniru, Hibya once told me that *serkarui* work hardest at the devotions they find most difficult. 'Swimming hardest where the current flows most weakly.' Am I this most painful devotion?

Her *bakzhinu duritzi?*"

"Do you ask this because you are male? And perhaps you have noticed that many of our sisters couple their hearts to other women?"

"I have . . . noticed this. But surely Hibya, after what she has lived, must find her devotion to me a special penance."

"We do not speak of penance. Service to the world is the obligation of all *serkarui*. What do you feel, Illuyanka? Is it spiritual devotion alone that binds her to you?"

"No, I believe not," he said after a pause. "But I have no sisters. I never knew my mother. I lack experience in searching a woman's heart."

"Do you not think it possible that it is your similarities that unite you, and not your differences? You, too, have lost family. And been subject to captivity. You, too, have suffered in the world yet are called to serve it. Nothing binds like shared wounds."

"*Duritzi kashyaru tzeroru-min kai yibasa yatzu eya,*" he said slowly. "Our most unbreakable binding is the illusion of liberty."

Her gaze deepened. "That is advanced wisdom even for me, and I have grown old in the mysteries. It has a ring of sadness coming from one so young."

"They were the first Keftiun words I heard Hibya utter."

The Kozhiniru meditated for a moment before answering. "The world is unbalanced by the desire for power, Illuyanka. The worship of the Goddess was once instinctual. Only when city-states like Gubel arose—artifacts of man's futile desire to possess the land, to build structures more eternal than the earth itself—did the ancient pieties begin to devolve. Man debased the gifts of the Goddess. Corrupted the very seed of her grasses and fauna by breeding and domestication, to feed the hosts of slaves who built their monuments. Hierarchy, endless cosmologies, pantheons of minor deities arose, subjugated to the punishing anger of a father god. And the people in terror of all."

"And the *serkarui?*"

"This is why we make our refuge in inaccessible places, where persecution cannot easily reach us. Yet still we serve the world—a world that would burn us alive. We serve because we know there is no evil but ignorance. The world seeks power without wisdom, Illuyanka. Both must be balanced by love. We survive to preserve the possibility of restoring that balance."

"So then *serkarui* are not sirens who charm men to their death in shoal waters? Demons who suck away the breath of babies while they sleep?"

She shook her head sadly. "That is how we are seen through the eyes of fear. In reality, our devotions of power are like the paddling of coracles. We use power without possessing it. If we tried, it would destroy us, like the mighty sea swamping a tiny boat. We never oppose the bourn, nor even attempt to redirect it. We learn merely to direct ourselves upon it. Only in that way can we perform the service which providence requires of us."

"And what is that?" he asked.

He demanded many answers for which she would not have believed him ready. She studied his face as she replied.

"To be the eyes of the world."

He considered this. "And what would you have of me, Kozhiniru? Only ask. I will vow you anything."

She smiled. "A *serkaru* is not initited by making vows, but by accepting them. What do I possess that you desire, Illuyanka? Gold? Copper? I would gladly give you our entire cargo, and the ship to carry it, if I could rely on the devotion I hope you will undertake."

He reddened. "My behavior shames me, Kozhiniru. For so long, my imagination saw in stolen goods the prospect of freedom. I preserved my will to live by weaving such dreams." He paused. "How foolish I was. How selfish I am."

He paused. "I have lived . . . an empty life. A little life. What time remains may be littler still." He struggled for the words. "But here, now, it is given me to know that my time is not contained by its seasons, nor my essence in the form of my past. I have come to believe it possible that love may be made eternal in the act of its expression. That limitless life may be experienced in a single breath."

She tried to conceal how much his answer moved her. "It was no simple thing for our navigator to see through your past, Luyan. It took Hibya only a moment. And Raya—your minstrel advocate. What seemed base avarice was really . . . how did she put it? 'The battered dawning of a desperate wonder.'"

He returned her smile.

"The Keftiu do not easily trust others," she said. "You saw it in the navigator. In our trade colonies, we deal on fair terms for copper and tin but avoid entaglements with the local peoples. The trade delegation is brought off every two years and replaced with a new company from the Aegean." Her face fell a bit. "Of course, all that will soon be at an end."

Luyan remained silent. She had not yet answered his question.

"What do we need of you? We need you to speak for us, Luyan. We need your intuition, your fluent, unaccented Akkadian. Your Anatolian appearance. We need your sex. All this and more we will need to convince the Canaanites of the truth. To persuade them to evacuate the coastal cities and towns before it is too late. We have been too long removed from our cousins in the Levant. Ours is the unannounced visit of ancient relatives. An imposition at best."

"My sex?"

"Female leaders and teachers have fallen into insignificance here. Canaan is a ridged patriarchy, both political and religious. They would never trust the word of a woman."

"And yet the Keftiu have not a single male god," he mused. He looked back up. "There must be more at stake than warning the Levantine. Forgive me, Kozhiniru, but what treasure are you so anxious to preserve?"

"Come. Rather than forgive your curiousity, let me satisfy it." She turned and removed the crossbar from a bulkhead door behind her.

He leaned to help her pull out a large hardwood box, surfaced in hammered gold, heavy despite the rollers on which it slid. The lid was topped with curved horns and flanked by winged owls with women's heads. Symbols of sacred wisdom.

The contents were wrapped in separate bolts of sea silk. An exquisite etched jade chalice, like the navigator's, with its north-finding needles. Then a nested disk astrolabe, other nautical instruments, and more than a dozen thinly hammered copper scrolls.

The first unrolled to a map of the Mediterranean in intricately tooled relief. Unlike the parchment charts, it contained a series of small chevrons struck in gold overlay marking the locations of coastal settlements in Libya, Siciliia, southern Iberia, and farther west. Most were near the Keftiun circular landmarks. At the very bottom of the vessel was a broad double slab of lustrous blue lapis lazuli, inscribed on one side in cuneiform and on the other in linear letters. A primer for translation from Keftiun to Akkadian.

The copper scrolls and their crisp detail could last for centuries, even millennia. Luyan wondered why they needed to be so durable. The Kozhiniru carefully unrolled another, and his brow knit. It depicted a land and seascape unknown to him. An ocean so vast the chart's borders could not contain its western and southern expanse. Along the right edge lay a complex coastline of continental proportions, with massive, ragged islands in the far north. The Kozhiniru lined it up to the left edge of the first.

Luyan was dumbfounded. They formed one continuous chart joined at the westernmost limit of the Mediterranean. A map of the world that lay beyond the Pillars of the Gods.

The hair on his neck bristled as he realized there were at least ten more scrolls of the same size.

She pointed to a line of chevrons stretching from the western coast of Iberia through its fabled mountains, along the shores of a great bay, upward through the peninsulas and lochs of northern island landmasses whose climate and terrain he could barely imagine.

All were Keftiun trading and mining colonies. All contained

serkarui communities.

Her trembling fingers hovered. "*Yakom tzeharui usuri.*"

"If your children, why must they be 'abandoned'?"

Her great age showed plainly as she refocused her eyes. "The sun sets in the Aegean, Illuyanka. Our culture will soon be no more. There will be no more relief, not another supply ship. No rotating home. With the destruction of Thera, our people in the outer world will be completely cut off. Unless we leave a record, posterity will not know they exist, will have no way to find them."

She carefully repacked the vessel, and Luyan helped her stow it in its locker.

"So," she smiled thinly, "are your questions answered?"

He could only bow his head.

She seemed to gather herself and spoke again with authority. "Here, in this *zhyuzhurai hitzwatu,* it is your right as a *serkaru* to question me and my responsibility to question you. We will share the *kirykmu,* and I will guide you in your devotions." She shut her eyes briefly. "For now, until we speak again in whispers, when you meditate, focus upon emptiness. Ask yourself how it differs from form. When your mind strays, gently and patiently restore it to that single thought."

"And the exercise of ecstatic motion I witnessed?"

"There are many experiences of *mahusuru,* from sneezing, to lovemaking, to . . . much deeper communion with the divine," she said. "We call that exercise *tzeroru-ti usurai.* The practice of conscious surrender. But you didn't witness—you took part. Did you not feel movement in your body, an involuntary urge to dance or sing?"

"Yes," he said. "When I was a child, I had a wooden puppet with strings on its hands and feet. But I felt a more than physical pull. I sensed a . . . connection to the others. To everything."

"You will participate again with us next time. Usually, it takes months of quiet sitting before an initiate is opened to the divine flow. Simply surrender. Expect nothing. Resist nothing."

"Do not try to direct the course of the bourn," he replied.

The Kozhiniru nodded. "We cannot alter providence, yet my long practice is not without fruit. Humble abilities to steer the course of the lives of those I cherish in small but meaningful ways."

Her face could no longer conceal her affection. She did not pull back when he reached for her hands. Another unknowing breach of ceremonial tradition. But the power of such innocence may be all that remained, she thought. All that stood against the ascendancy of what was soon to come. She intertwined her worn, scarred fingers with his.

"*Yibri.*"

She removed the cobra band from her arm and straightened the soft metal. Pulling her wrap back over her head, she lay the hawthorn sprig between the golden serpent and the silver knife in her right hand, then circled the triple wand slowly about. A silent invocation to the four winds.

"I offer you, Illuyanka of Cilicia, my humble and untiring service in your journey. These three things I vow." She dipped the objects in the water bowl. "I will never cease to purify you. I will never cease to edify you. I will never cease to beget you."

She planted her fingertip upon the deck and raised the triple wand over her head.

"And now may the earth and sea bear witness. I name you, Ser-Illuyanka, forever my kin. I welcome you, a courageous seeker of deliverance from the gods of this world, to the mysteries and devotions of our order. I bless you and consecrate you to the spirit of power." With an overhand motion, she flicked the wet knife, sprig, and serpent toward him. "To the spirit of love." She repeated the motion. "And to the spirit of wisdom," she said with a final sprinkling.

Her face broke and beamed, and the childlike light in her eyes returned. She cradled the sides of his damp head and kissed his nose, then presented him the golden serpent as a gift.

When she stood and parted the tapestries, Luyan saw all the *serkarui* lining the rails of the upper deck. Each in turn greeted him with a gift, a blessing, and a warm embrace. A cincture from one, a pair of sealskin leggings from another. A staff, precisely the height of his nose, from Raya; and from the healer, a waterproof bag containing dried herbs.

Finally, Hibya presented a new hooded seal cloak. She embraced him, touching her forehead to his and stroking his cheek.

"Ashyukui," she said, her face radiant. "Blessings."

10 Safe Space

"The whole aim of practical politics is to keep the populace alarmed (and hence clamorous to be led to safety) by menacing it with an endless series of hobgoblins, all of them imaginary."

—H.L. Mencken

9 March 1769
Lt. S. Singer, HMRN
At Sea

D arling Girl,
  I've found no heart for my quill these two days and more. Though scarce ever dispirited, I own I feel melancholic, and uncommon hipped. My misfortunes of these past weeks, unlooked-for as a winter squall, have given me a greater appreciation of what my mother's inner life must have been during that difficult time she established herself in England.

I wrote you earlier of shamans and *sorginak*, the Basque word for that sisterhood some call witches, of which Arima, indeed, was joint. I would fain acquaint you further with this race and its wisdom, and so with the nature of my first and most beloved teacher.

In the antique pieties of the Basques, *sorginak* referred to the devotees of Mary, or as who should say "Mari," that being their venerable name for the Mother of God, to whose dedication they are said to have built those longstanding circles of stone that inspire much conjecture. Over time, it has become hard to distinguish their true persons from their myth, and the word has taken on a disparaging significance.

Shamans and priests are masters of infinite befuddling fable. In truth, the *sorgin* is midwife and savior of infants left exposed to die; in myth, she is baby thief. In truth, she is pearl gatherer, living humble in coastal caves and uplands; in myth, she is web-footed river nymph, *murrúghach*, mermaid, *laminak*. She is Lilith, demoness married to the sea, and mother of monsters.

But herein lies another difference between shaman and *sorgin*, and by which they may be distinguished plain: in spinning endless apologue and appellation, the shaman sees to variegate the world, to divide and multiply futile thought until truth is hidden like a single grain of sand upon the ocean beach.

In contrast, *sorginak* are syncretists, not dividers. They purify expression, kneading and folding it like dough until less and less lies between thought and word; they seek to elevate the low and bring down the high and extract the wisdom which reveals itself in the balance. In short, where the shaman fain, through fear, to separate the faithful from the object of their faith, the *sorgin* would unify the human and the divine.

And what is expression? It is said of old that if what is within remains within, thence comes destruction; but if brought forth, then by the same one is saved. Expression is that self-liberating work of bringing without, of birthing the irreducible nature—the action by which essence begets essence. Yet here is a precious mystery: all essence is eternal, and all that is eternal is divine.

Again, it is said of old that when the word from above is sent forth below, it will not return void. Coiled within each of us is the expression of the causeless divine, begetting itself anew. This nature must in turn beget, must be expressed again, brought forth by our own will, to return in fullness to its eternal origin.

I say each of us, but I am not given to know whether this seed exists in all. Perhaps not, signifying the saying that not all that is sown is begotten, but all that is begotten was sown. But it seems to me one of pure heart must not shy from the effort, it being also said that if we fail to render ourselves equal to the divine, we cannot apprehend the divine; for like is known by like.

This rings of egregious blasphemy to the groveling lick-pages and idolaters of the modern Church; but I commend it to you, sweet girl, without hesitation because I know it will show a glim one day in your heart. Indeed, for the wisdom of the *sorginak* to grow within you—and mistake not, you are of that lineage—you must abandon timidity and open yourself like a flower to the sun.

The divine nature is like a watercourse, and humility our lifeboat. Yet it is also said that if we immure soul within body and abase the self and own to know nothing, to be capable of nothing; if we fear both earth and sea, if we scruple to ascend Mount Carmel, if we confess not knowledge of whence we come, and whither we hasten, from what bond we are prised, and from what death reborn—then we have not to do with God.

If these words require courage to hear, then perhaps in that their worth is proved. 'Tis fear which corrupts truth; fear which makes men cling to construct and form, comforting ritual and the multiplication of dead words; fear which drives men in insecurity to seek power over others. When we seek to control our neighbor, we enslave ourselves, condemn ourselves to living within the mind of another, and can by no means unbind ourselves from ignorance and our own dreadful casuistries.

I have come to know that there are mysteries which may remain veiled for an hundred lifetimes or reveal themselves in the blink of an eye. Of what knowledge I have been given, I will discover to you what I can in these letters. All that I have seen is but a glimpse; but in a fearless glimpse, all can be seen.

And these past months have taught me, for sure and all, that only love casts out fear.

I make no doubt you await the sequel of that disagreeable *rencontre* between Matthew Porter and Nessie, and so shall I stow my reflections and return to my history.

I say well *my* history, as come I now to play a relevant part, albeit still unborn.

Nessie's discontent was by no means diminished in the weeks after Porter's visit, and she advised with her own men of law on designs to frustrate the validity of Arima's marriage to Hagen, and even, were it possible, her naturalized residence in England. This, I add, would have rendered me a bastard.

She checked her hand, however, from the execution of these plans, the issue quite different should Arima have been carrying a male rather than a female babe. Hagen's death had jeopardized Nessie's control of the Singer estate, and the birth of a grandson would have materially improved her circumstances.

The interval was for Arima Singer, Matthew Porter, and Christopher Turnbull a welcome idyll, during which they established themselves at Portsmouth without interference. Matthew devoted himself to Arima's tutelage in English and to the management of her property and assets; while Christopher, to the delight of both his friends, took up painting, a talent he had hidden since childhood, and in which Arima much encouraged him.

Arima declared the upper floor of the house the office and atelier, securing a secluded working area for the men with the further advantage of access to their adjoining attic apartments. Christopher discouraged the servants from interrupting or disarranging their work; and Matthew undertook the maintenance of the entire suite, keeping it to a military standard of tidiness. These precautions provided them a discreet *solitude a deux* and were well received by the household staff, as they amounted to fewer stairs to climb and less work for the same wage.

One of Matthew's first tasks, after successfully converting a few of the smaller exotic pearls for Arima's account, was to call for a seamstress and corsetiere, she having been relying upon the few shifts of clothing tossed together in her hasty departure from Spain and her own not inconsiderable sewing skills. She was fitted for a number of dresses, insisting with little exception on mourning colors, and another cloak, her only being the crimson cape in which she had run off. The seamstress, to whom Arima's condition appeared during the measuring, estimated several garments to her largeness in the months to follow and offered to procure for her other essentials: hats, stockings, and smallclothes. She also recommended a reputable bootmaker. Arima's only peculiar request was for a pair of kidskin gloves in a pale beige, not quite pink colour; and the good woman visited several shops before she found the desired article.

Her replenished wardrobe gave Arima greater social access, and along of it many fascinating and agreeable diversions. As spring came on, the trio heard puppetry and recitals in the grand ruins and courtyards of the local gentry and passed afternoons lazily rowing in the small wherry they kept on the park lake or in rambling walks in the countryside.

Arima also spent much time at the local apothecary shop, learning the English for many traditional curative substances already familiar to her, although having little to say to our modern patent remedies, such as Daffy's Elixir and the divers marks of "female drops." The elderly apothecary, Mr. Fox, was at the outset quite charmed by Arima's looks and quaintness of speech, as well as, I make no doubt, her trade, as she spent lavishly and without bargain in the stocking of her dispensary. As her English improved over the months, he realized an unfeigned respect for her knowledge and skills, and in advising with her, went so far as to make important additions to his inventory and recommended applications.

Their evenings were spent at music, reading, and games. Arima's language lessons often took place in the atelier so to keep Christopher company as he painted; and his French, as well as his proper English grammar and spelling—though he was loath to own it—were much improved in the listening.

As Arima's condition progressed, she began to keep herself more to home and took pleasure in exercising her words with the servants, especially delighting in the management of the kitchen and sharing of *recettes* with the cook.

One Sunday afternoon in late April, Mr. Fox called unexpectedly at the house, no delivery from the apothecary being looked for, and Arima greeted him in the small parlor.

"I thank you for receiving me, mum," he began, picking at the brim of his hat. "My wife is uncommon distressed, you see. She's attending at the lying-in of young Missus Peabody, and there are complications. She's at a stand, and I thought you might be in the way of helping, if I may make so bold to ask."

Arima took a moment to process the English. She had learned from their conversations that Mrs. Fox was a midwife of longstanding practice among the yeoman and merchant families of the county.

"Yes, of course, I will do what can be done. They will accept . . . receive a foreign woman?" she asked as she tied her bonnet.

"Oh yes, mum. The lady is quite young, her first child, and her husband is beside himself. He's already sent two doctors away for offering to cut her."

Arima gathered some items from her dispensary cabinet into a string purse, and Fox escorted her to his waiting shay. During the short ride, he gave what information his wife had given him, but Arima displayed only a polite interest, extracting a pumice from her bag to smooth her fingernails.

Upon their arrival, they were taken in directly, Arima only stopping in the foyer to ask a bright-eyed young maidservant for a teapot.

The yellow-haired girl seemed confused. "Ye would like tea service, mistress?"

"No," Arima said patiently. "Bring me please the empty pot."

When she did, Arima charged it with a mixture of herbs: dead nettle, strong mint, hibiscus petals, hellebore, and smaller measures of valerian and ergot. She told the girl to bring it back to the kitchen and have the cook add a handful of ordinary black tea and plenty of sugar before its brewing.

Arima entered the birthing room alone. Before so much as looking at the patient, she made first for Fanny Fox. The midwife was seated facing the birthing chair, face worn and hands trembling, her apron crusted with effluvia. Arima took her wrist, looked into the weary eyes, clouded with cataracts, and addressed her in a soothing tone.

"Calm your heart, Mother, and tell me what you feel."

The old woman's jaw worked several times before she could speak. "It presents bad. A tricky breach, a leg jammin' low, and dry these seven hours and more. No fever yet, but she's flushed almost to apoplexy with pushing, and I fear for her. The doctors want either to cut her or quarter and pull the baby." Her eyes started to water. "The little leg hasn't kicked in hours, but neither she nor her husband will let the doctors near her with their knives and forceps."

The tea arrived, the young blond servant remaining to assist, and Arima directed that Fanny Fox take a cup first. It had a calming and restorative effect. Arima squeezed her arm.

"We are together now, Mother. Please let me help you." She glanced at the patient. "Has she received the poppy?"

Fanny shook her head. "The doctors were ready with their laudanum, but I whispered her to refuse it, weak as they both are."

"*Bien.* You are wise, Mother."

A second housemaid had been sponging the girl's swollen loins with water in an effort to keep them moist. Arima checked her hand.

"Please give her a cup of my tea, then bring me two fresh bowls of boiled water, clean and hot as possible. One with soap, the other with a handful of salt.

The servant looked at Fanny, who nodded, and she obeyed. The patient's eyes flashed with fear as Arima felt her for fever, remarking the ruddiness of her cheeks. When she spoke, she did so in an authoritative tone.

"Do you hear the ocean?" The girl did not appear to understand.

"Are your ears ringing, dear?" the elder midwife asked. She nodded weakly.

"You must drink as much of this tea as you can, and you must be brave now," Arima said. "Do you wish to save your baby?"

The girl nodded with greater vigor. Arima knelt to examine her belly, pushing firmly in several places. She placed a finger to her lips to silence the room and laid an ear, squeezing and manipulating the mass.

"Retain your wind," Arima said. The older chambermaid tittered, drawing a frown from Fanny Fox; but Arima merely smiled, lifted her head, and made an antic pantomime of filling her cheeks with air, crossing her eyes, and holding her breath. A spasm of laughter spread though the company of women, the patient included—a cathartic relief from fear and fatigue.

The girl dutifully held her breath. Arima resumed listening and auscultating, that is to say, thumping on particular areas of the belly. She asked for an empty candlestick and pressed her ear to its base while pushing it firmly into the upper left abdomen. She shut her eyes and listened intently, kneading with both hands, stopping, then kneading once more, drawing a grunt from the girl. Arima hushed her again and repeated the procedure.

As another contraction began, Fanny placed a hand to judge its strength and duration. Arima, for her part, was more interested to observe the patient's reaction in the face of the pain: her head lolled back, and she emitted a high-pitched wail of no great volume.

Arima rolled her sleeves and washed her hands with care. She sponged the girl with the soapy water, rinsed her with the salt solution, and then pulled a bottle of clear, clean olive oil from her bag and poured it over her own hand and wrist.

She looked now closely into the girl's eyes and asked in a penetrating whisper, "What is your name?"

"Emily," came the timid reply.

"And when did your mother die, Emily?" Arima asked.

The blond chambermaid placed a hand to her mouth.

Emily's eyes moistened. "These four years. She passed lying-in with my little brother, Henry."

"I am Arima." She took Emily's hand and placed it upon her own belly. The girl's eyes flared.

"We are not to be . . . we are not invalids, Emily. We are warriors. We battle . . ." Arima searched for the word. "We battle chaos. To bring order and light into the world. Do you understand, woman?"

Emily nodded.

"No pushing now, but be of courage! Will you be strong for your son?"

The girl held her eyes and set her jaw. She replied in a steady, determined voice, "Yes."

Narrowly folding her delicate hand, Arima began to explore the birth passage. She kept her other on top of Emily's belly and directed each servant to hold one of her feet, firmly to squeeze the soles each time she flinched or moaned.

Fanny Fox could see well enough to recognize an experienced practitioner. Arima withdrew her wrist, washed again, and asked for a pot of ordinary tea before pulling a chair next to the elder woman to advise with her.

"Mother, I have not the English needed. Are there no women of the house who know to speak French, Latin, or Spanish?"

The younger maid piped up. "Mister Peabody can talk foreign, and I 'eard the doctors prating away in Latin to one another. We could call 'em back, mistress."

"No. There must to be no more men in the room now. And we speak only in whispers."

The maid nodded, eager and wide-eyed.

"Please bring me paper and *crayon,*" Arima said. "And keep Emily drinking of my tea."

Laying the paper on a stool, she drew a nine-pointed figure, consisting of three offset triangles. Fanny Fox needed to hold it close to her poor eyes to make it out, and Arima searched them for recognition. Remarking none, she proceeded to write a Latin word outside each point, and within the bottom-most figured an infant lying on its back, legs drawn up.

Fanny studied it again and nodded. "We call that back transverse presentation, dear."

Arima repeated the words carefully to commit them to memory. She effaced and recreated the image, this time with the baby's bottom wedged tightly down into the point of the angle— representing the pelvic gap—its legs awkwardly crossed and one of its feet protruding.

The old women's eyes flared when Arima placed this before her nose. "It's not a normal footling breech, then! Poor little leg is tangled and blockin' the arse!" she whispered. "Probably broke as well, with all this pulling!"

Arima nodded. "The good news is the baby is weak, but the heart bats, and the . . . *cordon*? He turns not around the neck. But Emily should not be seating on this . . . birth chair. We must put her to the bed. *Renverse* her, yes, Mother?"

Fanny understood her words, fractured as they were. After giving Emily the basin—the hibiscus drew her water as it lowered the pressure of her blood—the maids removed the soft mattress from the bed and piled the board with several layers of quilts. On this, they laid a pile of cushions covered in fresh linen. Arima positioned Emily's hips on top, pelvis tilted upward toward the ceiling, and ordered the door bolted.

To the astonishment of the women, Arima removed her apron, gown, hoops, and corset. Naked, she again soaped and rinsed, then oiled her arm copiously to the elbow. She knelt between the girl's outstretched legs and spoke in a piercing whisper.

"This is our strongest moment, Emily. Together we frustrate *la mort*. Death. Make your mother proud." The girl nodded.

Working quickly before the next contraction, Arima supported the pelvis with her left hand and vined the oiled fingers of her right over and past the tiny protruding foot. With gentle pressure, she pushed the little leg back within the womb and clear of the other, eased by the oil, until only the baby's buttocks bulged, still wedged in the bony pelvic outlet. Emily grimaced and moaned, but did not cry out. Arima directed the attending women to lift the girl's hips as high as possible.

With her dry left hand, she felt for the baby's head through the skin of Emily's belly. She hooked a finger of her right into the infant's anus for traction and pushed inward and upward with a firm steady pressure while pressing down on its head from above. Emily wailed, and Arima wailed with her—a determined, controlled battle cry—and the baby rotated at last, head downward. Arima withdrew her hand just in time for the next contraction.

"Now. *Push,* woman!" Arima whispered fiercely.

A quarter hour later, it was indeed a boy, with a dislocated hip and a frail, threadlike keen; but it would live and flourish with time. Mrs. Fox took over, resetting the tiny leg in its socket while the maids shifted the new mother to a softer bed.

The old midwife embraced Arima and thanked her. She offered her the whole of her fee, but Arima refused even a portion and begged Mr. Fox to take his exhausted wife home straightaway.

Arima preferred to wait in the kitchen while the grateful father sent for a separate conveyance, where the blond housemaid who had assisted at the birth served her tea with a reverent air. She invited the girl to join her and asked her name.

"Mary, mistress. Mary Rosedew. As ye please, thank ye, mistress." She curtsied and hesitatingly sat, still staring wide.

Arima refused the biscuits. "You have a different sound of speaking. Your family, it is far from here?"

"Ayes, mistress. Foweymoor in Cornwall, and the other girls do chide me fer talkin' swain, much as I tries not to. I entered service when me tas and mam lost the farm."

"You are a mountain woman, like me."

Mary returned a shy smile. "Not wery grand mountains, mistress, but beautiful to us. And in anywise, it's 'ome. Our little place was nigh where's born the River Camel . . ." Arima remarked that she was babbling nervously, trying to work up the courage to touch on her true subject.

"Which it flows into the River Allen and then on into the sea." She trailed off and fell silent for a moment. "Fergive me fer askin', but 'ow did ye . . ." she blurted, looking nervously at the kitchen door, "'ow did ye *know,* mistress?"

Arima arched an eyebrow.

"I means to say, ye'd only just touched 'er belly! 'Ow did ye know it were a boy?"

Arima smiled. "Ah, I did not know—how could I? But women of this country are stronger in birthing when they desire and hope for a son. And have a greater force to live."

Mary looked skeptical. "But, beggin' yer pardon, mistress, ye knew other things." She dropped her voice to a whisper and leaned close, finally making eye contact. "Ye knew 'er mam 'ad died."

"If her mother were alive, she would be at the side of her daughter's birthing bed, no?"

Mary pondered this, and Arima continued. "When a woman must be strongest, she needs to bring her mother—the women of her race—to mind. Their *souvenirs*, their spirits, have power for her. This is also why no men must be present at birthing. A young woman can become . . . passive before a man. She may cry to him to end the pain, to rescue her. Only in a company of other women does her interior force see itself . . . show itself, yes?"

Mary nodded and sipped her tea. "When I was little, I was some taken with lore of spriggans an' piskies. Mam said 'twas all stuff, but dangerous, like."

Arima remarked to herself how verily unacquainted she yet was with the English language. "Springing in pis . . . ?"

"Spirits and water folk and such." Mary pulled a folded paper from her apron. As she laid it open on the table, Arima recognized the nine-pointed figure she had drawn for Fanny Fox.

Mary offered her a pencil stub, and Arima drew the remainder of the little representations within its points—the divers positions a foetus may take in the womb.

"You have seen such an image before, I think."

"Ayes, mistress." Her whisper softened. "The star part, but not wif' babies in. And, well . . ."

Mary took back the pencil and traced three coiling lines spiraling in the center of the figure. Arima nodded.

"It's me mamwyn's mark." Mary's eyes flashed, and her voice grew husky. "Me grandmother, ye see. The mark the bailiffs found upon 'er skin, which it got 'er burned fer a witch."

Arima took her hand. "Your grandmother, if she carried this sign, this full image, upon her body, she was a very wise woman, Mary. Did you know her well?"

"No, mistress. 'Twas long agone she was kilt, when me mam was naught but a little cheel 'erself. But ayes, Mamwyn was *an joan,* as they said backalong. A cunning woman, like. And Mam warned all us girls of this." She pointed to the paper. "As what the minister called 'the devil's mark.'"

Her hands were trembling, and Arima clasped them. "It is not a devil's mark, Mary. And it is not to be feared."

The girl met her eyes. "Oh no, mistress. I ain't afeared! I want to *know*! I beg ye learn me. Please." She indicated the writing at the tip of each point of the figure. "These tracin's, they're not jest 'bout babies, are 'em? They're . . . important, like."

Arima held her gaze sadly. The girl's mother had not so much as taught her to read. How destructive, she thought, had been the terror of the burning times, even across generations.

"I want to know what me mamwyn knew, and 'er mam before un, backalong to the *jamien* days," she said. "What ye did for our Emily 'twas *revedh,* mistress."

Mary's speech had grown more Cornish with her passion. *"Revedh?"*

"'Twas . . ." her eyes shone, "wonderful!"

"You have much courage, Mary," Arima said. "Do you wish to be a midwife?"

She nodded vigorously. "Ayes, mistress. I tent lyin's-in of me mam and two aunties, and now our Emily, and . . ." She hesitated with a slight blush. "I smelt yer 'erbs in the teapot before I give it to the cook to steep. I knows some, mistress, but not all."

Arima squeezed her hand to stem her rapid effusion of words. "You ask for knowledge. My heart is bound to give it, if only for your . . . mamwyn," she said. "But I am happy to do it, Mary. I will make arrangements. We will speak again soon, yes?"

"Oh, thank ye, mistress.! Yes! Thank ye!" Mary whispered and stood up to clear the table.

In the weeks that followed, Arima was called upon a number of times to act as midwife, the news of Emily Peabody's remarkable case becoming well and widely known in Portsmouth, in no small measure due to the admiring praise of the apothecary and his wife. The number of these requests also increased for the reason that she in no instance accepted payment, which was an uncommon blessing to poor women of the dockside district. Much as they became friends, Fanny Fox at length waited upon Arima to beg, on behalf of the county's other midwives, that she either cease her services or put a price upon them.

Arima solved this dilemma by limiting herself to cases in which other midwives called upon her special assistance, and to accept for training a small number of students, the first and most devoted of which was our Mary Rosedew, who joined the Singer establishment as a housemaid. Her lessons went well beyond knowledge of physic and childbirth, beginning with arts and letters, as well as a sound fundament of mathematics and languages. Gravidity began to limit Arima as the months passed, but she nonetheless also provided her pupils a grounding in certain corporal exercises and philosophical contemplation, edifying them body and soul.

She wrote twice to Nessie during this period, first in French and then, with Matthew's aid, in English, to convey her sincere best wishes, providing expressions of daughterly piety, and her desire that the two women should become acquainted; but she received no reply. It was a surprise to the entire household, therefore, when on a warm afternoon in late July, Bridger, with anxious apologies for the intrusion upon their lessons, asked whether Arima was at home to "the elder Mrs. Singer and her solicitor."

Arima, astonished, said she would be happy to receive Mother Singer. As soon as she could pin her hair and fix her bonnet, she descended to find Nessie seated not in the parlor, as was wont for guests, but along the great dining table, bolt upright in a fine black silk gown not unlike her own, with a middle-aged lawyer of nice raiment and sour countenance by her side.

I again write myself to sleep, dear one, and shall continue in the morning.

Affectionately yours,
S. Singer

11 Lotus Blossoms

Today she is humble Sister Ru,
Yesterday she was Teacher Wang.
Although born to wear delicate flowing silks,
Only woven hemp now shrouds her nakedness.

Leap out of the cauldron of right and wrong,
Cut off completely the road of life and death,
Then enter the tiger's lair and demon's palace
With a heart that feels not the slightest fear.

—Zhen Ru, c.1100

1602 BCE
Eastern Mediterranean

The Keftiun galley eased in north of the harbor of Gubel, visible from the heights of the city's acropolis, as a crewman cast his weighted line off the bow, sounding the depth. They anchored in five fathoms, a quarter mile off the rocks and coastal sea caves.

Hibya was included in the small advance party of *serkarui*. Perhaps for the diplomatic value of her family line, Luyan thought. He helped her prepare.

"We swim from here. The rocks are too treacherous for the ship to venture closer. We will make contact with the Canaanite sisterhood. They share connection with *serkarui* all down the Levantine. In the little time we have, we need to gather information on the political state of the coastal cities. We must learn who will trust us and whom we may trust," she said.

She refastened her cincture tightly over her sealskin leggings, then squeezed her feet into a pair of carved wooden sabots. Luyan had never seen anything like them. They had long fin-like projections at the toes, and Hibya unrolled and laced her cuffs down over them. Luyan suppressed a smile as she walked a few steps on deck in the strange paddles. It was the first awkward motion he had seen her make. She put on the long webbed gloves before diving into the water off the transom. He followed her.

Hibya darted through the water like a dolphin with the aid of the foot paddles and gloves, fastest when she kicked both legs in unison. Stopping to let him catch up, she dove deep and came up with a spiked, trumpet-shaped mollusk. The creature's name in

Keftiun was *nekushyu mayenku*, or "goddess comb." Luyan nearly pierced his skin when he tested a fingertip on one of the spikes. Handling the creature with her thick gloves, Hibya broke it open to show him its sack of dark viscous ink, the basis of the royal purple dye used in costly textiles.

The rest of the *serkarui* shore party were still preparing. Hibya signaled a deckhand to toss her coracle over the side and taught Luyan the precarious skill of tilting and boarding it from the water. She swam behind to steady the little craft as he pulled at the double-headed paddle.

The other five swimmers departed together off the prow. Hibya checked that her *labrysu* was tightly sheathed, then tilted the boat toward her and bit Luyan's lip in farewell. She kicked hard and soon overtook the group.

He reboarded the ship, stowed the coracle, then scrambled up the mast to follow Hibya's progress. Six wakes were starkly visible against the low morning sun as the swimmers negotiated the clumps of inshore rock. He watched until they disappeared beneath a natural archway.

He wished he were going with her. As short a distance as the rocks seemed from the masthead, he knew he lacked the endurance. He vowed to increase the length of his morning swims. He envied her exuberance, the joy of striking out upon her natural element.

But he would also worry until she returned safely. The time would pass more quickly for her, he thought. He looked for a task to distract himself.

Sliding down the backstay, he met the eye of the navigator. He did not seem overly busy, and his expression was not unfriendly. Luyan approached him and asked after Durzhyar's condition. The swelling was easing, and no corruption had set in. The navigator hoped he might be fit for duty in a few days. In the meanwhile, he invited Luyan to assist him.

Luyan accepted gratefully. He was unfamiliar with the Levantine coast and would be glad to learn something of its winds, shoals, and landmarks. To learn something of Gubel.

Countless generations ago, Gubel had been a Keftiun colony but was now the most important and jealously guarded of Egypt's trading partners. The Egyptians shipped papyrus, cotton, and grain to Gubel and in return received cedar and lapis lazuli, as well as wine, resins, and oils not produced in the Nile valley. Its culture and religion were a hodgepodge of Egyptian, Anatolian, and Syrian influences; its vernacular so long mixed with Amorite and other Semitic languages that it was no longer intelligible to Keftiun speakers.

As resources had been depleted, the once friendly relations between Keftius and Egypt had ruptured, and the Egyptians were left, for the moment, in tenuous control of the Eastern Mediterranean's remaining timber supplies. These were primarily the cedars in the mountains of northern Canaan. At their very foot lay Gubel.

The city's development had been along a large promontory that separated two natural harbors. Luyan spent several pleasant hours discussing the history and geography of the region with the navigator, who identified for him the temples and palaces high above the northern bay, aloof from the city's busy quotidian life. He showed Luyan some fundamentals of coastal navigation by juxtaposition of visible landmarks. He pointed to the pinnacle of the main palace and then to the tip of the harbor's north jetty. They were currently perfectly visually aligned from the ship's position. With his straight edge, the navigator drew a line through the two landmarks on his chart and extended it out into the sea.

Luyan immediately grasped the idea. "We are somewhere on this line!"

"Ayi." The navigator nodded. *"Kedo'shyo?* But where?"

"How can I know?"

"Do we not lie along many lines?"

Luyan sometimes found the pedantic method of the Keftiu frustrating: constant dialectic, questions answered with questions. He turned his head and looked absently aft toward the spoked wheel of the stern fin lever. His eyes flashed. The ship's position, like every point, was the center of a wheel. A hub from which an infinite number of spokes radiated. He scanned the coastline. A small lighthouse could be seen in line with the tip of a promontory a mile farther north. He located the land features on the map and passed another line through both, extending it offshore. Around the point where it crossed the first line, he drew a circle and looked up. The navigator smiled.

Luyan's sense of wonder began to overtake him. This was not an estimate within one *iter* or so, like the latitude and longitude read from the stars. Provided the map was accurate, this was their *precise* position off the coast, correct to perhaps a few dozen paces. With such a sacred possession—a god's-eye depiction of the earth and sea—the possibilities were endless.

He wished he could read the Keftiun number writings. What was the scale of the map? How did its lines relate to actual distance? He tried to find the words to ask.

"*Domin-mo orabi eya zhyaru tzo mayaru kai tufyu*? How much bigger are the land and sea than the papyrus?"

The navigator had anticipated his question. "Can you tell me how far we lie from the great tower?"

Luyan frowned. The high mountains prevented him from estimating the ship's distance from the nautical horizon.

"What if I told you that the tower was exactly one hundred paces in height?" the navigator said, holding out a charcoal and a scrap of papyrus.

Luyan drew the tower and the ship from a side perspective and considered them. He made a line between the ship and the base of the tower. He then extended a parallel line from the top of the tower to a point directly above the ship and another back down. He had created a rectangle whose long sides were the distance from the ship to the tower and whose short legs were the tower's height. He wrote the number one hundred in cuneiform next to each vertical line.

Luyan studied the rectangle for several minutes. He knew the height of its short sides but needed to know the length of its long sides. If he knew how high the tower *looked* from the ship, his mathematical mind hinted at a function, a relationship that could be called upon to calculate its distance.

The navigator was watching with a patient smile. Luyan shot a line between the tower's pinnacle and the galley. This cut the figure into two identical triangles, superimposed one upon the other. The relationship of the diagonal's length to the height of the tower would determine its distance from the ship. The navigator's indulgent expression began to fade to one of astonished respect.

A fixed relationship between two linear measurements, Luyan thought, that was dependent upon . . . what?

He imagined the ship farther out to sea. Its distance from the tower's base and pinnacle would be longer, but the height of the tower would remain the same. Something else changed however. The angle at the ship grew sharper, smaller. He drew a semicircle within it.

"We must measure this," he said and cocked his finger and thumb toward the tower. He did not know the Keftiun word for "angle."

The navigator produced a copper semicircle marked at regular intervals and invited Luyan to stand behind him. As he held the instrument's base parallel to the sea, he marked the point on the circle where the tower's top appeared, noted the angle, and wrote several lines on the papyrus. Although he could not read the Keftiun symbols, Luyan intuitively understood the calculation. The navigator read off the result in paces.

"*Vimyam zaiyam tzo kya.* Two thousand six hundred and nine." He squeezed Luyan's shoulder.

Luyan's respect grew more. He now knew the chart's scale. He could measure the distance between *any* two points on the land and sea.

"Ser-Luyan, you have a rare gift. Please keep the papyrus and charcoal, and come to me if you wish to learn more," the navigator said, rolling his map and putting away his instruments. He started to walk away but turned back with a tight jaw.

"Your presence honors us."

Luyan descended to the lower deck. Raya was engaged in preparations for the welcome feast for the Canaanite sisters. She was measuring out grains by the handful from storage baskets.

She discerned his anxiety. "Hibya will return safely. She is one of our best swimmers. Patience is the key to love, just as it is to baking. Come, I'll show you the preparation of the *banu.*"

She recited the recipe for the sacred *serkarui* bread. "Three waters, three grains, three airs."

She opened the lid of a large earthenware jar. Luyan crinkled his nose at the sour odor, like wet linen left too long below deck. She discarded some of the contents and stirred back in a handful of fresh buckwheat flour and tepid water.

"Each day we must refresh the mother and nurse her back to vigor before she breathes again."

Luyan could not imagine why anyone would want to breathe such a foul substance into food. Raya passed the jar to another *serkaru,* biting her nose playfully. Luyan did not know the young woman by name but had noticed her before. Her kinky hair hung in long braids. She was taller than most of the sisters, with a convexity of face, dark skin, and brown almond eyes that were strikingly unique. She sat down near the brazier, placed the jar between her crossed legs, and wrapped her sealskin cloak over all.

Raya directed the grinding in large stone mortars called *hawanerui.* Luyan took a shift at the arduous task. Raya showed him to push and roll the stone pestle instead of pounding. The grains of spelt were soon reduced to a fine flour. Other women were grinding buckwheat and a variety of wild millet, which, unlike the domesticated trade grain they called "eastern millet," was *ginyeru.* Fit for *serkaru* consumption.

A large cauldron was placed near the brazier. Raya measured into it several ladles of rainwater and then seawater, followed by an equal amount of ship's drinking water, poured first over her raised elbow.

"The three airs derive from the earth, the moon, and the sun—the breath of the mother, the scent of a maiden, and the heat of a fired oven." Raya beckoned the *serkaru* who had been warming the stone jar in her lap. Luyan, to his surprise, found the contents had expanded into a porous, gummy sponge.

"The mother's breath."

Luyan placed his face in the jar and inhaled. Its aroma was mild, less sour than it had been a few hours earlier. Alive, like warm spring moss. He now recognized it as yeast, its scent familiar from the communal kitchens in Tarsa where beer was made.

Raya poured a ladle of the reactivated mixture into the clay vessel, then the three flours, sifted through her fingers. Raya invited Luyan to help her knead.

They reached in together, pushed, folded, and pushed again, adding more flour when the dough became too moist, and a few drops of pistachio oil when too dry. As strong as his mariner's hands were, they began to cramp with the repetitive exertion. When satisfied, Raya covered the vessel with damp linen and gave it back to the dark girl, who encircled it reverently with her legs and cloak as she had done before.

"She will keep it warm for several hours," Raya said as they cleaned up. Her face lit again. "You have strong hands and a heart for food, I think."

He smiled back and shrugged. "I have never known such things as I have eaten on your ship."

"But we are so limited, this cooking area so small. Everything taken to sea must be dried or salted. I miss fresh vegetables most of all."

"The girl—the yeast keeper—she is your . . . special friend?" he whispered.

Raya burst out laughing at the phrasing.

"Yeast keeper!" Still chuckling, she nodded. "Anekti. She's mostly Egyptian. Is she not beautiful? I carry her *kyazusu.*"

"You are both beautiful. And beautiful together. What is

kyazusu?"

She knew no Akkadian word for it and began to unbuckle her cincture. Luyan covered her hand.

"Oh yes. The mark."

She nodded. "Mine," gesturing to her pubis, "and Anekti's." She pulled the cincture down the side of her hip and showed him a smaller version of the familar tattoo. The same interior spirals but with four points instead of nine.

"Why are the number of points on the star different for each *serkaru?*"

"It is not a star," Raya said. "It is a flower.

Our being is a lotus blossom,
Sown in murk and mud,
Sprouting pure from out the chaos
Rising upward toward the light."

A snatch from a *serkaru* children's song. It was not the first time Luyan noticed Raya's love of singing. She seemed to have music always in her head and ready upon her tongue.

"And as we grow in our beings," she said, "evolving in the *kirykmu,* the petals of the *kyazusu* are added to represent the opening of the blossom. This is a natural human process. Our practices merely guide it along a balanced path."

"But all have the three spiraling snakes in the center?"

Raya smiled. "The Kozhiniru loves you for your symbolic thinking. I have the mind of a poet. I am drawn more to the sublime devotions. *Kedosh meroya kom ya kozhmai . . .*"

Luyan had heard this preamble from the *serkarui* before. "But here is all that I am given to know." He was charmed by its humility.

Raya tapped her board to smooth the remaining buckwheat flour. She drew three curved lines spiraling toward the center, then three triangles around them, each rotated forty degrees from one another to create the nine-pointed figure.

She placed her finger at each point in turn and spoke their names. The words carried classical meanings, some much older than vernacular Keftiun.

Starting at the top, Raya said, "Three devotions of love: Meryu, Aryabu, and Aishyu." She continued counterclockwise. "Three of wisdom: Sishyasu, Ruyaku, and Onusuru. And finally, three devotions of power: Baturu, Kybanshyu, and Orshiyu."

"I know Aishyu," said Luyan. It was the familiar word for love. The passion which links two people. Loss of oneself in another.

"Yes, you do." She grinned. "Meryu is love for the divine. But you also know Aryabu, which is love in action. Sisterly—or brotherly—devotion. Giving of one's self for the community or protection of others at one's own risk. You demonstrated that you were alive to Aryabu when you saved Durzhyar."

Luyan processed this. "And the devotions of wisdom?"

"These are more difficult for me. Ruyaku is learning by willful action: observation, reasoning, and experience. You are already very gifted in this, Luyan. Sishyasu is a transformative understanding that cannot be expressed in words or symbols. It requires a willful stillness of mind to attain. Onusuru is the sublime wisdom—divine inspiration that flows to a submissive and open heart."

She moved on to the next set of three points. "The devotions of power are quite advanced mysteries, but I can tell you what I am given to know of their nature. I'll start with the Baturu. This is the power of begetting. To create where nothing existed before but the divine potential. The power to construct from what already exists is Orshiyu—building up, or edification. We build not only in the material world, but we build when we edify others, teaching by word or example. Like I am doing for you at this moment."

He smiled back. "What of Kybanshyu?"

Her face grew more serious. "This notion is rarely spoken of outside our order. *Kybanshyu* is the power of purification, of deconstruction. To guide the dissolution of ordered conditions back into chaos. And ultimately into unity, without which new creation could not occur. Because *Kybanshyu* is also called the destructive power, it is often misunderstood. We practice it when we purify our heart and mind and the world around us. Even in simple acts like sweeping or burning sage. It is not evil."

She paused. "Our devotions of power are never undertaken to gain ascendancy over others. They are an expression of our mindful participation in the great cycles of begetting, building, and destroying. The eternal equilibrium. Imbalance is the only source—the very definition—of evil."

Luyan pondered. "Even a slight imbalance?"

The mirth disappeared entirely from her eyes. "Evil and good are not opposites, Luyan. This is one of the devolved doctrines of the East, a dangerous oversimplification. In fact, evil may be born in the smallest of deviations from the highest good. Wisdom, slightly corrupted, is the most impenetrable ignorance. In the same way, hatred is not heartlessness, but defiled passion, imbalanced love. We hate because we wish to possess but lack the courage to surrender. Because we value another, but do not esteem ourselves."

"Is there not great danger, then, in pursuing perfection if it is so easy to fall short?" he asked.

Her eyes widened, then closed. She had spent her entire life in the disciplines of the *serkarui* and struggled at every point in her journey of understanding. She had never considered this question but sensed its importance. She stilled her mind, and the words of another *serkaru* song learned as a small child came to her. She sang it.

"Until each and all perfect our balance,
Paddling upon the water,
We pledge to balance one another,
None, no none shall drown."

It put Luyan in mind of the gentle care with which Hibya had steadied him in the coracle just hours earlier. He looked back at the figure.

"And the serpents in the center?"

"They represent the three practices: willful action, ecstatic action, and willful stillness. Each of the devotions falls within one of these categories. The three points of each triangle balance in these aspects. The unfolding of the petals is not a badge of rank, but of our state of being. An acknowledgement of our need for others to balance us as we advance in the mysteries."

He reflected. "So you carry your own *kyazusu* above your sex, and that of your beloved upon your hip."

She scanned his face. "Luyan, what Hibya has lived has made it difficult for her to surrender fully to anything . . . to anyone." She caught his eye. "But now, in the time that remains to us, she has found happiness. You are her *bakshinu ashyuki*. Her blessed devotion."

He nodded, but she placed her hand upon his arm. *"Li—kebi kozhma vi?* No—do you truly understand?"

He studied her in turn. "You love her too."

She hesitated for a bare moment. "She was—she is—very precious to me. I have now bound my life to Anekti's and have fulfillment. I pray only that Hibya might know the same."

The cry of a deckhand interrupted them. Swimmers had been spotted. Luyan embraced Raya and hurried up the companionway. They were still a long way off, beyond the nearest line of rocks. He ascended the mast and counted eight—not six—separate wakes. Two of the swimmers were pushing coracles.

Hibya and her party were returning with visitors from the sea caves of Canaan.

12 Heresy and Blessing

"Tyrants are seldom free. The cares and the instruments of their tyranny enslave them."

—George Santayana

10 March 1769
Lt. S. Singer, HMRN
At Sea

Dearest Girl,
    My salutations today are from the rough Bay of Biscay, having awoken as this lazy ship passed the latitude of the estuary of the River Loire, whose reference you may remember from the first of my letters. The sea air and honest shipboard commons—pease porridge with salt pork or beef and dense yellow cheese with the universal biscuit—have steadily improved my condition, as the unburdening of my heart to you in these letters purges my ill spirits. I spent an agreeable morning on deck and instructed the master's mate in some finer points of the sextant as he took his noon solars.

When I remarked our position, I was beset by a fond reverie in which I imagined myself commandeering this old vessel and putting single-handed into St. Nazaire, reprising the idyllic river journey of my childhood, perhaps sending for you and Eleanor to join me to live in happy serenity in France. But it will, alas, never be so as long as Blunt may still draw breath.

When I rested my quill for the night, I was relating events at the Portsmouth house, as I learned them from my mother, my uncles, and Mary Rosedew.

Nessie and her solicitor were seated at the great table, having called unexpectedly. Matthew Porter hurried to join and found Nessie following Mary with a suspicious glare as she served tea. He sat by Arima's side, directly across from the lawyer.

Nessie had not so much as acknowledged Arima's greeting, but the two women's eyes locked; Nessie to take Arima's measure, and Arima, for her part, gazing at the features of her lost Hagen, which appeared in the countenance and little manners of his mother.

Mary brought a small oblong box surfaced in red velvet and set it on the table. Arima covered it with her hands for a moment.

"Mother, I have long hoped for your visit, and I have been keeping for you a simple gift from Spain."

Matthew stood and delicately slid the box across the table; the solicitor reached to open it. Nessie's sideways glance became fixed. It contained the best specimen of Arima's large white teardrop pearls set in a pendant and chain of gold.

Nessie was silent for almost a minute before she again clenched her jaw and brow in their habitual dour figure and turned to her lawyer.

"Is it the gally presumption of this young person to farcify my family background? Make her to know that my son's property is no more gift to me than I am mother to her."

Matthew did not restrain his tongue. "Gracious madame, since is it you who choose to place the matter at issue, consider that my employer does no dishonor in offering a pearl merchant a pearl. Certainly, you are not so successfully distanced from Gweedore that you fail to account the stone's worth. Or mistake its origin."

Arima placed a hand on his arm. "No, she has reason. I offer what is already proper to her, for all that I am, and all I ever had, belonged to Hagen."

Nessie gave a derisive chortle. "And now Senõra generously bestows it upon his poor shucker mother, and me to be believing it not bought with his silver, but prised from the oyster with her own little hands, is it?"

"Not mine, but the hands of one of my many sisters."

Nessie's eyes widened, then narrowed again slowly.

"Ah, yes. I should have seen the way of it right off." She peered for several long moments at Arima with a new and different regard and then broke gradually into a deep-throated, rumbling laugh, which made Mary, still standing in wait, to quiver.

"Is ciaróg a aithníonn ciaróg, suiregan," Nessie mumbled, still chuckling.

"Yes, *kidek o aitortzen kidek, sorgin,*" Arima replied without a beat.

The dialects of Gaelic are sufficient related for a Cornish girl to take some measure of understanding from Irish. "One beetle recognizes another, my sad little siren" is what Mary thought Nessie to have said; but she was more mystified by Arima's reply— different in sound but so closely corresponding that she at first thought Arima was mocking the old woman. In fact, she'd uttered words of identical meaning in Basque.

What they signified, in plainest English, was "like knows like, witch."

But to be sure, Nessie had no greater liking for that English word than did Arima; the terms *suiregan* and *sorgin* carried an implication as common as their origin, and in so naming one another, the women acknowledged, however grudgingly, their own commonality.

Nessie at length addressed Arima directly, in a French that reminded her achingly of Hagen's. *"Il a mal fini, hein?* After all his running over the seas, he ended his life in the arms of a woman cut from the same cloth as the mother he despised."

"Mais non, c'est pas vrai ma mère," Arima replied. "He did not despise you. He longed for your blessing, and admired your wisdom and power more than he liked to admit. Will you balance those great gifts now with love, if not for me, then for his memory? If even for his child?"

Nessie sat in silence, her face a mask.

"Is it so strange," Arima continued, "that I should be drawn unknowingly to *your* son, a firstborn to the sisterhood, and he to another woman of our order?"

She paused for a moment, and her voice grew thick. "I see him in you, Mother, and I miss him so. I returned with him to save his life, and instead he died to save mine. Will you at least accept my love, if you cannot return it? I remain here to give you your grandchild, and a daughter, if you will have me, to care for you both, as well as little Eleanor. To be a companion to you across the lonely years."

Nessie's lip trembled, and for the briefest moment, Matthew and Mary thought she would break. She turned her head toward the wall and touched the edge of her lace handkerchief to the corner of her eye.

When she faced back round, she was of recomposed countenance; she blew her nose volubly and aggressively before continuing in English.

"Yes, and to bear me pearls. What color is the little pearl you carry within you, I wonder? Be it a pink one, with nothing more than a hungry mouth and a dowry to pay? Or perhaps a blue whom you can enchant with Spanish siren song to seize for yourself the whole of a hard-won family fortune," she said. "Well, I won't abide it, of that you may be sure." She touched her solicitor's arm.

The brass knocker was heard faintly in the background, and Bridger went to answer the door. The solicitor cleared his throat and began to speak in a nasal voice of disagreeable pitch.

"I am Archibald Spence. My London cabinet acts for Mrs. Neassa Singer under instruction to clarify certain matters. Among them, the legal validity of the purported marriage of the late Lieutenant Hagen Singer and Madamoiselle Arima Zarazua," here he gave the slightest inclination of his head and glanced at her over his spectacles, "the lady's right of possession of these premises and, if necessary, her status as alien resident of Great Britain."

Matthew Porter broke in. "If we are to hold a session at law, should not my employer also have the benefit of counsel?"

"This is no session, my good sir, I assure you, but more in the line of a discussion to set forth our respective positions with a view toward resolving them. We have already extended the courtesy of sending notice to the late lieutenant's solicitor, who we are informed now acts for the lady. I believe you may find he has just arrived," Spence said.

As if prompted, old Shelby was announced and entered with a flushed and harried air, his old-fashioned high-front wig slightly askew, and burdened by two ponderous satchels of cracked leather. Porter whispered Bridger to fetch Turnbull and Arima's papers from his office.

The butler left the lawyers already in active discourse as he ran up the stairs. Christopher was occupied with the finishing touches on an oil of Portsmouth harbour; his brush took a false stroke and an oath escaped his lips when Bridger precipitated through the door.

"Forgive me, Mr. Turnbull, but its old lady Singer and the solicitors. They're in the parlor talking Latin nineteen to the dozen. Mr. Porter would like you to gather our Mrs. Singer's legal papers and come join him," said Bridger.

Christopher furrowed his brow and studied on the matter for a moment as he removed his painting smock and cleaned his spotted hands with spirits. "Which one's winning?"

"Winning, Mr. Turnbull?"

"Which lawyer? Old Shelby can fire off the Latin like a goose shits. I'll wager he turns the winning phrase."

Carrying a large portfolio under his arm, Christopher followed Bridger down into the dining room and stood his imposing form behind Arima's chair, as eager to lend her his support as he was to adjudge the linguistic repartee.

Spence was in mid-argument. "Let us see if we cannot dispose of the matter of the premises. Surely, Mister Shelby, sir, you are not asserting that the lady is vested with title or property rights in the domicile? Can we agree that, at the very most, she has a tenancy— *dominion utile?*

Shelby rummaged in the portfolio and found Hagen's letter expressing his wish that Arima have the house. Spence began shaking his head before he finished reading it.

"No. This carries no force as a last will and testament, sir. It is neither witnessed nor properly attested."

"Surely sir," Shelby retorted, "you did not overlook the wording '*if* I should die.' Not a testament, perhaps, but clearly a deathbed gift. A writing expressing the intent that the donee shall retain the property if, and only if, death ensues. Fully enforceable, sir—*donatio mortis causa.*"

"That got 'im in the cods," Christopher said under his breath, and Matthew shot him a sharp glance as he passed Shelby the marriage certificate.

"In any event, the point is moot," Shelby continued, his hand trembling with age as he shewed the certificate to Spence, "as my client's right to the domicile arises under jointure—they were married, sir."

Spence read the Latin writing and turned it back. "Hmm," he said, "a Roman Catholic marriage, witnessed in a rural chapel on the Continent. Have you any evidence that it has been solemnized by the Church of England? License obtained? Banns published? The union registered in the records of Lieutenant Singer's home parish?"

Shelby replied promptly. "A foreign marriage, legally binding where performed, is equally valid in England, sir. *Lex loci contractus.*"

"'At's right, mate! Licks loco!" Christopher interjected with his thick finger pointed at Spence. "That was Hagen Singer. But just you leave off callin' him 'lieutenant.' He died the commander of a king's man o' war, and that gave him the title of captain, by right, custom, and courtesy. I lay you've never done military service, 'ave you, cully?"

Spence ignored the question and turned back to Shelby. "*Lex loci contractus* is a tenuous common law doctrine at best, and there are moves afoot in Parliament at this very moment, sir, that would render such an elopement unlawful. If your position rests solely upon this papist frippery, I'm afraid—"

"It does not, sir." Adjusting his spectacles, Shelby extracted an ornate canvas cover, licked his finger, and unfolded it. "This is a letter of information from the Admiralty office, under seal, referencing an excerpt from the ship's log of His Majesty's frigate *Merrow.* You will note that Post Captain Norton made an entry, sworn under signature, that the union was avowed before him aboard ship on the 19th of November *ultimo.* The commander of a British vessel of war on foreign station is the direct representative of the king in all matters temporal and spiritual, and his attestation carries the full weight of the union's solemnization by the Church of England. *Per verba de praesenti,* my dear sir."

Christopher failed to fully stifle the expulsion of a shrill whoop and slapped his fist into his hand.

Arima could read no reaction on the London lawyer's face. She studied his delicate powdered bob, blue tinted *demi-lunette* spectacles, and massive brocade cuffs as he casually withdrew several pages from the neat pile in front of him. With an air of condescension, he passed them across to his provincial colleague.

Old Shelby, far less *au courant* in the article of fashion, was put gradually out of countenance as he read through the long document.

"Permit me to give you a *precis*, my dear sir," Spence said. "Having already inspected the ship's log at the Admiralty office, we found the entry in question so nearly illegible that we pursued further inquiries into the state of Captain Norton's health at the time of its writing."

Porter frowned, and Shelby listened with a slack jaw, every one of his years appearing on his face.

"What you hold in your hand is the sworn and witnessed affidavit of Doctor Harlan Grimmer, ship's surgeon of the *Merrow* during its last commission. As you can see, he sheds considerable light upon the matter at issue."

A low growl could be heard in Christopher's chest. Matthew tightened his grip on the arm of his chair.

"His written testimony states," Spence continued, "that Captain Norton was unfit for duty on the date of the entry. Marsh fever, it seems. The captain's erratic scrawl and signature support this conclusion."

"He had not been relieved of duty," Matthew broke in sharply, "and was of sounder mind on his deathbed than is that tosspot surgeon of any Sunday morning."

Spence addressed him with a raptor-like turn of his head. "You witnessed the ceremony, then, did you Mister Porter?"

Matthew reddened but made no answer. Arima gave his arm a reassuring caress.

"Ah. I thought not."

Spence turned toward Nessie with a satisfied smirk; she had been peering out the window in a deep study during most of the proceedings.

He continued. "Doctor Grimmer next advances his learned opinion that Lieutenant—" He shot a glance at Christopher. "Er, that is to say, *Captain* Singer, was himself quite absent of mind, being far gone in the same calenture when he reported back to the ship; that he was likely not fully possessed of his wits when Madamoiselle Zarazua affected to marry him; and, most alarming of all, that having witnessed the young lady practice upon him numerous miasmatic banes, arcane tongues, and other black arts, he believed her to have not only robbed Singer of his God-given free will, but likely to have been the cause of both officers' deaths, as well as the origin of the very illness that laid low the ship's company."

"Lies!" Christopher barked, slapping a chair.

Matthew placed a hand on his friend's shoulder as he rose to his feet. "Mr. Spence, you may be sure that I *will* take my oath to contradict the backbiting calumny of that ruin of a surgeon. I eagerly await the day he is called to support such ridiculous statements before the magistrate, and you may tell him that if he does not hang for perjury, I will, by God, call him out and make him to answer for it myself!"

Spence replied without a hint of recoil. "You may find that difficult, Mister Porter, as Doctor Grimmer is no longer with us. He died the day he swore this affidavit."

"Liver grown, I make no doubt," said Christopher.

"It makes no odds, sir," Spence shot back. "Mister Shelby will advise with you on the probative value of a dying declaration."

He neatly folded the document back into its cover with prim motions of his spidery fingers.

Shelby's morose words followed a few moments of rumination. "They can enter the affidavit as testimony despite it being hearsay, and Grimmer not subject to cross-examination on its content."

"Simply put, sir," Spence said, "this document represents admissible and nigh unchallengeable evidence of Captain Singer's lack of mental capacity to have consented to the marital union. *Non compos mentis. Matrimonium ab invito non est matrimonium.*"

Arima's mouth fell open in disbelief. Until then, she had followed the complex English dialogue only by gross impression, but she clearly understood the Latin despite its Anglican pronunciation. She looked coldly at Nessie and addressed her in that same language.

"Scilicet, Mater, medicus erat vanidicus et adpotus! That surgeon was a liar and a drunk, and you must know it, Mother! Your son's mind was as clear as his heart on the day we married! Will *your* conscience ever be clear again if you do this? Will you bastardize your own grandchild?"

Still looking out the window, Nessie replied slowly. *"Dependet, sororcula, dependet."*

"Quid dependet, Mater? On what does it depend? On whether girl or boy? You address me as little sister, but is this the act of a wise woman of the sisterhood? *Quod actio saga sororna?"*

The room was silent for several moments, all awaiting Nessie's answer. Her gaze retained its distance. At length, she turned to meet Arima's eye.

"It hangs upon you, *sororcula.* Not upon the babe alone, but upon its mother as well. *Dum vidua et casta vixerit."*

She nodded to Spence, who produced the last of his papers.

The conditions of the contract of settlement, despite heroic negotiation by Shelby, were severe. Arima would renounce all claim to control over Singer family assets and would remain at the Portsmouth house, subject strictly to Nessie's supervision, at an allowance of five pounds per month. Arima would be responsible for the maintenance and quotidian operation of the domicile; she would christen and raise the child in the Anglican faith; she would remain a widow and chaste.

Nessie would have authority on all decisions regarding staffing of the establishment—it being specified that Matthew and Christopher were to be turned out—as well as over the child's educational, vocational, and social formation. Arima would at all times, in public, speak only the English language.

Arima prevailed in only a few points, and upon these her insistence was unshakable. Nessie would under no circumstances offer to remove the baby from her direct and private care during its tender years, it not being the Basque custom to relegate the close duties of maternity to nursemaids. Christopher and Matthew, while residing elsewhere, would remain in Arima's employ at their current salaries, she would choose her own midwife, and Mary Rosedew would stay on at the house—all this to be at Arima's own expense.

To her final condition, Nessie agreed with surprising readiness: the girl Eleanor Singer would reside in the Portsmouth house as well, under Arima's daily care, and in companionship to her own child.

Grimmer's affidavit would be held back, and no challenge lodged against the validity of the marriage, for only so long as Arima complied fully with Nessie's terms, and further provided the baby was male. Should that not be the case, all promises were to be null and void, and Arima would return to Spain, taking her natural daughter with her.

Arima signed the document in bold, determined strokes, stood, and held it out to Nessie, avoiding the lawyer's reach and compelling her to take it with her own hand.

"*Ecce haeresis summa tua,*" Arima said in a penetrating whisper.

Matthew thought to have noticed a minute passage of fear and disconsolation in Nessie's eyes. "Yes," he added in English, "your greatest heresy indeed, madame, and by your own lights, not your first. But what signifies a bit of apostasy to one whose god is mammon, eh?"

Nessie's visage clouded in quick anger, and before she could have the satisfaction of giving it voice, Matthew superseded her.

"Come, Chris, it seems we stand in another dead man's house made prize by Neassa Laughlin, and we are," he paused to bow deeply to Nessie, "no longer welcome here."

These last words he uttered in a mocking brogue. After heartily embracing Arima, the two men turned and took their leave.

In synthesis, then, to preserve the recognition of her marriage and her child's legitimacy, which is to say my own, Arima was reduced to little more than a governess and domestic manager in Nessie's employ.

For Arima, the remaining weeks before my birth stretched out in dark distinction to the agreeable months which preceded. Nessie took up residence in Portsmouth immediately to see that the terms of the arrangement were followed to the letter. Arima was from that time kept almost entirely to the upper chambers, and Bridger was under Nessie's strict instruction to admit no visitors, which he most reluctantly obeyed.

Her sole sources of solace were the support and increasingly intimate friendship of Mary Rosedew and her new charge, Eleanor, then four years old. Despite their reduction, Arima made her circumstances bearable and passed her days in sewing, reading, and instructing Mary in the principles and subtleties of that tradition in which they both partook.

I touched upon several of those very principles in my last letter, their operation now manifest in my history. First, Nessie's use of her power to so closely control another became her own bondage. She rendered herself nigh a prisoner in the house to supervise and regulate Arima's daily life; her every waking imagination became entangled with Arima's subject: how great her discontent, what preventions it might inspire, how sincere her intent to keep her bargain, what conspiracies with Mary; yea, even Arima's meditations fretted Nessie to distraction—all demonstrating that when we reach for dominion over others, we enslave ourselves.

And yes, Nessie's error did indeed penetrate the fundament of her own doctrine. In setting her face so hard against the event of my being born female instead of male, she was denying not only the value her sisterhood placed on the sex, but the principled distinction it held between providence on the one hand and fortune on the other.

By providence, I mean to say divine order, or the will of God, if you prefer, so long as your god be none other than the purest immutable good. While necessity may be the mother of invention, it is but the servant of providence, as the divine will is ministered by those events which are verily inevitable.

Fortune, on the contrary, is the carriage of that which is without order: the idol of operation, chaos expressed in base delusion, and empty in its being. If wisdom can be said to have a purpose, it lies in the insight that all events arise either from providence or fortune, and in the capacity to distinguish them while never pretending to the power to control either. This is no mean philosophy of consolation, but the core understanding which makes possible a life upon the watercourse way; and in its repudiation lay Nessie's heresy.

Do not imagine Arima, however, to have entered blindly into her new estate. To be sure, Nessie's actions were a betrayal of the most sacred values of her sisterhood, and the duty peculiar to a member of such eminence and gnosis; yet for all that, she *was* of that lineage, and herein lies our second demonstration. I have proposed that good and bad are not opposites, but that the greatest evil often arises from the slightest imbalance, the scarce corruption of the most excellent wisdom, benevolence, or righteousness; and this was how Arima believed the matter to lie in Nessie.

Although she had chosen a worldly route, Nessie was the eldest of the surviving women of her bloodline and the most senior in rank of the Donegal community. She was possessed of prodigious learning and discernment—an uncommon powerful *suiregan,* to use her own word. Her venal acts Arima attributed to backwardness of heart, perhaps the unhealed lesion of some past inconstancy or loss. She knew love to be the sole and necessary counterweight to the spirits of wisdom and power, and Nessie was plainly in lack of balance.

It became Arima's hope, therefore, to provide Nessie that balance, as members of her sisterhood were wont to do one for another, and love her unrequited. To love her until the elder woman might one day, with the blessing, rediscover the same capacity within herself, and suffer this last of her petals to unfold. Whether this was naught but a fond notion would appear in time; my mother was not by nature capable of sustained spite, at all events.

Other sacred duties of a sage consisted with Nessie's status, unsubject to embarrassment by her paralysis of heart. The women of the house—Nessie, Arima, as well as Mary—shared certain prerogatives by grace of common heritance, though long separated by distance, time, and tongue. Among these were the right to draw upon the learning of their elders, and to do so *tête-à-tête,* in a privy discourse of whispers which at once imparted and proved wisdom. Arima knew that Nessie could not refuse her this, no matter how coldly she might use her in daily life; no more could she impede the tutelage of Mary Rosedew.

You may puzzle as to why the sisters share knowledge only in whisper and shade, and these missives may themselves seem scant indices of fuller teachings. For the very causes I have stated, whether written in letters of gold or stinking with error, there is grave danger in setting these words to paper, to permit expression to pretend to permanence, when time is the very corruption of man.

If indeed the basest evil may be removed from the purest good by only the tiniest grain of misunderstanding, then my negligent shortcomings may be the seed of demons; yet even could I avoid the smallest admixture of imperfection, the effect of my words upon a psyche which is *a priori* maleficent may bear worse issue than the casting of pearls before swine. Should the evil man hear this doctrine of the bourn—that all things arise either from chaos or providence—might not he abandon all care to the consequences of his own actions? Might not such knowledge serve only to whet the edge of his natural vice and give license to his most dissolute inclinations?

Yet neither may I wholly neglect its expression, dear girl, as fortune dictates that this narrative, however flawed, must take the place of that whispering congress which would otherwise be our mutual devotion; and I pray these seeds, unwatered and unwatched by the loving eye of your gardener, may nonetheless grow full within you.

And what of your gardener? Registered in the local parish office by Frances Fox, attending midwife, was on August 20, 1751 at Portsmouth, to Mrs. Arima Singer, wife of the late Captain Hagen Singer of the Royal Navy, the birth of a healthy baby boy.

In accord with Arima's desire, a bed had been specially set up in Christopher's old atelier, and the lying-in was tolerably uneventful, though old Fanny Fox's worsening blindness had made welcome the assistance of Mary Rosedew.

I was Christened Sebastian X. Singer a week later at the recently renovated Cathedral Church of St. Thomas of Canterbury and was sealed well and proper—and legitimate—in the Anglican faith. Nessie was not content with the name, rightly deeming it to carry a papist as well as a continental suggestion, St. Sebastian being a popular object of Catholic devotion, and Francis Xavier both Basque and Jesuit. She would have been no less disarranged had she known that Arima intended the *X* to stand not for Xavier, but *Xixili*, a name of some tradition in her family, and by which she addressed me only in strictest privacy.

Nessie did not attend at my birth, but once I was bathed and swaddled, and posed no risk of noisome insult, she lost no time in groping me. Arima kept me tightly in her arms while suffering

Nessie to reach beneath my little blanket and handle me through my diaper. To hear Arima tell it, the thoroughness of the examination was worthy to a newly elected pope, and so rough Nessie's grasp that it drew from me a hearty wail. This, and the palpable contours she found, soundly satisfied her on the question of my sex.

I will reserve for my next letter my early recollections, they being much a memoir of a cloistered but happy childhood. I remark that Arima's relationship with my grandmother yielded little improvement in the face of her efforts and despite the happy event of Nessie's preference being realized in my birth. Arima oft invoked her right to "sitting in" during and after her pregnancy, and Nessie performed the duty with neither discernible reticence nor relish.

The content of those dialogues is sacrosanct, but Arima went so far as to tell me she found Nessie a teacher of substantial parts, and in showing submission to her in spiritual matters, she attempted to bridge the immense chasm of distrust that separated them. They gave Arima occasion to lay bare her heart and motives and to call to Nessie's mind obligations, longstanding in their sisterhood, of devotion to community and family. To what avail did not appear, however; at times, it seemed to Arima that Nessie was verily of two persons: the evenhanded guide of privy whisper, and the mawkish, spiteful matriarch of quotidian life.

How often and sore tempted was Arima to pack off with her little treasures—child, friends, and fortune—and return to the mountains of Gipuzkoa. Howbeit, it had been taught her that everyone who embarks upon a life in the bourn will experience at some point a difficulty through which the divine would prove her, a vocation or task which would call upon the inclinations and abilities in which she was most lacking—the *debozio desafiatzaile*, as the Basque *sorginak* called it; and she came to certainty that Nessie indeed was, for her, precisely that "challenging devotion." If Nessie understood the corollary—that opening her own heart to

Arima was, as she would term it in Irish, her own *deabhóid dúshlánach*, she gave no sign.

The ship pitches wildly tonight in the great bay, as you can no doubt divine from my hand. I will write you again tomorrow, dear girl.

Your devoted,
S. Singer

13 Inner Treasures

You've seen a baker rolling dough.
He kneads it gently at first,
then more roughly. He pounds it on the board.
It softly groans under his palms.

This is how your desire
tangles with a desired one.

A great mutual embrace
is always happening between the eternal
and what dies, between essence and accident.

—Excerpt from Rumi,
The Book of Love: Poems of Ecstasy and Longing
13th Century

1602 BCE
Eastern Mediterranean
The Middle Bronze Age

L uyan arrived back on the upper deck just as the swimmers
were mounting the port gallery.

Hibya cleared the gunwale first and turned back to assist the two visitors. The Canaanite women were naked, just as tanned but covered with more abrasion scars than the *serkarui* Luyan knew. Their hair, still slick with seawater, appeared thicker and more brown than black. The Kozhiniru welcomed them. Their Keftiun was understandable but archaic. Clearly not their first language. The *serkarui,* each in turn, greeted the visitors and introduced themselves.

The Canaanites took a special interest in Luyan, last in the reception line. Ethtar, the taller, greeted him uncertainly in Akkadian, instead of with the guttural *"ashyukui"* she offered the others. She looked curiously into his olive eyes, which matched her own. When he lowered his head to name himself, she fingered his red locks.

"Kizzuwadnu? Cilician?"

Luyan nodded and returned their order's greeting challenge.

"Kyom yaru etz maiteru."

"Myeni yatzmi etz zhikai shl'myeni," Ethtar responded with a smirk and a raised eyebrow.

The younger visitor met Raya's eyes. Both giggled, and their laughter infected even the elder *serkarui* with restrained smiles. Luyan started to color.

Had he said it wrong? He reviewed his words in his mind: "As above, so below."

He seized upon the bawdy double meaning, so closely following her reference to his red hair. The implication of "like therefore knows like" was also becoming clear, as her own drying tresses revealed auburn streaks.

Luyan smiled despite himself, then joined in the laugh. The tension broke in a wave of companionable mirth.

There was neither mockery nor blasphemy in their humor. Despite his maleness, his presence was a familiar benchmark for the Canaanites. A catalyst of reconnection for the two long-separated *serkaru* communities. Ethtar urged her younger comrade toward him, then took a handful of almonds and a long swallow of wine before repairing to the Kozhineru's compartment in the forepeak.

"Ashyukui," Luyan said to the girl, then followed with the Akkadian *"shulmu."*

She gave her name as Quarta. She had been born to a group of "deep river" *serkarui* several miles inland but was now living with the coastal community. Mobility was common among the Levantine *serkurui* in their constant struggle against isolation. Her gold pendant earrings were tiny approximations of the Keftiun *labrysu.*

She was curious about his own provenance, and they conversed fluently in high Akkadian. Hibya soon found an excuse to join them, placing an arm around Luyan's neck, and directed the conversation back into Keftiun. One by one, the others formed a circle, talking over one another in their excitement. Several times Quarta turned to Luyan to translate portions of their "whisper words," her term for the Keftiun language, now spoken by the Canaanite *serkarui* only in private ritual. His own fascination was tempered by a sense of melancholy, as one witnessing a meeting in the afterlife, the first acquaintance of the newly dead with their distant ancestors.

Communal devotions were planned that evening on the upper deck. They would be Luyan's first formal exercises as an initiated *serkaru.*

The Canaanites had brought a rich hamper of gifts, pushed in their coracles. Wine, shellfish, and a variety of wild roots and fresh vegetables. Luyan assisted willingly, and his mouth watered as he cleaned the wild broccoli, watercress and baby cabbage—a specific hunger born of long weeks at sea eating dried and preserved foods. There were also baskets of fresh pomegranates and several dozen fat squab.

Raya took charge of the preparations. There were variations in the dietary laws between the *serkaru* communities, and hospitality required caution. The Kozhiniru had warned Raya that the blood of birds and animals was not acceptable to the Canaanite sisters. Raya had no difficulty with this particular restriction, as brining of game was not uncommon in the Aegean to produce a more tender, subtle-tasting meat. She plucked and cleaned the squab and placed them in a tub of seawater to draw the blood from their flesh.

When the vegetables were cleaned and cut, Raya beckoned Luyan and opened the clay baking vessel. It was full to the brim, the dough nearly tripled in size, spongy and light. Together they formed it into a large round loaf, resealed the vessel, and piled it with hot coals to bake.

Luyan wiped his hands and noticed Quarta and Ethtar watching him. Ethtar turned sharply and strode away when he met her eye.

"Have I offended her?" he whispered to Raya.

Quarta quickly changed the subject. "I have never been on a big ship before. Your cooking area is almost as spacious as that of our great cave. May I help in some way?"

Raya shook her head. "It is our devotion to serve you tonight. Please do visit with us while we work, though."

She complimented the squab as she hung them to dry. Quarta told her that a large flock lived in the overhanging rock grottoes near her home upriver. She reached into the damp basket of shellfish, removed some oysters and, using her two hands, the biggest mussel Luyan had ever seen. It was fan shaped and multicolored and narrowed to a sharp point at the joint of its shell, where a long brown beard of fibers trailed. Hibya's eyes lit. She took Luyan's hand and combed his fingers through the fringe. The texture was finer than baby's hair. He pulled at the fibers, twisting them around his finger, but even in small bunches of three or four strands, he found them difficult to tear.

"It is the sea silk mussel," Hibya said. "The creature uses its beard to cling to the rocks. The strands are fine enough to penetrate the tiny pores of the stone, yet so strong they resist the pounding of the most powerful waves. When brushed and soaked in lemon juice, the silk turns a beautiful golden color."

Raya took a thin knife, worked under the shell, then opened it with a twist. The inside was coated in an exquisite mother-of-pearl. The quivering mussel itself was big enough to feed several people.

"Unfortunately, the flesh is tough when cooked and does not have much flavor," Quarta said. "We harvest them for their shell, their beards, and their occasional pearls."

Raya smirked. She cut beneath the mussel to remove the meat and sliced it into thin strips, which she coated in buckwheat flour seasoned with oregano and crushed hazelnuts. She poured olive oil into the flat bottom of a copper cauldron and tossed in a handful of garlic and red pepper. When they had simmered for a while, she fished out the aromatics and stoked the coals.

The coated slices of mussel sizzled as she layered them in the hot oil. The aroma made Luyan's mouth water again. After one turning, she lifted them out, brown and crisp, and laid them on a platter. She squeezed lemon over them and gave one to Quarta and one to Luyan to try. Hibya frowned and got a sample of her own.

Luyan's face lit up as he bit into the crunchy cutlet, the smoky sweetness of the hazelnut balancing the slight bitterness of the mussel's flesh, the garlic and pepper imparting a savor that the meat itself lacked.

Quarta licked her lips. "I have never tasted anything so good. Thank you for teaching me this, Raya."

"Oh, but we are not finished. We cannot waste this oil, flavored with so much goodness from land and sea," Raya said.

She took four of the squab, cut each in half down the backbone, and placed them skin side down in the cauldron, four at a time. Their fat sputtered and rendered as they browned. She restacked them, covered the veseel, and banked the coals around it to finish them by roasting.

Luyan's interest in *serkarui* cooking was beginning to rival his keenness for Keftiun navigation. When the birds were done, Raya removed them to a platter. To the fat and juices in the cauldron, she added bulrush starch, scraped all into a thick beige paste with a sumptuous, nutty aroma, and deglazed the vessel with fresh pomegranate juice. Luyan watched the mixture reduce down to a glistening ruby-red sauce that coated the wooden spoon. His stomach growled as she ladled it over the squab.

Several loaves of the hot, crusty bread were ready, as well as boiled greens, the crispy strips of great mussel, and a golden stew of oysters and mushrooms flavored with saffron. They summoned the rowers and crewmen below deck to eat, then ascended the companionway with the Kozhiniru and the other *serkarui* to meditate.

Luyan's legs stiffened as they had the last time, but soon a not unpleasant numbness came over them. He channeled his breath through his sinuses as Hibya had taught him, fixed his eyes on the deck, and recalled the Kozhiniru's instruction. He inhaled slowly. Keeping his eyes partially open discouraged random images. When they came, he tried to erase them.

It was a frustrating process. He remembered the Kozhiniru's admonition to be patient with himself and gently drew his attention back again and again. Instead of focusing on emptiness, he was attempting to empty his mind, and he realized his folly. He willfully sought to experience nothingness, to *feel* it rise and fall in his belly, stoked like a burning coal as he breathed. He stopped picturing the idea as something outside of himself. His breathing became more even, and his concentration narrowed.

The images that did arise began to change, to flow from a more timeless current. He reminisced upon the long summer afternoons of his childhood, sitting bird watch in his family's olive groves. The flocks of starlings would descend in a wheeling, perfect sphere and settle in a single tree. Luyan remembered his fascination at their approach, the raucous battle as the birds at the back rotated forward to push for primacy in the feed. Once roosted, they settled, the boiling cacophony reduced to stillness in a single moment, like a blown candle. The individual birds became distinguishable then, their bright yellow beaks framed by their purple body feathers.

Lying back against the piles of stone, cleared for cultivation generations before, he sometimes became so mesmerized that he missed his timing. After picking off and devouring the insects, the birds had already begun to peck and spoil the ripening olive fruits before Luyan remembered to cast his stone and drive them away. They quickly settled again. The starlings were as devious as they were persistent and soon recognized a pattern of sound or motion as harmless if it was repeated.

Just so were the random thoughts Luyan wrestled from his mind. Like the birds, they were distracting in the spiral buzz of their approach, the charm of their individual attributes. Both could be useful friends. Or destructive nuisances, should the mind become capitvated.

What he had learned then served him now. There was no point becoming frustrated. No use flinging a stone at any particular bird. If he felled one, the flock quailed no faster and returned just as quickly. Most efficient was the way of least resistance. A handful of small pebbles, cast one at a time, with minimum force and perfectly timed. Flung at that precise moment when the birds had fulfilled their purpose but before they could do harm. Acceptance that they would come back. Confidence that they would scatter once again.

Dwelling on the connection, he had another insight. The memory was itself a construction of his mind, empty in its very being. The imprint of events long past. Those birds were dead; that boy now a man on a ship, separated by many years and hundreds of miles from his olive grove.

One idea gave rise to the next. An endless chain—a wheel. Breathing out, he released this image as well. And before the next could surface, he himself knew a great emergence. Like breaking out upon a frothy sea after a long, deep dive. Everything around him became more distinct, more present. Not the new experience he had been expecting. Instead, a liberation from experience, a shattering of separation between himself and the sensory world.

He had not learned to push thought aside. He had broken his attachment to it. Thought, he understood, was mere construct, wholly conditioned by his mind. Something which took many forms but was utterly empty in its nature.

He stood on the edge of what seemed a limitless chasm. But free from any hint of fear. The truth was there, had always been there, hidden in plain view. How did form differ from emptiness? The question itself embodied delusion—*kebulu* in Keftiun. A riddle to be discarded, not answered.

The Kozhiniru tapped the floor to mark the end of the meditation. The *serkarui* now readied themselves for *tzeroru-ti usurai*—the exercise of ecstatic surrender.

Luyan stretched his legs, stood up, and joined the loose circle. *Tzeroru-ti usurai*, he knew, was done with eyes closed. When all were still and ready, the Kozhiniru gave the simple command to begin.

"Yako."

The exercise started slowly. Here a resonance, there a slow dervish or a worshipful raising of the arms. Luyan stood quietly, waiting to feel his limbs lighten as they had last time. Experimentally, he raised them himself, as if inviting the gods to take him. When nothing happened for several minutes, he remembered the Kozhiniru's admonition to expect nothing. He exhaled deliberately and simply opened his heart, tilting his head toward the sky. Almost imperceptibly, a slight heaviness began to affect his body, gradually bending him at the waist. He neither followed nor resisted. His hands, as of their own accord, folded into a prayer position.

His chest began to tighten with the god-fear. This was no superstitious fancy, like the gaze of a stone idol or the appearance of clouds after a prayer for rain. This was a tangible encounter with the divine. He searched for meaning in the motions as he was pulled downward. Although he could resist, he could not do so without stopping the exercise, breaking the connection made possible by surrender of his will. He was brought to his knees, slow and graceful, arms stretched over his head, then lowered flat upon the deck in supplication. The movements were almost pleasurable, like a deep stretch after a long, satisfying sleep, and as he submitted more fully, they became more subtle.

He was drawn back to his feet, spinning, hands and wrists circling, falling in with the rhythm of the women. A low hum sounded in his chest, the new base note of their chord. Quarta slowed as she circled past him. Together their harmony rose and led the choral toward its perfect resolution.

The exercise ceased as it had begun, leaving Luyan empty of all feeling but deep gratitude.

A few more moments of quiet and platters of food began to emerge from the lower deck—their turn at dinner. The *serkarui* ringed the deck, backs to the bulkheads, and ate from platters on their laps. The Kozhiniru took a central place at the threshold of the passenger deck, with Ethtar next to her. Quarta sat close to the brazier, clustered with Luyan, Hibya, and Raya.

Raya looked worn from cooking for two sittings. She relaxed now and permitted her companions to serve her. The meal started with the steaming oyster-and-mushroom stew, which Luyan found went especially well with the warm *banu,* torn and passed from hand to hand. Only Ethtar—and Quarta at her prompting—refused the bread. Luyan wondered what restriction may have been violated in its making.

Ethtar had no objection to the wine, however, and held her

glass to be refilled numerous times. Each person had the social obligation to watch the cups of her neighbors carefully. It was traditional among both communities that no one should pour their own drink.

Raya was concerned that the guests had rejected the bread. She asked Quarta if it was not baked in accordance with their tradition. Quarta seemed reticent to answer in front of Luyan. She finally admitted that the use of leaven was highly sensitive among Canaanite groups. It was never employed in the presence of a man.

"Do you have no male *serkarui*?" asked Luyan.

"There are once-born sons, but our coastal communities never keep them. For generations now, they have been given up to the world," Quarta answered in Akkadian. "And the sacred bread should never be touched by men before it is fully baked. The yeast culture should not even be opened in their presence. Ethtar noticed you kneading the dough. This is . . . corrupting among us," she said with a sheepish look.

Hibya turned to Raya and repeated the Akkadian word questioningly. "Corrupting?"

"Luginyeri'shyi," Raya translated for her, apparently a little irked at the suggestion. She turned to Quarta.

"What is the basis of such a doctrine? Our *banu* is the purest of foods, uncorrupted by domestic grains, wholly edifying to the body. It contains a balance of the Mother's wild gifts, including her sacred breath—what you call 'leaven.' Its making is an expression of divine balance. And men are a part of that balance."

Hibya tapped Raya's arm to remind her that Quarta was their guest. She also shifted herself toward Luyan until her hip touched his.

"We do not hate men," Quarta said, her eyes following the motion. "But you must understand that our coastal *serkarui* have suffered much conflict with the Canaanite ruling class. Ethtar's community has been depleted and is full of twice-born *serkarui* of Amorite and Anatolian blood. These cultures do not value women, whether young or old. They especially mistrust the *serkarui*. There have been generations of persecutions, of purges . . ." She glanced over at Ethtar.

She continued in her Keftiun whisper words. "It is different upriver. We have retained more of our Aegean traditions. The villages and clans fear us, but it is a respectful fear. We coexist with their shamans. Provide healing and midwifery when needed. We trade pearls, salt, and purple with the women of the farms in exchange for their *naki gantsui*."

This last term left Hibya and Raya staring at one another. Luyan assumed it was another disparity of dialect. The hosts avoided pointing out these little differences whenever they could glean their guests' meaning from context.

"Inner . . . internal jewels?" Hibya guessed. "Do you mean to say *nakaru-min gantzui*?"

"Umm, well, you know . . . milk, eggs, butter . . ." Quarta explained.

"You would say *nakarui-i gantzui*," interrupted Ethar, in a volume that betrayed her wine. The group realized their conversation had become the center of attention, hushed voices drawing notice as they so often do in a crowd.

Ethtar laughed at her own jest, a vulgar play on words whose specific meaning in Keftiun was "kidney stones." She tapped her cup on the deck.

"*Onshyeru-min ganzui*," the Kozhiniru said as she filled it. "Women's treasures. But *naku-min ganzui* is just as correct. 'Inner treasures.' In rural villages, women have the right to the earnings from eggs and milk and all things made from them. That is theirs to keep."

"But why 'inner'?" Hibya asked.

"Not, as many believe, because they are domestic products, produced inside the home. It is because they are all gifts of the Goddess derived from the bodies of her creatures. As Quarta said, eggs, milk, and cheese. But also seeds and perennial plantings, honey, and even pearls. Pearls are the *naku-min ganzui* of the *serkarui*. We gather them from the sea, from the bodies of the mollusks. The term also means 'portable wealth.'" She looked deliberately at Ethtar, who was beginning to rock slightly from her wine. "They come from a body and can be concealed in a body," the Kozhiniru continued. "This is the nature of 'women's wealth.'"

Quarta nodded in agreement. "Upriver, we smelt our silver ingots into ceremonial bowls and other containers. During times of persecution, we coat the silver with wet clay and fire them to make them resemble valueless earthen vessels. In this way, our 'inner treasure' remains safe if our grottoes are pillaged." An impatient grunt from Ethtar. "But of course, it is worse in the seaside communities," she finished quickly, looking away.

"Freshwater *serkarui*," Ethtar mumbled into her cup. "Even your pearls are twisted."

Quarta stared fixedly forward, seeming more embarrassed for Ethtar than hurt by her sarcasm.

The Kozhiniru changed the subject as the savory cutlets of mussel appeared, arranged elegantly on platters of their own shells. "Tell us what you think of Raya's preparation of the beautiful mussels you brought us, Ethtar," she said.

Raya watched as Ethtar took a slice and crunched into it.

"Makes me thirsty" was her only comment. But after draining her wine, she ate several more.

The rest of the company enjoyed them as well. Just as they disappeared, the squab and vegetables were brought out. Like most of the shipboard travelers, Luyan went first for the bright leafy greens, boiled until just tender in seawater. Their fresh, bitter flavor was deeply satisfying. There were peeled bulrush roots and onions roasted in olive oil and vinegar. But when he bit into the squab, its crisp brown skin glazed with the deep red pomegranate sauce and dusted with toasted almonds, it became clear that cooking was as much a spiritual devotion for the *serkarui* as their other arts. Raya watched his face as he took his first small sip of wine. The pairing was transporting. He could only nod in his rapture, and she smiled back.

Even Ethtar acknowledged her enjoyment. *"Yibri,"* she said, staring cross-eyed at the leg joint as she chewed.

Raya bowed. "The freshness of your gifts makes all the difference."

Platters of tea and honeyed seed cakes were passed to end the meal, and the company broke up into smaller groups.

Quarta apologized for Ethtar's behavior. "She spent almost two hours with your Kozhiniru, and they reached no agreement. Of all her family, Ethtar is the sole survivor of a long series of persecutions by the temple authorities at Gubel. She has made many sacrifices to safeguard the remnant of *serkarui* which she now leads. She will be difficult to convince. But without her word, the seaside communities around Gubel will remain where they are and will not take refuge upriver."

"It is our goal not just to save the *serkarui*, but the coastal cities and villages as well," Hibya said. "And we seek a home for our people's treasure, safe from Thera's destruction and the world."

They watched as two younger *serkarui* helped Ethtar to bed. Her wine seemed to affect her from the legs up, Luyan mused. The women had as much trouble avoiding her dexterous groping as keeping her upright.

The Kozhiniru joined them as they finished their tea. "Ethtar will be more reasonable in the morning, of course," she said, "but her trust has been so broken by the world that she has little left for even her ancient cousins."

Quarta spoke softly. "Kozhiniru, if I understand, not much time remains. Ask it of me, and I will go and prepare a place for your company upriver. Our grottoes are large, and I know you would be welcome."

"Ser-Quarta, your love is beyond doubt, and I bless you for it, but we have more to do than to run and hide. Do you know any other members of the seaside community who have contacts in Gubel?"

Quarta thought for a moment. "None as senior as Ethtar. But, Kozhiniru, no priest or lord of our land—no man at all—would consider the counsel of a woman." She glanced over at Talyera and the knot of young noblewomen seated aft. "Even if you were to form an alliance by marriage, the counsel of a wife here, even a royal wife, is of almost no consequence." She lowered her voice. "The northern influence—the cult of Ēl, the father god—has too strong a hold. They fashion their religion after their Amorite overlords, and their clothing after their Egyptian trading partners. There is no room left for veneration of the Goddess or life in the *tzeroro yridinu*," she said. "If Ethtar has made you feel unwelcome, it is because we ourselves are outsiders here."

"Nonetheless, it is our duty to try," the Kozhiniru said. "We will see in the morning if Ethtar has a change of heart." She took her hand. "I sense a purity in your devotion, Ser-Quarta. You have deep respect for the truth, yet you journey lightly upon the bourn. Will you be first in my *zhyuzhurai hitzwatu* at sunrise?"

Quarta reddened at the unexpected honor. She gave an eager nod.

14 Pivot Point

Where the ocean meets the sky . . . she dove into the vast waters
And searched the seabed below, but she could not see the bottom.
Realizing that she would not escape death,
She pined for her beloved home, for she was, after all, a woman.

"My cherished son, please do not doubt, and comfort my soul.
Now I shall depart beneath these waves
Which mindlessly wash the rocks, signifying nothing.
As a mere spirit, I can see you no more,
But by night, in your dreams—
And so I hate the dawn."

—Excerpts from *Ama (The Pearl Diver)*
Traditional 13th Century Japanese Noh play

11 March 1769
Lt. S. Singer, HMRN
At Sea

My Dear Girl,
 I have kept my own counsel during this voyage, as passengers are wont to do on a merchant vessel, being used with little respect by the seamen. Howbeit, to paraphrase our *sorginak,* salt knows salt, and I have drawn the attention of a small number of the crew, my seamanship proving more difficult to conceal than other aspects of my being.

One of these is Dennis Daniels, the midshipman of the sextant who I mentioned before, an agreeable youth from Surrey who is the nephew of the owner. Dennis longs for a naval warrant but lacks the necessary family interest. He has taken to sitting with me on the forepeak in good weather to hear tales of my service on the American station. My career making a short narrative, discourse soon progresses to the broader subjects of our lives and families; and we find one another quite good company.

We are often joined by the bosun, Jeroen Herrema, who has seen merchant service in the Pacific with the VOC, or Dutch East India Company, as we know it. His looks belie his apellation, however, he being a native of Japan and "Jeroen Herrema" easier to pronounce in Dutch than his original name—Jiro Hiruma. He is beardless, like I am, with fine black hair not dissimilar to the Basque's. His dark almond-shaped eyes are at their most charming when he smiles, and portray a singular wit and compassion.

I am fascinated by Jeroen and would question him daylong on the subject of his homeland, as I knew almost nothing of it. He is a polite and interested listener, but, alas, I usually draw little from him in the speaking line. He is content to share his pipe with Dennis and hear our histories, which I formerly attributed to a lack of English or a reticence to use it for shame of his accent.

The case was altered one afternoon when I mentioned the *sorgin danza* festival in Lasarte-Oria, which featured in my first letter. I had been discoursing upon the *sorginak* of Gipuzkoa, their making of salt and soap, their gathering of medicinal herbs and ocean and river shellfish; and as I recounted the practice of the village men to dress in female garb and dance at the *sorgin* festival, Jeroen's eyes grew wide, and he pressed me on numerous minute points. I asked him the reason for his curiosity, and he at length opened up, proving of much better English than I had supposed.

Jeroen was born in a region called Noto, a sea-swept peninsula in western Japan known for its fine lacquer work. While on a marketing journey to Edo, the capital city, he took traffic with Dutch traders, who much prized his family's wares. He became enamored of their society, language, and faith and in time asked to be baptized. A change in rule several years ago made Christians no longer welcome on the Japanese mainland, and Jeroen shipped out on a Dutch merchant vessel. Sadly, he would be put to death if he were ever to return, for a kind of cultural traitor.

In his coastal homelands live a group of women known, by their more respectful name, as Amasan—which first methought in my ignorance he had said "Amazon"—or sometimes merely Ama. These make their livelihood diving for abalone, pearls, and seaweed, existing on the margent of society. They are nonetheless widely revered by the Japanese people and feature in their arts and letters.

Jeroen was particularly intriqued by the *sorgin dantza* because there exists a similar festival in Noto linked to almost identical lore and myth. Just as Basque ritual invokes the mystical joining of the land and sea in the forms of the earth mother Mari and the great sea serpent Maju-Sugarr, so the Japanese mark the same union and pray for the conjugal visitation of their own sea dragon, Mizuchi-

Susanoo, upon their local deities.

To Jeroen's mind, however, the most astonishing parallel lay in the fact that in both ceremonies, the male participants don female dress and paint. Nearly as amazed he was to learn that communities not dissimilar to his Amasan span the coast of Europe and that myths of sea sirens spring from the fancy of mariners in the Atlantic as often as in the Pacific. Indeed, mermaid sightings of creditable report reach far back in our nautical history, though I have remarked their diminution during my own lifetime. This I attribute, in passing, to the invention of the portable ship's telescope, which permits their identification as mere pearl divers (or other natural creatures) at a safe standoff from the rocks and shoals where they appear.

Jeroen delights in giving me a little small foundation in his beautiful language, and I in improving his English, and we have became fast friends. It seems he was much taken in his youth by a girl of the Ama. He never tires of describing her, nor of asking me to recount as much as I know of the *sorginak*. We muse at great length upon their related subjects: the whisper-song that echoes through the caves of the Pyrenees; the "sea whistle" of the Amasan as they expel breath through their sinus cavities after a deep dive; red bean rice traditional to both festivals; food generally; the taste of fresh abalone. As we near Gipuzkoa, my suspicion grows that Jeoren has a mind to jump ship and discover it for himself, and I rue that I will never be able to do the same in Japan, so closely guarded is that island nation from outsiders.

My earliest memory is of playing with my Uncle Christopher's paint pots, left in the atelier after his hasty departure, and the sharp smell of turpentine as Mary Rosedew tidied my hands of them. It was doubtless little Eleanor who had opened and left them on the floor; she adored the bright colors and loved to illustrate scraps of wrapping paper when not at her little easel and canvas.

I recall my wonder at the Christmas decor in the parlor of the modest dockside row house which Christopher and Matthew had rented in St. Anne's parish after their summary eviction by Nessie Their landlady, a liberal-minded naval widow, occupied the basement apartments and provided meals and what little domestic support the two men needed. I remember my delight as I unbundled the shining foil from the poppets Christopher had carved and hand painted for Eleanor and I. We visited their house frequently, and the contrast between its atmosphere of easy amity and the hushed tension of the Singer home was another of my most primary impressions; the very lines of my mother's visage seemed to soften when alone with these, her two dearest friends.

It was Mary Rosedew who first dubbed me "Selkie," as I splashed in the bath. "Ye swim like a selkie," she said. It's prepossessing resonance in her native Cornish, as well as its preference, in Nessie's view, to Sebastian, proved persuasive; and the name quickly took hold with Matthew and Christopher and, at length, Arima as well.

In keeping with Nessie's agreement, I enjoyed a closer intimacy with my mother at the Portsmouth house than is usual to English children, especially sons. I cherish memories of bathing and breakfasting together in the atelier, my presence at her boudoir and toilette. I exalted when she solicited my child's opinion of her clothing for the day and gave me to choose of her perfumes and combs. Arima often kept me present during Mary's formational exercises, and I now recognize what a privilege and influence this was. I remember the day—I can have been no more than five years old—when Mary received upon her body the first elements of that figure which would, though overlaid additions, become what she knew as her "mamwyn's mark." I bit my fingers as I watched Arima raze and then repeatedly prick the skin of her venereal mount with the vivid blue dye.

That evening, when my mother stood up in our high-backed copper washtub, I pointed to her own tattoo, whose outline appeared though the fringe of her sex, thinned by the streaming bathwater. She patiently permitted me to imprint the whole of the figure in my mind, and I remember feeling reassured that her jabbing of Mary had not been some form of punishment. As I grew older, I glimpsed it only during our swimming lessons in the sweet waters of Hampshire's upland streams, which Arima preferred for their purity and isolation. But she made me and Eleanor draw and redraw the symbol, and my earliest letters were in the reciting and writing of the titles of each of its points in Basque and Greek.

The topmost points stand for the three devotions of wisdom, which in Greek are *henosis*, *epignosis*, and *epistemosis*. Descending to the right in a clockwise direction are the devotions of love, *agape*, *eros*, and *latreia*. And finally on the lower left side, the devotions of power, *hagnizó*, *sunthesis*, and *poiéōma*. But trusting you to safeguard these letters from the eyes of others, the figure may be rendered, titled with the classic word forms, thus:

It would be years before I apprehended the nuances of these terms, and indeed, a single lifetime of living practice may not be sufficient to their complete understanding.

In teaching, Arima sought always to profit from context and example, native curiosity, and dialectic. During one of Mary's midwifery lessons, as they were shifting the bed linen and swabbing the floor of the birthing chamber, Mary, who had a healer's keen mind for patterns of symptom and recovery, observed that women are more often stricken with childbed fevers after a breech birth.

"And why do you suppose that is?" Arima asked.

Mary pondered. "Perhaps the strainin' warms the body?"

"Do other forms of exertion cause fever?"

Mary furled her brow but made no reply.

"If no cause is evident, look for correlates," Arima said. "What else is present at difficult births?"

Mary slowed her scrubbing. "Why, there's more bleedin', and doctors is most often called in . . ."

Arima prompted her. "May it be that fever arises from what is introduced into the body, and not what issues from it?"

"Instruments!" exclaimed Mary after a pause. "It's only surgeons use forceps an' such. May they be the cause?"

"Yes, good, but more likely their lack of cleanliness," Arima replied. "Midwives attend one woman at a time and stay with her throughout her labor. We enter a birthing room with fresh linens, boiled water, soap, and mops and fling wide the windows to bring sunlight and sweet air. Even the ancient Romans knew that corruption breeds malady. Our surgeons have forgotten this. They wear filth and dried blood as a token of their pride, carrying it from one patient to the next like bees bearing pollen amongst the flowers." She mused. "I often wonder, as I watch the honeybees, whether the mechanism of what we call infection may be similar."

"Their physical philosophy comes second to antique learnin', then, is it?" Mary asked.

Arima shook her head. "Not at all, Mary. It is no flaw in the scientific method. It is a failure to apply it with humility, unbiased by pride or presuppositions, with a mind that is quietly observant and open to inspiration."

"So they weigh too heavy in *epistemosis*?" She dropped her voice as she carefully pronounced the classical word, which signifies the attainment of knowledge by deliberate mental and physical process—observation, reason, and experimentation.

"Yes," said Arima. "The mind can become shackled by unbalanced objectification. In our relation to the natural world, there is a fine line between observation and manipulation. Observation and experiment are necessary to the discovery of truth. But manipulation, even if unintended, not only alters its object, but hobbles the observer with prejudice and cherished delusions."

Mary reflected. "So truth is discovered not just by *using* the mind, but also by its purification."

Arima's visage composed itself in that smile which was the meed and delight of her students.

As my own maturity put a finer point on my understanding, the import of Arima's lesson appeared. Arima sought to convey that *epistemosis* must be balanced by the devotions of *hentosis*, that controlled stillness which unifies the mind with its object, and *epignosis*, inspired wisdom attainable only by surrender to the divine will.

My mother's learning, along with Mary's progress in letters and mathematics, left Eleanor and I in no need of tutors. We took our daily lessons together, forming a sort of little colloquium unto ourselves. Nessie examined us each week, foremost in English, on which she sometimes corrected Arima and Mary nearly as often as the children. She also compelled us to recite our kings and Bible books, me to demonstrate my sums, and Eleanor her drawing and music.

I was breeched early, which I believe discomfited me, as I had taken childish pride in my little gowns, many of which were tuckings of Eleanor's garments; I cannot remember a time that I did not worship her and wish to emulate her in every manner. Nonetheless, and principally for love of my uncles' attention, I relished the formation they gave me in the manly arts. These commenced as games but increased in rigor as I grew into older childhood.

I liked swordplay of all things, I think principally because Matthew and Christopher differed in their preferred techniques and often disputed comically on the subject. Matthew had been trained in the linear Italian and French styles of *passé* and *reprise* with long rapier, now made popular in England by Domenico Angelo, but less common among the British military when I was young. Christopher, on the other hand, loved to swing his broad cavalry saber, and what he lacked in finesse he made up in slashing power and zeal overall. As much for my entertainment as instruction, they would often spar, Christopher attacking with feigned antic rage and animal growls, Matthew exaggerating his *repartée* into near ballet to further frustrate him. I favored the grace of Matthew's style, as well as the weight of the rapier compared to the much heavier saber, since by the age of seven or eight it already appeared I would not inherit my father's bulk and stature.

I remember practicing in the late spring of my eighth year one warm afternoon in the yard of the Singer house, which was as near as Nessie suffered my uncles' presence. I was laying into the gatepost with my little wooden short sword while Matthew and Chrisopher took shade on an iron bench. Arima was sitting with Nessie in quiet conversation before one of the broad upper windows, as much to keep an eye upon me as to profit from what little breeze there was.

The neighbor boy—an overgrown, mutton-headed barbarian of ten or eleven years whose father, according to the public narrative, had been away at sea since before his birth—scaled the fence with a tree branch in hand and engaged me with a swat upon my backside. I had little previous contact with other boys and looked to my uncles in astonishment as I rubbed the stinging area. They exchanged concerned glances.

"Show 'im your best form, Selkie," Christopher called out, then in a menacing aside to the lad, "and you mind 'is age and size, you 'ear me there?"

"Do be careful, my dear," Matthew added.

I took my pose, and we fenced to cries of encouragement from my uncles, the watchful eyes of the women upon us. At first, I followed my instincts, jumping clear of his weapon, but soon remembering my lessons, awaited my chance to close for a touch. Every one of the boy's chopping blows reverberated up my little arm with a painful crack as I blocked and parried; and when my shock at length gave way to anger, I made a blind, impetuous lunge and ran my eye into the tip of his stick.

I saw stars, dropped my sword, held my face and began to weep.

The two men seemed to swap natures of a sudden: the routinely gruff Christopher stumbled toward me with a maternal shriek, and Matthew delivered my opponent a boot in the breeches as he ran for the garden gate.

"Ahow! Let uncle see the peeper . . . there's a lamb!" Christopher mewed, himself close to tears.

"No crying now, young man!" Matthew said in a military tone. "You'll dish that little huff out well and proper next time."

I struggled to stop sobbing and looked up at the window for my mother. She was already flying down the stairs, and only Nessie's face appeared. Through my one uninjured eye, I could see that she was laughing.

Arima crouched to swab and examine me. By good fortune, I had shut my eyes tightly before my advance; no splinters of wood had pierced the orbit, and no permanent damage done. She bandaged it for a few days until its redness and sensitivity to light diminished, and I meantime cut what Matthew called "a dashing figure" and enjoyed an honorarium of attentions from Eleanor.

For all that, as I supped alone with Arima that evening, she discerned in me a moroseness that I could not hide.

"Zer gertatzen da, maite nirea? What's wrong my love?"

"Why did Nana Nessie laugh at me, ama?"

She frowned. "When did she laugh at you?"

"From the window today. When I was hurt," I said.

She covered my hand in hers. "I'll give you a comfortable draught, and we will put you and that eye to bed early. Tomorrow morning we will attend Nana Nessie at her toilette." She checked my dressing and kissed my forehead. "And tomorrow afternoon you start learning the *benetako trebezia*."

I knew the Basque words, which grossly signified "true skill," but had never heard the expression.

"*Zer da hori, ama*? *Eskrima*? What is that, Mama? Fencing?"

"Much more than swordplay. A better way to defend yourself with weapons." She smiled. "And more beautiful, too."

Eleanor was nearly eleven by then, and we'd slept apart since I'd been breeched. Even so, I quietly climbed into bed with her that night. She cosseted my back, and I at length broke my silence.

"Is Nana Nessie mean-spirited, do you think?" I whispered.

She didn't answer for a time, and I half thought she had fallen asleep.

"Harpies ain't in it."

Eleanor was a superbly clever mimic, an ability I believe must be related to her musical gifts. She could reproduce the precise manner of speech of nearly any person, even birdsong, and never stammered when she did so. In our privy moments, she would sometimes imitate the cant cadences of Mary Rosedew or Uncle Christopher. This was by no means to mock them, but instead for the thrill of imagining Nessie's mortification had she heard it.

"The mopsie old harrigan hates the world, and scarce less herself."

"Eleanor!" I turned my face to hers in the dark. "You can't mean such things of your own Mama!"

"Well, she does, is all. She's worse than mean-spirited. She's hateful. She despises me, that much is sure."

It brought me low when she spoke thus. "Why do you say so?"

"She didn't want a girl," she replied in her native voice. "I knew it always, and when Papa and Hagen—your dad—passed on, it was worse. She looks at me almost as if it's my fault. As though . . . she wishes I'd never been born," she said with chilling dispassion.

I turned in the bed and pressed my face to her chest. "Oh! Don't even think it! It's too terrible!"

"Mind your eye," she said, hushing me and smoothing my

bandage. "It's all right, really. Before Arima came, I was alone with her in that big London house most of the time. I love how things are now, here with you and Arima and Mary."

Her words were soothing, and I was quickly succumbing to my mother's draught and the exhaustion of the day. "I love you, Eleanor," I breathed.

"I love you, too, poppet." She kissed my forehead, my last memory before falling into a deep sleep.

The morning breeze woke me. Eleanor was up betimes, sitting before the open window and fingering the imaginary keyboard she'd figured in chalk atop her dressing table. This was her usual manner of musical excercise and composition; she possessed the capacity to precisely imagine the sounds of each note and disliked—another of her little particularities—to play anything not of polished execution on the pianoforte in the parlor.

I lay still and watched her. A tiny corner of her bottom lip prised between her teeth; dusky blond ringlets dancing to her nodding rhythm, now revealing the deep study in her delicate gray eyes when she brushed it back. On occasion, her state of concentration was so deep she would forget to swallow her saliva, and make tiny slurpings or swab her chin with her sleeve. I could not then imagine another creature so perfect.

Arima came in to rouse and ready us. She dropped a weak tincture of rosemary and pine into my eye, renewed the dressing, and secured it with my little tricorne hat before helping me into my waistcoat and tunic.

When we entered the grand bedroom on the second level, Nessie was already rouged and endeavoring, with nettled waves of her hand, to keep the powder out of her second cup of tea as Mary seated her wig.

She regarded us as she sipped and then exclaimed, "Ah! Our wounded hero! How is that eye this morning?"

"Better, thank you, Nana," I said meekly. She glanced at Arima, who confirmed with a nod.

My gaze followed Eleanor as she moved off to the dressing table to tell and arrange Nessie's hairpins, she keeping a meticulous mental digest of each by long-held habitude.

Nessie gestured to a little side table where the tea tray was set, along with a pot of chocolate and a dumbwaiter of soda breads and condiments, Nessie preferring to breakfast sparingly; and we sat and served ourselves. I picked at a dry scone, having little appetite.

"Mother," Arima said, "were you not concerned to see Selkie injured by the neighbor's boy yesterday?"

Mary kept her eyes fixed on her work as she perfumed Nessie's nape and shoulders.

"That little demon next door was raised like a red Indian," Nessie said and turned to me. "Best you learn to cope, my boy. A creature like that is a force of nature. Recognize dumb animal malice when you see it."

I nodded.

But Arima was not finished. "You may have given the impression of amusement, which I think confused your grandson. Do assure Selkie that it was not he you were laughing at, if you please, Mother," she said with barely veiled anger.

Nessie faced her, then regarded me with cool complaisance. "Oh no, my dear, there's nothing comical about a poke in the eye! I was having a bit of a crack at those two fond friends of your mother's, is all. One day you'll understand how verily theatrical it is to see longshanks top it the man while his broke-lance sergeant turns weeping wet nurse."

She chuckled again with mirth at the memory as she examined herself in the table mirror and applied a beauty mark below her eye.

Nessie had precious little ability to communicate with a child, and I was confused by her sarcasm.

"Do you mean you were laughing at Uncle Matthew and Uncle Christopher?" I asked.

"I am not happy to hear you call them uncles. Do you suppose them to be your family?" she asked, her good humor vanishing.

"Stop that foolish fiddling with those hairpins, Eleanor!"

Arima grasped my shoulder tightly. I believe she desired me to gain experience in defending myself morally, as well as corporally.

"No, Nana," I replied.

Nessie turned her head from the mirror and looked at me. "No, Nana, what?"

"If they were family, they would be invited into the house, is what I suppose," I said, meeting her steely eyes.

She locked my stare in a contest that lasted several silent moments. "Indeed!" she said at length in a narrow baritone.

Eleanor interrupted the stand. "How many uncles have I, Mama?"

Nessie broke contact and turned to her daughter. "What? What possesses you to pose such an impertinent question?"

Eleanor continued nonplussed. "Because I can't remember any visiting the house." Her eyes lost their softness and took on an almost serpentine cold. "Ever."

Nessie's brogue worsened as it was wont with anger. "You! As for you, you will go back to your room! And no piano for three days!" she sputtered. "March, girl!"

Eleanor walked slowly past me with a satisfied grin, her head held high.

"And you, my boy!" Nessie said, turning back to me, my resolution nearly crumbling in the pause. Her voice softened. "You come here and give Nana a buss on the cheek, and mind the powder."

I warily complied. She seemed to take a perverse delight in my having stood up to her.

"Quite the little gamecock we have here!" she said to Arima, her smile returning. "I'll tell you what it is, my Selkie. We'll engage you a proper fencing master, and you'll soon exact vengeance on young Goliath next door."

"Ama is going to teach me—" I blurted without forethought. I held back the name of the practice, knowing Nessie had a distaste for Basque being spoken in her presence.

"Spanish swordsmanship, Mother," Arima interjected. "Quite popular among continental military officers. The girls of my village learn some fundamentals for our own protection."

Nessie addressed me with a smirk. "Your *ama* takes me for a bit of a flat at times, Selkie. As she knows quite well, the roots of *la verdadera destreza* are much older than Galician arms. Indeed, than Spain itself. But I forget she dislikes the Spanish. What did she call the practice in Basque? Something that sounds like our Irish *bataireacht traenáil*, I make no doubt."

"Benetako trebezia," Arima said. "And I am again humbled by your knowledge, Mother. But may our traditions not serve our sons as well as our daughters?"

Nessie considered. "Well, not in the yard. It would be unseemly as well as indiscreet. You may have Bridger clear the furniture from the grand salon. Be sure he rolls the carpets."

That afternoon, Eleanor and I spun with delight upon the broad expanse of empty floor in the high-ceilinged salon, which now resembled a ballet studio. Arima entered with three ashwood closet poles, trimmed to the heigth of our noses, mine being the shortest.

We warmed up with stretches and exercises to strengthen the belly and lower back and then learned to stand in a frontal pose, legs spread comfortably at shoulder width. I made Arima to know I was not fully content with the longstaff, for it seemed to me a step backward from the sword, in the use of which I already had a base.

"Well," Arima said, "try holding it by the end like a sword."

I found it impossibly heavy, grunting to raise the tip just a few inches off the floor.

"Now find the pivot point." She moved her hand to the very center of her staff and balanced it on the tip of one finger. We imitated her, and the difference was distinct—the object seemed almost weightless. Using a hand-over-hand motion, Arima spun hers in front of her body like a windmill, and Eleanor and I cried out in delight.

"Like our bodies, every weapon, whether sword or staff or battle ax, has a balance point. Cultivating awareness of balance is the basis of *benetako trebezia.*" She made a graceful turn, whirling the staff behind her back, then over her head and back in front.

She urged us to go slowly as we imitated her movements. "You can always add speed to good form. But you cannot add good form to speed."

Unlike Matthew's swordsmanship, which required memorization of static postures and linear forms, Arima's method taught sensible awareness of the reach of a weapon around the body's central balance point. I sought to feel this relationship, leaving my mind clear to observe my opponent's actions.

"Watch his feet, not his hands," she said. "No matter its dimensions, a weapon's maximum power is at its tip. Imagine your opponent surrounded by a great sphere formed by the end of his reach in all directions and his balance point at the center. Circle it, moving side to side. This forces him to adjust his stance to keep his equilibrium."

"But what if his reach is greater than mine, Ama?" I was mindful of my last encounter.

"Then you must bridge the gap, keeping clear of his weapon's tip while placing him within range of your own."

Over the following months, we practiced ever more complex forms with the longstaff. My mother insisted that during the early stages of my training I suspend the practice of swordsmanship to avoid confusion of method. We learned that when we swung a weapon around its balance point—pushing with one hand while pulling with the other—we doubled its power, further augmented by centrifugal force from the other articulations of our body: hips, waist, shoulders, elbows, and wrists. I sparred with Eleanor, who was inspired more by the dance-like grace of the movements than their application, but also with Mary and Arima, who put me through more rigorous paces.

After the passage of a year and more, we found ourselves one rainy afternoon at my uncles' house; the smart array of edged weapons hanging above their mantle inspired me to once again press Arima on when I might graduate from longstaff to sword.

"You already have, my love."

"But, Ama, a sword is not a staff."

"It is a weapon with a tip and a pivot point. The sole difference is that it does not balance at the middle of its length."

She asked Matthew for the loan of his short sword. He demurred at first, concerned for its sharpness, and offered his wooden practice piece.

"No," Arima said. "I want him to experience the real weapon."

They settled upon his grandfather's short rapier, of transitional Dutch design, preferable for its lack of a knuckle guard, which permitted me to grip with two hands if I chose. I took it carefully and struck the pointed-toe lunging pose Matthew had taught me. The sword weighed heavily upon my slender wrist.

"Find the pivot point," Arima said.

I laid it upon my finger. It balanced at a position on its grip below the cross guard, which I placed one hand below and one above.

"Now release that awkward stance and find your body's equilibrium."

I shifted to my natural posture, ready for motion in any direction.

"Good. Show me your first spiral exercise," she said.

I shut my eyes and let my body follow the familiar pattern. I spun the rapier around its balance point in flashing butterfly figures as I turned a full circle. Christopher gasped at the deadly flurry. I finished the exercise with a stylized flourish, one knee to the floor and the sword athwart my shoulders.

My uncles looked at me with mouths agape. Arima had it right. Sword or staff, it was all one.

I leave you here for tonight, my dear. I shall beg more paper from the ship's purser and continue tomorrow.

Your affectionate,
Selkie

15 Life Devotions

For if the will has nothing to employ it, and love has no present object with which to busy itself, the soul finds itself without either support or occupation, its solitude and aridity cause it great distress, and its thoughts involve it in the severest conflict.

—Teresa of Ávila, *The Life of Saint Teresa of Ávila by Herself*

1602 BCE
Eastern Mediterranean

After the welcoming feast, Hibya and Luyan went back to their hammock. The looming end of their journey had begun to settle upon them. Hibya distracted herself by toying with Luyan's hair.

"Your locks have grown."

Luyan had given up trying to detangle them. But daily washing had made them softer and redder. Hibya held them up behind his head in a bunch. They were almost long enough to wear Keftiun style.

He cupped the back of her neck, and she winced. The long swim, after weeks of confinement, had left her sore. He riffled his fingertips against the knotted muscles. She moaned gently.

"The healer gave me this," she said, pulling a small vial from her belt.

Luyan squeezed out a few drops. A strong, calming scent of lavender and camphorous laurel resin. He rubbed the oil into her neck and shoulders, felt the cooling, numbing effect on his own fingers.

He stepped down from the hammock and spread his cloak on the deck. Their usual prelude to lovemaking. Stiff as she was, she hopped down and lay back, eyes eager. He smiled and turned her onto her stomach.

He chafed his rough hands together to warm them, then coated them with the oil. Straddling her legs, he pushed his thumbs alongside her backbone. A firm upward traction toward her head. He flattened his palms, twisted down and sideways on her upper shoulders, pausing when she groaned.

"*E'yibri?*"

She nodded. "Don't stop, it feels good."

Unused to passive physicality, she at first supplemented his motions, stretching and working with his touch.

"Relax and accept it," he said. "Like in *tzeroru-ti usurai.*"

Ecstatic submission. She got the point, and the knots melted under his strong fingers.

He folded her arm behind her, raising her shoulder blade to access the muscles beneath. He repeated on the other side, then began a full-palmed, twisting motion, heavy and low on her spine. Her knees bent with the pleasure of the deep, cracking release. He continued, kneading her buttocks and thighs, the powerful muscle groups used in her long-distance, two-legged kicking style.

Her eyes were closed in rapture. She opened them languidly, reached back and laced her fingers in his.

"You have a healer's hands. Where did you learn these techniques?"

"When I was a boy in Tarsa," he said. "In the public baths. And also on the ships, for the soldiers and . . ." He could not bring to mind a Keftiun word for "master."

She tried to imagine what his former life must have been. She sat up, and bit his lip tenderly.

"On Thera, there are hot springs where the *serkarui* soak after their exertions. It makes your muscles supple and your skin so soft. I promise I will—"

She stopped. A promise to take him there would be impossible to keep.

"I vow that as long as I am alive, no one will ever own you again, Illuyanka."

His face showed a shadow of conflict. "What did it mean earlier, when you touched your hip to mine? Quarta seemed to understand. Raya told me some *serkarui* bind themselves to others by marking their bodies. In Cilicia, such markings are a sign of ownership."

She opened her cincture and placed her fingertips upon her *kyazusu.*

"It's true. When *serkaru* women are joined in love, they mark their hips with a smaller image of the *kyazusu* of her partner."

"And if a man is in love with a *serkaru?*"

She lowered her eyes. "It is not enough to love a woman's *kyazusu.*"

He would not be deflected. *"Ya aishya Hibya ... yulu ... Hibya."*

"You love all of Hibya?" she repeated. Her playful smile faded as he held her gaze. "I think you mean *like.* You meant to say you *like everything* about me. *Aishyara,* not *aishya.* And *minyuli,* not *yulu.* Say, '*Ya aishyara va-minyuli.* I like everything about you.'"

He would not lapse into a language lesson. He had eagerly repeated hundreds of her phrases in their shared night space, sometimes until the dawn crept through the scupper. But this time, he stood by the expression of his heart, plain and correct.

"Ya aishya'v."

Her fingers tightened. After an interval so long he feared he had blundered, she looked up into his eyes.

"Tzo ya aishya'v, Illuyanka," she whispered in return.

Hours later, after a joining of almost reckless abandonment, Luyan lay reflecting upon her nine-pointed marking.

"I would place this figure upon my hip?"

"Yes. Well, no." She looked into his eyes. "Yes, but in a particular place. A place special to women."

"How can I know, then?"

She bit her lip, then turned him on his side and wrapped him with her legs. He instinctively began to roll belly down to enter her again, but she stopped him. She explored his flank and found his pelvis's widest point. Less prominent than a woman's, but just as hard.

It did not take him long to understand. She expelled her breath in a moan when his hip found its precise placement. He responded to her grappling rhythm, soon discovering its shades and subtleties, his body's every muscle engaged. Hibya controlled the intensity. She withheld the crushing reciprocal pressure another woman would have desired, instead returning long, gingerly strokes of her smooth thigh.

She grabbed a handful of his matted locks, and her familiar flush as she peaked cost him his own control.

They lay back, breathless. Luyan explored his hip, the point of his body that had pleasured her.

"So I will mark myself here?"

It was several moments before she could respond. "Not . . . exactly."

She sooted the tip of her finger on her cauldron, dotted the center of her *kyazusu*, and embraced him again, leaving a black imprint on his hip several inches above the erotic juncture.

"That is where you may mark yourself," she said. "It is the spot where my *kyazusu* meets your body when we are joined. The markings will touch when we do, you see? It is not a sign of ownership. If you take mine, and I yours, we share a commitment to balance one another always. A life devotion." She met his eyes. "One that I desire as well, *yam aishymi.*"

"But I have no *kyazusu* to give you back."

They barely slept that night. By the time the sun rose fully, Raya was completing the last of hundreds of tiny pricks on Luyan's body with a long needle-like bronze instrument. She moistend its tip again with wine and dipped it a final time in the mixture of burned charcoal and crushed lapis lazuli. Then she scrubbed her work with a square of soapy linen.

"There," she said. "The redness and swelling will go away in a few days. Don't rub or scratch before the scabs fall."

Hibya released his hand and helped him carefully replace his loincloth. They mounted to the upper deck just as Quarta was emerging from the parted curtains at the forepeak. Her face radiated bliss. She stopped to embrace them.

"Such a blessing to sit in her presence. It was like one of the ancient mothers come back from the golden West, alive before me. Not just an icon on a silk tapestry. But I fear what is to come."

Luyan said, "The Kozhiniru believes much can be saved if the message is passed quickly along the coastal communities."

Ethtar appeared. Risen with the sun despite all she'd imbibed the night before. She dove into the sea and swam a full circuit of the ship before performing her ablutions. Luyan reflected on the swimming ability of women, the *serkarui* in particular. Hibya had explained that females were naturally more buoyant, enduring of cold, and less prone to blacking out under the pressure of deep water.

Still dripping, Ethtar strode toward them. She flashed a sincere smile of greeting at Luyan, then touched her forehead to Quarta's, holding the back of her neck for a moment before entering the Kozhiniru's whisper cave. Quarta met Luyan's eyes.

"Yes," she said. "I carry her *kyazusu* despite the differences in our ages. Her greatest fear is that I will abandon her and return upriver. Only her stubborn leadership has kept Gubel's seaside community together in the face of the northern persecutions. There is little trust between her and the worldly people of our region. There are much larger, more stable sisterhoods farther south, which I know would receive the Kozhiniru's message with open hearts and minds. But Gubel is the key to the coastal cities, and I fear there may not be time for you to reach them by sea."

Quarta often fell back into Akkadian as Luyan pressed her for details of Canaanite politics and protocol. More than an hour passed before Anekti approached them.

"The Kozhiniru wishes you to join her," she said to Luyan.

"But isn't Ethtar still with her?"

Anekti nodded. "She asks it. I am to summon Talyera as well."

Luyan entered the forepeak. Ethtar and the Kozhiniru were seated in meditation.

Ethtar spoke softly. *"Ashyukui, Ser-Luyan."* It appeared she had been weeping.

Talyera joined them, lilac and myrrh filling the tiny space. Ethtar gave up her cushion and slid in next to Luyan.

"We have much to discuss," the Kozhiniru said. "Ser-Ethtar has reached certain decisions, and we must act on them quickly."

After this latest session with the Kozhiniru, Ethtar's demeanor was more open, more receptive. Luyan tried to imagine what it must have represented. The meeting of two *serkaru* leaders, each great in her own right. For Ethtar, the revisitation of an ancient touchstone, both humbling and affirming.

"Ser-Ethtar has offered her assistance and good offices here in Gubel," the Kozhiniru continued. "We are uncertain of our reception. But it is clear that our delegation must be led by men. We need to warn the coastal population of the coming destruction and find shelter for our people and treasure. Ser-Ethtar is not optimistic, but she is willing to exert what influence she has."

Talyera spoke. "I have no illusions about my role. I am willing and ready to be offered in marriage to any house of the Levant, if an alliance will benefit our mission."

Ethtar spoke solemnly. "You may not know what sacrifice you make, Lady Talyera. The role of women here is not what it is in Keftius. Both the sun and moon are male deities in Canaan, eternally at war with one another. The very notion of female wisdom is belittled. Your ancient royal bloodline may be thought desirable, but you would have little ability to promote our objectives. In truth, we will be fortunate to leave with our lives. My rank provides me a certain access, some limited influence. But I fear it will not be enough."

"As may be," Talyera said. "Our lives and heritage are forfeit where they lay. I will do what can be done."

Luyan regretted his former judgment of her. Though different from the *serkarui*, her devotion to her people was just as disciplined and courageous.

The Kozhiniru turned to him. "Ser-Luyan, you understand our fate, the danger the world faces. You understand *all* that is at stake." His throat constricted. "Will you serve your order by leading the delegation?" She paused. "Will you act for me?"

Luyan held her eyes for a moment. "Even were the life you have restored to me not yours to take, Kozhiniru, I would gladly risk any danger for you. But I have lived most of my life as a servant and am not used to high courts. I fear I may fail you."

"You have grown in wisdom and confidence, Ser-Luyan. You are educated and resourceful. Your insight into our ways is profound. Who you are is neither bound nor defined by what you may have been. The Goddess has brought you to us. Will you trust her and cast aside your fear?"

She spoke again before he could.

"I do not demand it of you, Luyan. Should things go badly ashore, you may never be able to rejoin the ship. If you elect to remain aboard, the navigator is willing to appoint you sailing master. The ship is yours, if you want it, and may the Goddess preserve you. Consider it my heartfelt reparation for the death of your father and family. You are free to choose."

Luyan swallowed but did not hesitate. "I will go with the delegation, Kozhiniru."

She nodded gravely. They continued in hushed voices for another hour. The Kozhiniru formally appointed Luyan her personal emissary, as well as consul to the noble houses of Keftius. This made him the direct representative of both their temple and their court. The navigator would accompany and advise and provide the delegation the weight of academic status.

Ethtar told all she knew of the city ruler and high priest. She had a number of contacts among the noblewoman, as well as certain influential tribal leaders.

"Lady Talyera, please tell the navigator that I will be on the passenger deck before the evening meal to brief him and the other nobles," the Kozhiniru said.

Talyera bowed and left. The priestess continued in a more intimate tone.

"Luyan, Ser-Ethtar will be your kozhiniru once you go ashore. She is far advanced in our mysteries and bears the same obligation to instruct and guide as I do. She shares our purpose. She will stand beside you without reservation. I have explained your presence on the ship, how you came to be initiated into our order. I have asked her, for the sake of her people and my humble authority, to embrace you fully as *serkaru*. And I ask you to open yourself to her. There is much we have not had time to teach you."

Luyan bowed to Ethtar. In reply, she tapped her fingers over her heart.

The Kozhiniru continued, "I told you there were many devotions of ecstasy, many uses of the *tzeroru-ti usurai*. With it, we can test the divine will. Receive answers to our questions. This is a very advanced practice and dangerous for a recent initiate. But your participation may be critical to your understanding when it is most needed."

Luyan said, "I am willing, Kozhiniru."

They sat quietly for several minutes. The presence of the two *serkaru* teachers lent a synchronous clarity to his meditation. Ethtar's energy poured like boiling honey through his belly and loins. The Kozhiniru's was a crystalline flare before his mind's eye.

Finally, the Kozhiniru stood. "Divine Mother, we open our hearts and minds. Give these your children to know and express your will." She took their hands.

The invocation was not necessary for Ethtar, but helped Luyan grasp the purpose of the exercise. The Kozhiniru turned to him. "We now surrender ourselves to the divine, to seek guidance over our actions. An aid to navigation upon the bourn, if you will." She smiled.

"Are you to prophesy, Kozhiniru?"

"Prophesy is very different," Ethtar interjected. A prophet speaks for the Goddess. It is a crowning coupling with the divine, which usually closely precedes the death of the one so gifted."

"Now we shall speak not *for* the Goddess, but *to* her,' the Kozhiniru said. "We will frame a question and judge whether she has truly answered by comparing our experiences. Set aside your trepidation, Luyan. No harm will come to one purified by trust."

Ethtar squeezed his hand and closed her eyes and, after a few breaths, spoke. "Meri-heshtharu, what words or symbols would you have guide our delegation at Gubel?"

For the first time, Luyan heard spoken the sacred *serkarun* name of the Goddess. It resonated with names he knew. A breathtaking, ancient shibboleth.

The Kozhiniru said, "Begin."

The *tzeroru-ti usurai* commenced almost at once. Less expansive, more directed in its vitality than the group exercises. No spinning or dancing was evoked. His head lifted as though a golden thread were pulling him upward. He recalled the instruction to submit his mind as well as his body. He released the complexities that plagued him. His worry for Hibya, the strain between the communities, the imminent sense of disaster. The god-fear.

And as he surrendered his will, the divine will made itself known. The sunlight filtered into the forepeak, mottled by the sway of the tapestries. It seemed to coalesce, spiral within his chest, behind his eyes. It held no menace. Instead of constricting, it expanded him, rooted him in the confidence of its eternal companionship.

The answer to the question was clear. The serpent was the sign under which they were to greet the leaders of Gubel. The serpent would be there to provide the words, the wisdom to face their task. The outcome was not given them to know, but their fate was in the hands of the Goddess. They would not be alone.

"Finish," the Kozhiniru said. They had no need of words to confirm or interpret an answer all three had received so clearly.

Ethtar smiled and breathed a deep sigh of relief. "They have not worshipped the symbol of the serpent for many generations. It stands for wisdom, and wisdom is their only salvation now. At least it will leave no doubt. Our way is clear, Kozhiniru."

At that moment, six hundred miles to the northwest, its shores and peaks still covered with meters of ash from its last eruption, Thera stirred again.

The Kozhiniru had been right. Hundreds of *serkarui* had survived deep in the sacred caves of Thera, praying for their people's deliverance. The earth under their feet now trembled, then dissolved and swallowed them as the magma chamber melted through from below. The lava streamed into the central caldera and kissed the oceans for the first time in ten millennia, creating a plume of steam more than twenty miles high, bearing millions of tons of sulfurous acid into the stratosphere. More seawater flooded down through the new fissures, instantly sealed in by the hot liquid stone and mixing with new magma boiling up from below, creating a pressure chamber of immense proportions.

The base of the island was now a colossal incendiary, a league in diameter. It was only a matter of days before the next surge of magma would set it off, and a hundred cubic miles of molten and solid rock would blast upward and outward, sending the island's mountainous walls crashing into the ocean to catastrophic effect.

Thera's next outburst would change the map of the known world.

16 Pulse of the Heart

"There is a land of the living and a land of the dead, and the bridge is love, the only survival, the only meaning."

—Thornton Wilder

12 March 1769
Lt. S. Singer, HMRN
At Sea

My Dear Girl,
    Our lookout sighted land this morning, which came as welcome news, though we are still one or two days from reaching soundings off Donostia. Jeroen questions me on many matters, forgetting in his mounting excitement that, despite my roots, I have never before sailed the Bay of Biscay nor set foot in Spain.

But as my mother's native land draws nearer, her presence follows; I sense her lively eyes upon my actions, an awareness which rivals the intimacy we shared when I was a small child, as if I could reach up once more from that warm bath and hang upon her neck, catch the droplets falling from her hair upon my tongue, and hear again her soft Basque whisper.

With promise of ill-looking scars, my wounds are mainly healed, though I fret they may yet cause me misery. I have little idea of where, or how far, I must journey once we disembark, or by what means I might find Arima's family. My honest Jeroen has pledged his companionship for as long as I may wish it, asking only that I endeavor to interpret, if no fist as a guide. He grows more attached to me by the day, a condition I must deny finding disagreeable, as I recognize in him a likeness of spirit which would lie regardless of other *interesses*, and still, or perhaps all the more, were he fully sensible of my deeper nature and attributes.

But such ambiguities. Like overcast skies, they urge me heed closer my compass, for the voyage these letters chart is one of discovery, my dear, of unconcealed truth in the face of all you may have from the mouths of others upon my subject.

My last discoursed upon my later childhood and my maturing love for your mother, Eleanor. I believe that she loved me in her turn, but as I grew from the poppet with whom she shared bed and robe to assume what would become my place in the realm of manhood, the respective tracks of our sentiments diverged. I am convinced the same genius which frees her aesthetic imagination also binds her spirit; and the richness of her inner life may deny her the mental—I say not moral—faculty of empathy. I was all the more devoted for it. To love Eleanor is to see past that fragility of human response, and mistake it not for a numbed or crippled heart.

And alas, enter Captain Sir George Blunt. Long as I have avoided it, I must now write of your father. He is the only son of the late Rear Admiral Sir William Henry Blunt, heir of an English clan of minor nobility, but no small estate, whose familial manse is in Surrey. I know the Blunts have residences in London, and it seems to me Brighton as well. Nessie made his acquaintance through the remnants of her circle of London society, and I remember the day he first called at Portsmouth in my eleventh year. Over the course of several visits, Blunt made gestures to Nessie which, even in my immature discernment, seemed decidedly courtly, he some ten years a widower, and the two much of an age. His family had purchased his commission before the war with Spain, and during that conflict he'd been promoted and knighted, being well designed for active service, as his scarred face attested. I daresay Nessie indulged herself in imaginings of a title or indeed one day a peerage in the family.

Blunt impressed me as an overlarge, box-headed, slab-sided person of self-indulgent affectations, among these a crude patronizing of women and children. As I made my leg, he ripped off my hat and tussled my hair.

"Lo there, this must be the little man of the house, of whom I've received such fine report. No niceties amongst family my boy!

Think of me as your uncle—ha!" He turned to Nessie as if I'd gone suddenly deaf. "A bit delicate for nearly twelve, eh? He'll be curtsying next. Well, better a bitchy dog than a doggy bitch, I always say, what? Haha!" Wing shooting and fox hunting were the least unsavory of Sir George's enthusiasms.

But he surpassed himself in unciousness when he laid eyes upon fifteen-year-old Eleanor. Nessie had theretofore hesitated in presenting her, both for the financial liability a daughter represented and shame of what she termed her "little tendencies."

She need not have scrupled. Blunt was smitten by Eleanor from the outset; he took her slender hands in his hammy fists and pronounced her his "petal," she exhibiting her habitude of gazing at the point of her interlocuter's chin and never quite at the eyes. He never from that day ceased to use her as one might an injured sparrow—not, at all events, until their wedding night.

If Nessie was wounded by Blunt's precipitous shift of affection to her daughter—his junior by nearly thirty years—she gave no sign, a family peerage appearing the thing, principally; and for this I doubted I should ever forgive her. She agreed to the union.

And so, in the late summer of 1764, a few weeks after our return from that sojourn in France which I recounted in the first of these letters, and the very week I entered the Naval Academy, our Eleanor Singer became Eleanor, Lady Blunt, in a modest but quite *comme il faut* ceremony at Portsmouth Cathedral, a house reception following. In attendance were a number of my Laughlin great aunts who had overstayed their summer visit and could by no means be induced to quit the establishment before the wedding.

Indeed, my solitary ray of light that day was my great aunt Rhona, who arrived late to the ceremony from her side trip to Salisbury. Seated in the pew behind me, she gave my shoulder a comforting squeeze at the precise moment Eleanor stammered her vows. I did not immediately recognize her, having last seen her at the age of seven and retaining the principal impression of her long burnished copper hair, now flecked with gray and obscured by a powdered *perruque* in concession to Nessie. When she lifted a tiny corner of the wig and held a conspiratorial finger to her lips, I nearly burst out in laughter, as my early memories of her wit and charming good humour came flooding back, a tonic to my heart.

Later, in the garden, Rhona beckoned. She complimented me on my naval cadet's uniform and likeness to Hagen and presented me with a little beribboned box and regrets for missing my birthday. It contained three interlocked bands, two of gold and a middle circle of pure silver. She demonstrated how they rolled upon the finger to lie in a single nested ring of lustrous yellow, the lap of silver peeking out between. It being a whit large, she gave me also a gold neck chain of her own, that I might carry the ring under my shirt until the day it fit me. I embraced and thanked her warmly and was more grateful still for her company, her jocund frame a welcome counterweight to Nessie's presence, so different was she from her sister.

"With all my heart, *mo mhuirnín*. I've one or two more gifts I desire you to accept before you bundle off to sailor school," she said with her infectious smile.

The reception was breaking up, and we walked arm in arm through the garden doors into the drawing room, where my mother was conversing genially with a small knot of Laughlin cousins. I showed them my ring, and all praised its virtues, Arima clasping Rhona's hand and thanking her with an intense and searching smile. Having met on only a few prior occasions, the two women had taken a deep and immediate admiration in one another, and I remember Arima once saying that the *beauté caché* of Nessie's soul appeared upon the face of her sister. That's as may be, but in my view, Rhona's beauty remained all her own, and Nessie's better hidden.

The wedding gifts had been packed up, but two boxes still stood upon the drawing room table. Rhona gave me to open the first, an oblong mahogany presentation case that held a long-handled antique rapier of magnificent workmanship. I scarce breathed as Rhona explained that it had been made for my great-grandfather in the last century, and that now it was to be mine.

"May it profit you, the thing, as it did your ancestors," she said in response to my ardent expressions of gratitude. "And may you employ it with as much justice and more grace."

Wrought of burled onyx and ivory, the hilt lacked a knuckle guard, as featured in most modern rapiers, and its curious double pommel invited the free use of both hands, which well suited my physical frame and the style Arima had taught me. One of its gleaming steel quillons hooked toward, and the other away from the hilt, permitting me to trap my opponent's sword in either direction while protecting my hands. The blade was light and of slender taper but shaving sharp along its entire length. It came with a scabbard and belt, in which Rhona had punched another hole to fit my slender waist, and I was pleased that despite the weapon's overall length, much was taken up by the double handle, and it did not drag the ground when I wore it.

As I tested its delicate balance with several cautious passes, I made an inward vow to protect the beautiful sword as much as ever it may do me. My eternal love was sealed, however, when Rhona shewed me its secret: pulling back against the quillons with one hand as though drawing a bow while twisting firmly with the other, the handle parted to produce a separate dirk, turning one weapon into two. Her cousins applauded boisterously at the little parlor trick, and Mary passed more tea as I practiced the use of the mechanism.

Only a square cherrywood box remained on the table, which Arima gently pushed toward me. With a questioning glance, I opened it to find a brace of heavy pistols bedded in red velvet—the very ones which my father had received upon leaving for the academy twenty-five years earlier, and which had guarded him throughout his navel service. I at once abandoned my manly grandeur and embraced my dear mother, knowing the gift was among the few surviving relics of Hagen her fated journey from Spain had left to her.

"Ah, I nearly forgot!" Rhona said and sent Mary to her room to retrieve her last gift. It was an elegantly embroidered bag of oiled sailcloth with leather handles.

"What is it you English sailors say for the bag of valuables, the purse which holds all you would need if you abandoned ship . . . a 'ditty bag,' is it? Well, this one is yours."

I was overwhelmed with her kind generosity. The fine needlework must have taken months, and while decorative ditty bags were a point of pride for seamen, the deep purple pleated silk lining was exceptional. Rhona informed me that the lining could be easily removed if needed, but she hoped I'd leave it in for her souvenir.

Before her early departure the next day, Rhona led me to a secluded nook of the atelier and sat with me on cushions, in much the way of Arima and Nessie when in privy council. I was a bit muddled by the formality of the meeting.

She asked me if there was anything I needed, materially or morally, that she could provide, or any question she could answer in the short time she had. Still suffering from that paralysis of sentiment Eleanor's abrupt marriage had caused me, I was at misery to search my heart, and made no answer.

She pressed her hand to my breast, over the triple ring which hung there below my shirt. I started, but her manner was so bright and kind that my unease melted straightaway. Indeed, the very feel of her hand over my heart and the sound of her voice had a soothing, purifying virtue.

Her smile remained, but her mien grew intense. "I beg you not hate my sister overmuch, and that you remember that the burden of great wisdom can imbalance an injured soul." She paused a moment and studied my face. "You suffer, *mo mhuirnín*, and your tests are not yet over," she said. "But come the needed time, don you that ring and cast off all else—mark you my words—*all* else save your sword and ditty, and the purse your mother gave you, and you search me out, do you hear?"

I was confused, but I nodded. She bade me repeat her words exactly, which I did, and this visibly satisfied her. "Well and good, then. Make your way to any port in Donegal, some one of many women there will spy that ring and address you. Identify yourself to her, and she will reunite us."

I smiled. "Now embrace me," she said. "We shall meet again, *a chuisle mo chroi.*"

After she left, I asked Mary Rosedew the meaning of that Gaelic phrase, but my poor rendering made it difficult for her to recognize it with her Cornish, and she was in any case not certain it was, like many Gaelic expressions, precisely Englishable. She suggested I put it to Nessie, which I did that same afternoon over tea.

The old woman pondered for a moment, her face lined in a manner I had rarely seen and which may have approached sadness.

"I suppose it was from Rhona you heard those words?"

I owned that it was.

"Well, *a chuisle mo chroi* signifies 'the pulse of my heart,' which it's a sentimental expression among the fonder sort of Irish." She sipped her tea. *"Mo chroi',* forsooth. It may interest you to know that it was to my late husband, your grandfather, David, that my good sister, Rhona, first spoke of her heart. There's a heart that pulses fast and is a whit too easily warmed, you may understand. A heart, Selkie," she met my eye with a piercing glance, "is not a thing to be trusted. Not one's own, nay, much less that of another."

I was taken aback to notice a wetness in her eye.

Eleanor remained at the house, which now became one of several residences in the convenience of which Blunt indulged himself, dividing his attentions between his new wife, his gun dogs at Surry, and a variegated host of young persons in London, where his vicious bachelor life continued unabated. His sojourns at Portsmouth soon took on a spontaneous infrequency, and even Nessie's admiration for his character began at length to blunt itself, if a Birmingham pun may be forgiven me, she keeping more to May Fair to avoid his company.

As was required of students, I took up principal lodgings at the

Naval Academy by the dockyards but was permitted to visit back at the house on Sundays and holidays, thus never long deprived of home and family. My studies posed me little challenge and much enjoyment. The grounding in French, history, and mathematics provided me by Arima placed me well ahead of the first year cadets and left me leisure to excel in navigation and seamanship, which I liked of all things. I was most pleased by our practical exercises of a Saturday on the training hulks and above all the short ventures out into the Channel on the academy cutters. I was well regarded by most of the class, which I think less for my amiability than my status as a Portsmouth native with local knowledge and society—a useful companion on liberty.

When not carousing, the principal diversion of the young gentleman, as we for better or worse referred to ourselves, was fighting; and despite my every attempt to avoid it, I was called out on a handful of occasions during my first year. These little frays rarely rose to the seriousness of mortal dueling; pistols were never employed, and satisfaction was invariably claimed at first blood, if not before.

Howbeit I found a certain fascination in observing the role such exercises played in the social formation of young men; the code of mature male honor seeded by the divers little insults and challenges, the repartee of seconds, negotiation of terms, the worded and reworded apologies. As well for me that fisticuffs and wrestling are not fit forms of gentlemanly combat, as my stature increased little; but Rhona's gift and Arima's training served me admirably, and I found I had carefully to check the nuances of my swordsmanship to avoid injuring my opponents or even quickly humiliating them. More than once, after an honorable showing, I feigned defeat, needlessly yielding to young men for whom I held no animus or some furtive affection. My native passions have ever urged me to conciliate rather than conquer unless justice may definitively not be so served.

During my Sunday visits home, I began to notice subtle changes in Eleanor's demeanor within weeks of her nuptials, the magnification of her native reticence to communicate being one, and I at length put the matter before Arima. The relationship between my mother and I was such that little or nothing was ordinarily withheld, and her hesitation in responding concerned me.

"The condition of marriage can be a shock to a young girl, above all one of Eleanor's sensitivity," she said. "There is of course the disparity of age, and Sir George's . . . limitations and predilections."

I stared at her. I had never known my mother, in her life, to equivocate, and her English was by then as good or better than my own.

"What precisely do you mean, Mother?" But try as I might, I could extract no more from her on the subject.

It was that Christmas I next saw Eleanor and her husband together. Blunt was seeped in sherry by midday and, when not bellowing off-key from the window at each visiting band of carolers, was impatiently pressing Eleanor to accompany unidentified melodies on the pianoforte, his recollections commonly limited to a few disconnected notes.

"No, no, that's not it!" he roared imperiously. "Shut your cow eyes and just listen, will you? Pom POM! Pompum pom pom pum POM POM! The *Christmas* song, for all love!"

Eleanor's hands were trembling, and she was reaching a state of anxiety I had not seen since her childhood, which would soon set her to rocking in the corner with her wrists over her ears.

Nessie had left hours earlier, after Blunt had begun drinking, to visit her gift boxes upon the vicar. I was about to intervene when we were saved by the doorbell and Bridger's voluble announcement.

"Lieutenant Matthew Porter and Sergeant Christopher Turnbull of His Majesty's marine regiments, to pay their brief respects of the day, if you please, sir."

Bridger's reference to their retired military ranks was calculated, I believe, to draw Blunt's interest from his awkward persecution of Eleanor.

"Ah ha!" he said, "Arima's redcoats! Do come in my good men, and happy Christmas to you both! Bridger, there, put up the sherry and bring down some rum."

Arima was delighted at their appearance. She asked Eleanor to see to their tastefully bundled gifts—colorful marzipan sculptures, sugared almonds, preserved fruits and gingerbread, together with jars of Christopher's own black currant jelly—while she made formal introductions.

"May I name Captain Sir George Blunt of the Royal Navy," she said.

Blunt made a wink at Arima and an unsteady bow. "Your servant, gentlemen. I was regretfully deprived of the honor of making your acquaintance at the wedding reception."

Matthew spoke for both, knowing that rank and nobility were among Christopher's aversions. "I assume the good widow Singer had a generous surfeit of friends already packing the guest list, and though we were sorry to be absent, we hear the affair was quite the thing. I give you joy of your marriage, Sir George," he said, accepting and raising his grog. "And a happy Christmas to you."

"Do stay awhile, my good sirs," Blunt said after draining his cup.

Christopher looked uneasily about.

"Nessie is not here," Arima assured him.

"Posh!" said Blunt. "What's that to it? The lord of the manor invites you, eh? There's no refusing, haha!" He placed an arm around Christopher, who visibly suppressed a wince.

My uncles stayed to dinner, much to Nessie's discomfiture. Finding them there upon her return, she coldly retired without a word. Eleanor took the opposite end of the table from her husband, she having become the reluctant lady of the house, at least during his erratic visits. Blunt seated my uncles at his sides and next at hand myself and Bridger, it being our custom to include the staff in Christmas celebrations, and the family to serve them at table. Arima and Mary Rosedew joined Eleanor. Though a coarse display of etiquette, the women no doubt found the separation by sex agreeable, having no desire to be nearer to Blunt.

A line of capital wines accompanied, spoils of our party tour in France: white Anjou with the oysters, a rich red Chinon with the goose, superb Porto to follow pudding. The men partook of all, but I had little appetite. I was disadvantaged, as all three had significant sea service, including several actions, and spoke in that nautical manner of their mutual acquaintances—those officers with whom they'd shipped at one time or another. Indeed, I was stricken to be included in Blunt's table talk when he asked, in what he imagined to be a hushed tone, our opinion of his "little harem," tossing his massive head in the direction of the ladies.

My face clouded. Matthew clapped a hand to my shoulder and whispered me with a strained smile.

"Steady on, it's all the bottle talking."

Blunt did not fail to notice my discountenance, however, and amused himself with a farcical apology.

"Do forgive me, young Singer, for forgetting to include you in the reference!"

I replied coldly. "I beg your pardon, sir?"

Christopher intervened. "Cap'n's just talkin' facetious, is all, ain't that right, Sir George?" He refilled Blunt's glass with forced jocularity. "Little Christmas jest, all in bonhomie." He set the bottle down firmly and raised a toast. "To our fine ladies!"

"Hear him!" responded the men. I stood to pour and made my way to the end. Eleanor had not even sipped at her glass. Mary gave me a meaningful look and pressed my hand, and I glanced toward the kitchen.

I stepped out on pretext of retrieving another bottle of Porto, and Mary followed with a tray of cleared flatware and remains.

"Selkie," she said with a troubled air, "may we sit together?"

I hesitated. "You mean . . . ?"

"Ayes," she said. "I'm askin' fer a council in whisper. Will you oblige me?"

We sat on flour sacks in the corner of the pantry. Mary stilled herself in contemplation for a few moments before beginning.

"I'm brae worried for our Eleanor, Selkie. Each time Sir George is in the 'ouse, she gets some drawn in. Scarce talks a'tall. It's as 'er glim is blinkin' out, like. She ain't touched the piano in weeks." She bit her lip. "The last few days since 'e's in for Christmas, she won't even bathe of a mornin'. When I finally got 'er shift off n 'er, there was such bruises, Selkie!" Her eyes went wide on these last words. "I'm afeared to tell Arima of it!"

"Why should you be? Arima has a strong bearing," I said.

"Atlas ain't in it." Mary's formation in the classics had not proven unfruitful. "But it's 'er power frets me, too. What she might do to the stuggy cack if she found 'im out. She dotes on that girl like she does you, Selkie." Her eyes flashed again. "And she'd kill or die fer you."

I sighed deeply, quieted my mind, attempting to banish the vengeful ire that I felt, and fixed my eyes on hers. Mary had come to me as a counselor, not a protector; she deserved my comfort and guidance as much as Blunt did my blade.

"But there's more, Mary, isn't there? What else has happened?"

She hesitated, then lowered her whisper. "I faced 'im down on it. 'Sir George,' says I in 'umble manner, 'these bruises of Eleanor—has yer 'onor remarked 'em? You don't suppose she's fallin' off the bed in 'er sleep, do you, sir?'" She blushed as she paused. "'E frames me with 'is oogly leer and says, 'Me little petal's too delicate fer that stoney bed. She may need to sleep with somethin' softer against her skin. Somethin' with more stuffin' to cushion the falls, like,' says 'e. And there 'e gropes me some sinful. In back."

I fought the urge to precipitate out to the dining room and call the brute to account on the instant.

"God fergive me, I even thought of it." She blotted a tear with her apron. "Of acting as makeshift fer the girl, you understand, when Blunt were drunk of a night. If that's what it took."

I clasped her hand and shook my head.

"I dreaded it on enterin' service," she continued. "But I wouldn't be the first 'ousemaid bedded by a master, and if it guarded our poor Eleanor from such abuse . . ." She stifled a sob as her pitch heightened with emotion. "She's not fit fer it, Selkie. It shall addle 'er. And do fer what's left."

We sat in quiet again for several minutes before I spoke.

"Mary, you are family. I love you, as I know Eleanor does. I cannot suffer such a sacrifice as you propose, and if Blunt offers you any further insult, I pray you tell me." I searched my mind and heart for the necessary words. "You are not alone in this, Mary. We are together."

I vowed to visit more often, above all when Blunt was in Portsmouth. After the table was cleared and Blunt snoring soundly in an armchair before the fire, I drew my uncles aside to the front parlor to advise with them.

As to Mary's disclosures, I was bound to secrecy, but presented my own concerns on the subject. They too had noticed Eleanor's plight, and their worldly impression confirmed what I already knew. I recounted Arima's mention of Blunt's "limitations and predilections." Matthew and Christopher regarded one another.

"Arima is a wise woman," Christopher said. "But she's puttin' it kindly. Your Cap'n Blunt has a reputation in the naval service, Selkie."

"And in London society," Matthew added.

"He takes his pleasure from his position, and it makes no odds with who, so long as he can subjugate 'em," Christopher said.

I stared blankly.

Matthew tried to put it into comprehensible terms. "Selkie, many ship's captains relish the abuse of power, especially at sea. But there is a breed that extends this distorted delight to the dark of their cabin, if you understand me." I feared I was beginning to. "To such men, the gender of . . . I shan't say their 'paramours,' as affection doesn't enter into it, but . . . the objects of their lust, is often indifferent."

I reflected. "So Sir George is, as who should say a pederast?" My face betrayed my regret for choosing the word the instant I let it slip. Christopher was gracious enough to return me only a reassuring chuckle.

Matthew smiled. "No, no, my dear. Blunt is by no means like us. His behavior is not an expression of love, unorthodox or otherwise. It arises instead from a deep self-vitiation, I think. A compulsion to inflict pain or dominance without which he cannot . . . fulfill his bodily desires. Junior midshipmen while at sea, poor working girls, or boys, onshore—it's all one. Whether penury, youth, or lack of rank, it's helplessness that draws him, like a hawk to a crippled field mouse."

"Oh, Eleanor," I sighed with a miserable shudder.

"Listen now, love." Christopher turned my chair to face his. "This is serious business. I know you want to protect her, and we're full in it, at your service. Just say the word. But mind this—you are no more secure than she is from 'is likes. Blunt's a dangerous sort, Selkie. Powerful of body, position, and purse, and without a godly scruple to 'is bosom. Be grateful when 'e sates 'imself numb with drink, and wha'ever else his blood craves. He's liver-grown and gouty, and, I make no doubt, battling impotence. It's 'is frustration is most dangerous to Eleanor, if you take my meaning."

I nodded slowly. "I must call him out."

"No, sir," Matthew responded with the firmness of command. "As skilled as you are with that pretty little rapier, you will not sue for a meeting. You are thirteen and half his size. And he is deadly—the killer of three men that I've heard of—and beastly unwilling to give quarter."

Christopher glowered. "You just leave 'im to me, if it comes down to it."

"Send for us at any hour, my dear," Matthew said. I embraced them both tenderly before seeing them quietly to the door. It was snowing and too late for a shay. The companions turned up the collars of their coats and linked arms for their long walk back to the dockside through the deserted streets.

Deep in reflection, I stood watching them through the side window until they vanished in the night. I have never ceased to be thankful for the presence of these two fine men in my life, not only for the link to the father I never knew, but the unassuming insight they provided of that adult male realm into which I found myself thrust.

The house was dark and cold as I stepped back through the hallway. Thinking all were abed, I was startled to hear a snort and creak and scarcely perceived Blunt restlessly stirring in his chair by the dying embers of the fire, muttering unintelligible words of discontented tone. Without lighting a candle, I strode to the sideboard, poured a full gill of rum into a noggin, and held it to his lips.

"Happy Christmas, Uncle," I whispered. He took two semiconscious swallows before, to my consternation, his eyes fluttered open and tried to fix me with a bleary gaze.

"Petal?" he croaked. "Ah, there's my simple little piece." He clutched my throat with alarming strength, wrested the cup from my hand, and pulled me to my knees between his legs. "Put that stuttery gob to some use," he mumbled as he tossed off the rum.

Forgive me for leaving you here, but I find myself incapable of moralizing and empty of further narrative for now. I have written the night away and think to take a turn on deck for what the dawn may discover.

Your affectionate,
S. Singer

17 Spring of God

We are what we always were in Salem, but now the little crazy children are jangling the keys of the kingdom, and common vengeance writes the law!

—Arthur Miller, *The Crucible*

1602 BCE
Eastern Mediterranean
The Middle Bronze Age

The ship swept slowly into Gubel's harbor against the morning land breeze. A skiff with two harbormaster's agents pulled out to meet them. The navigator paid double the demanded fee and requested a mooring in an uncrowded area near the entrance, in case a hurried departure proved necessary.

A barge took off the delegation. There was a landing on the shore directly below the upper tower, but it would have required a steep climb up the stone stairway to reach the palace and administrative buildings. Instead, they were set on a dock off the main promontory and met by a small retinue of local officials and guardsmen, who accompanied them as they wound their way up the peninsula and through the port, making the more gradual and public ascent toward the acropolis.

Ethtar had left Quarta on board after their private farewell and swum into shore ahead of the party to arrange an audience with the city lord and high priest. Amid the sights and sounds of the great city, Luyan reflected upon his parting with Hibya. She had betrayed no anxiety.

"Nothing could keep us apart, my love." A brave smile and what they had come to call a "Cilician kiss."

He wished himself a measure of her certitude.

The navigator and Luyan were dressed in full Keftiun ceremonial garb and accompanied by four of the strongest rowers, armed with swords. Anekti had her *labrysu*, hidden under her authentic Egyptian robes. They rendezvoused with Ethtar as appointed. She wore the typical courtly garb of the Levantine and was accompanied by the wife of the high priest.

In train, the group approached the main palace. Luyan looked with wonder at the massive pillars and roof timbers, its entrance surrounded by Egyptianesque stilae. In the reliefs, he recognized the "smiting" or "thunder" god, known in Canaan by his Amorite name, Ba'Ēl Hadad. He was a broad-shouldered warrior figure raising a club in one hand and a forked bolt of lightning in the other. Luyan had never before seen him wearing the high, pointed crown of lower Egypt, however. It imparted an alien air to the familiar image. A blasphemous hybrid of northern and southern beliefs.

"He is one of many Ba'Ēl—the municipal gods of the Levantine," Ethtar said. "They have usurped the goddesses. Reduced them to the status of concubines, with feminized versions of the names of their male consorts. The ruling god of the Levantine pantheon is Ēl, their most high father god. Sometimes he is called Ēl-lohim, 'father of the host of gods.' Images of him are rare, as some sects consider it sacrilege to make idols of him. When he is depicted, it is most often as an old man with a long gray beard, sometimes with bull's horns."

"The name of the city Gubel means 'spring of Ēl' in old Amorite," Luyan added for the Keftiun speakers.

The navigator nodded and slowed to study the architecture, a reinterpretation of Egyptian design. Its resemblance to the palaces of Keftius and Thera was more than coincidental. The ancient relationship of the Egyptian and Keftiun cultures already existed when the Keftiu had colonized Canaan many generations before. The massive columns were capped with vivid frescoes of red-and-blue falcon's wings and glyphs depicting the city's founding, its great families, and its noteworthy battles. The Canaanites dressed in an imitation Egyptian style. There was no shortage of real Egyptians, however, and the harbor was crowded with merchant ships from the Nile cities. Gubel's role as Egypt's primary trading partner was apparent.

The high priest's wife demonstrated an amicable but cautious respect for Ethtar. She led the entourage to the entrance of the city palace and waited at the foot of the steps while the guards summoned the doorkeeper, who ran down and bowed to her. She mentioned the arrangements for an audience with the city lord. He escorted the delegation into the main hall. There Ethtar greeted the chief attendant and dictated to him names, titles, and other information necessary to introduce each visitor.

They were invited to wait on benches, and Ethtar took the opportunity to further brief Luyan on what to expect. The city ruler was Adad-Sin. He did not hold himself out as king, as he was under the protection of two greater powers: the Egyptian Pharaoh and King Indilimgur of Ebla, the Amorite capital to the northeast. Indilimgur not only shielded Gubel from the Hittites, but also provided it with lapis lazuli from overland trading partners farther east. The blue stone was primary among the exports that made Gubel so important to Egypt. Indeed, the city's protector goddess, Ba'Ēl-at Gubel, was sometimes called the "Lady of the Blue Stone." After paying initial respects to the city ruler, the delegation would pass across for a visit to the temple named for her.

The ancient shrine had originally been dedicated to Ishtar. But the mother of wisdom had lost status over the centuries, and the temple goddess was now little more than the consort of Ba'Ēl Hadad. Ba'Ēl-at Gubel's descent in the pantheon did nothing to mute her popularity with merchants and rural farmers, however. Her temple formed the highest point of the acropolis and commanded a sweeping westward view of the sea.

After a short wait, the delegation was summoned into the palace's great hall, its thick columns draped with purple tapestries, where Adad-Sin sat upon a raised platform before a writing table of polished ebony.

Luyan was surprised to see that was a spare man with an unhealthy, jaundiced complexion. He'd imagined all noblemen to be fat with rich food and indolence. Adad-Sin's attire was semiformal, the meeting a mere part of his daily administrative schedule. He wore a draped Egyptian-style headdress, decorated loincloth, and colorful sleeveless linen robe. A gold chest plate was visible upon a chain around his neck, dipicting a falcon's outstretched wings spanning from a central cartouche with simplified hieroglyphics. Beneath each wing was a figure of a horned bull.

On Adad-Sin's thigh was bound a gold ceremonial dagger, elaborately etched. Comparing its workmanship and hieroglyphics to the more crudely wrought breast plate, Luyan concluded that the dagger was likely of authentic Egyptian origin, a token of the authority delegated him by that great southern power. He was surrounded by a few court officials of various rank. But no women.

The lord navigator was introduced first, by his administrative rank and the name of his Keftiun royal house. He presented his gift—a necklace of amber stones set in gold. Adad-Sin acknowledged with a polite nod.

Next, Luyan was introduced. He was surprised to hear that he had been assigned a priestly rank as well as the title of emissary of the high priestess of Keftius, whom the attendant referred to as the "Kozhiniru-Entu," combining her Keftiun and Akkadian titles. The city ruler studied Luyan with curiosity but made no overt reference to his visibly Anatolian—and potentially Hittite— features. He showed particular interest when Luyan opened a small ebony chest compressing a dozen swatches of sea silk, which poured out with the material's characteristic drama.

Adad-Sin gave no acknowledgment of the high priest's wife as she broke in to formally present Ethtar. He was familiar with the local *serkaru* leader. He impatiently interrupted the introductions to address her directly.

"Yes, the queen of our mermaids." His grin reminded Luyan of a spoiled child.

The attendants opened her chest of pearls at the foot of the platform. After pausing to be certain her gift was noted, she replied with a bow of her head.

"Far too dangerous a title in these times, my lord."

Adad-Sin searched her face for sarcasm. Although he bore her no personal dislike, she clearly made his court officials uneasy. He continued in a fluid vernacular, a personal aside to a fellow Canaanite leader.

"Yes, for all our blessings in trade, I wriggle like a fish in a basket," he said. "Beset by alliances, both human and divine. From the north, the Amorites, whose gods and patronage I must court in exchange for lapis lazuli and their protection from the Hittites. From the south, an insatiable Egyptian appetite for the blue stone, as well as our cedar and oils. I must demonstrate allegiance to Pharoah as well or face conquest. Meanwhile, the timber supplies dwindle, and the farther east we cut, the more our crews are ravaged by growing hordes of Habiru bandits."

Ethtar smiled in recognition of this confidence. An acknowledgement of his respect, if not affection. She nodded at Luyan, who presented Talyera, with a description of her descendancy from the Keftiun ruling houses.

She was dressed in a full floor-length skirt, fitted tightly at the waist and belling out in alternating layers of purple and yellow. Her hair was coiled in the traditional manner, a number of hanging ringlets held by a gold band around her forehead. She wore a formal corselette and short vest that accentuated the narrowness of her waist and the prominence of her exposed bosom. On both her upper arms and her ankles were coiled golden serpents.

Adad-Sin eyed her keenly. "I am pleased to see that the fashions of Egypt are still so well preserved at the courts of Keftius. I do not understand why a beautiful girl would wrap herself in so many serpents, however," he said, turning to Ethtar with a twisted smirk.

Talyera had the breeding to respond to the compliment and ignore the sarcasm. *"Tudah hod, enia,"* she replied in courtly Akkadian. "Grateful thanks, my lord."

Ethtar interjected. "Our noble visitors are from your ancient motherland, my lord, where even the great Goddess entwines herself with serpents."

Repartee was one of Adad-Sin's many diplomatic talents. "Yes. Yet even Ishtar herself fears of them," he said with a pointed glance at Luyan. The quote was from a well-known Luwian myth.

Taking Talyera's measure one final time, he turned his eyes to Anekti. Noting upon this closer inspection the authenticity of her wrap, layered wig, and the classic Nubian contours of her face, he sat up slightly in his seat and addressed her in enthusiastic Egyptian.

"*Iiwy em hotep nefer weret sat-Kemet!* Welcome in the very greatest peace, daughter of Egypt!"

"*Aw ibek neb-i herey-tep, em hotep nefer.* Greetings, my lord mayor, in great peace," she replied cordially but coolly.

Anekti's introduction assigned her no formal title other than "lady." But it referenced her family roots—house names of distinctly Egyptian, not Semitic, origin. It also highlighted her role as liaison between those houses, the temple of Keftius, and the Kozhiniru-Entu. Her presence in the delegation appeared to have the effect the Kozhiniru had hoped—casting Adad-Sin in the shadow of potential accountability to his Egyptian masters.

In a gesture uncharacteristic for female visitors to a Canaanite court, but quite proper in Egypt, Anekti removed one of her gold cobra armbands and, instead of laying it at Adad-Sin's feet, stepped toward him and placed it in his hand. He reluctantly took it, assessing her again with his unrevealing gaze.

"*Em heset net Wadjet, neb-i.* The blessings of Wadjet be upon you, my lord."

Adad-Sin masked a momentary look of alarm, passed the object with two fingers to one of his attendants, and perfunctorily switched to Akkadian for the words of welcome.

"We honor your long journey to our shores. We praise the value of your goods and pledge the reciprocation of your peaceful intentions. May the blessings of Ba'El Hadad and the Lady of Gubel be upon you and your ventures," he said with finality. He directed the safe mooring of their vessel and the provision of requisite hospitality.

He added a seeming afterthought. "Oh, I am informed through the household of our high priest that you would like to make a visit to our grand temple. My chief assistant will see to it."

"Thank you, my lord," Ethtar said with a bow.

She turned and kept pace with Luyan as they made their way out of the hall. It had been a preliminary reception. They had already made formal request for a longer audience, during which they hoped to impart their warning. But Adad-Sin had not mentioned it.

"The weasel!" Ethtar whispered in Keftiun. "How lowly he regards the women of his court. He will not so much as acknowledge the wife of his highest religious official, though she stands directly before him."

As they exited the great hall and rounded a corner, she turned to Luyan and continued in Akkadian. "Ser-Luyan, Adad-Sin has chosen not to acknowledge us as a diplomatic delegation, deliberately treating us with no more status than merchants. This despite the lavishness of our gifts and the rank of our members. Merchants would have thrown baskets of sesame seeds and olives at his feet, not pearls. His pledge of protection was especially weakly worded. Should things not go our way, there remains a real danger that your ship and its company may be seized."

"Has he so little respect for Keftius?" Luyan asked.

She sighed. "Our position is not hopeless. Anekti's presence was helpful. Her deliberatly addressing him as 'mayor' underscored his position as an Egyptian vassal. Her wording was polite but not subservient. You must likewise maintain a demeanor of superiority and patronage. Any show of weakness may be exploited, not only by Adad-Sin himself, but by the other members of his court. His political situation is very tenuous. He is leaving himself options should our presence here prove unwelcome to any of the many religious or political interests."

Luyan considered her words as the group was led down the pillared corridor and into a side room. On a low refectory table surrounded by cushioned couches, a generous meal had been set for them, hosted by Adad-Sin's chief assistant.

During the meal, Luyan was again impressed by Talyera's social and political abilities. She kept the conversation lively while subtly steering it away from controversial topics.

The chief assistant gave them a description of their afternoon destination, the famous Temple of Ba'Ēl-at Gubel, and asked with genuine curiosity about the state of religious and political life in the Keftiun Aegean. He lamented past days when the trade between Keftius and Gubel had been brisk, before the increased competition for timber and copper. He discreetly mentioned the stories of Keftius's western supplies and wondered aloud if the flow of goods might one day be reversed. In a manner nearly befitting a vendor, he lauded the quality of Canaanite wines and oils as he offered them copious samples of each during the meal.

He began to instruct them on the proper protocols for a special temple visit—an opportunity for private worship—and what form of offerings to make, both to the gods and the temple officials.

Ethtar informed him that she had already arranged for the high priest himself to greet them at the temple entrance. They would not need his guide services. He set his jaw at this, but the display of influence clearly impressed him. The temple would not be open to the public until the following day—the new year festival, when the city "king" was bound in heavenly marriage to Ba'Ēl-at Gubel. While Adad-Sin eschewed the title, the ritual required a human representative of Ba'Ēl, and the Canaanites expected the city ruler to stand in.

The ceremony, like many of Adad-Sin's public actions, carried dangerous implications. The Egyptians deemed the role of living god proper only to Pharaoh. The Semitic peoples, even many Amorites, increasingly recognized no god but Ēl, the one most high father.

Ethtar had drunk very little wine. "Our guests have important words to share with Adad-Sin and the high priest. This was arranged before their arrival. Can you tell us when these will take place?"

"I have no knowledge of the high priest's arrangements," the chief assistant said. "The city ruler has general audiences in the mornings. Perhaps you could come and wait upon him tomorrow before the festival?"

Ethtar cleared her throat. Before she could speak, Luyan interjected.

"No."

The man turned sharply toward him with knitted brow, but Luyan continued unabashed. "Emissaries of Keftius's royal house and temple will not sit on benches begging a mayor's leisure. Nor did we journey so far to sit at table with servants. Mark me well. Our gifts were not tribute. And the news we have to deliver is of the utmost importance to the coastal cities of the Levant. You will present us an invitation to formal audience under Adad-Sin's seal for a set hour tomorrow. Else we pay the respects to your shrine proper to representatives of your mother civilization and depart. You may explain the consequences to your master at your leisure. We have every reason to expect a more gracious reception at Surru and Sidon."

The official stood stiffly and leaned toward him. The navigator rose in turn. But Luyan merely leaned back and folded his hands across his stomach. It was a pose he had often seen his Cilician commander assume—an unmistakable posture of superiority in eastern Mediterranean culture.

After several moments, red and trembling, the official slapped his hands and forehead on the table in submission. He refilled the cups, bowed again, and clapped for his retinue.

"Please summon the attendant when you have finished your meal, my lords."

He left the room with a deflated and malicious expression. The entire Keftiun delegation exhaled as one.

Ethtar grinned. "You have truly cast away fear, my little brother. Well done."

"Tell me, Ethtar, what was the significance of that final exchange in Egyptian between Anekti and Adad-Sin?" Luyan asked.

She leaned into the table. "The disdain Adad-Sin showed

toward the cobra was his way of subtley belittling our feminine wisdom tradition. The Egyptian Wadjet is the same divinity worshiped under the sign of the serpent in Keftius. By invoking her Egyptian name, Anekti made clear that should Adad-Sin reject us, he rejects the ancient protector god of lower Egypt. Not a politic move when Ba'Ēl Hadad still wears Wadjet's crown. Oh, and by the way, our new year celebration tomorrow?" She smiled wryly. "It is also Wadjet's feast day."

Luyan turned these connections over in his mind. For all Tarsa's secular conflicts, they paled in comparison to Gubel. He was gripped by a growing sense of imminent upheaval, not only in the natural world, but among men and gods as well. Despite his first impression, he now had no doubt that Ethtar, the leader of a community at an epicenter of cultic turmoil, was a formidable kozhiniru in her own right.

"Ser-Ethtar," he said, "may I seek whisper counsel with you when time permits?"

She unhesitatingly made the captivating formal reply he had first received from Hibya. *"Kudaru Ser-Luyan'm yam kyīkoru yibasai.* May Ser-Luyan's request bind my heart. We will sit together after your temple visit."

"Will you not accompany us?" Luyan asked.

"I would not be permitted entrance."

"Another male privilege?"

"It's complicated. In times past, the city ruler was vested with the dual role of priest king—a function Adad-Sin stills serves on ritual occasions. But in recent years, King Indilimgur of Ebla has sought to consolidate power over the cities of Canaan by installing his own Amorite priests in their temples. Women are allowed access with certain ridiculous restrictions. But as a priestess of a rival sect—a 'nature cult,' to Semitic thinking—I am banned."

She stood up from the table.

"We are thus a Canaanite city with Keftiun descendancy, Egyptian culture, and a Semitic priesthood. This, Ser-Luyan, is a very fragile equilibrium."

18 A Singular Debutante

"Don't you know that a midnight hour comes when everyone has to take off his mask? Do you think life always lets itself be trifled with? Do you think you can sneak off a little before midnight to escape this?"

—Søren Kierkegaard

13 March 1769
Lt. S. Singer, HMRN
At Sea

S weet Girl,
      The blustery dawn only irritated my sleepless eyes, and the deck being crowded with the crew at holystoning and swabbing, I repaired below to continue to write. I found dear Jeoren waiting with a restorative potage prepared me with his own hands, having begged boiling water from the galley.

The ship so near to land, the last of our stores are being put to lavish common use. Jeroen made contribution from his small personal stock from Japan—a sort of dried morel and fat grains of white rice—to make what he calls *oya-ko*, a savory stew of chicken topped with an egg. He smiled as I took several eager spoonfuls, and as its warmth began to line my stomach, it occurred to me to ask him the meaning of the dish's name.

"Oya-ko means 'mother and child,'" he said with a grin. "You are eating both. Chicken and her egg, you see? Good for the blood, good for the stomach. Help you sleep, Selkie."

Finishing the dish after reflecting upon its etymology was among the most difficult moments of my voyage, but Jeroen's intentions were so sincerely well that I could not reject them, and I spooned it down quickly with feigned relish for his sake.

You will wonder that after the incident I last recounted, I should have chosen to continue to serve for my Eleanor, as it were, in *locum tenens,* and I cannot deny that the same was indescribably disagreeable; but you might understand, dear girl, if you had witnessed the relief upon her face that next morning. Blunt, in lieu of visiting his debauched frustration upon her bed, had spent the night unconscious in the drawing room chair, satiated in brain and body. Despite Arima's remedies, his backsore and crapulous condition kept him confined for much of the next day as well, which multiplied Eleanor's joy; and she blossomed as she passed the morning at games, an impromptu poesy recital, followed by a delightful lunch and an exploration of Christopher's lovely gift hamper of sweetmeats. It was the first time she had smiled in many weeks, and I was glad to suffer any hardship, be it again and again, to have provided her solace.

I thus was not, and am not, ashamed of my course. I reprised Blunt's generous serving of spirits that afternoon and evening at dinner, as well as my lubricious ministrations later that night, dousing the embers of his mind and body and accepting my stripes that Eleanor might be allowed to heal.

It was evident to me that Blunt was not, at least in every instance, wholly demented of my identity during our assignations despite the dark of the drawing room and his extreme drunkenness. My hair is long, but I wear it clubbed in naval fashion, and although Eleanor and I are much of a size, I contrived to remain clothed, as I might not have had these *rencontres* taken place in a bedroom, and there is no mistaking male array. He often gripped me by the collar and pawed at the buttons of my waistcoat; and so on until the holidays drew to their end. When he returned to London and I to the academy, the busily salacious quality of his parting embrace proved my impression, and I marvel I held my gorge.

I endeavored to shake off these images and lose myself in my studies, often resorting to the practices of contemplation and controlled breathing Arima had taught me. Greater liberty was enjoyed by senior students, and though I attempted to align my visits home with those of Blunt, his appearances came most often unannounced. This unpreventable quality of life began to tell upon me nearly as much as Eleanor, and she more than once called me to her bed, that we might cosset one another as had been our innocent wont in childhood.

I became increasingly remote and fractious over the subsequent year. Late in my second term, I was surprised to find myself calling out a bulky senior cadet named McKennis for a lighthearted remark upon my smaller physical stature.

"I say, Singer! Was that little coat tailored bespoke, or did your mum sew it at home, along of kitting your sister's poppets?"

I would ordinarily have overlooked such a harmless jibe or even joined the lackwit in his laugh. But no—out we went to the dueling ground.

The cold and offhand ruthlessness with which I bested the hapless fellow astonished me as much as the gasping cadre of witnesses. I unsworded him with a slash across his knuckles and spun to kick out his legs, leaving him on his back with the tip of my rapier at his throat.

I demanded his apology, which he was slow to voice; I daresay in hindsight this was due to the breathless shock of his heavy fall.

"Have your mum stitch that, then," I said flatly and took my satisfaction with a cruel nick to his jaw.

If any good can be thought to have resulted from my shameful display of animus, it is that I was never again to be called out for the remainder of my tenure at the academy. I willingly covered McKennis's surgeon's bill and received with guilt his needless letter of apology. I entered my final year of study in a hipped and nearly friendless condition.

The week of my graduation, London was in disarray with the repeal of the Stamp Act, and matters were heating up on the North American station. Nessie recommended I pass for lieutenant immediately. The two years nominal sea time which my degree conferred, added to the several my name already carried by grace of false muster enlistment, qualified me to sit for the examination; and its successful issue would position me to accept an early commission, an opportunity ofttimes presented by wartime service.

Accordingly, I posted up to London for oral review by the Admiralty board and returned to Portsmouth to find my written orders waiting for me. I was rated midshipman ordinary of HMS *Persephone*, a ninety-six-foot brig which had been bought out of the packet service. She was a vessel of beautiful lines, fast and weatherly, armed with twelve thirty-two pound cannonades and two nine-pound long guns. When first I set eyes on her in Portsmouth harbor on a sunny June morning in 1767, I felt the pall of the past months begin to lift from my heart.

Although ultimately meant for coastal patrol between Halifax and the Chesapeake Bay, it seemed likely that *Persephone*'s packet duties would continue for a year or more, as the shuttling of dispatches and dignitaries between England, Ireland, and the North American colonies was of immediate priority. This happy circumstance offered me the hope of some liberty in Portsmouth every three or four months.

Arima, Eleanor, and my uncles saw me off at the dock. I lifted my hat in grand officer-like manner as the blue-and-white signal of departure was run up, and my family waived their handkerchiefs until I was lost to sight beyond the harbor wall.

We made our way out of the Channel and traversed the Irish Sea, our first mission to deliver a retinue of Lord Townshend's adjuncts to Ulster before making south to clear the westerlies, across to Carolina, and up the New England coast to Halifax. I experienced a pleasant sentiment of proximity to Rhona when we rounded Ireland and clutched her triple ring through my waistcoat like a talisman.

I acquitted myself to good report on my first cruise, overcoming the prejudice often attached to midshipmen rated by graduation from the Naval Academy in lieu of sea service. I was grieved to miss visiting home after that short sortie, as we put in at Liverpool; but upon my second homecoming six months later, I disembarked at Portsmouth with ten glorious day's liberty and an acting commission, earned by my honorable conduct in several small actions against coastal smugglers and for commanding the successful carrying in to Halifax of a prize vessel taken off the outer banks. I did not deceive myself, however, that this early promotion, and in particular its hasty ratification by the Admiralty, was not due in some part to the interest exerted by the Singer and Blunt families.

Arima and Mary shed tears of joy upon seeing me, and Eleanor in disconsolation at my having been absent for nine months and more. She did not seem well, and as I held her trembling hands in mine, Arima met my eye with a concerned look. When I at length had my mother to myself and filled the gaps in my letters, she turned to Eleanor's subject. I was nearly eighteen, and I think for this reason she abandoned her former reticence and spoke openly.

She avowed that she had been aware of Eleanor's discontent, but not until after I left for sea did the full severity of the circumstances appear to her. Arima had taken to secretly dosing Blunt with hellebore during his visits in hope of reducing his aggressive impulses, but this had availed little. I told her I'd found better luck in strong spirits, and she could not suppress a bemused smile at our similarity of instinct. I chose not to burden her with the knowledge of my having resorted to further, more personal remedies, this in my life the only time I ever willfully withheld anything from my mother.

Eleanor had taken often to hiding under the bed when Blunt was at the house; she sometimes awoke and clambered hurriedly beneath it when he arrived in the dark morning hours. A childish evasion, perhaps, but it was more than once effective, as after ranting and calling out for her in his drunkenness, he often collapsed insensible and did not rouse till midday.

With Arima's patient questioning, Eleanor had gradually revealed the nature of her conjugal torment. Although oppressive withal in his carnal tastes, the worst of Blunt's brutality followed his failed attempts to consummate the act. This in mind, Arima had altered the composition of his tea in an effort to alleviate the worst of his impotence and left the hellebore to Eleanor.

After a gentle but thorough examination, and further

questioning on the subject of her lunar visitations, which had been wholly absent for nearly a year, and before that of no monthly regularity, Arima sadly concluded it unlikely Eleanor would ever bear children, regardless of her husband's capabilities, and the same was confirmed by Blunt's London physician. As he is wont, he re-wrought this news in his mind as reason to cast further blame and aggression upon my poor cousin, and I burned at the injustice of this, as her condition, Arima said, had most likely been caused by Blunt's abuses in the first instance.

"Is Nessie aware of these matters?"

Arima sighed. "There is very little of which your grandmother is unaware. She remains hopeful that Sir George will soon go to sea and remain away for a year or more."

"Yes," I said. "He is to command a ship of the line on the North American station. The vessel has been long delayed in fitting out, but it has left the yard and should be fully manned, watered, and provisioned any day now, God willing."

Arima shut her eyes in a brief prayer. "So may it be." She regarded me with some concern. "And you, my love, how long do you suppose you will be away this time?"

I could not surely tell, but it seemed my next cruise was again to be packet duty, delivering dispatches between Halifax, Ulster, and London and ferrying more passengers of rank. The ship had undergone a general reordering of officers and crew, in my case through the happy circumstance of my promotion, and I was to berth this time in a wardroom cabin. I had been confirmed Lieutenant Sebastian X. Singer, HMRN by a beautiful cover under seal of the Admiralty delivered to the house that morning, along with orders, failing at my peril, to "report to the captain of HMS *Persephone* at Portsmouth harbor to take up duties as second lieutenant thereof on Friday proximo."

Arima read the documents several times, nodding slowly with pride, and I think with a certain melancholy of her memory of the last Lieutenant Singer, HMRN. As she folded them back carefully, she begged I pass as much time with Eleanor as possible before my liberty ended; to this I gladly agreed.

"She was at her best when you were a little babe, playing Momma to you or the few pets Nessie permitted in the house. Motherhood would have done her so well." She sighed. "Well, she will always have us, yes?"

"*Bai,* Ama," I agreed, reverting to Basque, as I kissed her cheek. "*Beti etxekoak gara.* We are always family."

After dinner, I desired Eleanor to play for me, but she declined. Mary said she had not touched the piano in several months. I chose one of her most favorite books of sonnets and read to her in the parlor until she took my hand and bade me accompany her to bed. Blunt was not expected, and much time had passed since we had last closeted ourselves together.

The little rituals of our childhood gave her solace: we washed, separated by a screen, then combed out one another's hair, leaving the replaiting for the morrow, and crawled beneath the quilt, she in her shift and I in my long shirt. We shared sips of her bedtime tea and whispered reminiscence of happier days, diverting particulars of my time at sea, and hoped for future journeys together abroad. She clung tightly to me, and I was saddened to feel her hunger for the press of a body that desired nothing of her but the warmth of her embrace. Long into the night, in the security of my presence, her breathing slowed, and she tumbled into angelic sleep.

I stroked her hair and watched over her for a while. l know not what time I drifted off myself, but I was roused in stages, as from a dream within a dream, perceiving a sound which became more definite at each repeating. I thought them muddled snatches of song, thus:

> "*The very last time I saw my love*
> *She seemed to lie in pain,*
> *With sorrow, grief, and anguish*
> *Her heart was broke in twain:*

Oh! there's many a man that's worse than me,
Then why should she complain?
Oh! Love is such a killing thing!
Did you ever feel the pain?"

This seemed to echo from a great distance. When all went quiet, I dropped back off until I heard again, and from a nearer remove:

"I wish my love was a red rose,
And in the garden grew,
And I to be the gardener;
'Tis then I could be true."

Arima's hellebore still weighed heavily upon me, but my mind became sufficient clear to draw the figure of Blunt picking his way unsteadily up the road atop his massive chestnut gelding, bawling what few lines of song he could call from his besotted memory between the pauses, which most of these he got wrong or amused himself in their farcical distortion. I felt for Eleanor, and finding myself alone atop the bed, I turned toward the wall to reach below it. Indeed, she was hidden there and clung onto my hand as I lay on my stomach, only letting go when she heard Blunt without the door of the room, the peals of his song shaking the floor and ringing her crystal bed lamp.

"I wish I was at Exeter,
All seated on my ass,
With a bottle in my hand,
And on my knee a lass.
I'd call for liquor merrily."

"Here now!" he cried as he kicked open the door, briefly bathing my loose hair and back in the weak light, took another swig from the bottle, and wetly blew out his candle. Before I could turn over, he placed his knee between my shoulders, and began a

271

snatch from another of his grim drinking ballads.

"Now I like a drop myself,
When I can get it sly,
And you, my bonny bairn,
You'll like it well as I."

"Haha! You'll like it well as I!" He grabbed a handful of hair and twisted, poured brandy over my face, and much into my nose and mouth, nearly choking me.

"Daddy's shipping out betimes, petal, but just you think of this when I'm away." He drained the bottle, cast it to the floor, and began to unbuckle the knees of his breeches. "Give Daddy a spice of that velvet before he's off to serve king and country, eh? That shy little quim may be as broke as your wits, but let's see if you can't make a change and do one thing right."

The breeches fell heavy upon the back of my legs. "The last for a time must last for a time. Best you make it a good'un, d'you hear me there?"

He knocked me in the back of the head with his elbow, hard enough that I saw stars. The blow stopped my coughing and jolted me into a sort of lucid resolution. Eleanor was safe beneath the bed, and Blunt far from sated. I relaxed my body and fixed my mind and heart two feet below.

"I'll have more for you when I get back, petal mine," he said as he fumbled and then began singing again, his tuneless rhythm drowning out my whispered groans:

"You shall have a fishy
on a little dishy,
you shall have a fishy
when the boat comes in!"

He laughed again, and my mind was so oddly detached from my body that I reflected upon and almost pitied him, the profound loneliness of his self-amusement. I fought to grow quieter still, that Arima might not hear. As deeply as it tore me, I conspired in his rapid release, the sooner to end the performance.

"*Dance to your daddy, sing to your mummy . . .*" he croaked to the tempo of our motions. I shed not a tear, grieved only that Eleanor was compelled to hear it all.

"*Dance to your daddy, to your mummy sing,*
Dance to your daddy,
Dance to your daddy . . ."

What seemed like hours later, scarce before dawn lit the window, I untangled my limbs from Blunt's snoring, sweating hulk and made my way silently to my own chamber. There I attempted to wash him from my body and the myriad stains from my nightshirt. For the latter, I used cold water, as the service teaches is necessary to remove blood.

I was not without some qualms to have left Eleanor alone with him but experienced a novel and native instinct to tend my own charge. Perhaps firsts give rise to firsts, and injury to liberation; but in any wise, I felt no longer a spy in my own life, but a kind of singular debutante, and no shame in comforting myself after such a baptism.

In a fresh, dry shirt, I sat before my table mirror. Would that I were numbed—indeed, quite to the contrary, the edge of my sensibilities felt fresh whet—yet the face that gazed back was of carved expression. I pressed in vain with my fingertips to smooth the furrow in its brow, the tight drawn mouth, but they remained when Arima appeared behind me, dim and silent in the gray light, and began to comb and plait my hair. We exchanged not a word, nor did I meet her eye.

When she finished, she lay her cheek to my head, seeming to know that I could not linger. Mary rapped gently and entered to lay out my new uniform—a gift from Nessie—and I donned the fine silk stockings and the spotless white breeches and waistcoat with little conscious feeling. I fastened my sword, slipped into the piped frock coat, comforted by the weight of its rich blue broadcloth, and took up only my hat and ditty bag, thinking me I would send for my sea chest. After a wordless double embrace, I walked out, cocked my hat against the rising sun, and made for the dockyards.

I stayed a few nights at my uncles' house, where I received Arima the evening before I was to report to the *Persephone*. Eleanor did not choose to accompany her, nor was she at the dock to bid me farewell the day I sailed. The newly painted brig seemed to shine in the midmorning sun, its yards squared, rigging blacked, and taffrails varnished. I forced enthusiasm when the new members of the wardroom and forepeak were named to me and was surprised to find myself met by my former dueling opponent McKennis, still a midshipman despite his having been a year ahead of me at the academy. I took only meager joy in being presented as lieutenant for the first time.

We were bottled up some while in the Channel by persistent westerlies. Not until nearly two weeks later did my malaise begin to lift as we cleared Brest and made a rough crossing to Boston, where we lay over to await provisions and better weather, taking on a handful of passengers before departing.

Among these was a physician of uncommon refinement and intelligence, Dr. Löw Benjamin, who was making his return to England after a year spent lecturing at Harvard College. He dined with the officers in the wardroom, a courtesy extended to passengers of rank, giving me frequent occasion for discourse with him. He was a Royal Academy member, born and educated in Alsace before setting up a successful medical practice in London; and he gave uncommon great lots of his time and money to the town's charity hospitals.

While the doctor's English was superb, and of but mild and quaint accent, it pleased him to speak to me in French when he took a turn on the quarterdeck during my watches. His prodigious education extended to linguistics and the classics as well as physic and anatomy, of which he had made physiognomy his special study. I enjoyed his commentary on a wide range of subjects, among them history, philosophy, and what he termed hermeneutics, and he complimented me often on my appreciation. He seemed astonished to learn that my formal study had ended with the Naval Academy, where no more humanistic education was given than scarce necessary for young midshipmen to pass for gentlemen.

Without disclosing overmuch, I credited my mother for my early formation, and it seemed the more I spoke on her subject, the more he wished to know, and he a widower; but despite our increasing friendship, he did not press me. If I demurred in my responses, he did not reframe his questions; instead, his intelligent green eyes took on a bemused glint, as though challenged with a particularly fascinating riddle.

Before our next call in Halifax, we took a long leg south in fulfillment of our general commission to distress unlawful trade. One clear afternoon off Long Island, we found ourselves chased by two small ships. These were a brigantine and a sloop out of New York harbor, seeking to bring to and board us in search of colonial seamen shipped by impress and generally to demonstrate dissatisfaction over other perceived oppressions. The *Persephone's* compact dimensions no doubt emboldened them; they would never have offered such insult to one of our frigates.

Though faster on a bowline than either of our pursuers, the breeze was well abaft our port beam, and we fired several shots with our stern chaser in attempt to warn them off as they closed. Their persistent effrontery at length vexed the captain sufficient that he ordered us to come about and bear down upon them. Our long bow gun put a shot through the foresail of the brigantine, which hove to without striking its colors, drawing us into a small but serious melee when a number of their crew attempted to shoot their way onto our deck.

As typical in colonial actions, our officers were targeted first.

Lieutenant Chauncey Honeysett took a harpoon to the neck, and I suffered a splinter wound in my right side when a ball from one of their swivel guns tore through the quarterdeck taffrail; but the captain and I cut down two of the boarders, and we at length forced them to disengage. The sloop then came in range of our cannonade; we put a single broadside into its rigging before veering off, and both vessels gave up the chase. The dispatches we carried being our priority, we made all possible sail and pressed on for Nova Scotia.

To his credit, Doctor Benjamin emerged from below decks well in advance of the all clear to care for the hurt, as we did not carry a certificated surgeon. He could do nothing for Honeysett: the harpoon had opened the poor man's jugular, and he expired bloodless, his face as white as a mackerel's belly. As for me, the jagged, six-inch shard of oak had pierced my coat high on my flank below my raised sword arm and lodged between two ribs. I refused the doctor's examination until all other of my shipmates were attended to, which the crew mistaking for valor, I believe earned me no small measure of their esteem.

The good doctor was more perceptive, however. Recognizing, as I was soon to learn, the true basis of my reticence, he desired me, in a volume audible to most of the deck, to retire to my cabin.

"And remove that good coat and breeches, if you please, Mister Singer, before they soak up the last drop of your blood, sir! I shall attend you presently."

The wardroom steward, thinking this a call to his duty, made to follow me, but the doctor held him back on pretext of needing his assistance with Honeysett's body.

My head spun as I negotiated the companionway. When I removed my frock, the reason appeared: blood soaked the entire side of my vestments and breeches and puddled in my right boot. I despaired, and not only for my life; I would not—could not—remove aught but the waistcoat, but I unbloused my shirt and carefully furled it upon my midriff. I crossed my arm tightly over my chest and held the shirt up with my left hand, just far enough to expose the rough wooden missile protruding from the pulsing wound.

It was upon my cot in this delicate pose Benjamin found me when he entered my cabin not a minute later, bolting the door behind him and addressing me now in whispered French.

"*N'aie pas peur, cherie, tu ne caches que ce que j'ai su il y a longtemps.*" He said these words with the kindest and most gentle of miens, but they made my breath quicken and my eyes flash in panic.

"*Fais moi confiance.* Trust me. The privity of patient and physician is sacrosanct, my dear."

I make no doubt that my loss of blood played a hand, but the purity of Doctor Benjamin's unguarded, dignified beneficence emboldened me; so grand a soul indeed it took to pierce the veil of my life's most longstanding interdiction.

I suffered him to remove my shirt. I gripped the head ropes of my cot with both hands and looked away as he swabbed. He quickly and expertly arranged his instruments and was about to uncork the laudanum but stayed his hand as his eyes passed again over my torso. He handled and prodded me delicately in places I had not before noticed a deep, swelling tenderness.

"*Eh bien, une chose à la fois.* First things first." He turned back to my wound.

He placed a leather crop in my mouth, and I bit down hard while he carefully removed every particle of wood from the fissure in my ribs and stemmed the flow of blood. His confident, experienced hands reminded me of Arima's, and I endeavored to remain still despite the pain. After he bandaged me, I lowered my arms, and he demanded of me my breeches.

I hesitated again by reflex, but he spoke with compelling reassurance.

"My dear, you are not betrayed by what you conceal, but by what you cannot."

Here he traced the contours of my jaw and brow with his fingertips, the schooled assessment of a cranial anatomist, to be sure, but it seemed to me not without some fatherly affection.

I arched my back with difficulty and trembled as he peeled the breeches off. Even my smallclothes were bloodied. I uncinched the loincloth of thick cotton with which I habitually girded myself, in antique style, under my leggings. Beneath that now lay exposed what Rhona had called "the purse my mother gave me," affixed comfortably by thin bands of strong byssus silk about my waist and legs.

The doctor lifted the object. Arima had designed it to hinge easily upward for convenience, and he palpated and examined it with interest, almost as if it were a veritable part of my body.

"Singulier," he breathed in an admiring tone. *"Question de droit de patrimoine, sans doute?"*

I nodded. An issue of inheritance rights, certainly. "But . . ." I paused. *"Plus que ça."*

He placed it inverted upon my naked belly while he examined me in greater depth, posing questions I'd never thought to hear from the lips of any man, and which I answered with the unthinking impulse of a gallows confession.

As for the object, it had been patterned, stitched, and stuffed with loving care by my mother during her long months of confinement nearly twenty years before, cut from the soft kid leather of the pinkish gloves bought shortly after her arrival on those strange English shores. She'd nested both together for strength and bulk, removed all fingers but one, and packed the whole tight and heavy with the cuttings. A pair of smooth stones deep within the pouch completed the illusion. These simple measures, and the embedded carpet tack which had made me to wail upon her groping, had proved sufficient to prevail over Nessie's examination and, with a daily trifle of saddle soap and lavender oil, to carry me through a lifetime of deception.

"There!" The doctor smiled. "Perfectly healthy. And now there are plans and preventions to face, *cherie.*" He seated himself upon a locker and wiped his hands and brow. "Plans and preventions indeed, yes."

But as philosophy maintains, life will out over the best of these, and you, my dear girl, are that life. No officer's rank or impostured male attire could alter or long conceal the fact that I was fraught, pierced like a heart-shot doe with your sweet living being and with you I would soon grow great and gravid.

And so, uncertain still of what you may know or thought you knew, I can no longer defer what my history now demands I put before you plain, and there it is: I am your natural mother, if natural I be.

There is more to tell, if more you care to read, and in any case I will in faith write it out. But enough for now.

Your loving,
S. Singer

19 Swords and Cedars

Who is she that looketh forth as the morning,
fair as the moon, clear as the sun,
and terrible as an army with banners?

—Song of Solomon 6:10

1602 BCE
Eastern Mediterranean

At the front gate of the palace, the Keftiun delegation was met by a retinue of palace guards, who accompanied them on the short walk to the temple of Ba'Ēl-at Gubel. The path led west between sloped walls of gradually increasing height, past the reflecting pool on the south side, a flock of sacred sheep and goats on the north, toward the towering temple entrance. With no external columns, it seemed impossibly high and made lavish use of massive cedar timbers, the region's most important resource. Its gilded double doors were topped in a lattice transom of the same wood, which channeled the afternoon sea breeze back toward the delegation in fragrant wafts.

A party of minor priests and acolytes were waiting for them, along with the high priest's wife. As perfectly balanced as they were on their thick bronze hinges, it took three men to open each of the ponderous doors. Luyan was transfixed as the view unfolded before his eyes. The long central hall, lined with stone columns separating it from lower ceilinged galleries on each side, was penetrated by the western vista of the sea, the setting sun backing a life-sized bronze statue of Ba'Ēl-at, the mistress of Gubel. Mirrors of burnished silver were angled to illuminate her face with reflected sunlight. She stood erect with feet together, wearing the horned crown of Isis—inwardly curved bull's horns around an orb of gold, adorned by two bright feathers of cobalt blue.

The goddess was surrounded by waist high cartouches carved in relief with the names of prominent visitors, and columnar votive tables holding offerings: small statues, gold, copper, and lapis lazuli objects of masterful design.

The high priest appeared silently from a side chamber. An ancient man of nearly sixty, he wore a white linen wrap with a purple-and-gold border draped over one shoulder. On his head was a conical turban of dyed blue fabric, its base clamped by a stub-horned gold tiara.

He welcomed the party in the name of Ba'Ēl-at Gubel. His wife led Talyera and Anekti through the doors, stopping to give them linen scarves to drape over their hair. The women made an immediate right turn and walked along a side gallery where cedar latticework separated them from the male worshippers in the main hall. Ethtar remained outside.

The men were invited to perform ritual ablutions in a gilded vessel set upon a cedar tripod. The bowl had been filled with clear water from the exterior reflecting pool and contained petals of fragrant blue lilac. Each in turn, they splashed their hands, faces, necks, and ears, a minor priest reciting the necessary prayers of purification.

The navigator and Luyan processed behind the high priest down the main gallery, his acolytes abreast. Two attendants rolled out a limestone column capped with a votive table and placed it before the goddess.

The high priest turned to face the guests and asked the purpose of their visit. This was their cue to express their required devotion and also an opportunity to place special petitions before the priest, who would intercede with Ba'Ēl-at Gubel.

Luyan replied. "We come to pay homage on behalf of the sovereign ruling house and high temple of Keftius. We ask permission to present our humble gifts to the goddess and the temple, and we seek her blessings upon our endeavors here on the Levantine coast."

The old man looked pleased. Invoking the blessings of the Lady of Gubel not only during their visit to her city, but for their entire journey in the Levant, was a pious compliment indeed. And inclusion of "the temple" was a clear offer of emolument to the high priest himself—never unwelcome or impolitic.

The navigator held forth an olivewood box. Within was a foot-long solid gold bull, its gleaming horns curved inward in the sacred Keftiun semicircle. A murmur of appreciation was heard from the high priest's wife through the side gallery lattice. An assistant passed the idol to the elder priest, who grunted slightly with its weight. He faced Ba'Ēl-at Gubel, and raised it with a prayer in arcane temple Amorite. Then he set it upon the empty votive table with reverence.

The acolytes deposited cushions on the prayer platform. The high priest tossed incense into the brazier at the goddess's feet and bowed in ritual supplication as he continued his intercessory prayers. No animal sacrifice was possible the day before a major ceremony on the religious calendar, but Luyan and the navigator were each given a handful of incense to offer.

After permitting them several minutes for quiet reflection, the high priest assembled the recessional party and led the guests out. The women followed along the side corridor and rejoined the men at the temple entrance. Luyan took a final look down the hall at the strangely violet sunset before the great doors were slowly shut—an artifact of Thera's ash still circulating in the western sky.

The high priest's wife addressed him. "Husband, I know you are busy with preparations for the ceremony tomorrow, but would it be possible for our visitors to have a brief audience?"

The priest cast a crimped eye on Ethtar but nodded at the navigator and led them toward stone benches in a gazebo overlooking the sea.

The navigator spoke in Keftiun, compelling Luyan to translate.

"We thank you for your prayers, and we are especially sensible of the compliment you pay us in providing a private audience. Before we begin, may I beg you to accept this token of our esteem and gratitude." He brought out a small onyx box from under his cloak. The priest's face softened perceptibly when he opened it. It contained a large red amber stone of unusual clarity. Holding it to the last rays of the setting sun, his eyes widened at the play of light through the translucent gem.

"A rare gift indeed, my lords," he said, reluctantly closing the box with a last glance. "Tell me now, how may the temple assist you?"

The navigator continued through Luyan. "While we have journeyed far, our task here on the shores of the Levant is only beginning. We have come first to Gubel, knowing the influence you wield over all Canaan. We are one of many delegations that have sailed from the Aegean in recent months to alert the coastal regions of the greater sea to a terrible coming disaster. One that will not only flood the shores and river basins, but will have far graver consequences for many seasons to come."

The priest looked unimpressed. "Your oracles have prophesied this? Your priestesses?"

Without waiting for the navigator to respond, Luyan shook his head and spoke.

"This is no prophesy, my lord, but a warning. The deep places of the earth in Thera have shown signs for many months. Just weeks ago, the mountain cast a vast cloud that obscures the western skies even now. I witnessed this event with my own eyes." He turned toward the sea and the dusky violet arc on the horizon. "I doubt my lord has failed to notice the unusual afterglow of the sunset. This is but a foreshadowing of the destruction to come."

The priest cast an appraising eye upon him and addressed him directly. "But you—you are not Keftiun, are you? You look Anatolian, and you speak with a Cilician accent. One wonders how it came to be that you act as temple emissary of these sea priestesses." He cast a jaundiced glance at Ethtar. "You are barely old enough to hold priestly office yourself."

Luyan's eyes met Ethtar's for a moment. He knew he must tread carefully. The high priest was no minor official. He needed to acknowledge the jibe, but without returning an insult that would extinguish all hope of the man's goodwill.

"There are many wonders in these exceptional times, my lord," Luyan replied. "Our own delegation has marveled to find a city of

Canaanites, the descendants of Keftiun blood, clad in cheap Egyptian linens and worshipping rain gods. One wonders as well how it comes to be that Gubel's royalty have abandoned their most sacred religious duties."

The priest studied him sourly for a moment. "Adad-Sin is no king. Nor is he of sufficient piety to intercede with the gods." He leaned toward Luyan and pointedly added, "*Our* northern gods. And as for his Egyptianizing, it is just as embarrassing to Indilimgur as it is to the Canaanites."

Luyan was taken aback by the conversation's abrupt turn. He had not expected such unconcealed criticism from the Amorite priest toward the city ruler. The fragility of Adad-Sin's political situation was becoming evident.

Ethtar's raised eyebrows urged him to conciliate.

"My lord, the Kozhiniru-Entu is aware that your holy position makes it difficult for you to receive a foreign priestess, and we mean only respect in offering a male voice in her stead. Our lord navigator here is of the highest rank in our royal court and academy and can address any questions or reservations you may have. We need your support to convey the warning of the coming danger to Canaan. Other delegations have been sent to Egypt and Libya, but the fate of the Levantine coast may well hang upon your patronage, my lord. Little time remains."

The high priest was silent for several moments as he gazed out at the western sea.

"Throughout the northern Levant, my brothers in the service of Ba'Ēl have seen portents as well, predictors of great change, even destruction. They say a burning boulder, like a fiery snake from heaven, fell into the sacred lake at Aphek. A sign from Maridthu, or in the minds of wide-eyed rurals, the serpent goddess herself come to reclaim her land from Ēl."

He sighed. "If she spares us, I fear the earthly powers of this region will not. There are more swords left in the world than cedars." He turned his eyes slowly to Luyan. "If I agreed to help, what would you have of me?"

"We have requested a formal audience with Adad-Sin, in hope of convincing him of the truth of the warning we carry. But we have met resistance. Do you know why this might be so, my lord?"

The high priest nodded. "Tomorrow is a politically dangerous day for him. The timing of your arrival is surely either destiny or bad fortune. A reminder of his Canaanite roots at the moment he most needs to conciliate Egypt and the northern powers. I am of Amorite blood myself, but I serve this temple, dedicated to one of the last female deities venerated in these regions. The ceremony tomorrow represents not only the spiritual marriage of Ēl to the Lady of Gubel, but also the city's subjugation to the Amorite king. Should Adad-Sin fail in this demonstration of loyalty, he faces the possibility of deposition by Indilimgur. If he exhibits too complete an abandonment of the old ways, however, he risks an affront to Egypt, and even revolt by the rural Canaanites, who rely on the goddess for the fertility of their crops."

He turned to Ethtar. "You have made things more delicate by confronting him with your serpentine wisdom god. The image attests the common cultic roots of Egypt and Canaan. This is the worst possible time to remind the Amorites of that relationship."

"My lord, would you influence him to grant us a private audience in the forenoon, before the ceremony begins? Surely, our discussions need not be made public. If you supported the importance of our message, it might convince him," Luyan said.

The priest sighed. "Convince him, perhaps, but there's no telling of what. He has nearly as little trust in me as I have in him. And nothing is private in that court. Even his chief advisers have divided allegiances. The very fact that Adad-Sin has received you may be used against him by his enemies. They are very adept at swaying the opinion of the people." His face softened into genuine concern. "The bearers of bad news have historically not fared well in Gubel. Adad-Sin is more likely to seize your ship and behead you for bringing this evil to our shores than to thank you for warning us of it."

"Are you his enemy, my lord?" Luyan asked.

"You have a direct manner, young man." He reflected for a moment. "Adad-Sin is weak, but he is not without his virtues. It is no easy task being all things to all people. My first loyalty is to this ancient city and its goddess, and there is no telling how Egypt might react if Indilimgur were to enthrone an Amorite ruler here. No, I am not Adad-Sin's enemy," he said, casting his gaze toward the temple. "I am Gubel's friend."

The sun was finally fully set and the torches lining the path lit. The delegation were shown to the temple guest complex, where the high priest's wife had arranged a light supper and rooms for the night. During the meal, a messenger delivered a summons to attend Adad-Sin shortly after dawn.

Ethtar did not like its wording. It read more like a command than an invitation. As a precaution, she left the table early to swim out in the dark and warn the Kozhiniru. The ship would weigh anchor, row quietly out of the harbor during the night, and stand off and on at a safe distance offshore. Ethtar arranged to place three torches at the foot of the acropolis steps the following night if all was well with the delegation. If the signal were absent, the ship was to make sail immediately and set south down the coast without them.

By the time she returned, the meal had been over for several hours. She entered Luyan's chamber carrying a longstaff wrapped in linen and several scrolls in an oiled skin bag. Her hair was still clubbed and damp.

"*Ashyukui,*" she said. "The Kozhiniru sends her blessings as well as her message to the city lords. I have translated as best I could. You can read Akkadian in the old lettering?"

Luyan nodded. His cousins had tutored him in cuneiform. "It is the line writing of Keftius that mystifies me."

Ethtar smiled. "I would teach you if we had time. We must prepare for our morning audience with Adad-Sin. But first I have a promise to keep." She bolted the door and sat cross-legged in front of him.

Luyan mirrored her posture. She was nearly a head taller than him and carried an equivalent weight of lean muscle. Her shoulders were broad, considerably wider than her hips. She had a solid, determined jaw.

"The day has been full," she said. "Let us begin by meditating together."

He focused his eyes upon her navel, and she upon his. He exhaled slowly, and the birds in the olive grove appeared before his mind. He greeted them this time as amiable messengers of insight, not the pestering distraction they had once been. He breathed again and permitted his ideas of sense memory, form, even of self, to vanish with them. His fear of what the morning might hold began to spiral into nothingness.

"*Ser-Luyan, yam kyikoru-ti kahu, meroya vam kataru-min onshyeru'ch,*" Ethar began.

Luyan was moved by the wording of her invocation to whisper counsel. "Luyan, brother of my heart, behold this kinswoman of your tribe."

As he looked into her olive eyes, framed by her strong, perceptive brow, he found himself seized by a permeating, dulcet current. Different from his connection to Hibya, but equally powerful, this was his first encounter with *aishyu* in its kinetic manifestation—the perceptible love that bound all *serkarui*. Here was an unmistakable emanation of the human heart, surpassing all philosophy. The devotions, he realized, were more than exercises. They were a refinement, a reduction of human nature to its divine essence. *Aishyu* was love expressed, surpassing the limit of words. A dynamic experience that could be shared tangibly and directly.

"*Va'ashkyuka'y, Kahatu,*" he could only respond. "You bless me, Sister."

She tapped her heart. "What burden may I lift or share? What would you have of that which I am given to know?"

Luyan knew few of the ancient formulas. He replied with what seemed natural.

"I am inspired by your courage, your service to the sisterhood,

Ser-Ethtar." He paused to reflect. "I have learned much, overcome much in the past weeks. Yet still I feel . . . uprooted from the boundaries of my world. From the person I was. At such moments, I am plagued by doubt."

After a moment, she replied, "Who are we? From where do we come? To where do we hasten?" She smiled sadly. "These are the questions we all must face sooner or later. But for some of us, the universe poses them in a stark and painful manner and compels us to seek their answers at a young age."

"What I fear most is failing the Kozhiniru and my sisters. And Hibya."

Ethtar nodded. "It failure that I, too, most dread. Losing Quarta, as I have so many of my sisters, to the marauding fanaticism of this land. Losing my position in the community, the only family I have left. It took much self-reflection and submission of heart to recognize that I am—we all are—now in the hands of providence. The events we are living are no chaotic eddy of fortune. We all rise or sink together now, in the undeniable currents of the deep water. In this, if nothing else, you may take comfort."

"You and your sisters have suffered. I know your community no longer admits men into the mysteries. I am grateful that you have accepted me."

She switched into Akkadian. "It shames me to say it, but the divisions in this region are much older than the persecutions. Generations ago, when the stockpiling of food became vital to the cities, the shamans suppressed the rural fertility rites. The innocent diversity of nature worship was supplanted by monolithic granary temples, vengeful father gods who held power over rain and crops. Beliefs invented to control others, enslave others. To keep the people in constant fear of famine, flood, pestilence, and the end of days." She lowered her eyes. "Our traditions surrounding the leavening of bread, indeed all of our community's practices of ritual purity, derive from those times of upheaval."

Luyan smiled sadly. "The end of days."

"Yes," Ethtar sighed. "So long have we been menaced with the imagination that I resisted receiving the truth when it finally appeared from the west. I have much foolishness to make up for and little time to do it."

"We do not speak of atonement."

Ethar smiled. "You seek wisdom, but it is you who impart it to me, little brother. The Kozhiniru spoke the truth when she said you were *ituru ashyukyari.*"

"Born of immediate blessing?"

"Better to say 'an enlightened birth.' A rare being, begotten with no impediment to the unfolding of the nine devotions. One who may require only a single epiphany—sometimes a great trial or an unbidden change—which, like a lightning bolt, ignites insight."

Luyan reflected. "Such as the loss of loved ones?"

Ethtar held his gaze. "I grieve with you, Luyan. Some losses cannot be reconciled with providence. We strive to surrender our attachment to those who have departed this world while cherishing their memory. Your father would not want you to suffer each time his dear face appears before your mind's eye. He would desire it give you comfort and strength."

For Luyan, Ethtar's fellowship had a different quality from that of the other *serkarui.* Her imposing physical presence and confident, direct manner put him in mind of his older male cousins. It inspired a trust he had not known since their deaths. Even her auburn hair and olive eyes, so like his own, imparted a reassuring feeling of connection.

"I do my father an injustice. I never knew my mother and have no sense of her absence. But my father guided me, taught me Protected me. Yet I push his memory from my mind because his loss racks me so."

Ethtar nodded. "I, too, lost my mother at an early age. She died in the persecutions."

With unschooled instinct, Luyan quieted his mind, made a willful effort of concentration. With each exhalation, he stoked the *aishyu* still smoldering in his heart and directed its flow back to

Ethtar.

The result startled them both. Ethtar broke out in a deep-throated moan and bent nearly double, her eyes brimming with tears.

"E'yibri Kahatu?" Luyan asked, placing his hand upon her shoulder.

After a moment, she nodded, sitting upright. Eyes still lowered, she covered his hand with her own, heavy and equally calloused.

"Ayi, Kahu, it is quite all right. I have never tasted the *aishyu* of a brother. The love of any boy or man. How is it that it can be so much like that of my dearest sisters, yet at once so disquieting?"

He started to pull his hand away. "Is it corrupting, Ethtar? I would not deliberately give offense."

She looked into his eyes and gripped his hand tighter. "No, Luyan. How could the unselfish love of a brother and sister ever corrupt?" She paused. "Ser-Luyan, I permitted my preconceptions to offend you at the feast on the ship. I know now that your heart is purer than any bread. That what issues forth from my mouth can corrupt me more than anything I put into it. I ask your forgiveness."

"None is necessary. I pray only that we may trust in one another should my courage fail in these coming days."

She nodded. "You may give me your trust, *Kahu,* and accept mine. Though it is a rare virtue in this Canannite community, so full of twice-born itinerants who hide in our caves when it suits them and depart without a word when they miss their men. So few stay and support us when the pressure is greatest." Ethtar had a way of looking most angry when her voice sounded most helplessly sad.

"You have suffered many kinds of loss, have you not?" Luyan whispered. "Betrayal, rejection, jealousy—these are things of which I am perhaps fortunate to know little. The fate of a slave is such cosmic treachery, it burns away all notion of right over another."

"I have long known that insecurity is my greatest enemy. But to hear you put it that way—'right over another.' Manipulation is not counted among the sacred powers, and for good reason. It is essential delusion. It traps us within the experience of that which we seek to control. The natural world, our fellow human beings, even the self. And yet I grasp for it, and I suffer so when it eludes me."

"Ser-Ethtar, what can you tell me of the devotions of power? The Keftiun sisters are reticent to speak of them. Yet we are facing powers here in Canaan that threaten to overwhelm us."

She meditated for a moment and then said the familiar words. *"Meroya kom ya kozhmai* . . . here is all that I am given to know . . ."

Luyan reverently straightened his posture and placed his mind in a receptive state.

"Let us begin with *kybanshyu*. In this devotion, I have delved deepest," she said.

Luyan's stomach tingled. This was very different from the cautious awe with which the other *serkarui* discussed this most misunderstood of subjects—often called the destructive power.

"I think first of *kybanshyu* as the power of purification, the reversion of form to elemental chaos. Many *serkarui* mistake it for the opposite of *orshiyu,* the power to construct, build up, or edify. But do not forget that building up is an exercise of willful action, while *kybanshyu,* deconstruction, is a devotion of willful stillness. We purify the world around us as we clarify our minds through a wiping clean of elaboration, a concentrated effort of reduction. Its ultimate goal is peace. And limitless potential for regrowth."

"But if willful action is required to build something up, how can it not be required to tear down?" Luyan asked.

"Because there is no static construct. No permanent structure of mind or matter. All form is fluid and exists only within the flow of the *yridinu.* We chase it, as we ourselves move from state to state. But constancy of form, even from one moment to the next, is an artifact of the mind. This is not to say that nothing is real, but that the way the mind perceives form is like . . ."

"Watching a bird fly?"

She tilted her head and paused to consider his example. "Tell me why you say that."

"When I acted as lookout on my old ship, I used a viewing board, a thin wooden shingle with a tiny pinhole. It shaded my eyes from the sun and sharpened images at a distance. In idle moments, I sometimes tried to identify birds in flight. When I peered through the hole and turned my head at just the right speed, the bird would seem to float still in the sky. I could distinguish its plumage, its shape, its colors."

"And when you held yourself still?"

"The birds flew off," he said. "Like stray thoughts when I quiet my mind in meditation."

She nodded. "Meditation is an exercise of willful stillness, and it is one means of pursuing the devotion of *kybanshyu*. Persistent, determined action is required to build all the myriad forms around and within us, like the beautiful temple you just visited. But with a single moment of quiet clarity, we can remove the very cornerstone of the conditioned world. And all may be taken down in an instant."

Luyan was silent for a moment. "An awesome power. But you do not seem to find it dreadful, Ethtar."

She shrugged. "Perhaps I had more idols to tear down before my growth could begin. But there are many kinds of imbalance. My sisters find me too direct, too quick to shatter the beliefs of others ..." Rarely had she unburdened herself so openly in whisper counsel, even to her closest sisters.

"And what of creation, Ser-Ethtar?" Luyan asked. "The devotion of *baturu* is still a mystery to me. How can something be brought into being from nothing?"

"Of all the devotions of power, *baturu* is the one with which I have struggled most. The ecstatic action of begetting. The origin of all things seen and unseen. You have already far surpassed me in that, Luyan."

"How can that be?"

She gave no answer. The light of dawn was filtering through the sea silk banner drawn across the window.

It was time to prepare for their final meeting with Adad-Sin, upon which so much depended.

20 A Cry from the Gap

"Beauty is nothing but the beginning of terror."

—Rainer Maria Rilke (1875—1926)

14 March 1769
Off Donostia, Spain
Lt. S. Singer, HMRN

D ear Girl,
'Twas a life of uncanny duplicity she lived, perhaps
think you, but I hope better. I own it was a merry
pickle, but I gave of my best to bear up and live true to it, and my
disguise was no more miserable than the masks we wear one and
all. How verily do we know to whom we speak when we speak the
words "I love thee"? Worse still, when we hear them—how certain
to whom they are addressed?

And how many were complicit in my artifice? There you have
me. Before meeting Löw Benjamin, I may have said just two, those
being my mother and Mary Rosedew; dear old blind Fanny Fox
else perjured herself in signing my birth record, which I do not
imagine Arima would have suffered. This I never thought to ask
her. Howsoever, the doctor's discernment made plain that others
must have divined as well; assuredly Rhona, and if her silence
rendered her an accomplice, I bless her for it.

My good, liberal-spirited, and charming doctor—how fortunate
am I, born fatherless, to have yet been bestowed with so much
paternal love: Chris and Matthew, Löw, and they not all, as I will
tell.

But Löw, who will live always in my heart as the first man to
love me as a daughter, now proposed me a saving scheme. An
officer's uniform does precious little to hide one's form, and I was
certain soon to grow manifestly great, which would not do if I
remained on board the *Persephone*. He could have stretched a

point on the severity of my wound to get me invalided in Halifax, but Royal Navy lieutenants give birth in military hospitals as frequent as they do in sick berths; which is to say this was no solution.

He counseled me instead to bide my time and, by the letting out of my waistcoat, carry on until we were back well at sea for Ireland. To provide pretext for my confinement, I would pretend to fever. Seamen believe all such maladies transmissible, of which notion Löw would omit to disabuse them.

We lay over in Halifax for about two weeks, our captain to make report of the attack and its attending administration and to replenish our wardroom. By the time we were bound for Ulster, my wound was healing without complication, and my other condition near becoming evident. The doctor informed the captain that I was unfit for duty. The good man visited me but stood at a remove, and I feigned a fit of coughing to seal his reluctance.

"Fever, I'm afraid, sir," the doctor told him in his offhand, professional tone.

He frowned. "Rare on the North American station. Is it catching?"

"With this strain, I cannot tell. It may have passed by traffic from Carolina and the Caribbean," replied Löw. "As for the lesion, I still fret it may not be secure from crisis. It would be best all round if the lieutenant were put ashore as soon as ever possible."

The captain considered. "If the breeze holds, we are perhaps a fortnight out of Londonderry, our next port of call—three weeks at most. It has a military infirmary. Will that suffice, Doctor?"

"There's no telling. But it would be prudent to consider alternatives, Captain. Mister Singer's is not the only life in the balance. It is too late to turn back for Halifax, I take it?"

"Certainly. And our course lays along the northwest coast of Ulster, a thinly settled, windswept rock pile. More peril than haven," the captain said. "We are on packet duty, Doctor, and I am concerned to say that we are without authority to interrupt our scheduled sail plan to put in whenever it may suit us."

His concern seemed quite unfeigned, and he had the matter right. He witnessed my execution of a last will and testament—all my worldly estate to Arima and Eleanor, with Matthew and Christopher as trustees, and pin money to Nessie during her lifetime. Disdainful as I was of Nessie's contrivances, I'd never before considered what might happen if my true sex were made public, before or after my death. Control of the Singer fortune would likely revert entirely to Blunt as the nearest male relative, leaving Arima, like Eleanor, to subsist at his pleasure. I signed in hope I might yet find a way to avoid that outcome. The captain pledged his prayers and best efforts before returning to the quarterdeck, and I felt a wave of remorse for gulling such a fine officer.

Löw endeavored to put my mind to rest. "You have more than your scruples to protect now, *cherie*. The navy will survive without you for a time, I assure you."

I returned his warm smile, but was not without forebodings. Should I be marked a deserter after the doctor got me sick listed, the naval board might tar him an accomplice to that serious crime and refer the matter to the Old Bailey; and that I would not abide—not if it were ever so. Furthermore, a military hospital was out of the question. I needed to disembark discreetly while still fit to make my way to Rhona, with whom I could lie-in and be delivered in safety. Time was short and options few.

Neither could I long keep up the facade of illness. In that early stage, my condition was marked rather by restless energy than fatigue, and the confinement to my tiny cabin was disagreeable in the extreme. My gravidity was as much an intrusion upon my spirit as my flesh—neither felt now wholly my own. Löw's advice and care were a comfort, but my recollection of every morbid complication Arima had attended as midwife played before my eyes.

I praise always the courage of the many brave men I have served with, but what blue ruin, methought, dogs the life of a woman at all its stages: the maiden taunting her doom with each passionate surrender; the mother poured out like a drink offering for her children; and the crone—that lonely distillation of the hearts and wisdom of all who fell about her along the byways of time.

In the weeks that followed, the ship in its steady progress seemed in league with my body, drawing me powerless toward some end which my anxious mind could not envision, however certain.

On sighting the coast of Donegal, I scarce fought back madness. Rhona was at that moment so nigh that I fancied I could hear the clarion mirth in her voice. We hauled a point north to stay clear Tory Island, but were nonetheless sufficient close to speak fishing vessels. I imagined jumping ship and swimming, but this was fond fancy. Even in that midsummer season, the expanse of cold North Atlantic waters and the rocky surf would have overcome me despite all Arima's lessons.

The gulf stream kept mild and steady on our stern, and it would not be long before we rounded the northern peninsula of Inishowen and put into Loch Foyle, leaving me no means of evasion before we docked in the port of Londonderry. I informed Löw that it must be then or never. He set his jaw and sacrificed a valuable bag of saffron he had been guarding for a gift to his sister, which he mixed with spirits and applied to my face and exposed skin. The tincture turned me such an alarming shade of yellow that I prayed it might not be indelible. He bade me lay still and sent a boy to notify the captain that my condition had worsened.

The doctor stated that my liver appeared to be failing and believed the ship likely to require quarantine when it reached port. The captain's eyes widened at my spectacle. He could offer no argument save duty—the *Persephone* could not spare a launch nor put in before Londonderry. Nonetheless, in the end, the miserable prospect of quarantine, and the doctor's offer to accompany me ashore, won the day; we hailed a fishing boat out of Sheep's Haven Bay and I was lowered limply over the side on a bosun's chair.

The captain did not require of the doctor a formal undertaking. He agreed to log me as invalided, asking only that arrangement be made for report of my situation to the navy office, and on this much Löw gave his word. My ditty bag, sword, and boots were tossed into the fishing boat; my sea chest would ship on to London along with the doctor's dunnage. In a parting flourish, he advised, as he carefully descended the pitching accommodation ladder, that my bed clothing be burned and my cabin scrubbed with vinegar.

The good captain called out to thank the doctor and bid me again a full recovery before hastily hauling wind and parting northeast toward Malin Head. The fishermen, visibly discomfited to have been brought up under the lee of a British man-of-war, became hospitable when presented with a generous palmful of silver and the information that I was a child of the Donegal Laughlins, and Löw by no means an Englishman. Though Sheep's Haven was closer, I begged they put us into Loch Swilly and down to the cathedral town of Letterkenny. Much as I honored Löw his stubborn humanity—he cared not a whit for any authority but that of his own conscience—I fretted yet for how I might abscond without I cast disrepute upon him.

Once the *Persephone* was out of sight, I rose from my humble deckhouse berth and took the air, that little liberty an ecstasy after my long confinement. The fishermen navigated night and day, and it nigh rent my bowels to ride their boat as they shot the riptides and threaded the rocky shoals well after dusk, ignoring numerous lights which appeared to mark the safe channels, my nervous demeanor no small source of amusement. Once we entered the loch, the case was altered; they reefed sail and paid cautious attention to each navigation aid, carefully avoiding the spits and bars and sweeping clear of the flats. I learned later that the coastal markers were often falsely situated to lure English vessels to wreckage on the rocks.

We made a good dinner of salmon grilled over a peat fire on the open deck. Löw retired early, and I stayed awake pondering my circumstances. Close on midnight, as the boat rounded well clear of the treacherous sandy shallows of Inch on our east, we neared a large flat adjoining the western shore, and I took my decision.

Only one crewman was awake, and he manning the tiller. By the light of the full moon, I dashed off a brief note of thanks and farewell to Löw and another to Arima for him to post or deliver. I slid them both, along with my will, into Löw's pocket as he slept on a pile of netting in the deckhouse. I kissed him gently on the forehead and covered him with my coat before removing my boots and stockings and stuffing them into my ditty bag. After hastily doffing my waistcoat, shirt, breeches, and smallclothes, I gathered and cast all over the bow, save my curious purse, which Rhona had bade me keepsafe. Naked now but for my hat and the bandage about my bosom, I strapped on my sword, rolled Rhona's ring upon my finger, slung my ditty bag across my shoulders, and climbed atop the forward rail.

I balanced there for some moments, one hand upon the hilt of my rapier and the other upon my belly—upon you, my love—and regarded the moon's broken reflection upon the shimmering surface. Each tiny swell, indeed, each drop, if studied in isolation, contained her complete image, yet none could hold the essential nature. That, God willing, there would be time enough to discover; and I raised my gaze to face her directly and whispered the first of the little Basque prayers my mother had taught me, a plea for lunar wisdom:

"Illargui amandrea, zeruan ze iberri?"

Receiving no immediate answer, I dove headlong into the water, leaving my hat floating behind, and swam several dozen yards beneath the surface to render myself well clear of the boat before coming up to breathe.

The loch was warmer and calmer than the coastal ocean waters, and I had no difficulty in reaching the flats. There I emerged and precipitated across the sandy beach, through a patch of delicate ferns, and clambered up the mossy rocks that separated the loch from the salt marshes. My first impression of Donegal was how soft it felt beneath my naked feet.

A mellow pod of sleepy gray seals greeted me atop the pile. I crouched among them, listening to the fishermen raise their alarm in words I must assume signified "man overboard." The boat was already a quarter mile distant and more, but poor Löw would grieve only until he found my letter.

I shifted my belt athwart my shoulder to carry the sword high on my back like a quiver, lest it clatter on the stones. I unplaited and shook out my hair against the night chill and, taking my direction from the moon, made my way south and west over the marsh, praying I reached shelter before the sun exposed me.

In this, I failed. I was still in the open when the dawn broke upon the green of the rosses, and wholly overcome by the vision. I watched in reverence as the copper sun leisurely began to dispel the wisps of sea brume clinging to the earth like a scarce-remembered reverie. Sound carried far on that flat terrain, and I was torn from my worship by the echo of voices.

I bolted for a stand of hawthorn framed by the rising sun and hoped the glare might shield me from view until I made it. The cry of an astonished child reached my ear just as I leapt into the cover of its leaves and pinkish flowers, not entirely avoiding the spines. In outline, I perceived an old man and a boy of perhaps nine years approach the grove, speaking in hushed voices. I wished then that I had more Irish than the few expressions gleaned during Rhona's visits. Löw's bandage, which bound both my wound and the increasing feature of my bosom, had caught upon the thorns, and to free myself, I uncoiled and cast off its bitter end.

I crouched still and peeped between the foliage as the natives stealthily closed; the old man drew breath and fell to his knees when he remarked the blood-stained linen wrap hanging from the tree and exclaimed in a quivering voice, *"Bail ó dhia ort, murúch maith!"*

With a ritual delicacy fitting Veronica's Veil, they prised the bandage and folded it carefully, the old man giving it to the boy to kiss, who then opened his clasp knife and cut from it two neat strips, which they tied upon the hawthorn's outer branches with whispered prayers. Packing the rest away, the man deposited a small leather flask upon the ground before the tree, which he topped with a little pile of salt and a tarnished silver coin. My astonishment grew as the pair bowed at the waist and, retaining this posture, backed away some thirty yards distant. I reached out for their gifts, slipped the coin in my hair, shook off the salt, and uncorked the flask to find it full, much to my satisfaction, with a fine clear whiskey, which I sampled straightaway.

Fearing what the marvelous souls might make of an English mermaid, I called after them, *"Gu raibh maith agaibh!"* which struck my mind as signifying "thank you," but I could not recall if in Mary's or Rhona's specie of Gaelic.

As may be, upon the hearing they jumped and turned and fled with whoops of delight, clapping one another awkwardly upon the back. I treated my tongue to one more small taste of their pure spirit and broke into laughter myself, my head and heart a-spin with the wonder of my Donegal welcome.

At all events, I could neither roam the fields naked nor spend the day concealed in hawthorn. I untangled myself from the bushes and lay my ditty upon a sunny rock. The waxed sailcloth had admirably survived its immersion, and I undid the double closure to extract and don my stockings and boots. So close wedged were they that I carelessly tore away a corner of the purple silk with which Rhona had lined the bag. I discovered that the pleated material had been fixed with only four loose stitches and designed to easily remove. This I did and blessed her. The lining opened into a Brunswick gown, its folds concealing a matching petticoat and cap—traveling clothes of fine looks and serviceability.

I shook them out, dressed myself with furtive glances about, and replaced the bag's other contents. I knew not how I looked and was glad only to cover my nakedness, but the drape and fit of the garments upon my body felt at once alien and natural. I slung my bag and my sword belt across my shoulders and found walking difficult until I discovered how, with a slight gather at the waist, to keep my petticoat from dragging.

The delicacy of my new array encouraged me to keep to dry ground. I crossed a path and followed it south, divining that the signpost marked *Leitir Ceanainn* must point the road to Letterkenny. The rosses gave way to gentle hills and glens and more frequent stands of forest, all alive with the movement of cloud shadow. Entranced as I again was by the charm of that countryside, I was startled to hear the beat of trotting hooves behind me.

"Dia duit, Inion! Cárb as duit?" came what sounded a friendly greeting.

I turned to find a sharp-eyed young man on a piebald mare, his capital shortcoat and tweed caubeen bespeaking some means. No simple rustic, this, I remarked, and also that I was meeting his eye, which a young lady would not make so bold to do. I hastily bowed my head and forced a bashful smile, hoping he would pass along.

"Tháinig tú ó Ráth Maoláin?" he persisted. Though his every utterance rose in song, it seemed I had ignored a proper question. I remembered the Gaelic for the town of Rathmullan from a north-pointing signpost and shook my head. He cocked his own and fixed me with a quizzical grin.

Never having faced the frank admiration of a young man, I mistook his manner for challenge and reached over my shoulder to loosen the hilt of my rapier, hoping I might draw it from that awkward position without contriving to cut my own throat.

"Níl, Níl! Gabh mo leithscéal, Inion!" he cried with alarm, rearing his mount and turning to gallop off. My gesture had communicated much, and from the fear in his eyes, it appeared I was not the first girl with a sword he had vexed in Donegal.

"Wait!" I called. He pulled up and looked back, but did not approach. I pulled the flask from my bag and held it out with an amiable mien. Brow furrowed, he walked his mare slowly back, and I tossed the whiskey over. He caught it in one hand, pulled the cork, and tipped it up, still eyeing me suspiciously as he swallowed. He drained the half or more, and I shook my head when he made to return it.

"Thank you, English," he said. "How come you here, may I ask?"

"You speak my language well."

"Aye, but 'tis not well you speak it. Better to address a stranger in any tongue save the king's west of Derry."

"I am searching for my relations in Gweedore," I said. "Do you know the Laughlins?"

His face broke again into that impish smile. "The Laughlins and McLaughlins of Gweedore, is it? Well now, Gweedore's not what it once was, and that's a family too grand to pass much time there." He took another pull at the flask. "It's at Killybegs you'll find them. Them as worth findin'."

I held his gaze for a moment. His facetious manner seemed to flow more from lightness of heart than ill intent, and I saw no reason to distrust him.

He pressed the flask to his breast and bowed in his saddle. "Phelin Crossan at your service, Mistress Laughlin," he said.

"Singer, if you please," I replied, starting a gentlemanly leg and finishing with a clumsy curtsy. "My grandmother is a Laughlin." I looked around uneasily. "I would take it kindly, Mister Crossan, if you would direct me to the road to Killybegs."

"Well now," he replied, leaning over his horse and closing one eye. "D'ye see them little small hills just there?"

I looked to the south and the sprawling mountains many miles distant.

He sipped again. "Through them runs *an Bearnas Mór*, as you would say 'the Big Gap,' and that's your road to Killybegs."

I raised a brow.

He slowly dismounted, dusted off his saddle, and held the bridle with a courtly gesture.

After a moment's hesitation, I gathered my petticoat and climbed atop the gentle mare, taking care for my sword and remembering to keep both legs athwart the saddle in ladylike manner. How I should control the beast from that attitude I knew not, but Phelin took the reins from my hand with a flourish and walked ahead, leading at a brisk pace.

He was given to prodigious pressure of speech, and I was obliged to suffer much of his history and that of the region along the way; but I was discovering that men will labor for female attention like mules for apples, and he seemed to find my ear a fair bargain for his guide service.

His father administered the affairs of the Presbyterian rectory and glebe outside of Letterkenny, and he himself had held there the position of stable master those three years. If I willed, he would borrow two fast horses on pledge of his old mare (this being a form of contract I could only assume unique to Ireland) unless, of course, I wished to leave my sword as security, which he made no doubt I did not; or without I desired to share with him his saddle, which he made no doubt I did not, etc, etc.

I scanned the rosses in silence.

"All the same," he continued after a pause, "two horses is faster than one, and it teemin' with brigands and tinkers, the Gap."

It was afternoon before we crossed the river and neared the outskirts of Letterkenny. Phelin set me down in a stand of oak overlooking the church estates, and I gave him what little silver I had, the better to seal his pledge. True to his word, he was back before dusk with two fine, spirited Arab stallions. Contrary to my instinct, he assured me we were better to set out straightaway and enter the Blue Stack Mountains under cover of darkness, as the tenant brotherhoods and other bands of thieves that inhabited them were less active after sundown. He bid me fear not, however, for he avowed himself capable of threading the Gap with closed eyes, so long as the moon was full. I asked had he a weapon, and he showed me a sort of knotted cudgel sheathed on the side of his saddle.

I am at misery to put into words the beauty I beheld as the sun set beside those sprawling moss-covered heights and verdant vales, with many a cold, clear stream to drink from and fat brown trout catchable in two hands. Darkness fell in haste, however, and the friendly peaks became cold, looming hulks of black against the starry night sky. We tarried only long enough to water the horses and use our eyes to the gloom, and when we rode on, I left it to Phelin to search out the track while I scanned the ridges. Once the moon fully rose, we were able to canter, save where the path grew steep, and when we rounded into the deeper cuts, I could sense my companion's solicitude.

In the midst of the crossing, atop a high ridge overlooking the next pass, I noticed an unnatural twinkling of stars and fell back a bit. Phelin's lead increased, and as he turned in alone ahead of me, I drew my rapier and separated the dirk from its hilt. I removed my bonnet and was shaking out my hair just as I heard two pistol shots. Sitting on the reins, I slapped the horse with the flat of my sword and entered the pass at full gallop.

All my adult life I had been swallowing my voice to mimic the deep monotones of an English gentleman, but the cool mountain air now burst from my lungs, ringing the cliffs with the keen of a scalded banshee. I rode the dappled silver stallion full into the knot of men surrounding Phelin as they were endeavoring to dismount him, and I daresay the terrific sound and spectacle was to them more fabulous than an hundred sea fairies leaping into hawthorn. I swung both dirk and rapier, opening the face of one robber and slashing the pistol from the hand of another. All fled for their souls, howling pious oaths, and I doubled back, breathless, to attend to Phelin.

"I'm all right," he said. "The blaggards shot in the air to startle my mount and stop me." He straightened his cap. "Jesus and Mary, woman, how knew you to do that?" He appeared more daunted by me than his attackers.

I wiped my blades on the horse's neck and reassembled my sword before sheathing it behind my back. "When we cease to serve fear, we may make it serve us," I said, quoting my mother, and smiled at him in the moonlight, brashly meeting his eye. "Come now, Phelin Crossan, and guide a poor *suire* out of these mountains before those credulous cowards find their cods."

Out of the mountains we were and in sight of the busy town of Killybegs by midmorning. We slowed to a walk as we crossed over the new bridge, rode past the grain storehouse, and approached the harbor. Dozens of colorful fishing vessels were putting out into Donegal Bay and the ocean to the west: great deepwater doggers, venerable herring busses, smaller dories and wherries, and even a few skin-covered curraghs. I was admiring the antique design of one of the latter as it swept slowly past the dock when I remarked a pale, wraithlike girl in a singular hooded burgundy cloak standing at its prow, still and silent as a figurehead, and fixing me with an otherworldly stare.

Phelin shuddered and crossed himself. I prayed only we might find someone with knowledge of my family before all the traffic had departed. We inquired of a group of busy stevedores who, upon hearing the name Laughlin, pointed vaguely in the direction of the far end of the pier, where the biggest of the doggers were docked. The *petits cons* found leisure to comment upon my person as I dismounted, however, and Phelin grabbed my elbow as I spun round to address their effrontery.

He guided me past them as he whispered in my ear. "Mistress, you cannot be guttin' every poor craythur who admires a girl of beauty and bold bearing. Both are much valued here in Donegal."

I found myself blushing at his words, and hoping he would not notice, when came the welcome distraction of a tug at my sleeve. I turned to find the girl of the curragh, who had approached silent on bare feet. She was perhaps seventeen. The burgundy velvet hood contrasted astonishingly with her parchment-white skin, ethereal pink eyes, and silver hair. She neither curtsied nor named herself, but raised to me the back of her splayed fingers to exhibit a triple-banded ring identical to the one I wore, save all of silver.

"Ar an talamh, mar a dhéantar ar neamh," she said in a voice of almost childlike pitch.

I turned to Phelin, whose eyes were wide, his pretensions to sophistication failing him. "Sh–She's praying to you, Mistress," he said in a tremulous whisper.

I insisted he translate her words exactly.

"It's the Pater Noster. The Lord's prayer, in Irish. She said, 'On earth as 'tis in heaven.'"

I turned back and met the girl's gaze.

"Kidek o aitortzen kidek," I replied in Basque. "Like knows like." Her eyes lit with understanding.

In a gesture of penetrating innocence, she straightaway twined her warm alabaster fingers with mine and led me toward the end of the docks with determined steps. Phelin fell in behind in superstitious silence. The crew of one of the largest of the trawlers were stowing their gill nets for departure, and a large red-haired man in a thick oiled woolen tunic was squatting with his back toward us as we approached.

"She's been expecting you, has Mother," the man exclaimed in booming English. Only when he stood up and turned around did I realize he had been addressing me.

I was mute in my astonishment. I beheld the figure of myself, had I indeed been born my father's son: the wit and glint of eye, the strong, kind smile, the inviting breadth of shoulder. If not my male simulacrum, then Hagen's ghost, before me.

"Come here and give your uncle a hug."

No, not Hagen, nor the phantasm of my male self sprung free to haunt me, but Cormac McLaughlin. This was Rhona's son by David Singer, and Hagen's half brother. As he drew me to him and embraced me, I buried my cheek in the peat-scented wool of his tunic, felt the reassuring expanse of chest beneath it, and tasted, methought, a grain of the tender care of that father I never knew.

Rhona was not at Killybegs, but on Gola Island in the Gweedore Bay, where the family's shellfishing was principally done. Cormac would lose his tide if he did not make way at once. I bid a hasty farewell to the gallant Phelin Crossan, leaving him with two of my uncle's guineas, much of my gratitude, and no mention of our adventures in the Big Gap. I did pray I might see him more again.

Úna, the exquisite albino girl who scarce ceased holding my

hand since she had met me, shipped with us, and we took her leather curragh in tow. I learned her hooded garment served merely to protect her fragile skin from the sun, and not some ritual purpose. She had no English, but delighted in trying to teach me her Ulster Gaelic.

We passed south out of Donegal Bay, then pointed west and north, a fine moist breeze just abaft our port beam, and eased between the rocky shoals and small islands guarding Gweedore Bay. I took great pleasure in the fishing boat, with its rounded bow and stable bottom, slow but well suited to towing a heavy net in an offshore gale. I proposed Cormac several adjustments to the sail trim and even to the standing rigging, it seeming to me that the hull rode a bit by the stern at the waterline and that a tightening of the backstay to give the mast a slight sweep would make it faster on a bowline and provide a more efficient angle of attack when trawling.

Cormac listened to my observations with an admiring smile and invited me to take the wheel on several occasions. I felt no reluctance, and indeed an agreeable exhilaration, to cry out my orders to the boat crew in my natural voice, which had broken forth like a bottled genie in the Blue Stack Mountains. Neither had I any difficulty in opening myself to Uncle Cormac and made him to understand my entire history, witholding nothing; the light of paternal pride in his eyes as I recounted my formation and naval service gave me the deepest joy I have known in life.

The family, he told me, had recently bought a small sloop in hope of fitting it out for transatlantic merchant service, the embargo and new acts of taxation making salt fish so dear in Boston that the temptation to smuggle could not be denied. They lacked shipwrights with skills suited to repair of the larger vessel, however, as well as the navigation and blue-water seamanship to make the crossing; this to say nothing of a knowledge of how to service her guns.

"Until now, mind you," he said with his brilliant smile. "Just think of it! How's old King George to guess our lovely pilot was once a lieutenant in his Royal Navy, if indeed his brigs can catch her at all, at all."

Be assured I would have done anything for the man at that moment; yet that aside, the prospect of liberty to continue in the trade I so dearly love, indeed, to practice seamanship in the bosom of my family, and that without need to disguise the gender of my birth and heart, promised the resolution of a conflict for which I had offered many a forlorn prayer.

In short, methought perhaps I needed not choose between sea and sex, the dual moorings of my deepest nature. I could have wept with happiness at the notion as I lay my head upon a rough cot in the deckhouse and closed my eyes for much-needed rest, Úna's salty fingers running through my hair.

Howbeit my last conscious thought is always of you, my love. I drifted off thinking I could by no means go a-smuggling with a babe in my arms.

The next afternoon, off the craggy shores of Gola Island, the largest and westernmost in Gweedore Bay, Cormac hove to and transferred Úna, her crew, and I into the curragh, which its shallow draught would allow our approach and landfall. He would sail out to set his nets for the twilight run, fish the next several days, and come back to visit me within a fortnight.

Úna kept my hand clasped to her bosom, prating on in Irish as we stood at the round prow of the leather boat, the crew sweeping in careful strokes. As we neared the shore, my eyes followed her finger to the top of a high cliff, where a tall woman with flowing red hair stood vigil.

"*Siúr Roinseach.*"

My heart leapt to see Rhona hold high a corner of her cloak in welcome.

J.P. Jamin

21 Serpents of Fire

"If a Jew does not believe in miracles, he is not a realist."

—Simon Weisenthal

1602 BCE
Eastern Mediterranean

The summer day dawned clear, and its brightness would mask the signs of Thera's final warning while the new year celebrations lasted. But a mounting, blood-red afterglow would linger long past sunset.

The Etesians blew steady from the northwest, ten to fifteen knots at sea level. But twenty kilometers into the stratosphere, the forces were much different. A vast plume of dust and sulfurous acid was dispersing at nearly three times that speed, creating a sprawling lightning field as it and the dry southern Khamsin clashed. The volcanic ash carried its own warmth and spiraled with the weight of much colder air pressing from above—a miller's wheel that, by early evening, would roll the Levantine coast.

A coy whiff of what Thera still held and would soon hold back no more.

Ethtar and Luyan, the rest of the delegation behind them, stood at the base of the steps of Adad-Sin's high throne. Adad-Sin was dressed in full ceremonial garb for the day's rituals. The golden crown of Ba'Ēl at his elbow, his Egyptian dagger on his thigh. He was flanked by a dozen armed palace guards. His entire court was present.

He had an uneasy, displeased demeanor. That of a man who was not in full control of events.

Luyan held the Kozhiniru's staff. Around its top was coiled a gleaming copper serpent, affixed with wire. She whom the Egyptians call Wadjet. Goddess of wisdom and fertility. The

Canaanites, Amorites, and Keftiu all had their own names for her.

The moment had come to abandon diplomatic delicacy. The Kozhiniru had directed it. Her troubled dreams demanded it. Now was the needed time, she had written. Returning courtesy for courtesy, affront for affront, their message must be made known at all costs.

Ethtar held out the rudely worded summons received the evening before.

"Is it your custom, my lord, to send for your honored guests in the dawn hours like prisoners to judgment?"

"You have your audience, mermaid," Adad-Sin said. "On a day I can little afford the time to grant it. Is it the custom of Keftiun guests to make importunate demands of their hosts?"

"You must know, lord," Luyan broke in. "How many unanswered letters have you sent begging the support of your Egyptian masters? You, a descendant of the greatest sea power the world has ever known?"

"Speak not of my descendancy!" Adad-Sin snapped. "I strangle by my many roots! I need not another fanciful myth to finish the job!"

He sat back, his twisted leer reemerging. "You will, I think, regret the bad fortune your words have brought you."

He clapped, and the curtains were drawn from the western portico overlooking the harbor.

Luyan's stomach chilled. Their ship was not standing well offshore where it was meant to be. It was at single anchor in the middle of the main channel, flanked by two Egyptian war galleys. A third flagship blocked the harbor entrance. Startlingly close, he saw a circle of *serkarui* balanced on the rails, some standing, some on one knee. All wielding their poleaxes—a wordless threat to anyone who might try to board.

Performing their ancient duty. Protecting the Kozhiniru.

The side corridor filled with short, tethered steps. The Keftiun pilots filed by, flanked by Egyptian soldiers. Two crewmen were supporting Durzhyar. Luyan met his eye as he passed.

317

"There you see it, snakemaster," Adad-Sin said. "Your ship is taken. All who can navigate it are now lain prisoner. Will this change the tone of your warning, I wonder?"

"For your people's sake, my lord, I pray you attend better to its substance," Luyan said.

Talyera spoke as she gazed out of the portico. "From here it's your harbor that looks taken, my lord, not our ship. What accord did the Egyptians offer?"

She turned her lovely eyes to Adad-Sin. "The Kozhiniru to remain unmolested in pledge for the pilots, I think? Preserving the status until they receive orders?"

He glowered and turned to Luyan, as if the words of a woman needed translation.

"Your orders, my lord?" Talyera continued with raised eyebrow. "Or those of a higher authority?"

Adad-Sin gave a start as a dozen Egyptian swordsmen, all gripping sickle-shaped *kophesh*, stomped into the hall. They flanked Adad-Sin's royal guards, one for one.

The situation was evident. A senior Egyptian official was soon to arrive. Adad-Sin's ability to ensure his security was in question. Perhaps a great deal more.

"Little time may remain," Ethtar whispered. "Say what is needed."

Luyan went over the words of the Kozhiniru's message in his mind and opened himself to the current of *onusuru*. He glanced at the gleaming serpent topping the staff, trusting in Meri-heshtharu to give him voice.

"Shemi, Belu Adad-Sin. Hear me . . ."

He told of how and why they had come to the shores of Canaan. He foretold the coming destruction, the defilement of the air and skies, the massive wave that would flood the coasts, even as far as the Levant. He told of years of plague and famine, fallow fields, dead livestock, seas awash with sulfur and pumice instead of fish.

He told it in his highest, most poetic Akkadian, both rational and transcendent in its authority. He told it in the name of the

Kozhiniru-Entu. He told it, swore it, under the sign of Wadjet, of Meri-heshtharu. She whom they knew as Maridthu, beloved Ishtar, sacred Hathor.

Adad-Sin did not interrupt. Many of his courtiers stood frozen, and even the Egyptian guards sprang beads of sweat as they listened to Anekti's translation.

But the retinue of Amorites were unmoved. The foremost was Mabug-Rad, Adad-Sin's vizier and principal rival. He had been appointed directly from Ebla by King Indilimgur. Standing beside and behind him, Luyan saw the dour chief assistant, whom he had humiliated at table the day before.

When Luyan finished, Mabug-Rad spoke. "My lord, is their Aegean priestess more powerful than Ēl-lohim, the lord of hosts? Her vision clearer than that of the ancient of days?"

"Have not our own priests seen signs?" Adad-Sin asked noncommittally.

Mabug-Rad exhaled in disgust and loped toward Ethtar and Luyan like an accuser.

"Evil heralds a witch, it does not hunt her! Fiery serpents from heaven? Bloody dusk in the west? Do you not see that these demons come from the sea to escort this destruction? They do not warn us with these symbols! They curse us!"

He made an abrupt grab and pulled the staff from Luyan's hand. It clattered to the steps at Adad-Sin's feet, the idol and its trailing wires breaking loose. The Egyptians gasped and shrank away as the coiled metal serpent rolled down the steps with eccentric springing motions, the wire shards rattling as it seemed to slither this way and that of its own accord. So lifelike was the illusion that even Mabug-Rad jumped back.

The Egyptian soldiers reformed and fell silent. A tall, broad-shouldered Nubian of unmistakable authority had entered in the confusion. With a smile at Anekti, he picked up the copper idol and staff and began to repair them.

Naked from the waist up save for an elaborate gold chest plate, the Egyptian introduced himself.

"Nebamun-si-ahmose, Nebet," he said to Anekti with a courtly smile.

"Imey-er-a'hew Nebamun, a'nekh djet em heset net Wadjet! Live forever, Admiral Nebamun, in the favor of Wadjet!" she replied in the exclamatory tone of polite Egyptian greetings.

Adad-Sin rose out of his throne, but only so far, lest the Amorites think him too deferential to the Egyptian.

Nebamun waived off his words of welcome and switched to Akkadian. "I am not a pious man," he said, twisting the wires, "but there are those in Thebes who would not suffer such sacrilege against holy Wadjet on her very feast day."

"A regrettable mishap, Admiral," Adad-Sin said, coolly. "The day is sacred to Ba'Ēl as well, and to his consort, who watches over this city. Who protects our trade—and yours."

The Egyptian was a warrior, not a priest. "Pharaoh believes it is not protected enough. He is the god that should concern you most. He is the reason I am here. Shipments of cedar and lapis lazuli are diminishing by the month." He looked at Mabug-Rad. "How will your northern partners defend against the Hittites if they cannot control a roving rabble? Our Hyksos had origins no less humble than your Habiru bandits. Now they rule half our nation."

He handed the staff back to Luyan with a glance at his clubbed hair. "Or am I wrong, Lord Adad-Sin?" he continued. "Perhaps the wood and blue stone is going to new trading partners?" He shot out his lower lip and blinked in mock naiveté. "Or should I say, older ones? It was during the reign of your predecessor I last remember seeing a Keftiun ship in the harbor of Gubel." He placed his foot on the step. "Yes. Not long before he was deposed."

Adad-Sin shifted in his seat. Were their situation not so perilous, Luyan might feel sympathy for him. The man's throne was a razor.

"I assure you we are no trade delegation, my lord admiral," Luyan said. "We are one of many diplomatic missions that have sailed from Keftius in recent months—"

"To warn of ruin. Yes, I know," the Egyptian interrupted. "We have received word from Libya of your oracle. And another of your pretty ships was sighted off the Nile delta just before I sailed. None of that concerns me. But 'diplomacy' today may mean commerce tomorrow, and that does."

"They make it witness, not mere augury," Adad-Sin said. "Even my high priest considers these grave omens. The young Keftiun emissary here swears to have seen Thera's stirrings with his own eyes."

"Swears it by his owls and snakes! By Lillitu, mother of monsters!" the chief assistant spat from the cover of Mabug-Rad's shoulder.

The admiral's face clouded. The man had spoken without leave in a royal court, his words an impetuous insult to the oldest of Egyptian goddesses. An Egyptian soldier grabbed him by the hair, threw him to his knees, and poised the inner curve of his sword by his neck.

Luyan held the staff across his chest, and the Keftiun delegation took a few steps back. The situation was more volatile than he had first realized.

"No!" commanded Adad-Sin. "You will not enter my court and spill blood!"

All eyes were upon the city ruler, Nebamun's and Mabug-Rad's menacing him from either side of his throne.

"Bring him to me," Adad-Sin said to one of his own guardsman.

Begging and weeping, the assistant was dragged up the steps and forced again to his knees at the foot of the throne. Adad-Sin leaned in and raised the man's chin, staging a miraculous facial display. Contempt and paternal empathy flickered in turn, like the figures on a pinwheel.

Suddenly, he stood, snatched the straight sword from the soldier's belt, and plunged it down between the assistant's neck and shoulder, driving the blade into the hollow of his collarbone and cleanly through his heart. He fisted the scrolled handle to wedge the weapon tightly.

Barely a drop of blood seeped out as he kicked the man's body

J.P. Jamin

down the steps.

He stood with arms akimbo and scanned the entire company before sitting and reclining well back on his throne. "Not on this holy day," he added with a tone of afterthought and shut his eyes in a pretense of calm reflection.

The court, the Egyptian visitors, even the Amorites, maintained silence until Adad-Sin spoke again. He waited several minutes, attaching a masterful gravity to his next utterance.

"Now. We were discussing the value of our word," he said. "I give you mine, Admiral, that all cedars we cut, and all lapis we receive from our esteemed Amorite brothers," here he nodded toward Mabug-Rad, "shall be first and always at the disposal of the house of our Pharaoh."

Neither the Egyptian nor the Amorite replied.

Adad-Sin continued. "His excellency, the Keftiun emissary, says he is not here to discuss trade, but to warn us of danger." He paused again. "He has taken his oath as to both. What say you, Admiral?"

Nebamun considered for only a moment, before his diplomatic smile returned. "Their ship will remain in the harbor until we have departed. But if the Lady Anekti is prepared to give her pledge as well, then I am satisfied for now."

"Em ankh Per-o." Anekti exaggerated her Nubian accent for his benefit.

"Ah! There we have it, then!" Adad-Sin said, beaming with staged delight. "By Pharaoh's life! Does that satisfy you, Mabug-Rad, or do you require a higher god for her to swear by?"

Mabug-Rad darted a glance of pure malice at Luyan, then bowed once to Adad-Sin and once to Nebamun.

Adad followed with a series of rapid commands. Luyan's pilots and crew would remain ashore as guests, not prisoners, and Adad-Sin would reserve judgment on his warning until after the ceremony. The Egyptians and the Keftiu were both invited to the temple, the ceremony being open to all—even Habiru. It was a day of jubilee. A day of general amnesty and reconciliation for all the

322

peoples of Canaan.

"But, Admiral, no arms on the acropolis, please. Our own guards have things well in hand, yes?"

Nebamun's smile faded. After several moments silence, he ordered his swordsmen out of the hall and followed them.

Adad-Sin dismissed the remainder of the court and called for wine.

Yes, upon a razor he sits, Luyan thought. But even a *serkaru* had to admire his balance.

Back in his guest quarters, Luyan opened the door to Anekti's tap. She held a finger to her lips as she and Ethtar entered.

"I have tended and spoken to Durzhyar," Anekti whispered. "It was as Talyera thought. The Egyptians rowed in and blockaded the harbor before our ship could slip out. There was no bloodshed. Our pilots came off voluntarily at dawn in exchange for Nebamun's pledge not to board."

"But Durzhyar's wound . . ." Luyan said.

"It does well, just some dizziness," Anekti assured him. "Ser-Luyan, I breakfasted with the Egyptian admiral. His command is merely a vanguard. Pharaoh has report of southern incursions by the Hittites. Troops are readying to march north, and Adad-Sin's throne is in jeopardy."

"The least of this region's problems," Ethtar said.

"But not the least of ours," Anekti replied. "The admiral believes Adad-Sin will make an example of us to appease the Amorites, now that he has lost Egypt's confidence."

"Adad-Sin is unlikely to move against us until after the ceremony. We have at least a day," Ethtar said. "But your ship, and the Kozhiniru, are still trapped in the harbor."

"Ser-Anekti," said Luyan, "you have some influence with Nebamun. Do you think he could be convinced to let us depart?"

She shook her head. "He will blockade the port until further orders. And whatever they may be, you can be assured he will follow them." She averted her eyes. "He has offered to safeguard me personally for as long as he can, but there is no telling when Adad-Sin may again feel the need to flaunt his authority."

Luyan touched her hand. "Raya would want you to take Nebamun's protection."

"I would sooner take his head," she replied.

Ethtar smiled grimly. "The Kozhiniru was definite in her instructions. If Adad-Sin remains unconvinced of our warning, Luyan is to deliver it publicly at the ceremony."

He nodded. "For better or worse, our duty to the Canaanites will then be fulfilled, and we may act to preserve ourselves and our cargo."

"How are we to do that?" Anekti asked.

Luyan looked at Ethtar. "I think I can regain the ship unnoticed if I swim out quietly after dark. But our people stranded ashore— can you lead them overland to safety?"

Anekti frowned. "With respect, *Kahu*, I can swim farther, faster, and stealthier than you can."

Ethtar responded to her with sharp authority. "And with respect, *Kahatu*, we all have loved ones on that ship. You can neither navigate nor pilot it."

Anekti looked more abashed than Ethtar had intended. She squeezed her shoulder. "Hibya, Quarta, and your Raya will be safer on a coastal vessel then on horseback. They are *serkarui*. They can take to the water at any time and swim to shelter. We will ride the coast road down to Simmiltu Surru, north of Akka. Its sea grottoes shelter the largest *serkaru* community in the Levant. They will guide us to safety on the high ridges above."

"Let us pray Thera's wrath does not overtake us all before we get there," Anekti replied. She turned to Luyan. "We may not speak again, *Kahu*. The swim will be the least of your challenges. If you deliver our message at the temple without being killed or imprisoned, and make it to the ship afterward, there is another Egyptian fleet sailing up the coast, already blockading the port cities to the south."

She unscrolled a map upon her knees. "From the navigator. Do not put in at Surru, but follow the coastline carefully after you pass it. The chalk cliffs ascend in a gradual slope for two *iters*. Where the sea meets them, you will find the grottoes."

"Heave to, and we will swim out with coracles to take you off," said Ethtar.

Luyan studied the chart carefully before rolling it. He was grateful for his lessons in coastal navigation.

"*Meri-heshtharu kai'vak eyo, Kahatui.* May the Goddess be with you both, Sisters," he said.

"*Tzo kai'v, Kahu,*" they replied and embraced him.

At that moment, inside a dark public house in the teeming dockyard district of Gubel, one man smelled sweeter than the rest. His body was wrapped in a rough cloak, pulled up to hood his high, misshapen turban. He carried a basket of fresh loaves. All eyes were upon him.

He raised his cup, and the company followed suit.

"Blessings, stranger," they said. The man repeated the words, as one who had forgotten his own name, and sipped. All other cups contained wine, but he drank only water. No one called him "lord" or "king," which, for the purpose of the day, he surely was.

He took a large loaf from the basket and broke a corner before passing it to his right. Each man tore off a piece with eager reverence, squeezing the warm bread carefully. A skinny young dockworker at the end of the table barely contained a grin, and instead of eating like the rest, stealthily concealed the morsel in the folds of his loincloth.

The stranger rose. Armed palace guards parted the sweaty throng to let him pass. He would repeat the bread-and-water ritual at numerous hovels and public houses as he made his way up to the temple of Ba'El at Gubel.

The young dockworker waited as the room emptied, the crowd pushing one another to follow the procession. When no eyes were left to see, he pulled the ball of bread from his garments and tore it open. The royal seal of Adad-Sin lay in his palm. Carved in deeply veined lapis lazuli, its handle an enormous gray pearl, it was the instrument of authority bestowed upon the city ruler by his predecessors. The conveyance of the highest power in all of Canaan.

It was unique, and it had been concealed in but one of the dozens of loaves Adad-Sin carried in his journey through the bowels of the city, disguised as a commoner. With this ritual charade began Gubel's celebration of the new year. The orphaned prince, demented of his royal identity and lost in chaos, would be restored and bound in sacred marriage to the goddess. At the close of the ceremony, the lucky young dockworker would step from the line of worshippers at the temple steps to ransom the royal seal. His reward would be far greater than the price for which he might sell it. And he would enjoy the favor of the throne for the rest of his days.

At the same moment, the goddess was being prepared for her wedding night. A dozen priests had washed the statue and were anointing it with cedar oil. They dressed her in a black-and-white tunic and layered beads of rich blue lapis around her neck.

The temple floor was piled with sweet reeds, and a ritual bed of lilies lain down. They erected a canopied tent of silk on a frame of light balsa, its doors delicately balanced to blow open when the sea breeze filled the gallery from the west at sunset. The bridegroom could not enter the bedchamber until the goddess was willing.

Luyan had arrived early, ahead of the procession, and won a place near the foot of the steps. He was still carrying the Kozhiniru's staff, the serpentine figurine covered again in linen. Many visitors had traveled far to witness the ceremony. The crowd was a mixture of rich and poor, urban and rural, amicable and unruly. He found himself standing beside a knot of quiet sun-darkened men in woolen skirts and patterned yellow tunics, their wiry hair held back by white linen cords, their beards trimmed neat and round. The nearest surveyed him, smiled politely, and bowed.

"Prosperous new year, my lord. I am Sedu."

Before Luyan could reply, another group, dirty and probably drunk, began tussling with some Egyptian soldiers, arguing in a Semitic dialect Luyan had difficulty making out. The Egyptians were searching the tribesmen for weapons. A Canaanite behind him in the crowd muttered, "Habiru."

"They object to being touched by the uncircumcised," Sedu said.

Luyan turned back. "I have never before seen a Habiru. You understand their words?"

Sedu smiled and bowed again. "This day you have spoken to one. I beg only that you not confuse me with that riffraff."

"But you are Habiru as well?"

"My brothers and I are of the southern tribe, the Bint-Iamīna. We have served the kingdoms for generations and earned our independent estate by loyalty in battle and faithfulness to the one God most high. Those others are Similites. Northern Habiru. Driven from Mari and Ebla for their many crimes. They exist by raiding and banditry."

Luyan returned the bow and gave his name.

"Yes, Lord Luyan, I know who you are." Sedu smiled again. "You are Luyan of the dancing serpent. Emissary of the Kozhiniru-Entu and friend of our cave sisters."

"How is it you know that?"

"The people are speaking of nothing else. They are eager to hear your prophesy from your own lips. Above that, to see you work wonders. You will find them more credulous if you can manage one or two more."

Luyan met the man's eyes. "It was not prophesy. The deep places of the earth within Thera and Keftius contain evidence such catastrophe has happened before. Dozens of meters of stone and pumice burying ancient settlements. There are signs of another disaster very soon to come."

He stemmed his flow of words. Could he trust a stranger in this splintered city? He bid *onusuru*, the divine wisdom, to judge the

Habiru's motives and candor. The same discernment the Kozhiniru had used to weigh the heart of a young lookout at the mast of a Cilician ship, what seemed so long ago.

Sedu's smile faded as he lowered his voice. "As for me, I am a friend of Ethtar."

Luyan sensed nothing but openness from the Habiru. "Then you know she needs your help."

Sedu nodded. "The city gates are closed. So many have made the pilgrimage that it can contain no more. We have amassed fast horses for Ethtar and her company outside the south entrance. My brothers and I will escort them. We depart down the sea road the moment the ceremony ends."

The man had lifted half the burden from his mind. Luyan thanked him.

"It is family duty," Sedu whispered. "I am a once-born of the *serkarui.*"

There was an abrupt increase in the tempo and murmur of the assembly. The lyres and drums that had been playing since noon were overlain by the shriller rhythms of sistrum and clapper. Adad-Sin, still in the guise of the orphan king, had begun to ascend the stone pitch to the acropolis.

Only half an hour before sunset. The unhurried procession crossed onto the temple grounds. The high priest appeared atop the steps in full ceremonial dress, holding a scroll, looking strangely haggard. He nodded when he spotted Luyan.

The music reached a crescendo and then came to an abrupt stop when Adad-Sin reached the bottom step. He looked up and dropped his empty basket. In a deep staccatto, the high priest began to read from the scroll—an abridgment of the Amorite myth of the restoration of the son of Daguna.

"Shemi! Hear! Hear, and remember yourself!

You are Adad-Sin, lord of storms, lord of heaven.
Smite once again the enemies of your people!

Let the earth feel once more your gentle rains.

You are Kumarbi, castrator of the sun!
Recall the day you spat from your mouth
The genitals of Šamaš, like lukewarm curds.

Cast off your forgetfulness, oh my son!
Take again to your bosom your consort;
To your mighty body your rightful array!

The mantle of Ba'Ēl, the Lord Ēl,
The horns of Ēl-lohim, the Lord of hosts,
The chariot of the ancient of days!"

With each line, Adad-Sin mounted another step. After each triplet, he shed another garment. First his rough cloak to unveil royal purple robes. Then his turban to reveal the gleaming horned crown. At the top, the priest anointed his head with oil. Finally, Adad-Sin removed the robe and entered the temple in only a black-and-white linen shift.

A coldness ran in Luyan's belly. The prayer made promiscuous use of sacred myth, invoked powerful gods. Hurrian, Hittite, and Amorite names, intermixed without caution, without a thought to blasphemy. The multiplication of endless cosmologies, the Kozhiniru had said. Religion as he knew it was meant to reduce uncertainty, to impart clarity over forces greater than the believer. He closed his eyes, breathed slowly to detach himself from his imaginings.

Adad-Sin entered the temple. The sun had set, but the western skies remained arched in vivid crimson, like a rainbow bleeding out in sacrifice to the one god not yet named.

The evening sea breeze was late in coming. The air was thick, warmer than it had been at midday, a dank hint of rot and rust settling from above. A nervous silence blanketed the crowd.

The spectators below the stairs had no view through the open temple doors, down the central gallery within. Nearly an hour after sunset, the unnatural afterglow remained in the west, and the temple mirrors bathed the marriage tent with its reflection. Against the burgundy smolder, those on the higher steps and terraces of the surrounding buildings saw the silhouette of Adad-Sin standing impatiently before it.

In the span of a moment, all flickered out. A rolling darkness doused the twilight in the west, and the stars fanned into blackness, a curtain drawn angrily across the heavens.

Sheet lightning blinked over the sea, momentarily illuminating the anxious face of the high priest. Luyan began counting, the reflexive habit of mariners, and a crackle of thunder followed before he reached three. The storm was upon them. His ears popped, and a stream of reeds, fabric, and debris shot from the great doors of the temple on the back of a monstrous, screaming wind. It caught the high priest's linen wrap and swept him off his feet. The din masked the sound of his neck snapping as his head hit the stone steps.

Luyan ran to him, shielded from the wind by the lower stairs. The priest's turban had blown off. Blood streamed from an ear, matting his long gray hair and beard. His eyes were fixed upon Luyan, lips moving. Luyan removed his own cloak and balled it to cushion the old man's head, then bent close to listen.

"Within. Her prophesy . . . her oracle!" The priest's jaw worked silently as he fought to say more. "Tell them!" he croaked. "Warn . . . them . . ." His eyes flared, then closed in a stony, lopsided wink.

The clouds above spidered and cracked with lightning. In a spreading wave, the people began writhing and screaming. Driving rain pounded the coast, and with it blew Thera's ash, condensing into millions of acid-soaked gobbets, each glowing violet blue with the storm's discharge. They spiraled from the sky like serpentine dancers. While the light of their fire was harmless, the corrosive sulfur was not. Over the whole of the acropolis, exposed skin, eyes, and lungs were burning beneath the torrent.

Sedu and the other Bint-Iamīna grabbed Luyan's elbows. There was nothing more he could do for the priest, but he bore one last duty to Gubel. They mounted the steps with him, stopping midway in the dry arc sheltered by the eaves of the temple. He turned and noticed the Amorite vizier Mabug-Rad shoving out from the crowd, a dagger in hand. He bolted up the steps in Luyan's direction.

Mindful stillness, Luyan thought. He would not turn and run, would not be stabbed in the back. He needed the people's trust, not their contempt. One deep ocean breath. Unmoving as a statue, he stood and watched and timed his blow.

Mabug-Rad raised the weapon over his head. The moment before his foot touched the step below him, Luyan swept the Amorite's ankle with the bottom of the staff. With a crazed roar, he toppled forward, and Luyan spun the staff upward into his jaw, knocking him aside. One of the Habiru kicked away the dagger and planted a foot on the man's chest.

Still squirming with rage, Mabug-Rad looked beyond Luyan and barked, "Kill him! Kill him now!"

Luyan and Sedu turned. Adad-Sin was standing a few steps behind them, flanked by four of his palace guards, their swords drawn.

Luyan raised his staff in the defensive diagonal he had learned from Hibya. The Habiru drew hidden daggers from their robes, ready to protect, but no attack came upon Luyan. Instead, one of the palace guards spun and swung his sword at Adad-Sin's neck.

The destructive power left no gap between thought and action, and the bottom of Luyan's staff began moving as the sword did. Their tips collided within inches of Adad-Sin's throat, deflecting the strike, giving the other guards the moment they needed to react. All three buried their swords into the traitorous assassin, and Adad-Sin was left wide-eyed and gasping but unharmed.

The scene was threatening to devolve into chaos. Luyan saw the Egyptian soldiers clustered around their admiral. A large Amorite contingent, some visitors of rank from Ebla and Mari, began to encircle Mabug-Rad, and the Habiru holding him poised a dagger at his eye.

"Stop!" commanded Adad-Sin.

He clapped a hand to Luyan's shoulder and spoke into his ear. "You have twice preserved my life today! Preserve now my people. Deliver your message. Neither the Egyptians nor Amorites will molest you while I live!"

Luyan met his eye. He discerned the man's basic goodness, risen above the mire of regional conflict. Like Raya's lotus blossom. He felt the presence of the Kozhiniru, strangely near. He mounted a few more steps and turned toward the assembly. When the top of his staff peeked above the stairs, the tunneled wind whipped off its linen cover. The copper idol began to glow, the violet discharge skipping along its coiled length and spouting upward like a comet's tail.

"*Uṣṣuru!*" Luyan cried.

And listen they did. The rain-burned worshippers began to bunch around Luyan as they realized there was shelter from heaven's bite in the lee of the temple steps, under the protection of the luminous serpent.

22 Bread and Blood

The soul replied, saying, "What binds me has been slain, and what imprisons me has been destroyed; my desire has been brought to an end, and ignorance has died. Still bound in this world, I was set loose from all worlds; while in this form, released from the very form of heaven and freed from that chain of forgetfulness which is the essence of time. From this hour on, for the span of eternity, let the words be yours; I remain at peace."

Gospel of Mary (Papyrus Berolinensis)
2nd Century AD

15 March 1769
Lt. S. Singer, HMRN
Donostia, Spain

Dear Daughter,
    Well, we are at moorings in Saint Sebastian, waiting for the harbor launch, and I may have little further leisure to write for a time. My exile continues, but I run now with an unburdened heart and a beguiled Japanese boy, sweet of soul and countenance, from whom my man's livery has failed to fully conceal a mermaid's heart.

I will soon end his confusion.

Howbeit to understand why I have fled again so disguised, you must know that there was yet tying off to be done when I reached Gweedore, and 'tis a history I owe you.

Rhona shone with happiness when I stepped out of the curragh and into her arms. It pleased her to see her gown again.

"The color suits you, though I own I'm a bit taller. Did the skirts drag?"

I recounted my journey in detail, from Löw Benjamin to Phelin Crossan, but she laughed most hearty at the homage paid me in the hawthorn hedge. "A new clootie ring is born! And they'll be chasing cows for months from Rathmullan to Letterkenny!"

I smiled along politely. She explained that in native belief, when a *murúch,* or sea maid, is sighted on land, it is a rare blessing, although an evil omen upon the water. Hawthorn is a sacred tree known to be home to fairies and good people of all species, and the tying of rags to the branches is common, each an offered prayer for health, wealth, or love. The old man and the boy had likely been tracking me at a distance, keeping out of sight lest I transform into a cow, which is as mermaids red of hair or cap are wont to disguise themselves on dry land. I recalled an almost identical Basque legend, which held that Mari oft transformed herself into such a creature, and her sacred caves guarded by a redheaded bovine which roamed the *akelarre*.

I spent my first night on Gola Island in a thatched stone hut in the little village where the family salted fish and shucked pearl oysters. Rhona examined me carefully, Úna's presence at once comforting and oddly provocative. Rhona noticed my diffidence with a slight smile as the girl helped me disrobe.

"Úna holds herself blessed to be first to spy you in Donegal, and the family looking out for you these twelve months. I've never seen our little sister of the caves so taken," she said as she palpated my naked belly. "Perhaps she makes it providence that joins two kindred souls, their beauty both long shrouded from the sun." She washed her hands. "Like knows like, does it not?"

I wondered how earnest Rhona's notion might be as she gently probed me. Úna met her eyes in wordless question and traced a figure just above my sex with the tip of her snowy finger, making a sapid warmth shoot into my stomach and up my spine. Rhona spoke some soft words, and Úna stood at the head of the bed until she finished.

Rhona addressed me again in English when at length she stood. "Never mind now. Four months gone, and all looks well. How d'ye feel?"

"Ambuscaded," I said. "And not eager of further confinement."

"Ah, there your fear's mistaken. Donegal women don't know the meaning of lying' in. You'll be workin' along of us till your last month. Then you'll take to the caves, learn our domestic rites, while we await the birth. You're born of a woman of exalted lineage, though Arima would never say it, the humble soul."

I glanced down and placed my hand on my belly.

"Aye," Rhona said. "The *leanbh* will share in that blood." Her brow furrowed, and she continued in a whisper. "And in Blunt's, will it not?"

I froze at the mention, but Úna's tender fingers brushing my temples gave me the power to nod. Putting the image from my mind, I met Rhona's eye.

"And Cormac," I said. "Do tell how I come to share his blood?"

She sighed and took my hand to help me up. We sat on low stools by the peat fire, its loamy smoke drawn off by the strong Atlantic wind as it scoured the stone chimney cap. Úna poured tea and sat down nearer to me, seeming for all the world to discern our every meaning as we spoke despite her absence of English. When she pulled back her hood to drink, I reached to touch her hair; she held my eye, the corners of her lips twitching in the merest suspicion of a curve, while I extracted a yard and more of thick, wavy silver tresses.

"That's her smilin'," said Rhona. "She feels much and shows it little." At this last, she leaned to comb out Úna's hair with her fingers, grinning sweetly, as if on her behalf.

"Is she like—?"

"No, *a chuisle*," answered Rhona before I could utter Eleanor's name. "Úna suffers from no impediment. 'Tis only the sun she shrinks from, the pallor of her." She took Úna's face in her hands and touched her forehead to hers. "Ah, but you should see her in the moonlight, Selkie!"

"How is it she seems to understand my English?"

"She speaks only Irish, but any language signifies when she chooses to open her heart to the speaker," Rhona replied.

"Did she receive church schooling?"

"Scarce any. She was expelled from a Catholic orphanage when she was only six. She's uncommon in more than her looks and a terror to the devolved pieties."

Rhona explained that while instructing the orphans on the nature of divinity, a priest had asked if there was anything impossible to God. Little Úna had raised her hand and volunteered that there were in fact two things God could not do. Over unchecked laughter from the other children, the priest had smugly challenged her to name them.

"God cannot lie."

"Why not?"

"Because the word of God is truth." She spoke looking down at her desk.

The priest had grown quiet along with the orphans. Heady stuff for a six-year-old.

"And what is the second?"

Úna's preternatural red eyes fixed him, then, like stove doors opening in a dark room.

"She cannot see your sin through the blood of Jesus."

"Magic, you wonder?" said Rhona. "Well, her little performance was followed by a speedy vanishing act, to be sure. Witness of the divine feminine aside, her most alarming blasphemy was implying she saw certain sins that God did not. That priest transferred back to Dublin shortly after, and I found the little one wandering in the Donegal Diamond."

Úna took Rhona's wrist and turned her head to me. *"Inis di an Cormaic, Siúr Roinseach,"* she said in her chiming voice.

"Aye, Siúr Úna," Rhona replied, "I have not forgotten. Let us speak of my Cormac." She drained her cup and cleared her throat.

I scarce credited myself equal to framing my history in all its blushing particulars when first I took up my quill. For my part, my resolution has won a melancholic sort of liberation; but I pray these letters discover what you would know, my girl, without they overmuch shock your sensibilities.

Howbeit, that duty Rhona long ago fulfilled in advocating Nessie's marriage by no means embarrassed her inclination, or indeed privilege, to pursue her own natural union with David. This ancient right, as who should say *droit de partage,* was the price a sister paid to depart for married life in the world: if she would not herself contribute a child to the community, then she willingly suffered some dissemination—the *bon mot* indeed—of her chosen mate for its increase.

Their several meetings rose to no height of love on Rhona's part, but founded an erotic bond that lasted well into David's marriage. Nessie could not have failed to discern it, though Rhona would have made no secret.

The menace the liaison posed to Nessie's ambitions, however, was manifest. For these, she had abandoned the Communion of the Roman Church; but unlike her father, she had also sacrificed a fellowship older and more defining than any religion, and at length the very country of her birth. In Nessie's mind, she had paid too much, and gone too far, to remain subject to the rule of the grove. She'd earned for herself a life—a civilized English life—untouched by the breath of scandal.

For Rhona, the matter ended with Cormac's conception; but Nessie, lacking in that easy passion which influenced, for better or worse, Rhona's every decision, was pierced each time she saw its glow in her husband's eye. The knowledge that Rhona had a healthy son in Donegal bit her all the deeper after Eleanor's birth, and deeper still upon Hagen's death. Having witnessed Nessie's jealousies, and the way the bitter artistry of her mind could turn such thoughts, I felt for the first time some measure of sympathy for her.

All this Rhona related to me without a trace of shame or regret, but for her sister's misery. For my part, no catechism withstood in judgment when I learned of the practice—the higher good of the community coming before private right, and a woman's body her own to serve either as she chose. Indeed, the moral liberty with which she spoke of it eased my lingering conflict over my chosen defense of Eleanor. I began to believe I might one day hold that act as noble as I hold its issue precious, however unable I may be to forgive Blunt.

Nessie had never consented to meet or correspond with Cormac.

"More's the pity," said Rhona. "A *leanbh* firstborn to the

sisterhood is the child of all. Cormac is as much Nessie's son as my own. He's the very figure of Hagen. And her David. He has love to spare for us both."

"Did Nessie very much love David?"

Rhona considered. "I think she loved what David represented for her. When our father—your great-grandfather Seamus—made his Protestant confession, he preserved the rights of all our family, our properties, livelihood. Our very mode of being. But he did so at a great cost to himself. He was rejected by his friends. Cut off, by his lights, from eternal salvation. Nessie was more devoted to him than any of us. She alone would accompany him to the Anglican church of a Sunday when she was little, to hold his hand on his empty pew. He was no more welcome there than among his former Catholic mates at the public house—the hypocrites all. I think Nessie made her own conversion just to share in his loneliness. And that ambitious nature: that's her desirin' to prove some nobility in his abnegation. Her talents could well serve this struggling community, if only she would quit that empty London house and come be the leader for which I'm so poor a proxy."

"Self-isolation seems one of her talents."

Rhona sighed. "Aye, but she takes no joy in the loneliness, Selkie. Nessie's is a heart betrayed by its own faculty of mercy. A heart which gave all to honor our father, and the giving in the end insufficient."

Her eyes grew distant as she paused to sip her tea.

"A boy chided her in the road one Sunday as she was walking to services with Seamus. 'Off to take the king's biscuit with that feckin' heretic?' shouts the foul mouthed little guttersnipe. Nessie was perhaps seven years old.

"'Aye! And to hell, if that's where your pope sends a girl for lovin' her Da!' replied she."

Rhona held her knuckle to her lips for a moment. "Seamus used to weep into his whiskey when he told of it."

Una became my guide and constant companion over the days

which followed. We ranged Gweedore Bay in her curragh, from the flat southern estuary and salt marshes, to towering Bloody Foreland in the north. The many islands between vary much in size, Gola being the largest, and each is a study in contrasts, their Atlantic faces ripped into countless sea caves moaning in the relentless wind, a stone's throw from serene protected inlets.

Deep within the most inaccessible of the oceanside caverns lay the refuge and sacred spaces of *na siúracha*, as Úna called the sisterhood. She was uncertain of my swimming abilities and mindful of my condition, and as the curragh made what seemed a perilous approach, standing off from the rocky surf only by vigorous and skillful oarsmanship, a group of women, clothed in singular garments of sealskin against the cold water and jagged stones, swam out to meet us. They pushed a tiny boat—little more than a willow frame hulled with hide—in which they ferried us safely into the caves.

Úna led me along a vast network of grottoes, where she was greeted with cordial respect by women of all ages. Some squatted in circles shucking oysters or making salt; others performed domestic duties, washing or cooking in large copper kettles, and still others sat in silent meditation. In one large cave, dappled with sunlight from its high fissures, a dozen or so were fencing with knotted wood staves, and I searched my memory for Nessie's Irish term, so similar to the Basque *benetako trebetzia.*

"Is é sin bataireacht traenáil?" I ventured.

Úna's eyes glinted, and several of the women laughed in good-natured approval and doubtless some amusement at my manner of speech.

"Tá sé, deirfiúr Béarla!" one replied. "That it is, English sister!"

A pointed stare from Úna silenced the lot. *"Caecilia!"* she said, her voice ringing through the caverns.

The women stopped and faced her in respectful order, one and all.

"Siúr Caecilia!" she titled me.

I understood in part: their playful reference had

discountenanced her, and I was moved by the deference they showed her despite her young age. What baffled me, however, was that Úna had been acquainted with me only as Selkie, yet she presented me as "Caecilia." This is the Latin form of my original name, Xixili.

Úna could not have known of it. No one knew of it; indeed, none but Arima and I had *ever* known it—that Basque name evinced only by the middle initial X upon my birth record. Her understanding of languages she could not speak, and now this divining of secrets, such inexplicable discernment I had never before seen demonstrated.

"Bail duit, Siúr Caecilia," said the sisters as they lined up to greet me with a kiss on each corner of my mouth. I returned their blessings.

We exited the grottoes via a different route, passing some caverns that were alive with fire, laughter, and song of numinous beauty, and others so empty it seemed nary a seal had ever inhabited. I surveyed the few possessions of the *siúracha*. Each had multiple purposes: their staves doubled as tent poles or brooms, their cauldrons as bread ovens, the sealskins as bedding, carpet, shelter, and kit. None were fixtures, but all portable, indeed, designed for hasty departure—transport by water on a swimmer's back or in the little skin boats—and to leave no trace behind.

It was slack tide when we emerged into the open air. The swimmers easily pushed us around a small promontory to the protected inlet where Úna's vessel was waiting. The moment the curragh cleared its shelter, the six rowers were at misery against the heavy southwest winds and ignorant of the safe use of their gaff-rigged sail in a heavy breeze. I bade them keep us head to wind, then hefted my skirts and shimmied partway up the mast to unbind the canvas. The crew swore oaths for fear the boat would capsize should the sail set sudden. I punched several tie points with my dirk and threaded the jack cords to shape an efficient double reef.

I sprang aft to take the tiller and sheet, bore off two points, and as the canvas caught the breeze and bellied out with a stiff crack, I ordered the crew to ship oars and sit upon the windward rail to counter the roll. With mortal confidence, Úna repeated my commands in Irish—and this a further mystery, as by way of proving her understanding I had been alternating between English and Basque.

The piggish little curragh at length found its line and began to cut across the wind on a wide but speedy tack, kicking up such a wake that I called for a spare sealskin to wrap myself and Úna. The galloping slap of the leather hull upon the waves prised from her a fulsome grin and frank, childlike laughter.

I shouted my order to come about, this time in Latin. Upon Úna's translation, the crew sprang as one, ducked the swinging boom as we crossed the wind, and smoothly mounted the opposite rail.

"*Quomodo potestis intelligere me?*" I asked, my lips to Úna's ear. "How is it that you can understand me?"

She turned, still beaming with excitement. "*Tuigim go maith, mar go bhfuil tú álainn!*"

I merely shrugged and smiled back.

After our choppy westward tack, we made it back to the lee of Gola in short time on a single beam reach, where we were pleased to find Cormac waiting. Úna leapt into his embrace before me—a vision of a brown bear holding a porcelain doll—and he took distinct pleasure in her rapid recount of my use of her curragh as a racing yacht. He gave me the glad news that I was to go inspect our smuggling vessel.

The venerable little sloop had been careened on the calm deserted beach of Bo, a small island near the river's mouth. Cormac and I were pulled across the next morning; he had already ferried over a handful of trustworthy shipwrights and carpenters from Donegal.

I found its hull more or less intact but in need of bracing and replacement of midships timber. The most delicate bit would be the fabrication of a new sternpost and rudder. Surprisingly, the masts were in fair condition, as they likely had never submerged under the rocky shallows from which the ship had been salvaged. The eight small guns were rusty, but not honeycombed, and with grinding and redrilling, they would answer.

I made report of all to Cormac, who nodded gravely and translated for the workmen. I digested the lumber, ironwork, cordage, and other materials that were necessary, and he determined to send as well for a forge and smith. Lacking the resources of an established shipyard, the refitting of the vessel would require several months, and I knew I should have taken to the caves before then to be delivered. I accordingly made all effort to direct the work while I could, at the same time selecting and training the crew.

My greatest pleasure was in the unhurried evenings I passed with Cormac, polishing his knowledge of chart and sextant and projecting the gain and adventure we might share. He was a prodigious seaman and coastal navigator of long experience, but he put it plain he meant to rely upon me to command.

I made no objection but guarded my wonder over what I should do once you were born, my love.

Since my arrival, I had often admired Mount Errigal, whose rose-colored summit stands watch over Gweedore from the east. At Rhona's urging, I chose to take a respite from work and worry and make the short pilgrimage before I became overgrown.

Úna accompanied me, and we ascended a portion of its western face, which gave over the whole of the coast and the sea—a glorious vista which alone merited the journey. Our horses were by then as weary as I, but Úna insisted we circle the entire mountain, she reciting in turn the sacred name for each of its aspects, which varied much with the points of the compass from which we viewed them.

I made several attempts to press the lateness of the hour, but Úna seemed a creature somehow prised from the cycle of time and its concerns, and her unhurried pace made plain she meant to benight us on the mountain. Having watered and unladen our mounts, we watched the twilight from a cairn of ancient stones atop a western rise; and she murmured a prayer as the last rays of the sun seemed to ignite Errigal's peaks with the very pink that blazed in her eyes.

We sat in stillness until the moon rose, and Úna led me carefully up the slope, across a high ledge, and into a dark crevice. She set a bed of blankets upon the smooth stone and left me to rest my swelling ankles. I declined her offer to light her little lamp, being fatigued in the extreme, and fell asleep straightaway.

I found myself covered by Úna's red felt cloak when I awoke several hours later. The wind was piping complex chords in the deep chambers of the mountain, overlain by a supernal harmony that could only have been Úna's voice.

I lay there bathed in the sublime music for a time before opening my eyes. Into the vertical crevasse and upon my face, the rays of the waning moon fell true, and its broken orb framed the naked figure of Úna, turning graceful circles upon the perilous ledge.

Soundless, so not to embarrass her devotions, I crept out. The lunar radiance upon her lambent skin and hair robbed me of my breath. Her eyes remained closed all the while, but when she slowed to curl her toes over the very edge, her back in a balletic arch, ivory breasts and arms uplifted toward the heavens, I felt the nudge of her heart. She gave no sign, but she knew I was there.

Her ecstasy beckoned. I say not I joined involuntary, but with conscious surrender of will, my body was caught up of its own; I stepped out of my garments, shut my eyes, and trusted to the divine dance.

An hour later, the rapturous movements ceased, leaving me sensible only of a blissful purgation and clarity, and we retreated within the cavern.

"On peut rester debout pour se parler un peu? May we stay up and speak awhile?"

Úna nodded without hesitation in response to my French,

opened and lit her lamp—a little scallop shell wrought in silver, its bright wick floating in train oil.

Determined to solve this mystery, I took her hands, looked into her eyes, made deep violet by the flame, and repeated my earlier question.

"How is it, Úna, that you can understand me?"

I sighed when she again replied, *"Tuigim go maith, a ghra mo chroi, mar go bhfuil tú álainn."*

I comprehended no better than before and smiled hopelessly. "How am I meant to decipher such a charming oracle?"

Úna kept hold of my hands, folded her legs, and shut her eyes. On the instant, that purity of awareness which still lingered seemed to focus in my belly, burning like sunlight through a lens.

She reached out and clapped her cupped hands gently upon my ears.

"Éiste!" she commanded in a piecing whisper that rang off the smooth granite walls.

The fire seemed to coil up my spine like a serpent.

"Éiste!" she repeated as she clapped my ears again, and this time the sound seemed to shatter into many distinct tongues. But still my mind resisted the significance.

On her third reprise, she tapped the middle of my forehead with the tip of her finger. *"Éiste!"*

And then it burst brilliant behind my eyes, and I gasped, and the word echoed backward through my mind.

"Éiste! Escucha. Entend! Enzun! Audite! Eyshto!" It turned like a wheel of voices from antiquity.

The meaning was all one, however.

"Hear!"

And hear I did, the significance of all Úna's Irish now flooding my understanding. The cave, and my mind, grew quiet.

"Tuigim go maith, a ghra mo chroi, mar go bhfuil tú álainn," she whispered again with an angelic smile, and I seized it straightaway.

"I understand you well, love of my heart, because you are so beautiful."

Come September, the low hills blushed with lavender, and the doubt bit harder as my time grew near and I more mindful of my dilemma. Once delivered, would my babe be firstborn to the sisterhood, to remain with me until weaned and then reared in remote Donegal among the *siúracha*? Or would I give you up to the world, to be named and raised by adoptive parents of some great town or city—to lead what Nessie would call a "civilized" life? Was I even capable of so alienating my own child, a stranger among strangers, and I to see you no more again?

Yet unwed as I was, and late in living my very womanhood, what sort of mother could I make? This was no mere voice of Christian scruple; I pondered equally how, if I kept the babe, I dare risk command of an undocumented merchant vessel, as likely to finish dancing at a rope's end as setting up my carriage. What mother would scarce consider such a choice? But God forgive me, I sore desired it.

I had done of my best for our sloop. She swam off her blocks at high tide, sound of hull and rudder. Cormac piloted her, under a single topsail and my anxious eye, to a protected inlet on the south shore of Gola, where she would lay at single anchor until her crew completed her rigging and painting.

We christened the vessel the *Murúch na Raghniohie*, or "Mermaid of Ray," which, to Cormac's boundless self-amusement, I had myself been dubbed in Donegal legend after my visitation in the hawthorn bush. We called her simply the *Ray* for brevity.

Rhona escorted me to the deepest of Gola's caverns, reserved for the most revered of the *siúrnach* devotions, childbirth among them. She put aside other duties to keep me company during the last few weeks, and I passed the time in pleasant discourse with her and the other sisters, learning the rituals of purification, making of sacred bread, and surrounded by the sweet rhapsodies of their ancient song and whispered prayer.

She put the question to me one night over her needlework.

"What would you have it be, then?"

"I don't mind. Girl, perhaps," I answered, thinking she meant the sex of the babe.

Her smile flickered. "But whether born to *na siúrnach* or the world is the question."

"Must I decide now?"

"If it's a once-born child you're wanting, then you've to be initiated into the mysteries before the birth," she replied. "I'm willin' if you are."

"I'm far from ready."

"You're far overdue for it. Arima would have passed you in years ago had you not been compelled to keep up appearances for that sister of mine." She lowered her needlework. "You're a *breith cumasach*, at all events—a gifted birth. Úna sees it, and she's another. Your initiation would be but recognition."

I recalled Úna's tracing on my body, astonished at my lack of *an comharthasiúre*, the mark of the sisterhood, like the one my mother bore.

"And if I give the child up to the world?"

"Easier done if a boy, but is that really your desire?"

I felt you turn within me, embraced my belly, and lowered my head in silence. Rhona produced a letter, folded and sealed.

"Perhaps this will help you decide, oh girl of many names. It's been bouncin' between Donegal and Letterkenny for some weeks and just brought to hand this morning."

As she passed it to me, I recognized my mother's fine copperplate hand on the cover. "Mme. Alaba Laughlin, Donegal." It was in reply to the note I had left with Löw and read as follows:

Dearest Alaba,

I bless and thank you for the kindness of your correspondence informing me of the death of Lt. Sebastian Singer, HMRN. As a mother, I felt the comfort of Providence to receive the news from the hand of a niece instead of a stranger, and to know his spirit walked on in familial lands.

And how blessed to know you are to be a mother yourself! You are in capable hands with Rhona, though I pray you may afterward visit England. Our Nessie moved back to London when she heard the news of Sebastian and has not visited since. Its only Eleanor and I here in the Portsmouth house now, as Mary has gone back to Cornwall to practice as a midwife, and Sir George remains long at sea. Eleanor would so love to hold your baby and would mind it as long as you might wish or require.

No need to choose between your family and the world, *cherie*. Should you travel all the seven seas, she would care for it as her own, I hope you understand, and I for them both.

Do visit. I long to see you, my Alaba.

Love always,

Arima

"Beautiful word, *alaba*," Rhona said as I folded the letter. "Basque for 'daughter,' I'm imagining?"

I nodded.

"Just so. Clever girl, informin' her that way. Sebastian dies a hero, not a deserter, and his pretty Irish cousin writes his mum to tell of it."

I smiled, and not just for Rhona's comment. Arima had divined my dilemma and presented a resolution. I had at last some hope, dear one—a way I might give you a life in the world that need not be among strangers nor carry the stigma of illegitimacy; nor, above all, forever separate us.

A lovely hope it was. But what of Blunt?

The birth was without concerning incident, and though the grottoes of Gola may still echo with my cries, I have always found such descriptions an oppressive machination for a mother to practice upon her child. I wish to recount only my joy when first I held you to my bosom, the scent of your silky hair, the petal down of your skin as I pressed it to mine, sweeter than a thousand first kisses. I fell to imagining the resemblance of your features: the fullness of Arima's lips, Rhona's playful brow, my own high cheeks, which dimpled when you smiled.

You were, and are, the most beautiful creature, the very breath of divine grace. I knew then I could never abandon you to strangers. My path was clear.

You will always be both my daughter and Eleanor's, but in accordance with custom, I left it for her, your worldly mother, to name you. I followed all the requirements, weaning you from my own breast at three months to thence rely on other nursing mothers of the sisterhood until you were placed in your new home. Only then did I submit to rituals of purification and formal induction.

Of these I will describe what I can, as I had not time during my sojourn to set down my discoveries in a grammar, or *grimoire*, as Arima would call it. Unlike education read from a primer, a *suire*'s formation requires the writing of one; but these letters must stand for my record of what little I am given to know and pass on.

The Donegal communities are not the oldest in Europe, but believe themselves to have best preserved the ancient doctrine and ritual, they being the remnant pushed to the most isolated northwestern regions of the continent; persecuted first by native Druids, then by the early Celtic Christians, and finally by the Roman Church, which suppressed all three.

The initiation ceremony, *saorghlanadh inishuire,* is a ritual of physical and spiritual purification. In former times, it took place on Inishuire itself, a secluded island in the middle of Loch Finn, or the "Beautiful Lake." This had been the home of the Chríonmháthair—the leading woman of the Donegal sisterhood—who there performed whisper counsel in a small underground cavern.

Siúrnach tradition holds that the sixty-ninth Chríonmháthair, then ninety years old and lame with age, was the victim of a shameful murder by Druid clansmen. By happenstance, a hunting party were paddling past the island when they spied the Chríonmháthair being transported along the shore on the back of her burly grandson. The cowards released a hail of arrows from the boats, piercing them both. Bleeding badly, he kept hold of the old woman and made to flee but, after another cruel volley, stumbled into the water and died with her.

The sisters relocated farther northwest, as they had many times before, and Beautiful Lake came to be known as Red Lake for the innocent blood spilled there. *Siúrnach* initiation moved to a rocky grove on a plain near the mouth of the Gweedore River, named "Beautiful Stones," or Carrick Finn, in remembrance of the former site.

And to Carrick Finn I was taken one morning, gentle thunder rumbling over the Bloody Foreland as I was pulled across the bay. The rites normally coincided with the first rainfall of a maiden's flux; but I had waited the required time after weaning, and my fertility now evinced itself anew, concerning me for the gossamer robe of white silk I wore, already damp in the drizzle.

We arrived at the circle, a slight elevation in sight of Errigal and the sea, where the women lay a cordon of silk banners between the stones, a private space under the high gray canopy of sky, and shed their garments. I climbed onto an elevated table stone, my bare feet cold on the wet slate, and each sister stepped up in turn to bestow a singular open-mouthed kiss, drawing the breath from my lungs, then exhaling it back within, warm and heady. My clinging wet robe concealed neither my form nor the crimson streak of my lunar condition. The sisters peeled it from my body. Rhona placed a silver knife in my left hand, a gold hoop in my right, and a wreath of hawthorn upon my head.

Úna sat on her heels before me, holding a large polished bowl of pure silver, and looked up with that newfound smile, her eyes made red by the somber skies.

"Oscailt amach, a ghra mo chroi," she said.

I obeyed, dropping my head back and spreading my legs and arms to catch the running rain.

Another languid roll of thunder sounded as Úna slid the bowl beneath me.

Caiscín is one of those many Irish words that is not precisely

Englishable. It signifies "wild grain bread" or "Easter bread," which I daresay is rooted in its taking three days to rise.

And three sleepless days I was rooted, with the silver bowl of dough in my lap, before resurrecting from that pit beneath the ancient standing stone. I meditated, sweated, and fasted in the tiny *purgatorium,* with only water and what little air drew in past a brazier of smoking sage and kelp. I saw visions which will never leave my memory; yet by the third morning, I had forgotten my very self.

When the sisters at length tilted back the stone, I handed up the bowl, and Rhona bent low to descend the little steps. She posed a series of ritual questions which I am bound by oath not to write and, after an hour's discourse, bestowed the blessing of initiation. It made me, formally and forever, a *suire* of her order, a sworn servant of the world, and a devotee of its liberation from delusion.

Words cannot describe my sensibility of renewed being as I emerged into the fresh air and rich aroma of the *caiscín* baking over a peat fire. Three waters, three grains, and three airs. That, and three days to rise, is the simple *recette.* Its broad round crust was scored with the nine-pointed *comharthasiúre.* There was dandelion wine to accompany the sacred feast, and we laughed and sang around the fire until dawn.

I slept most of the way back across the bay, my head cradled in Úna's bosom. My memory is more vivid, however, of the following days and nights I passed with her in Gola's deep grottoes, entangled atop piled sealskins, bathing in the rocky cascades, the fathomless, salty partaking. In those breathy kisses expired a lifetime of dubiety and vexation, the first love expressed to me, and verily me, denuded of disguise, absent of constraint.

Indeed, my silver siren was no more bound by chivalry than I. She demonstrated her desire with the candor of innocence, and my heart soared to discover a specie of passion more forceful in the offering than the taking.

At Cormac's urging, Rhona at length deranged our bliss. Come to inform me that the sloop was ready, she discovered me lying bravely still as Úna placed the final touches with razor, needle, and ink upon my *comharthasiúre*.

I embraced them both tenderly in anticipation of my early return from England, and I boarded the *Ray* an hour before the ebb, the mark's raw sting an agreeable *memoire*.

The sloop was laden with linen and provisions, undutied and quite common to English import. The *Ray* proved sweet and weatherly, and the short shakedown cruise useful in preparing her and her crew for future Atlantic crossings.

And of course our most precious cargo was you, my love.

Traffic picked up within sight of the English coast. I shifted into the nondescript costume of a merchant captain against presenting the singular spectacle of a female at the helm, and Cormac not yet equal to piloting the Channel.

We docked at Portsmouth by the first light of dawn. I gave Cormac instruction for dealing with the harbormaster and tradesmen. Unless matters went wrong, I would be back aboard by the next afternoon tide and directed we be unladen, watered, and provisioned before then—no leisure to drive hard bargains. I strapped my sword belt, slung my ditty, and merged with the dockyard throng—mainly stevedores and fish merchants at that early hour—cradling you beneath my coat, unaccustomed to the pepper of English voices. Once on the main road, I roused a hack shay.

I made the driver to stop a small distance from the house, wondering how I might call without revealing myself to the servants. Arima was in the side garden cutting herbs for an early breakfast.

She looked up as I approached.

But I must interrupt my tale of arrival with another, dear girl. Jeroen does not like the prospect of registering his disembarkation here in Gipuzkoa, and neither do I carry money or papers necessary to clear customs. I will find a way to get us discreetly ashore and finish this letter when settled.

23 Ladder of the Rock

"This far you may come and no farther;
here is where your proud waves halt."

Job 38:11

1602 BCE
Eastern Mediterranean

"Shall we worship the god of death?" Luyan began.

A confused murmur. He raised his voice. "Shall we make offering to Mot?"

"Ēl forbid! Never! No!" The people were confused, splitting into factions, but all objected to the unthinkable. More and more began to gather. Some who had taken shelter in the outer buildings emerged, running the gauntlet of burning rain to hear Luyan's message.

He hurled his voice above the din. "And yet that is what you do!"

A pause. "Your complacence in the face of the coming destruction is no less! You turn your faces from the earth, your ears from the voice of the Goddess. In your ruler's own words, you flip like fish in a basket!"

Sedu and the Bint-Iamīna pulled closer to him. Mabug-Rad was massaging his swollen jaw with a vengeful scowl, speaking into the ears of the other Amorites. Similite Habiru were standing with the rural pilgrims and the Egyptians. The urban Canaanites seemed lost; even the residents of Gubel avoided Adad-Sin's gaze.

Mabug-Rad cried out. "It is you who would confound us! Indilimgur is the father of Canaan! Ēl, the ancient of days, is the father of all gods!"

"Keftius gave birth to Canaan!" Luyan retorted. "And the earth, who speaks now in warning, is she not our mother—and yours? Can you secure enough of her gifts in your temple granaries at Ugarit and Megiddo to sustain you through years of drought and famine? Can you safeguard the grain from mildew? Her leaven breathes life into the bread of her children. It is poison to those who would hoard her bounty to gain power!"

The seedy Similite leader spoke. "There is only one god! He is Ēl-Dārû, invisible and eternal! All Habiru worship him, even your Iamīnite servants who stand there at your side!"

Sedu broke in. "The Bint-Iamīna serve no one but God, Similite! A freedom won honorably, unlike your pillaged life of exile! But have we not other names for him? Is he not also Alapu‘Ēl, the bull god? Ēl-Shadû, god of the mountains? You make him invisible because you haven't a scrap of parchment saved from your desert fires on which to figure him. But how few generations ago were you prostrate before stone images of an old man with horns upon his head?"

The Similite had reached the limit of his theology. Luyan continued. "There is no time left to us for debate. If your roots lend credit to my warning, know that they stand before you. Keftius is the bull, transmuted into your Ba'Ēl. Its horns are the horns of your altar." He turned to the Egyptians and raised his voice. "The horns of the *labrysu* are the horns of your Apis! Your Hathor!"

Many of all factions gasped at the blasphemy. Having overcome his own pious dread, Luyan saw no further point in cautious words. When we break our bondage to fear, the Kozhiniru had said, we may make it our servant.

He turned to face Adad-Sin. "Have you never wondered, lord, about the source of your Canaanite myth of the twin mountains, Tharumagi and Targhizizi? Why they are said to support the heavens and hold back the seas, yet are nowhere to be found in the Levant?" Adad-Sin made no reply.

Luyan faced the crowd again. "The story is but a lost shadow of your Aegean origins. The sacred space between the twin peaks of Mount Ida on Keftius is where all things join. They are the eternal horns that raise the depths and tear down the heights. It is better to efface wisdom entirely than to corrupt it, and it is only wisdom now that will save you!"

Here he pounded the staff into the steps. In a blinding bolt, the discharge leapt from the copper serpent to the pinnacle of the temple roof. The assembly reacted as one, with shrieks, prayers, and prostrations.

Luyan paused again and shut his eyes. The wind was beginning to relent. He could speak now and be heard by all. He could speak now with authority.

He gathered his breath one last time and delivered his warning.

An hour later, the rains had stopped, and the city was clearing as fast as the skies. The country dwellers and Similites had departed for the mountains. Adad-Sin had sent out his best riders with torches to warn the cities and villages of the Levantine coast. Sedu and his Iamīnite Habiru had left to escort Ethtar's company south along the ocean road. In the courtyard of the temple, smudge pots and torches were relit. Acolytes were reverently caring for the body of the high priest. A red moon came into view in the southeast.

The Egyptians were the only remaining problem. Despite Adad-Sin's orders, they had armed themselves, and a full cohort of Nebamun's soldiers ringed the acropolis. Nebamun ordered Mabug-Rad guarded until he determined what to do about his attempted assassination of the city ruler. No nobles or officials of rank, whether Canaanite, Amorite, or Keftiun, were being permitted to leave the temple complex. But Luyan needed to reach the ship.

He paid his last respects to the high priest. He felt special sympathy for one whose life was poured out in devotion to a foreign goddess. As he squatted over the body, a young acolyte asked him of the high priest's last words.

Luyan had not had time to consider them. " 'Within . . . her prophesy. Her oracle,' he said."

The acolyte seemed confused and looked over his shoulder at the great doors. "No oracle has spoken in the temple of Ba'Ēl-at Gubel for generations," he said. "Especially not a female."

"I assumed he was speaking of the goddess herself," Luyan said.

The young man shook his head. "An oracle is a human being through whom the gods speak. Prophesy given within the sacred confines of a temple."

Luyan rose slowly to his feet and looked up the steps. He mounted them quickly. Near the top, Adad-Sin was speaking with Nebamun. Mabug-Rad and the Amorites were standing off to one side, nursing their burns.

"We must enter the sanctuary," Luyan said.

Adad-Sin shook his head. "It is a shambles, and the goddess lies upon her face. The priests must repair the disarray, rededicate and re-sanctify it before we may enter."

"Please, my lord," Luyan said. "I believe the high priest bade us go in. His last words as he died. I believe he received an oracle before the storm began and would have us hear it."

Adad-Sin looked doubtful but ordered his guards to accompany them.

"We enter together," Nebamun said to the Amorites.

They brought more torches, righted and lit the braziers as they made their way down the central gallery. The reeds and silk tent had been blown out by the strong winds, and the ornate cedar latticework splintered and scattered about the stone floor. Copper moonlight filtered through the many gaps in the roof.

The statue of the goddess lay facedown, her feet propped upon her heavy limestone pedestal. She had not been blown over by the storm, but lowered with ropes suspended from the beams above before the canopy was placed over the marriage bed. She was to have retained the position throughout the ceremony, a hidden ritual symbolizing Ba'Ēl's dominance.

Luyan heard a cough in the darkness. He seized a torch and circled around the rubble.

Sitting cross-legged against the pedestal and facing the portico that gave upon the moonlit sea—facing west toward Keftius and Thera—was the Kozhiniru, her eyes swollen shut.

She had braced her back against the stone as she confronted the full force of the sulfurous torrent, to avoid being blown down the gallery and out the temple doors. Luyan dropped to his knees and took her wrist. Her skin was raw, but she betrayed no pain. She turned her head weakly. He could not tell if she was trying to open her eyes.

Nebamun's voice boomed behind him. "What deception is this? We left her on your ship, surrounded by her guardswomen!"

"Be assured King Indilimgur will hear of this latest abomination of Adad-Sin!" Mabug-Rad said. "A foreign priestess in the sanctuary of the temple! May he soon install a ruler on the throne of Gubel who would not suffer such desecration."

Luyan opened his mouth, but the Kozhiniru spoke first.

"Indilimgur will not sit long enough on the throne of Ebla to see Adad-Sin's successor." Her voice had an unfamiliar, watery resonance.

"Silence the witch!" Mabug-Rad cried. "Has she not wrought enough destruction this day?"

"Sever his head if he utters another word," Nebamun said. The nearest soldier's hand sprang to the grip of his *kophesh*. "It is death to silence one who speaks for the gods."

"I beg you continue, Kozhiniru Entu," said Adad-Sin. He called for a skin of fresh water, and Luyan held it to her lips. "What have you come to tell us? What is the fate of our Amorite king?"

"Indilimgur has but a handful of years remaining. Ebla nears its final destruction," she said.

"Will it be at the hands of the Hittites, holy one?" asked Nebamun.

"It will. But fear not, Egyptian. Soon after Thera has had its way, on this very hill you shall erect a Theban temple, a temple of your obelisks. The Hittites will not rule long in the Levant." She inclined her head toward Luyan. "Nor in Cilicia, my son. Yet another handful of seasons and the Hittite ruler, too, shall be no more. Your homeland freed by yet another king. The world sees itself through the eyes of its heaven. Warring gods and warring men beget one another in endless revolution. As above, so below."

Sorrow and awe battled within him. This was the Kozhiniru's broken body, but the voice in her mouth was that of the divine. Miraculous as it was, he knew she would not survive it.

"Kozhiniru," he said, "these are momentous matters. But they cannot be what brought you swimming from our ship in a storm."

"The truth of these prophesies will unfold before you in a short time. I give them that you may believe what I speak next. Things more dim and distant. And more momentous still."

"We listen, holy one," said Nebamun.

She spoke of her lost children. The other great empires of the Mediterranean would survive Thera's calamity, now that the warning was received. But it would destroy the Keftiu and strand their colonies in the far great West, beyond the Pillars of the Gods. Nebamun, a mariner, could barely conceive it. The others not at all. But Luyan knew the truth and prayed they set her words to memory.

"Find them, lords," she said. "Let them not remain adrift for more than a few generations, without a lifeline to their home waters. If they do, they will forget their faith and culture. Forget their very bloodline. But how to make ships and smelt bronze into blades, these things they will not forget. They have more wood and copper at their feet than is left in all the six kingdoms." She paused, her voice cracking, and Luyan gave her another swallow.

"They will remember. And return from the western seas generations hence. Countless thousands, abandoned and homeless, in search of the roots of their ancient empire. Finding it gone they will despoil yours. And that calamity you shall not survive."

She went silent. Luyan looked at the faces of Adad-Sin and Nebamun. Fear he saw, and even some understanding. But nothing to which he could entrust so great a consequence. So much depended on where they might lodge this knowledge and the treasure that was its key. His work was not done. He needed to evade Nebamun's soldiers and regain the ship.

But one more question remained, its answer not for Canaanite ears.

"My lords, she is dying. Let me fulfill my private obligations, I pray you."

Adad-Sin replied graciously, "Certainly, Lord Luyan. We shall await you without."

He stood and led the company back down the corridor, leaving Luyan and the old woman bathed in the light of his single torch.

He held the waterskin again to her lips, but she was too weak to drink.

"Kozhiniru," he asked, "what has the Goddess shown you of our future? What will become of the *serkaru*?"

"You see it yourself, Iluyanka," she said, now in her own voice. "A distant time when man will become his own disaster. When the wilds can be stripped no further, and even the farthest grottoes will no longer shelter or sustain us. A time when we will be driven forth to be in the world, but not of it. And hold our whispers in our hearts."

"Will this destroy us?"

"Never our essence. Merely yet another change in its expression. The watercourse lives in us, as we live in it. Destruction never comes from bringing forth what is within, Iluyanka." Her voice began to fade. "Whether word or action, expression will be our salvation."

The Goddess would speak no more through her. She clutched feebly at his hand.

Her voice grew thinner. "Your obligation here is done, and well done, *Kahu*. My coracle is below, at the foot of the cliff, where the torches were to be lain. Go back to the ship and preserve your treasure." Her cough was no more than a deep rattle.

"Be peaceful in your mind, Mother. I will lodge the chest high and deep, safe from Thera's wrath and what is to follow," Luyan said, his tears gathering.

She forced her eyes open, and through the slits they gleamed in the moonlight like the healer's coppered honey.

"Yes, my son. But it is a greater treasure of which I speak. Go to her. Preserve yourselves above all. The most wondrous bringing forth . . ."

Her eyes shut fully and opened no more.

Luyan did not rejoin Adad-Sin at the temple entrance. In a bittersweet figure of Hibya's passion, he bound the old woman's lifeless arms and ankles tightly around his back and climbed out the western portico into the darkness. The cliff was left wet and scoured by the storm, and it took all his masthead skills to balance his beloved burden and find handholds in the rock.

At last, he dropped heavily into the sand, made his way along the base to the stairs, and found the coracle in the moonlight. He placed her body inside and wrapped it tenderly in the sealskin covering. Many smaller vessels had been beached or broken up by the heavy winds. Looking about for Egyptians, he pushed the little boat quietly into the harbor and kicked off. He prayed he might swim as well as he climbed.

A wisping, sulfurous brume rolled upon the water. It burned his eyes but concealed his movements from the Egyptian ships as he pushed the coracle ahead of him. It took him half an hour. Panting quietly, he neared the Keftiun vessel as it lay gently pitching in the dark. There were no rowers on the outer galleries to extend him an oar, and the scuttle doors would be sealed tight from within. He craned his neck and saw Hibya squatting on one knee on the taffrail, leaning on her poleax in the moonlight.

The *serkarui* were still at guard. A ruse to fool the Egyptians? Or did they truly believe the Kozhiniru to yet be aboard? He needed to alert Hibya without raising the alarm. The nearest Egyptian vessel was no more than two hundred paces away. He directed his love and whispered her name.

She sprang to her feet and pointed her ax toward the dark, foggy water. About to call out to the other *serkarui*, she was touched by his familiar presence.

"Luyan?"

"*Ayi, yam aishymi!* Open the rowing gallery scuttle!"

As casually as possible, she pretended to stretch and climbed slowly off the taffrail. A weary sentry taking a break. Once down, she crouched and ran to the companionway and down to the lower deck. She unlatched the scuttle door and clambered quietly through, her head appearing over the gallery rail just above Luyan. She strained eagerly for him, her smile uncontained, but it froze upon her lips when she made out the outlines of the coracle in the fog.

She could not risk calling down any more *serkarui*. Luyan levered the coracle upward and pushed its end toward her. His stomach wrenched as it nearly slipped back off the rail—a splash that would have surely given them away—but Hibya managed to hold it. When it was safely aboard, she reached out for Luyan.

With fervid reverence, she tenderly bit his mouth, his face. But she did not weep.

"You knew?" Luyan asked, holding her head in his hands.

She nodded. "She went off before the storm. Ordered us not to follow. But to double our anchor and act as if we guarded her still. The Goddess was already on her lips. Her prophesy could not be denied, and we knew her life was near its end." She placed her hand upon the body and looked into Luyan's eyes. "Thank you, *yam aishymi*, for returning her. A *serkaru* should never be interred within the earth. Now she can be tended by her sisters. Surrendered properly to her next journey on the waters."

He squeezed her hand. "We have little time. We cannot risk the sound of rowing, and the sea breeze is against us. We have no choice but to slip both our anchors. Our only advantage is the ebb tide. We must drift slowly on the outgoing current toward the harbor entrance, making as much distance as we can before the Egyptian flagship takes notice. Only then do we raise sail, and pray our tack carries us clear of the jetty."

She nodded, took a dagger, and dove noiselessly into the water. She cut the cables of both anchors below the waterline before resurfacing. They were not likely to need them again.

Hibya passed the word for the *serkarui* to remain at their posts along the rails, making no sign of their departure. Luyan kept low as he crept on deck and untethered the port steering paddle. Slowly, almost imperceptibly, the retreating tide carried the ship through the darkened harbor and toward the sea. Luyan steered to pass between the stern of the Egyptian flagship and the rock jetty at the harbor mouth.

The ruse almost succeeded. The two flanking ships took no notice as the Keftiuns drifted silently past, but the flagship raised the alarm when the dark hulk appeared, crossing her stern against the shimmering waters. A hail of Egyptian arrows peppered the side and flew whining over the deck. The *serkarui*, as one, crouched low and shielded their chests with their *labrysu*.

Luyan ran to loose the bunts and brailing lines, and the sail fell and filled. He hauled with all his weight upon the sheet and gave it to a crewman to tie off. The deckhands knelt behind the bulwarks, but Luyan needed to stay standing to lever the massive steering oar. Hibya stood between him and the Egyptian archers. She deflected several arrows with the broad side of her *labrysu*.

The Egyptians had hauled anchor and begun rowing to close. But cutting the breeze on a close tack, the slender Keftiun ship shot through the narrowing gap and out into the choppy sea, passing within feet of the jagged promontory.

The heel lessened, and the ship picked up speed as Luyan turned her southward and helped the crewmen re-sheet the sail. On their fast beam reach, they would pass Surru shortly after dawn and be in sight of the sea caves by midmorning.

Luyan greeted the sunrise from the masthead, scanning anxiously for Egyptian warships. He welcomed the morning land breeze, which would provide the ship seaward leeway and a good offing from the rocky island port of Surru and coastal traffic. Egyptian galleys liked to hug the shoreline. With the navigational ability the Keftiu had given him, he was not so limited.

Despite himself, his eyes turned west, where Thera's titanic bow lay strung and drawn. For the hundredth time, he prayed they might reach safety before it was loosed.

He slid down the backstay and adjusted the steering paddles. Hibya appeared at the companionway and greeted him with a Cilician kiss and a cup of tea. She'd stood watch with him most of the night as he steered due south, keeping the star Kolchab off their stern. As the moon set, the *serkarui* had released the Kozhiniru's naked body over the side with a hymn that was dolorous and haunting.

Luyan sipped gratefully. "Is all well below?"

"The passengers are at table and will come back on deck when you deem it safe. But the lower holds are flooding slowly. Nearly three hands of water. The crew cannot locate the leak."

He reflected. "The storm did more damage than we thought. The buffeting in the harbor must have loosened the seams of the hull. There is little point bailing. Let us hope the ship survives our need for her. It will not be long."

"And the cargo?" she asked.

"We will be swimming off, pushing the crew and passengers in coracles. Little can be carried."

She nodded. "What matters most is in the forepeak."

He stroked her hair. "What matters most we carry within us."

She smiled. A crewman called out. The tower of Surru was in sight. Luyan retrieved the navigator's angle from the instrument locker and took its height and bearing. Consulting the chart and compass, he drew a line, calculated the tower's distance, and marked their position. His course was laid to bypass the port island well offshore and approach within an *iter* of the caves.

He thought of the navigator, of Durzhyar. He prayed that Ethtar had brought them safely to Simmiltu Surru. Within a few hours, he would know. He felt the pressure of the short, uncertain time. But the god-fear was gone.

The bright limestone cliffs came in sight off the port bow as the sun was nearing its height. Luyan fell off southeast, making for the point where they rose to their highest and touched the sea.

They had avoided the Egyptians. He looked at the chart one last time. Three small islands—there they were, just ahead. A moderate surf slapped the arched chalk tunnels that penetrated the cliffs in a deep network. He hove the ship to, motionless in the water, steering and sail power perfectly balanced. A willful stillness.

He went aloft—perhaps the last time in his life he would climb a mast—removed his loincloth, and waived it. For several minutes he saw no sign of life, and his heart began to sink. Then a knot of more than twenty coracles shot into sight from between two huge limestone pillars, as if delivered from the loins of an elephant god. They were pushed by dozens of *serkaru* swimmers. The wind picked up suddenly, and his garment blew out of his hand.

Rare for the summer, the northern gale blew steady as the last of the passengers and crew were taken off the ship. Even with the combined efforts of the Surruian and Keftiun *serkarui,* it had been long work, and the afternoon sun was beginning to dip. Ethtar stood with Luyan and Hibya on the upper deck.

"Sedu and the Bint-Iamīna will guide the Keftiu inland," Ethtar said. "They will take refuge in the mountains on the other side of the River Yirdenu. At a place called Rephra-Ahk. Your people will be safe there."

"And your *serkarui?*" asked Hibya.

"The message has spread down the coast. All are fleeing to higher ground. The great ridge above these caves—the ladder of Surru—is the loftiest place for many *iters,*" Ethtar said.

Raya, Anekti, and Quarta boarded over the taffrail. "You are still aboard?" Raya asked. "Beach the ship on that sandy inlet, if you wish, Luyan, but may it not be better to just abandon it here and swim off with us?"

Luyan shook his head. "I have one more duty to perform to the south, in the high caves of Mount Karam-Ēl, and a heavy burden which a coracle cannot carry. It will be faster sailing with this wind at my back."

"At our back," Hibya said.

Raya looked at her with concern before her smile returned. "Yes, time is short. You will find us again?"

"We wander bewildered, but never lost. Forever will find us all," Hibya replied. A snatch from one of Raya's beloved childhood songs. It drew the intended laugh. They all embraced, Luyan and Ethtar more firmly than any.

"Make haste now," Ethtar said, turning to fight back a tear.

She was first into the clear blue sea. After the others followed, Luyan unbound the steering paddles and made full sail. Once his course was set, he refastened them with thick rope. He needed make no more adjustments. In less than three hours, the northern wind would drive them hard onto the broad sandy promontory at the foot of Karam-Ēl. The vineyard of god.

Hibya and Luyan pulled the precious chest from its cache in the forepeak and sat together upon it. Their first moment of rest since he had regained the ship. Luyan met her golden eyes and covered her hand with his own. The hand she rested often now upon her belly.

He looked back. In the distance, atop the high ridge of Simmilu Surru, the Ladder of the Rock, stood a lone man on horseback. Luyan's keen eyes made out a yellow tunic and an arm extended in farewell. Naked as Hibya now, he had nothing to wave with. But he was sure the Iamīnite knew he could see clearly.

The sun was setting when the long climb was finally complete. Luyan and Hibya were pulling the chest up the last of the piney ridges in a rope sling, ripping it with hurried regret through the delicate flowered bushes, guiding it carefully along the smooth basalt cliffs, when it happened.

The air went abruptly dead, as though a thick door had been slammed shut. Hibya turned to Luyan. He saw her lips move but could not make out her words. He breathed in, as though through a thin reed, and the sound came.

It seemed he heard it first with his skin, the hairs on his forearm like grain in a windy field. A deep hum resonated within his ears, then resolved into a towering rumble. The very fabric of the firmament seemed to split about him, tearing slowly from west to east. It did not stop or relent. It was the mere rolling echo of a far greater bellow, two hundred leagues distant, that had occurred nearly an hour before. The wave would follow, thirty minutes behind the sound.

Luyan managed not to drop the rope. He and Hibya heaved together, and the heavy chest gained the ledge. They had found a suitable cave, high and deep in the rock. They nestled the box in the dark of its farthest corner and piled stones of pumice and basalt against it. Safe kept by one volcano from the ravages of another.

They huddled for a time, hands over one another's ears, and Luyan kissed away her tears. At last, the sound diminished in gradual waves, as though the gods were weeping themselves to sleep.

The setting sun shone directly into the cave, turning Hibya's eyes deep copper. Luyan took her hand, and they stepped out onto the ledge. Not a breath of wind stirred where the green slopes ran down to the turquoise bay. No birds or insects could be heard in the silent air.

A gentle hissing reached them from the beach far below. The surf was receding, cautious and steady, a dream wound back, to be reimagined before the waking day. The seabed stripped nude, no thought to its shame. Out and farther out, nearly a mile distant.

For the briefest moment, all was still.

24 An Imperfect Divinity

"Let us live for the beauty of our own reality."

—Tom Robbins

15 March 1769
Lt. S. Singer, HMRN
Donostia, Spain
(continued)

W e mingled with the crew as they pooled at the gangway for liberty and contrived to evade the port officials with no great difficulty. By grace of the wide floppy brim of Jeroen's hat and my local accent of Basque speech, we drew little suspicion. With the last of my silver—I accepted none from my uncles, and Jeroen sacrificed his pay when he jumped ship—I have secured us a modest room at a little inn high in the hills, where I write now over a cup of excellent coffee.

And so once more again in England.

There were no servants remaining at the Portsmouth house. Nessie had dismissed some and taken the rest back to London nearly a year before, breaking off all correspondence with Eleanor and Arima when she'd learned of her grandson's demise. Because I'd been reported dead, and would almost certainly be taken up for a deserter should anyone learn otherwise, Arima hurried us within and directly to her room. She embraced me, then rocked you in her arms while I gave a precis of my sojourn in Donegal.

"She is so beautiful," she said, kissing your forehead for the hundredth time. "No name yet?"

"No, that's for Eleanor." She met my eye and nodded.

We spoke on quietly of her life in Portsmouth, the ease she and Eleanor felt in the absence of Nessie, and especially Blunt, who had been on the American station for over a year in command of HMS

Viceroy, a ship of the line. She missed Mary but took great pride in her becoming a midwife and relocating to practice in Cornwall.

As a prevention before leaving, Mary had written out a certificate of registry for you, declaring the birth of a daughter to Eleanor, Lady Blunt, dated three months prior, in the event of any question as to your legitimacy.

I was delighted to learn that Dr. Löw Benjamin had been of assistance to Mary in recommending her for her midwifery license, which were becoming increasingly difficult to get. He'd delivered my letter to Arima personally and stayed the following several weeks in Portsmouth to gain her better acquaintance. I had never before seen my mother blush, but she did so in the most charming manner as she discussed their correspondence. Löw posted down at least monthly to call upon her while I was away, and, she informed me, had proposed marriage during his last visit.

I had suspected him already smitten with my description of Arima during our voyage. She had been alone all of my life and was most certainly deserving of the solace of companionship in her later years.

She shook her head as I stated this and held my eye. "No, it is not possible. I made promises long ago to your grandmother that I would remain unmarried. Your father was the one love and devotion of my life, Xixili."

I was on the verge of pointing out that she had known my father not a score of weeks, but the penetrating quality of her regard checked me. Understanding came in a burst, as it had in the caverns of Donegal: I *was* the fruit of that life devotion, her long vigil in England, her long-suffering service to his family; all had been expressions of her love for Hagen.

She smiled, placed her hand upon my head, and kissed my blinking face, as much in confirmation of what had passed between us as of the initiation which had opened me to receiving it.

"Sor Xixili," she whispered.

"Sor Arima," I responded.

Low as we were speaking in that early morning hour, our

presence roused Eleanor, and I trailed off as I noticed her, stock still at the open door of Arima's room, gazing at me with furrowed brow.

I stood up. "Eleanor . . ."

She disappeared in haste, and we heard a row from her room up the hallway.

I looked questioningly at Arima.

"She has barely spoken of you since you left. Like me, she had notice from the Admiralty that you had been lost. You named her as your second of kin," Arima said. "I had to tell her the full truth."

A damned thing to overlook. I followed toward her room and found her ransacking her armoire, a pile of her pretty gowns and dresses already upon the bed. She began hurling them at me.

"Here!" she sobbed. "Take them! They are my best, and as that great beast well knows, we are much of a size!" She broke down, sitting at the side of her bed, her wrists pressed to her ears, clenched nails cutting into her palms.

I was filled with confusion and shame. I squatted before her and took her wrists gently, as Arima had so often done in her childhood. I was certain I had failed her in so many ways: the lifelong deception, the abandonment, even the assignation with Blunt—its horrid memory can only have festered for her, and I could not imagine what sentiments it must have inspired.

"Eleanor, I'm so very sorry. I should have stayed at your side, defended you. I know what a disappointment I am. Your Sebastian may be lost, but love, I would still die to protect you!"

She shook off my hands and slapped at me.

"Oh, can you?" she cried. "*Can* you truly be as stupid a woman as you were a man?"

She rose to her feet. "Protect *me*? It should have been *I* who protected *you*! You're my little cousin! My *niece*, for all love! I cowered there under that bed, paralyzed as I've been all my life, and let you . . . let you . . ." Here she gave a cry of unmixed rage.

"And to learn that you were always and verily as I'd imagined— my baby girl, my poppet. I must have known it somewhere in my heart. I could never understand why I so resented you for playing the man, topping it the little grandson Nessie always wanted " She wound down to quiet sobs. "Oh Christ, Selkie, I feel so low."

She wiped her eyes with her sleeve, and she looked fully and frankly into mine. "I wonder can you ever forgive me?" she whispered. "I doubt I shall ever forgive myself."

I stood and crushed her against me, the full-body embrace of a sister, heart upon heart, and with nothing left to hide. That clarity of the *saorghlanadh inishuire* again gripped me, as is its wont when needed most.

"Eleanor, we do not speak of forgiveness. I need to beg an uncommon service of you."

I turned to take you from Arima and tenderly held you out.

The words came to me, as if fully formed. "Eleanor, Lady Blunt, this is the natural daughter of your husband. A girl also of your own bloodline and the issue of the love we share. Can you conceive to protect her, as she was conceived in my desperate attempt to protect you?"

Her eyes shone with a brilliance I had never before seen in them as she gathered you from my arms. She glanced up, and Arima and I both smiled. She stroked your face and removed your bonnet to touch your hair, now grown out in soft ringlets.

"What's her name?" she asked reverently.

Arima knew the drill better than I.

"This child has no name but the one you will give it," she said slowly, translating the formal Basque words in her mind. "If you accept it, you swear to do so as fully your own, legitimate in the eyes of God and the law."

Eleanor rocked you gently and reflected for several minutes upon the import of the words.

"I accept her," she said at last, her voice thick with emotion.

Arima nudged me out of the bedroom to give you and Eleanor time to bond. I turned back at the door and looked again upon your sweet face. There was a warmth in Eleanor's eyes as she cosseted you. She seemed for the first time fully present in the moment, at length wholly connected to something outside that inner world that had been her habitat and refuge.

"The next few hours will be the most difficult," Arima said. "Best to take a walk, get out of the house. Perhaps you may go visit Matthew and Christopher? They know everything and would be unhappy to miss you. I will help Eleanor settle in with the baby."

She kissed me and held my face. "You took the right decision, *alaba*."

I followed her advice. But though I had left my dunnage and heavy boots with Eleanor, each step away from the house—from you— felt as if I were yanking my foot out of wet sand. The misery of separation left me little mind to reflect upon the danger of my position.

I was still in male array, the simple green frock coat, loose Nanking trousers, and clogs of a merchant captain and in danger of being recognized. Yet my reticence to expose my true sex in Portsmouth lingered, so long hidden to secure Nessie's financial position. Little I then cared for her interests, but a secret safeguarded over a lifetime takes on its own motive force of habitude and is not readily abandoned.

As I turned up the main road toward the dockside district, a passing carriage slowed. I instinctively pulled my hat down over my face, but the window opened, and I heard a familiar voice cry out.

"Singer? Surely, it can't be you? Stop, driver!"

I walked on hurriedly, feigning deafness, but heavy boot steps approached me from behind, and at just a few paces, I recognized the unmistakable voice of McKennis, still in midshipman's uniform.

"Mister Singer! Sebastian Singer, as sure as I'm born! Tarry, will you, sir, and greet your old shipmate!"

There was nothing else for it. I turned around, affected a casual smile, and found my male voice. "Hallo, McKennis! Trust I see you well?"

"Prime, sir, prime! But can I trust my eyes that I see you alive? We were told you never made it back after we put you off with that Jew doctor. You're reported lost at sea this year and more." As dull as he was, his countenance was beginning to migrate from surprise to suspicious confusion. He still carried the scar of our school-day duel on his jaw—a strawberry crescent, like he'd been licking at the bottom of a jam pot.

"Invalided in Ulster," I said, not having thoroughly considered a cover story. "Damned serious condition. Only back on my feet this past month and returned on the next merchant."

He frowned sceptically. "That old Irish sloop by the market yard?"

My blood froze. He had been to the docks. Seen the *Ray*. He was not only aware of my presence in Portsmouth, but knew my means of escape. I endeavored to change the subject.

"But what about you, old boy? Still a middle? You must have passed for lieutenant by now, eh?"

His face regained its habitual slackness. "Second go round, yeah. But I'm afraid I need more family interest than I've got to rate a commission."

His brow furrowed again; one imagined one could smell the wood burning in McKennis's head when he thought too hard. "Bless me—if I'd known you was alive, I'd have asked you to put the word in with the captain."

I hesitated. "Which captain is that?"

He chuckled. "Why, your uncle George, don't you know? We're just back in to Chatham from station duty. I was transferred to his *Viceroy* in Halifax."

My mind reeled. Blunt was back in London. There was no telling how long before he might make his way down to Portsmouth. Indeed, he may already had done.

The embers were smoldering again. "But how came this mistaken report of your death?"

"Well, 'lost at sea' is a bit of a stretch, McKennis. You remember those fishermen you put me off with?"

He nodded. "Daft Irish buggers. Not a word of the king's among them. I didn't like it at the time."

I tried to tell as small a lie as might answer. "Well, you read it right. They put in to Loch Swilly after dark. Bad tide race off those salt marshes, and I went overboard in my fever. I washed up on a nearby sandbank, but by then they were long gone. Some natives found me the next morning, and I was laid up in a little thatched hut sipping their sovereign remedies for some long weeks before I began to recover. A near run thing."

"All's well that ends well, what?" he said after another pause, not looking fully convinced. "Well, your uncle will be glad to hear of it. Off to London to report in at the Admiralty, I take it, then?"

I ignored the question. "Is Sir George still in London or back in Portsmouth?"

He shrugged. "Dunno, sir. I was dispatched down straightaway after paying out. Been carting about since yesterday delivering Admiralty covers. I'm to tutor at the academy! Not much chance for advancement, but better than being beached without pay," he said. "If I see him in town, I'll carry him your compliments."

"I'm hopeful I'll run into him first. Bit of a surprise, eh?" I forced another smile. "Well, better not keep that fine carriage idle. All the best, McKennis," I said, pumping his hand.

I had an agreeable reunion with my uncles. Matthew appeared comfortably domesticated and Christopher a bit rounder and less military in bearing. Matthew had at length succeeded in imposing some measure of polish upon his partner's manner of speech—but we do emulate those we love, in the end. Their little house, like the streets of Portsmouth, seemed to me somehow smaller and closer after the broad rosses and sea cliffs of Donegal. We made an early dinner, and I took particular relish in my first proper English pudding in many months.

I advised with them on my position. Matthew was of the opinion that if taken up, and the story I gave McKennis proved insufficient, I should reveal my true sex to the Admiralty, and as who should say plead my belly. My gravidness would likely be adjudged as having been either a veritable condition of invalidity or as justifying of my desertion. At all events, as a woman, I might avoid hanging. This did not appeal to me, however, as it might blow back upon Löw, casting him complicit in my deceits.

Christopher saw the matter more simply. I had jumped ship under pretense of sickness. A foremast jack might beg off with a flogging if he returned voluntary and quick, but as an officer gone a year and more, there was nothing for it but to get away and stay away.

"All your Singers and Blunts combined wouldn't be able to help you, dear. You're not the first tar to disguise her sex at sea. But the courts martial make examples of officers who run, and an Admiralty embarrassed by your little masquerade will not be inclined toward clemency," Chris said. "You've given more than your due to king and country, Selkie. Let it go and with a clear conscience. You've been hiding for half your life. You owe it to yourself to fully live the rest of it. Live it as who you are and pursuing what you love."

He might have been, perhaps was at heart, speaking of his own life. Matthew laughed as he wiped back a tear.

"Takes our niece in trouble to make this one wax sentimental."

But the remarks put me again in mind of Blunt. Mary's birth certificate would support your legal status as Eleanor's child. The chronology was neat; he had merely to believe that the doctors had been gainsaid on her barrenness and that you were born while he was sea. He would not be the first sailor to return home surprised by a new child at his hearth.

That's if he were inclined to believe you were his, of course. What irony of English law that the truth is harder proved than a lie. Before I could quit the country for good, I needed to assure myself that Blunt would be going to sea again and soon. Even should he accept you, the man's unchecked presence would make family life as unbearable for you as for Eleanor. But perhaps, methought, I underestimated her, thinking back to the maternal confidence, the protective purpose in her eyes when first she held you.

My uncles and I parted with a promise to see one another again before I left, and I walked slowly back to the house in the late afternoon light, unable to shake my dark forebodings. It may have been a prescient waft of what awaited me, or my conflict of heart over again abandoning a helpless loved one, but I began to quicken my steps as I neared the house.

Turning the corner, I saw the main door and gate left open, and thin black smoke rising from an upper window—the window of Eleanor's bedroom.

The house was silent, but guests had recently been received in the salon, a warm teapot and a half-empty decanter of sherry on the low table. A speckled trail of blood led across the floor and out the door. Before I could start up the stairs, I heard the front door close and Arima's stricken voice behind me.

"*Ai ene!* I was gone for not ten minutes!"

"What happened, Ama? Where is the baby?"

"I don't know! I stepped out just to find a hack to send you the message, to warn you to stay away." She followed me up the stairs. "Sir George and Nessie called. But all seemed well when I left. We were sitting to tea; Eleanor and the baby were in her room. I had not yet given them the news."

Eleanor's room was a wet, smoldering shambles, but neither she nor you were within it. The drapes and some of the bedclothes were scorched, the door shattered, one thick post sprung in.

I cried out, "Eleanor!"

"We are here," came a calm voice from Arima's room at the end of the hall.

Fanning our faces and coughing, we entered. The window was open, and the air within was fresh, though smelling of burnt hair. Eleanor was kneeling before what might have been an Egyptian mummy, slathering it with balm from Arima's apothecary case, which lay open before her.

The mummy was Nessie, sitting up against the footboard of the bed. She was wrapped in a damp sheet, blistered burns visible on her neck and lower jaw, legs twisted and unmoving. You nestled in her one uninjured arm, quiet and alert.

"Mother!" Arima fell to her knees before her.

"Where is Blunt?" I demanded, having satisfied myself that you were unharmed.

"Gone, for now," said Nessie. "And so should you be, Selkie."

"What happened?" Arima asked as she examined her burns.

"She saved us. The baby and me both," Eleanor said.

Nessie shielded your face with her hand and coughed weakly. "Sir George and I posted down from London together. We bumped into a tumid simpleton of a midshipman at the Blue Anchor who said he had seen you, Selkie, alive and well and walking by the house in civilian array."

Arima held a mug of water to her lips. "We neither of us credited it at first," Nessie continued, "but he took his oath on it. I'd have wanted time to advise with Arima, to understand what it meant, though I sensed my sister's hand in it. Blunt was already ordering a hack shay, however. I thought it better I be with him when he called here."

"I sent Eleanor to her room when they rang," said Arima. "He kept demanding why she did not come down to greet her husband. But I wanted to explain things calmly before he saw the baby. And I needed to warn you away, Selkie. He said nothing about your having been spotted in Portsmouth."

"His calm was all pretense," said Nessie to Arima. "He believed you'd been hiding Selkie. Harboring a deserter, closeted upstairs with Eleanor in her bedroom."

"As little time as he spends here, he's jealous of anything, anyone in my life but him," Eleanor said, taking you from Nessie. "He knows how we loved one another as children, Selkie. How close we have always been."

The scene began to appear. "So he went upstairs. Smashed in the door the moment Arima stepped out?" I looked at Nessie.

"I don't mount stairs as speedily as once I did. Nor will again," Nessie said, glancing at her legs. "But I wasn't far behind when I heard the crash and his brute bellow—"

Eleanor mimicked Blunt's deep voice. "So! It's a deserter's cuckold you'll make me, is it, you drooling little whore? His boots still under your very bed and his bastard in your arms! I'll incinerate you with it ere it takes another breath in my house!" She stopped and kissed your head.

Nessie continued. "When I reached the room, he had taken up the glass oil lamp lighting the bed table and was about to smash it over both of them. My brave girl was covering the babe with her body. The pride I feel now to think of it."

Her blue eyes sparkled, and her countenance broke with a smile I had never before seen, smelted fine from the dour dross of decades. Eleanor turned busily to the bed to shift your clout, discomposed by the novelty of her mother's kindness.

Nessie coughed. "At all events, I wasn't having it. I vaulted on from behind and choked him with my arm. He struck back and broke the lamp over me, though praise God a good bit got on himself as well. I was aflame shoulder to arse, but hung on for spite and love, thinking only to make Eleanor a lane to get the babe out."

She coughed again, and Arima frowned at the fluid sound. "That she did, running past just before Blunt threw himself backward into the door post, which is what broke me."

I fell to my knees beside her. "Nana . . ."

"Ah, never mind, Selkie, dear. I feel nothing below my bosom, and for that I'm grateful. The animal had that cutlass of his raised over me when Eleanor returned with a stout broomstick. She blocked his stroke handy and delivered a crack to the chin that sent him reeling, all the while screaming bloody murder. Well, that must've knocked the devil out and some sense in, for he fled his guilty ruin. My Eleanor doused the flames, pulled me here, and tended to my burns."

She smiled at Arima. "And thanks to my other daughter for

teaching her physic. And the way of using a fine bit of oak."

Much passed between the two women in that brief moment. The love of a mother for a daughter-in-law, acknowledged after long years of denial. The repentance of a sister for her sins against another, and regret for its terrible price. The women shut their eyes and exchanged that coursing form of *agape* shared amongst the sisterhood.

I was surprised to feel its essence as well. I reeled from the draught of such long-reserved affection. My heart resonated, amplified it in reply. And in that moment, I loved her back, the old woman, God help me. The presence of a third initiated sister in such proximity could not be concealed, and Nessie turned to me, perplexed and astonished.

"Selkie, dear, tell Nana true now," she said slowly. "Is that babe yours or Blunt's?"

I only smiled in reply.

Her eyes flared. "'Tis both, then," she whispered. "Born in Donegal? There's why I discerned Rhona's hand in it!" A tear formed in her eye as she coughed again, but the gravel gave way to rumbling laugher. "Well, there's no fooling me, is there? Not much!"

Her painful chuckling trailed off as she contemplated the significance of the situation to Blunt.

"So he doesn't know . . . he mistook you . . . oh Jesus, girl, what have you done?" But her eyes twinkled with admiration.

"Show me," she said after a pause.

"Nana?"

"Show me, if you please, what Arima hid so clever and Rhona made sublime. If you've the kindness, it will settle out my thinking, which is more than I deserve."

I needed to shift my clothes in any case, as I was determined to pay a formal visit to Captain Sir George Blunt. I stood up and let fall my garments. Wordlessly, the three women fixed their eyes upon my *comaithsiúre*, the scabs fresh fallen from each of its nine petals.

"All is in balance. I beg your forgiveness, my daughters. And I thank you, every one," she said at length. "And now will I rest a bit?"

We placed Nessie in Eleanor's bed. She would recover from the burns, even given her age, Arima said, but she would never regain the use of her legs, her back being broken clean.

I retrieved one of my formal uniforms, the waistcoat and tight breeches requiring me to first bind my bosom and don my old device. I strapped on my sword and was brushing the hat when I heard a loud knock at the door.

My mother opened it, and I was surprised to see Cormac step into the foyer, backed by Matthew and Christopher.

"We were concerned at your message and came immediately," Matthew said to Arima.

"And encountered this very fit-looking gentleman millin' about in front when we arrived," Christopher interjected.

Arima stared at Cormac as if at a vision. Before I could make introductions, she stepped to him and took his face in her hands.

"Yes," Matthew said. "We both remarked the resemblance. It's quite astonishing."

"Hagen's brother," Arima whispered.

"Cormac McLaughlin. Your servant, madame."

"Well, it appears there are acquaintances to be made here," I said to Cormac, "not the least of which is your stepmother, whom you will find upstairs. May I have a word with my English uncles in the kitchen?"

Christopher, still gaping at my Irish uncle, made no sign of moving, and Matthew pulled him firmly by the elbow.

I recounted events and came straight to the point.

"There's nothing else for it now. I can't suffer this. And I don't care if I hang for desertion after. But I haven't the frame to murder him in his bed. I'm bound to force a meeting. Will you, either of you, act as second for me? I haven't dueled since the academy."

"Jesus wept!" Christopher said after a moment of shock. "You can't mean to fight Blunt! I own he wants killing, but let me deal with him, for all love. Let it go. Get on with your life, Selkie, like we talked about."

"I'm not thirteen anymore, Uncle. This *is* me getting on with it. It's neither Sebastian's honor nor a women's vengeance. It's my baby's safety, my family's well-being in the balance."

"We're family as well."

"Indeed, Matthew. You are both *my* family, and this is for *me* to do. If it goes wrong, I'll need you here to watch over the others. Either way, I won't be."

At length, they gave in to my determination, and their advice proved indispensible. I was in want of an equitable meeting, with matched pistols and at close range. I could not call Blunt out myself, or I might be denounced and arrested for desertion before the duel took place. But I worried that even if the challenge were issued through my seconds, my position, or my uncles', might be compromised.

"I'll get him there," said Matthew. "Although I worry for what may happen after. I would not put it past him to arrange for you to be taken up in the event you best or kill him."

The long deferred acquaintance of her stepson affected Nessie deeply. To the surprise of all, she insisted on returning to Ireland with him. Since my connection to the *Ray,* and to Donegal, was now too well known, I demanded Cormac sail without me on the dark morning tide. He gingerly transferred Nessie into a chaise, with only the dunnage she had brought from London. I said nothing of my intentions, but made my farewells to Eleanor, and most bitterly to you, sweet girl.

Arima searched my eyes as I held you and, through the roil of my sentiments, divined my purpose.

"Xixili," she said. "Find safety, I beg you. I will stay and protect the baby."

"Ama," I whispered. "You can no more protect her from Blunt than you could Eleanor."

Her countenance withered at my words, thoughtless, though not unkindly meant, and a tear sprang from her eye.

"Or you?"

I shook my head vigorously. "No. No, Ama. It was my choice to make. And never your duty to shield me from its issue." I rocked you in one arm as I wiped her cheek with my thumb. "No more 'tis now."

She struggled to compose herself, wishing me not to part thus. She lost herself for a moment in your calming smile.

"Another woman of our line born unbeknownst," she said. "Are we no longer safer in the farthest grottoes than hidden in the world's plain sight?"

I pondered this. "We are born to be its eyes, are we not?" I gazed down at you in my turn. "However much you hid of me, I was never abandoned."

She made no reply, but cradled my face and held my eye, as though to swaddle me once more and all in that ranging certainty of her presence I'd known throughout my life. At length, she took you gently from my arms.

But as I lived, I would not abandon you to Blunt. Thinking him likely licking his wounds at one of the dockside naval haunts, Matthew, Chris, and I rode along with Nessie. As the carriage pulled away, she flung a final glance at the home she had made, so long ago with her handsome Scottish parson.

"There's nothing for me to go back to in London," she said. "The pearls of my foolish, stubborn heart have been there in Donegal these many years. I've been too long away from home, and what remains for me to do remains there."

She coughed. "Harbor no fear for our sisters in Portsmouth. There burns more of me in my Eleanor than you might credit, and the fire of love withal. Our dear Arima saw to that, long balancing my burden while bearing her own." The tears of her smoke-damaged eyes glistened harder. "She merits better company than mine in the years to come. Do, will you, make her to know she's released from all arrangements. *Libérée et déchargée,* aye?"

I hushed her with a spoonful of laudanum. She scanned my clothing and sword as she swallowed and grasped my hand with surprising strength.

"Will I tell you what I'm given to know of the destructive power?"

I made no reply.

"Well, I will, and it's this. *Hagnizó* can reduce the world to dust. But only forgiveness will free your heart."

"Mo ghrá thú, Nana," I said and kissed her forehead.

My last sight of my grandmother was across the expanse of Cormac's shoulder as he carried her, wrapped in a blanket, up the gangplank of the *Ray*.

Dawn found us in a secluded depression on the far north commons, Matthew at my side and Christopher holding the box of my father's pistols. Blunt had yet to arrive. I prayed it would be he who appeared, and not a file of soldiers or a cohort of thief takers to arrest me. Matthew had found him late the night before, drinking away the pain of his burns in an officers' club by the dockyard.

"I gave the scoundrel a choice," he said. "He could make a private answer to an honorable challenge or denounce you, in which case I would see him reputed throughout the service as a sodomite. That bit did it. Christopher and I know more than enough witnesses happy to see him taken up under article twenty-eight. Glass houses are delicate places."

The threat had also won me choice of first-round weapons, a concession from the challenged party, but I was quickly understanding it was no advantage. I placed an impractical, sentimental trust in my father's familiar pistols; but if a single exchange of ball resulted in no satisfaction, I would be left fighting the monster with heavy sabers.

"I'm afraid these are not proper modern dueling pieces,' said Christopher as he worked the locks of Hagen's old dragoons. "They're a matched brace but awfully heavy, and hardly a hair trigger." He grunted as the hammer fell stiffly. "She'll be slow to lift this," he said to Matthew. "Best start with arms already raised, eh?"

"No," Matthew said, turning to me. "Stand side on with your arm down and let Blunt lift his for the snap shot when the handkerchief drops. You'll make a small target, and he's most likely to miss or graze you. Then bear up, raise your pistol slowly, and take careful aim. If he moves off the line before receiving your fire, I'll shoot him dead myself."

A carriage came into view, cutting the morning fog in the distance. The first to stumble out as it pulled up was an ill-looking naval surgeon. He was staying at the same club and all that could be recruited on short notice. I sorely wished he were Löw but hoped Blunt had drunk as much.

Howbeit Sir George was an exceptionally seasoned tosspot, and a few hours' sleep were sufficient to restore him to a tolerable conscious state of odium. He exited the conveyance on steady feet, itching at his burnt neck with a malignant eye.

The seconds met to negotiate final terms, mark off the ground, and superintend the charging of the pistols. I found these niceties detestable and longed to simply join issue.

They settled on ten paces. A respectable number, but I would have preferred a lesser remove. I was better off dead than wounded if Blunt were left alive.

We took our weapons and toed the scratch, and I presented my profile as Matthew had counseled. I struggled to control the flutter in my belly, my eyes on the handkerchief as it was lifted and dropped.

Blunt fired so hastily that I never saw him raise his arm. I was aware only of the report and a lashing pain across my midriff, as though from a riding whip. I buckled but kept my feet rooted. There was no time, no point, in concerning myself with my wound. Be it mortal or not, I had only that one moment to accomplish my purpose. I gritted my teeth as I slowly raised my pistol and took deliberate aim, dead on at his breast. Exhaling slowly, I gave the trigger a deft and steady squeeze.

He doubled over, though I seemed to see the discharge before I heard it, a firework of searing flashes in my right eye, and the report, gassy and dull.

It may have been the modern polished grain powder, not in use when the old dragoons were manufactured, or just mere metal fatigue, but the pistol had misfired, the breech blown back in my face, the weak ball spat low into Blunt's groin—a forceful punch, but not enough to penetrate the broadcloth of his breeches.

He stomped and bellowed and was warned to keep his mark. Neither of us owned satisfaction; it was not yet finished. Matthew handed me one of Blunt's matched sabers and a handkerchief to swab the blood from my eye. As no medical aid was permitted until the issue was resolved, I stuffed it discreetly in my sleeve.

We touched swords, and fear crept in. His first pass stunned me with its power and speed, and I barely parried one hacking blow before scrambling crab wise out of the path of the next. Blood and tears obscured my injured eye, and my waistcoat was a study in crimson from his grazing shot. The still-small voice of doubt told me that I most assuredly could not keep this up for long, and my ears seemed to pulse with mocking laughter.

He slashed at my side, looking to press the advantage of my injury. I scarce contrived to raise the ponderous saber to block him, the blow ringing the failing muscles of my arm. But along of the pain, Arima's wisdom flooded in, dousing my panic.

This was no house-yard bully, and I was no longer that eye-injured eight-year-old. Blunt might kill me, or blood loss—but fear would not.

Find the balance point, I told myself. I dodged again, Blunt's great bulk beginning to check him, and slid my finger up the heavy sword. Its weight equaled at a spot above its short handle, on the blade itself. I swore inwardly—I would quite sever my hand should I grip it there. Ducking another breathless blow, I pulled Matthew's handkerchief from my sleeve, wrapped it tight around my palm, and sought to quiet my mind, remembering I need find my own balance point as well as the weapon's; that the power to destroy lies in willful stillness.

I shifted my grip, assumed a natural stance, and faced Blunt. He raised his cutlass again with a wheezing roar, clearly determined to slaughter me before his wind gave out. I deflected the blow, my blade in perfect equilibrium and light as a feather on its sharp pivot as I crouched and spun toward him.

My motion bridged the orbit of his weapon's tip, and I executed a turning figure eight, slashing upward from low and close, and sliced his inner thigh to the bone. The circular momentum carried me around again on the rise, and the second sweep of my blade, had he not already begun to crumple from the first, would surely have half beheaded him.

Instead, it bisected his upper face—eye, nose, and brow. He completed his heavy fall in a fine cloud of blood.

I could honorably do no more; but the fountain which pulsed from his loins gave me to hope my task was finished, and I left him to his surgeon. I dropped the saber, my palm bleeding through the shredded handkerchief. Matthew sprang to my side.

"And now you must run, my girl!" he whispered, stuffing my waistcoat with wads of clean bandage and overlaying it with his own to hide the damage.

Chris helped me back into my coat and hat, and they rushed me, limp and muddled, into the waiting shay with only my ditty, my rapier, and an anonymous ticket of passage on this Spain-bound merchant, sailing with the morning tide.

And so I depart a nameless exile, not fully certain Blunt is dead. I shall not return to my lovely British Isles until neither he nor King George may anymore discomfit me.

Forgiveness is power, Nessie said. Forgiveness is liberation, though she was overlong in learning it.

Power perhaps. But balance before all, and if we turn each cheek, return good for evil, and prayer for every persecution, then what is left to us to repay a simple kindness? Mistake me not—I would like it of all things, a purging shake of dust from off my sandals. But I, in the moment, feel sufficient free, and think me instead to forgive myself, now. To tend once again my own charge, and order my world not by power, but by spirit.

That spirit which Jeroen saw through construct and form, pretense and performance, and tasted pure last night, in the dark of our tiny room in Donostia. That spirit which woke us this morning, happy in one another's arms, with not a farthing for another night's lodging and no idea of where to get one. Yet the sunshine streaming through the window, and the knowledge that we were neither of us alone in the predicament, seemed wealth enough for a lifetime, and most sacred magic.

But even once stripped of fearful fallacy, is there not yet power in magic, you may ask, and what is left for a witch to say of it? Only what my little history reveals: true magic is neither pure nor perfect, and arises only when divinity meets passion. The passion of David for Rhona, of Arima for Hagen, the sacred *élan* of Úna's passion for me.

How can power be at once imperfect and divine, ask you, when omnipotence and perfection are both qualities of God? Perhaps therein lies magic's most impenetrable, circular mystery. A fragmentary fiction which points us to a flawless truth? Or a force whose essence is delusion, and delusion its force?

But until that veil is raised, we remain upon this stage, our most pernicious roles being those we play in the mind and judgment of others. Perhaps Nessie has got it right. The greatest magic may indeed lie in mercy—the saintly choice to close my eyes to the miserable self-deceits of the world, aspiring to be as uncondemning as little Úna's blood-blind Goddess. But nobler still would be liberation from my own moral construct, and life in the confidence of a heart uncondemned.

Accordingly, in the light of this fine morning I stood before the cracked glass, naked in body and spirit, ready to don once and forevermore the fabric of my sex and abide no further delusions, neither in my mind nor Jeroen's. If a body scarred by swivel gun and pistol ball, it also bears the badge of childbirth. If one eye be ringed with a speckled tattoo of burned powder, the brow ever creased by the mantle of naval service, it is also a countenance which, like my mother's, can be transfigured by the scarcest sensibility of happiness. I slid into the one red gown of Eleanor's I had packed; and I say no more than that I think it must please my man.

Searching deeper in my ditty for overlooked coins, Arima's leather contrivance which had so long filled my breeches rolled out upon the table, worthless now, to me or anyone. I shrugged and offered to sell my rapier, but Jeroen demurred, naming it our "last useful possession." His quaint wit never fails me. I laughed with delight at our poverty and, making to confirm the notion, drew the sword and cleaved the leather object in two.

Our mouths gaped, and our eyes shone, as its long hidden pair of stones rolled free: matched teardrop pearls of prodigious size and a magic pink luster.

So there it is, my little primer, for what you may make of it. Imperfect, but I think not incomplete. To write more, I must know, not imagine, the unfolding of your nature. That remains for you to discover, and but one *grimoire* to write, though a thousand you may read.

Begin yours, my love.
S. Singer

Epilogue

October 2015
Kuzaki, Japan

Yumi apologized to Chika on the train ride back to university. But she shut her mother out, from then on fulfilling only the most basic filial obligations. No further visits to Kuzaki. Graduations, her rewarding work at the pediatric hospital in Kobe, marriage and divorce—not once did she write home of these things. And she never opened the letters stuffed with ten thousand yen notes, still smelling of the fish market.

Yet, like footsteps in sand, the imprint of her mother's nature remained. In the way Yumi defied the senior resident to perform a tracheotomy on a boy suffering allergic asphyxiation. The gentle whisper song with which she soothed a feverish little girl to sleep, long after the nurses' shift was over. In the patient way she bears pain.

In her unrestrained abandonment, when she makes love.

She turns her face down, full into the water, and crawls deeper along the sandy bottom.

"The sea holds a multitude of Amas' tears."

There had been no derision in her mother's words. No intent to mock Yumi's wretchedness. She should have known it then, recognized the paraphrase of the ancient song. The Ama are singing it now as they pick over the ashes. Once any unburnt bones are removed, they will commit what is left to the outgoing tide.

Water is a woman's essence; the sea born of her tears.
Nothing in the universe more soft and yielding,
Yet unsurpassed for wearing down the high places,
Etching away the stony and hard.
It can give life or take it.
It flows in the places men reject.

Her finger touches something on the seabed, and she opens her eyes. There, in a patch of seaweed, the spiral folds of an *awabi*. Rare in such shallows. She floats still a moment, then digs, pulls her head clear of the water and sucks it from its perfect shell.

It tastes of her last tear as she swallows.

Still living—it tastes of her mother.

Acknowledgements

This novel could not have been written without the support of my family and friends, named, unnamed and misnamed. Special recognition falls to my copy editor Jenny Quinlan, and my many academic editors and beta readers, most notably including Matthew Krumholtz, Ph.D, Marie Helene Nadeau, Ph.D., Franz Gutwenger, Ayna Koryakina, Esq., M.A., Lawrence Bass, M.D., and Professor Raphael Douady, Ph.D. Without them the book's historical, scientific, and linguistic content would not ring as true. Any errors are my own.

Cover art is by Maciek Zielinski (www.maciekzielinski.com).

About the Author

J.P. Jamin is a native New Yorker and the author of several nonfiction works in the fields of law and economics. A lifelong love of sailing, history, philosophy, cooking, and parenting two brilliant daughters inspired *The Seas Come Still*, Jamin's first novel.

Twitter: @JPJaminNY